PHOBIA

Dean Crawford

© 2019 Dean Crawford
Publisher: Fictum Ltd
The right of Dean Crawford to be identified as author of this Work has been asserted by him in accordance with sections 77 and 78 of the Copyright, Designs and Patents Act 1988.
All rights reserved.

www.deancrawfordbooks.com

1

London

Nobody is looking at you. Nobody is interested. Nobody cares.

Honor McVey kept her head down as she was buffeted by the hot breath of the London Underground. A train burst from the darkened maw of a tunnel to her right, aged Victorian brickwork giving way to a brightly lit subterranean platform and ranks of impatient commuters. The air was stale and heavy, the last of the summer heat trapped in the city's tunnels. The commingled scents of metal, grease and electrical charge competed with wafts of aftershave and perfume as the train whined to a halt and the doors hissed open. A flood of suits, glowing mobile phones and briefcases poured out of the interior, and Honor was swept up by a similar crowd, all jostling for space as they boarded.

Don't make eye contact.

The seats were all taken by suits hiding behind their broadsheets and teenagers hiding behind closed eyes and headphones, tinny-sounding music emanating from within. Nobody offered her a seat. Honor gripped a handrail and held on, one commuter's back pressed against her chest, another man hemming her in from behind. The air was even hotter in the confines of the train, and her heart skipped a beat as she missed a breath.

Breathe. In through the nose, out through the mouth. Count your heartbeats. You've got this.

The swaying motion of the train, the dense air and the close confines threatened to shatter Honor's fragile shell and she closed her eyes, pictured another place, another time, somewhere when everything was just fine and she wouldn't have to see what she was about to see. Distraction was, she had been told, the best way to avert anxiety; not so easy when she was crammed like a sardine in a metal tube, hurtling along a centuries-old tunnel, deep below ground. The heat intensified. Keeping her eyes closed wasn't an option, she realised, as she almost fell against the man in front of her.

She caught her reflection in the blackened windows, the darkened Victorian-brick tunnels flickering by on the far side. Blonde hair in a neat ponytail, charcoal-grey suit, white shirt, five-foot-nothing. She looked like any other commuter on their way to work. The difference was that they would be behind desks, or at tills, or on workshop floors, safe places. They wouldn't have to see what she would witness.

Two stops, and three hundred and twelve heartbeats later, the train pulled into Monument. The doors opened and she followed the crowd off the train, across the platform and up the escalators, crammed once again between men who always seemed so much taller than she was. Ninety-eight beats later, she walked out of Monument Station and sucked in a lungful of fresh air as she closed her eyes and stood for a moment, rigid amid the bustling morning crowds near London Bridge.

The streets were crammed with vehicles all noisily hurrying somewhere, their headlights lost in a foggy gloom that enshrouded the city. The air was damp but mild, the streets alternately lined with modern tower blocks and two-hundred-year old architecture, contemporary steel and glass warring with Georgian stone, all rising up to vanish into the grey murk above.

Honor gathered herself together and crossed the junction at Monument, headed south beside the A3 toward her unavoidable meeting with death. Ahead of her was London Bridge and the wind-flecked waters of the Thames, a sheet of beaten lead flowing ever eastward. The odours of water, mud and old stone gusted between the buildings, filling her lungs with the breath of the city.

London had a presence all of its own, ingrained with the ages, pounded into the cobbles, alleys and pavements. She could sense the immense antiquity around her as she passed a monument to the Great Fire of London, then descended onto Lower Thames Street. The sweep of the Thames was not visible from here, the street lined with office blocks, but amid them towered the ancient spire of St Magnus the Martyr church. She looked up at the medieval heights vanishing into the fog and swayed with vertigo.

Honor came to a halt on the opposite side of the street and took a breath. It was time. She wasn't sure that she was truly ready, but as her cognitive therapist had told her, it would never feel like the right time.

Honor crossed the street to where a police cordon surrounded the church. The street was sealed off at both ends, keeping traffic and onlookers at bay. Two sets of ambulance hazard lights flickered a kaleidoscopic display through the mist as she approached two police constables manning the cordon, the distinctive red and white check-flash of their otherwise black uniforms marking them out as City of London Police. The constables turned to her as she reached them, and she pulled out her warrant card, along with her blue cordon card.

'Honor McVey, Detective Sergeant.'

'Ma'am,' came the immediate response as one of the uniforms lifted the cordon for her. 'It's this way. We're keeping the public as far away from the scene as we can.'

The constable led her toward the church, and Honor saw three detectives, probably a Homicide Assessment Team out of Bishopsgate, standing around something on the pavement at their feet

'D.S. McVey,' the constable announced, as though she were royalty of some kind. The detectives looked up at her, all three of them registering a flicker of surprise - or maybe concern, she couldn't be sure. One of them was unknown to her, unusual in a small CID force.

'It's an honour,' Detective Constable Danny Green greeted her with a broad south- London accent and a cheeky grin. 'Good to see you back.'

Danny's brief embrace was welcome and she couldn't help the smile that caused her cheeks to ache as she returned it. Danny was in his thirties, with thick, unkempt brown hair above piercing grey eyes that missed nothing. Tall, somewhat arrogant and with a permanent five-o-clock shadow on his jaw, Danny was considered a safe pair of hands, with ten years in CID.

'This is DC Samir Raaya,' he introduced the younger man next to him, 'fresh out of MET direct-entry training, now attached to City, so he's being led by the hand, by me. You're welcome.'

Samir was dark-eyed, black hair crossing his scalp in a fashionable sweep and an eager-to-please expression on his features. He looked like he should be fronting a boy- band, not standing in the fog at a crime scene. He shook her hand deferentially.

The third man was all too familiar to her.

'Honor,' Detective Constable Colin Hansen greeted her coolly, his handshake limp, without passion. 'I'm Supervisory Officer, CAD's been updated, I put you down as the Investigating Officer when I heard you'd been assigned.'

Disappointment. Honor could see it in his eyes. Hansen was only a few inches taller than her, stocky but short, and seemed forever to be trying to make up for it. He'd been made up to acting-Detective Sergeant in her absence, but that would now be rescinded. Promotions were rare in such a small force. Short, black hair framed a round face with small, dark eyes. Honor decided not to make waves.

'I got called in,' she said by way of an explanation. 'First day back so I'm going to follow your lead, for now.' She looked down at the pavement, where a damp spot revealed the likely location of the crime. 'What are we looking at here? The DI was pretty vague.'

Danny gestured to the damp spot.

'Local building firm called it in an hour ago,' he explained. 'The body's been here since some time during the night. We were on-call with the HAT car so we headed straight down.' Bishopsgate had recently been assigned a single Homicide Assessment Team vehicle, which was shared between the four Major Incident Teams stationed there. 'We're already searching for local CCTV coverage, but unfortunately none of the cameras are set to cover the scene of the crime.'

Honor frowned. 'Why not? The body was found here, right? Is it in the ambulance?'

Danny Green smiled without humour and pointed one finger straight up. Honor tilted her head back and the world swayed around her.

'Oh, Jesus, you've *got* to be kidding me?'

The sky above was a featureless ghost grey, the magnificent church spire soaring into the gloom, but she could see a faint patch of darkness alongside it and realised that it was the body of a man. She was looking up at his feet, and he was hanging from something. The fog between the church and the opposite ends of the street was dense enough to conceal the body from sight, but that wouldn't last for long.

'Welcome back,' Danny said with a cheery wink. 'It's all yours.'

Honor's stomach back-flipped inside her. Her first thought was to insist that another Investigating Officer take the case, maybe Hansen, but after what had happened, turning down a case now might be the end of everything. Sympathy or no, the DCI would write her off active duty and she'd be behind a desk for the rest of her career. Honor steeled herself.

'How long before we can get the body down?'

'Scene examiner's already on site and the specialist search team will be here soon, shouldn't be too long,' Danny said, knowing that she would want the body down before the media could get a handle on the story. 'We got an ICEFLO camera to do the rounds but there's nothing out of the ordinary, except for the victim, obviously.'

'Obviously,' Hansen echoed. 'First glance, it's a suicide.' 'Who found the body?'

'Site manager, Gary Wheeler, at seven-thirty am,' Samir replied, keen to join in as he glanced at his notebook. 'Called it in right away, we got here, scene examiner showed up about ten minutes ago. As the Senior Investigating Officer, DI Harper said she was assigning you the case.'

Honor nodded, her mind already racing. Detective Inspector Katy Harper had suggested she take the first case that came along, get right back into things, throw herself in at the deep end. Her cognitive therapist had felt otherwise, but Honor was suffering from cabin fever and had to get out of the apartment for a bit, even if it was a risk for her.

'Do we have a name?'

'Nothing yet,' Hansen replied. 'Once we get the body down, we should be able to identify the victim. They're wearing a suit, could have done this after a hard day on the trading floor, lost a billion on commodity stock or something. Wouldn't be the first time.'

Honor frowned inwardly. The body of the victim could have been in situ for many hours, perhaps since the previous nightfall, which presented a number of difficulties for the investigation that she had been assigned to lead. The pathologist would have to establish the time of death, while the laborious task of trawling through hours of CCTV to try to identify the time that the victim arrived at the church would be down to her team of three, as Hansen would almost certainly be returned to his own Major Incident Team, the force desperately short of detectives.

'Canvassing? Witnesses?'

'No witnesses yet,' Raaya replied. 'Not enough uniforms to send anybody knocking on doors, so it's down to us.'

'Standard,' Honor agreed. It was going to be a long day. 'Danny, can you try to ID the victim, take a look for missing persons reports north and south of the water? The victim might not be from our borough. And see what CCTV assets we can get on the approaches to the church. I'll go take a look at the scene with Samir and handle the door-to-door afterward.'

'Will do,' Danny said with a surprised smile, relieved that he was being spared the drudgery of canvassing the local area for information. Most detective sergeants would have sent the DCs out for that. *Win hearts and minds*, Honor thought as she turned to leave with Samir. She was coming back after a long layoff and she was going to need a good team behind her to pull through – Danny was the only face that was both friendly *and* familiar.

'Is there any point heading up there again?' Hansen asked. 'I've already tagged it as a suicide – the guy didn't levitate onto that rope.'

'I just need to see it all for myself, before signing off on it,' Honor replied. 'It won't take long.'

It wasn't a request, and she didn't wait for Hansen's response as Samir led her toward the church entrance. Built in the 11th century, the church was close to a thousand years old. To her left lay Whitechapel, the dark warren of the city where once Jack the Ripper carved his name as the most famous serial killer in history. Less than half a kilometre from the Tower of London and the wall, she was acutely aware of the city's ancient past all around her as they walked into the church.

'Where's Gary Wheeler?' she asked Samir.

Her voice echoed through the vaulted interior, the air weighted with antiquity. Aged pews were arranged over a stone floor of engraved tombs that had lain at rest for centuries, worn smooth by the passage of countless pious feet.

'Just over there,' Raaya gestured with a nod of his head. 'Giving a statement to the uniform.'

Honor made her way across to Gary Wheeler, her heels clicking on the cool stone. Somehow, after the cramped tube journey, the airy church and the scent of polished wood seemed comforting.

Wheeler was a big, thick-set man with a thick moustache, curly receding hair and a ruddy complexion. A large belly hung over a utility belt, a yellow hard-hat perched at a jaunty angle on his head as he turned to them. Honor showed him her warrant card and introduced herself, then let Wheeler do the talking.

'I didn't even see him until I got up into the steeple,' he explained as a young female officer jotted down his statement. 'Damned near scared the life out of me. It's not every day you open a door to see a dead body hanging in mid-air.'

'And you saw the body how, exactly?'

'From the belfry,' Wheeler replied. 'I opened the baffles to get out onto the scaffolding, and there he was, danglin' right there in front of me.'

'Could anybody else have got into the building before you?' Honor asked.

'Sure,' Wheeler nodded. 'The site's locked overnight and has camera coverage, but it's not Fort Knox, y'know? Guess he had to have got in, otherwise he wouldn't be hanging there now, would he?'

'Was there any sign of break-and-enter into the site?'

Wheeler nodded. 'Lock's been forced on the church doors. Brute force job, not professional. Looks like he got in here to top himself.'

'Are you contracted to Tower Hamlets or Southwark?'

'Hamlets,' Wheeler replied. 'Been working for 'em for twenty years. I've seen some stuff in that time, but nothin' like this.'

'Who else has access?'

'Site manager, Jenson Cooper,' Gary said. 'He's on his way over.'

Honor nodded. She directed the uniform to get statements from both men before she joined Raaya as they headed for the belfry, Hansen following silently behind.

'Guy wants to commit suicide, he could throw himself under a train or off London Bridge,' she said. 'But no, he breaks into a church and hangs himself from the bell tower. Why?'

'Statement?' Raaya offered. 'A need to be seen for some reason?'

Honor walked with mechanical efficiency to an open door to the belfry. There were already forensics officers in customary clean-suits combing the door for evidence, but they waved Honor through. The temptation to ask them to take the body down first was overwhelming, but she knew that to do so would be a break in procedure that could fail the case with the CPS.

The climb to the top was arduous, narrow twisting staircases of stone leading her to the upper heights of the tower. There, a single belfry door was opened out onto narrow gantries that were surrounded by walls of clear plastic tied to scaffolding poles.

'Did he get outside through these doors?' she asked, more to distract herself than anything else.

'Yes,' Raaya replied, not mocking her question. 'Once inside the church, there was little to stop him from getting up there onto the scaffolding.'

Raaya gestured in a deferential "ladies first" manner. Reluctantly, as though tracing the steps to her doom, she edged toward the opening. The cold air from outside hit Honor as she reached the tiny opening. Beyond was a three-foot wide, wood-planked walkway of scaffolding that surrounded the belfry, to which had been strapped three eight-inch wide scaffolding planks, each stacked atop the other, each about ten feet long. Two forensics officers dressed in white suits were working on the walkway, taking samples.

Beyond, the scaffolding planks extended out into the misty air, a hundred and fifty feet above the city streets. Honor, her legs unsteady, sucked in a breath and stepped out onto the narrow walkway.

The world seemed to tilt around her as a hot flush plunged through her body. The fog was lifting and she was treated to a plunging, vertiginous view to the street far below. If she leaned forward even a little, she knew that she would topple over without any means to grab hold of anything to break her fall. Nausea poisoned her throat and she felt herself start to fall to one side.

'Oh shit.'

She jerked away from the view and the back of her head smacked onto the unyielding stone of the belfry.

'Are you all right?'

Honor closed her eyes and tried to catch her breath as she struggled back inside, feeling her way with her hands and trying not to catch Samir's eye.

'I'll be fine,' she insisted. 'Risk assessment is too great; we can't work out there. Heights aren't my thing, anyway.' 'Mine either,' Raaya replied. 'I'll go.'

Raaya was younger than her by a few years, with an open face and soft dark eyes. He wasn't being a hero or trying to impress her. In fact, he wasn't actually looking at her at all as he steeled himself, and then stepped through the doorway onto the scaffolding outside.

'Not great for a first day back on the job, Honor,' Hansen uttered as he strolled past her and out onto the scaffolding with his hands in his pockets, clearly unafraid, his small black eyes glistening with delight. 'You sure you're up for all this, so soon? I can ask DI Russell to take the case.'

'No, thanks.'

Honor backed away from the stone arch, and instead walked around the edge of the belfry's interior to where she could better see the victim. She could just make out the two forensics personnel out on the scaffolding, carefully searching for prints and evidence, before the fire brigade would be called in to bring the man down from the grisly heights. Honor edged along the interior of the belfry to where she could see through the next opening.

From her vantage point she could see the body dangling from a noose out on the edge of the scaffolding boards. He was young, maybe thirty, with thick black hair and a slightly tanned complexion, perhaps Mediterranean in origin. The man's jaw and head were twisted at an awkward angle, his tongue bloated and swollen into a purple mass that bulged between his lips. One eye stared up into the foggy sky, while the other was rolled up to reveal the white. She wondered who he had been, who his family were, the loved ones who might even now be waiting to hear from him. Not for the first time, she wondered what might have led such a young man to take his own life in such a dramatic way, dangling from a twenty-foot rope out over the streets far below…

Honor stared at the rope for a moment, and in that instant the entire scene before her changed shape. The moment of revelation. The dawning of new and terrifying possibility. She had felt it before on numerous cases, both as a detective constable and later as a sergeant. The hairs on the back of her neck went up and she felt little insects of loathing scuttle beneath her skin.

She waited for several minutes until Samir ducked back inside. His features were flushed, and he sat down on one of the beams and took a few breaths to compose himself.

'Are you okay?' she asked.

He nodded. 'Just as soon as I'm sure I'm not going to throw up.' 'Did they say anything?'

Samir shook his head, ran his hand through his hair. Hansen sauntered back into the belfry, his hands still in his pockets.

'No immediate signs of struggle, nothing to suggest a second party. Just like I said, a suicide.'

Honor said nothing. She already knew that this was no suicide, although clearly the forensics teams and Hansen had not yet come to the same conclusion.

A constable appeared in the tower behind them and caught Honor's gaze. 'We've got somebody downstairs, ma'am, a family member.'

Honor didn't hesitate. Within a minute she was out of the belfry and back on blessed *terra firma*, where officers were now struggling to console and restrain a young woman with long black hair. Large crowds had gathered nearby in the rush-hour traffic, and Honor glanced up to see the hanged man clearly visible as the fog began to lift, the sun trying to break though. Honor made her way across the street, and as officers held the woman back from the crime scene, she placed one hand firmly on the woman's shoulder and turned her gently around.

'My name is Detective Sergeant Honor McVey,' she said, her warrant card in her hand. 'I'm the investigating officer. How do you know the victim?'

The woman's eyes were thick with tears that had smeared her mascara. She was dressed in a business suit and looked as though she was on her way to work when she had encountered the scene.

'That's my husband,' she sobbed. 'What happened? Why would he do this?'

Honor kept her voice calm, hoping to draw as much information about their victim from the wife before she succumbed to shock. She also didn't want to tip her hand too quickly that her husband might have been murdered, as the woman herself might be a suspect.

'We were hoping that you might be able to tell us,' she replied. 'Do you know of any reason why your husband would choose to take his own life?'

The woman shook her head vigorously.

'We've never been happier!' she sobbed. 'We're recently married and he's been promoted at work! This is the last thing that he'd do!'

Honor noted the woman's use of present tense, a clear indicator that her husband's death had not yet sunk in, and a possible primary indicator of innocence.

'Sometimes people don't tell us about everything that's going on in their lives,' Honor said, as gently as she could. 'Is it at all possible that your husband was hiding something from you, from everyone, that might lead him to…?'

'You don't understand!' the woman snapped back. 'Sebby *couldn't* have done this to himself, he's not capable of it!'

Honor didn't rise to the woman's anger, knowing to keep her own emotions as neutral as possible. Standard procedure – believe a first-account witness, investigate afterward.

'People under terrible stress can do things that we can't begin to…'

'That's not what I mean!' the woman insisted through her tears. 'Sebastian couldn't have gone up there, he couldn't even bear living in a first-floor flat! He's absolutely terrified of heights!'

2

'How long before the body is down? We don't want a bloody circus up there.'

Honor walked through the main doors of Bishopsgate Police Station, affectionately known as "B-Gate", a large, grey-stone building in the heart of the city's old town, with Samir, Hansen and Danny right behind her. By now the fog was clearing to reveal bright autumn sunshine in a powder-blue sky. The morning had also revealed a flood of phone calls from journalists eager for a bite on a new "incident" story unfolding at St Magnus.

'Fire crews are in the belfry, pulling the body in,' Danny replied.

Honor nodded as they were buzzed through the building's lobby and into the interior. She led the way past the newly refurbished custody suite and custody bridge, behind which were the new fingerprint scanning rooms. Fifteen cells adjoined the bridge, beyond which were the endless corridors of the station's vast interior, which extended all the way back to New Street. The original station had been built in 1866, where once Catherine Eddowes had been held for drunk and disorderly in Houndsditch before being released, only to become the fifth victim of Jack the Ripper. Rebuilt prior to World War Two, the new building was structurally reinforced and had survived a direct bomb hit during the conflict. Now, it served as CP-6 and was rapidly taking over from CP-5 at Wood Street as the City of London Police's centre of activity.

'Canvassing hasn't pulled anything in yet, but it's not a residential area so we're going to need the MET to assist us. I need that CCTV footage, and anything else we can grab from all ingress routes into Lower Thames Street.'

'Footage is on the way,' Danny confirmed, keeping pace with her demands with a sedate lack of ostentation. 'Might take a few hours to collate everything, but there's no way anybody could have got into that church without being caught on at least one camera.'

The four of them huddled into an elevator as Samir hit the button for the second floor, where the CID offices were located. Honor took a soft breath, because she didn't want the others to notice her anxiety as the elevator door closed with a gentle ping, the four of them standing within inches of one another.

The basement of Bishopsgate held the firing range, the floor above the muster room, canteen and custody suite. CID held court on the second floor, with offices above and the top, seventh floor, what had once been the restraining suite. A former City Police hospital, the upper floor had long been said to be haunted by the ghost of Evelyn Rolfe, a nurse killed by the direct bomb-hit in World War Two. Even Honor got shivers walking around up there, late at night.

'The pathologist will perform the autopsy by the morning,' Samir said as he checked his notes. 'Cause of death is a no-brainer, but we can't be too careful.'

'Agreed,' Hansen nodded, 'it's pretty clear the guy hanged himself.'

Honor spoke up, more to distract herself from the ever-closing walls of the elevator than anything else.

'He didn't hang himself,' she said. 'He was murdered.'

Hansen, Samir and Danny looked at her.

'What makes you say that?' Samir asked.

The elevator door pinged open and Honor led the way down a corridor to their offices.

'What do we know about our victim, and where's the wife now?'

'Sebastian Dukas,' Danny replied, in his hands a series of scribbled notes taken from the wife's brief questioning, 'aged thirty-two, Greek heritage, works for a national bank, not one of the big ones in the district. No priors, nothing on CRIMINT. Wife is Katarina Dukas, thirty, graphic designer, clean as a whistle. She's with an FLO in the custody suite. They live in Clapham, rented apartment, married last year.'

Honor reached her office and dropped her bag into her seat, her mind turning over the information as she considered her options. Normally the DCI would conduct an interview with Katarina Dukas, as they would have taken control of the investigation, but with no actual crime on the record yet there was no formal protocol in place. Honor knew that was about to change, but she didn't want to tip her hand to the victim's wife yet. What Katarina knew about her husband's unfortunate demise might affect how she replied when questioned, and Honor wanted the unvarnished truth from her before she was told that her husband had been murdered. Until she alibied out, Katarina was a person of interest in the case, as were all the victim's nearest and dearest.

'I'll talk to the DI about getting an incident room set up,' Honor said. 'I want the media out of this for as long as possible. They can't have failed to notice the body, but it'll look like a suicide to them so we'll stick with "we can't comment on an on-going investigation" and let them sweat the details out.'

'How do you know it's a homicide?' Hansen demanded. 'You couldn't even get out on that scaffolding, but now you're telling me that guy was murdered?' Danny noticed the accusation and shot Hansen a hot look.

'I went out on the scaffolding,' Samir replied quietly. 'It didn't further our knowledge, did it?'

'Says the direct-entrant,' Hansen shot back. 'What the hell would you know? You haven't even been part of a full-blown homicide case yet. You've never even walked a beat.'

'Can it,' Danny snapped and put himself in front of Hansen.

Hansen said nothing but his eyes wobbled with panic as Danny got in his face. 'Hansen,' Honor said, her voice calm, 'as you pointed out, I'm the Investigating Officer now. I'll update the CRIS database with what I know, so that everybody can understand how Sebastian Dukas was murdered. Is that sufficient for you?'

Hansen nodded. Danny smirked at him but said nothing.

Honor didn't want to talk about her suspicions with them right now. Her thoughts were dominated by the sight of Sebastian's face, his tongue bulging from his grimacing features, and by the grief-stricken wife, Katarina, her confusion and angst. It had been six months since Honor had been forced to confront such emotionally taxing scenes, a poison that laced the veins.

'We'll need to start sifting through that CCTV as soon as it arrives. Samir, you handle everything east of the church. Danny, you watch the west. I'll take anything north or coming off London Bridge, and update CRIS and EAB with what we know.'

'Will do,' Danny said, leaving the office with Samir.

'Hansen, go see DI Harper and find out where she wants you.'

Hansen stared at her for a moment, his confidence returning as Danny got out of earshot. 'This isn't your office yet, Honor.'

Honor couldn't help herself. She leaned on her desk with both hands. 'It certainly isn't yours, Colin.'

For a moment she thought that he might bite, but then Hansen turned and walked out of the office. Honor took a moment to breathe again. First day back, and already she was into a homicide and a pissing contest with Hansen, but at least she could tell that both Samir and Danny were switched-on and eager to get to work. Unlike Hansen, she detected no sense of rivalry from them, no bitterness at her return, filling a vacant slot that either man might have coveted. The limited size of the City of London Police made promotions hard to come by, progression difficult for even the best officers, and so many were often lost to more lucrative posts across the MET and further afield.

Most people thought that the Metropolitan Police Service covered the entire city of London, and in some respects that was true, but the "square mile" was in fact covered by its own territorial police force, the City of London Police.

Operated by a little over a thousand staff, the force was the smallest in the country and was responsible for the City and the Middle and Inner Temples, as the local Inns of Court were commonly known. In recent years, a barrage of resignations and swingeing budget cuts had reduced the Metropolitan Police Force's numbers to a shadow of their former self, and while the same cuts had hit the City Police, they had increasingly found themselves taking on major crimes from the overstretched MET. The result was Bishopsgate's Major Crimes Support Unit of four small City Police MITs that ran homicide investigations in and around the square mile, taking the pressure off the MET's own MIT force. Bishopsgate was one of four boroughs within their jurisdiction, headed up by DI Katy Harper and DCI Tom Mitchell.

Detective Inspector Katy Harper held court in an office just down the corridor from Honor. Although older and more experienced, Katy Harper had been unfortunate in missing the promotions boat on three occasions, most often pipped at the post by male colleagues in a world that existed long before the *#metoo* movement. Her anger at being denied promotion radiated itself down through the ranks with seismic force, preventing any female officer from suffering the same fate, an asset that now benefited Honor as she knocked on the open door of Katy's office. The door was rarely closed.

'Honor,' DI Harper said with a cautious smile. 'Welcome back.'

Honor walked in as Harper gestured with a wave of one hand to a chair opposite. Petite, slim, with bobbed auburn hair and thin lips, the DI was famous for a desk piled high with mountains of paperwork, files and other paraphernalia from which she might ambush anybody walking past her door who looked like they should be working harder. It was said that she had not taken a day off in six years, even after spraining an ankle at home. Instead, she had taken a taxi direct from A&E to her desk, and was known to sleep on a sagging leather couch tucked against one wall of the office when handling particularly difficult cases.

'St Martyr's,' Harper said.

'Thirty-two-year-old victim,' Honor replied, 'swinging from a noose off scaffolding on the steeple. Wife's in the custody suite with a FLO, forensics are done and the body's off to the morgue for autopsy. We're going to need an incident room.'

Harper's left eyebrow jumped up and hovered for a moment.

'You going to justify that? CRIS has it listed as a suspected suicide; city suit takes a dive and checks out of life.'

CRIS was the Crime Reporting system used by City CID to log and report crimes, and which most detectives used to update their work on any given case. Hansen had already logged the case on the system and tagged it as a suicide.

'The crime was staged to appear a suicide,' Honor said. 'We've only got one Homicide Assessment Team vehicle.'

'We're handing over to MIT 4 this morning,' Honor pointed out. 'We won't need the wheels. This is a fresh case and it's already got the attention of the media; it'll be on the news before noon. We need to be ready to move or we'll be facing lots of horrible questions and no decent answers.'

'Make it worth my while.'

Honor sucked in a breath.

'The victim was hanged from a rope almost twenty feet long. Hangings need a rope that is a specific length, based on the weight of the victim. Too short, and they asphyxiate slowly on the end of the rope or are able to free themselves if they're not bound. Too long, and the drop tears the head clean off the body, decapitating the victim.' Harper winced. 'Sebastian Dukas did not hang himself, he was lowered into position, either already dead or left to die. Given that he was not bound by the wrists and could plausibly have saved himself, it's my assessment that Sebastian Dukas was already dead before he was hanged.'

Harper watched her for a long moment.

'You've been watching too many horror movies,' she finally said with interest, 'but I don't doubt that you're right. I once read they screwed up the rope length when they hanged Saddam Hussein, took his head clean off. If you're right, how does that affect the nature of this case?'

Honor didn't hold back, willingly allowing herself to fly by the seat of her pants. This was speculation time, a chance to share ideas and see what revelations they could uncover.

'Highly visible corpse,' she said, 'positioned to display as clearly as possible to crowds as soon as the sun came up. The fog could have scuppered that plan, if it *was* the plan, but it also concealed the body until later in the morning. Our

HAT vehicle didn't arrive until rush-hour was already in full swing.'

'You think the weather played a part? That's elaborate.'

'Getting a body or an unwilling victim two hundred feet above the ground and hanging them from scaffolding is already elaborate. This was planned, methodically. I don't believe anybody could kill a victim and then just concoct that display on the fly. Given Sebastian's Mediterranean ancestry, this could be a hate crime.'

'I agree, in principal,' Harper said. 'But it could also be the result of drugs, alcohol, anything.'

'There was too much to do. The perpetrator had to break into the church, get the body up into the steeple, strap scaffolding planks together, secure them, hang the victim and then get out, all without being seen.'

Harper inclined her head.

'True, but the square mile doesn't have a large residential population. That means that a suspect could have picked the location purposefully, and maybe even the means of displaying the victim: CCTV cameras point down to the streets, not up to the tops of buildings, so even if you capture them on the footage we're not necessarily going to capture evidence of a crime.'

'Both backs my point and opposes it,' Honor said. 'The weather provided further cover against the perpetrator's work being discovered before he was ready – nobody would have seen the body hanging there, the fog was thick overnight. It's only this morning that it showed up, so with the lack of witnesses and poor visibility he could *theoretically* have taken his time. But it seems unlikely that he would have come up with something so complex, at least not if we're considering an opportunistic killer.'

Harper nodded, and Honor could see the unease in her eyes.

'I don't like the sound of it,' the DI said after a moment's thought. 'Chances of another killing, that it's not random?'

'We need to talk to the wife, Katarina,' Honor said, 'but right now there's nothing to suggest anything obvious in their lives that would warrant Sebastian being hanged in the middle of the square mile. They seem like an ordinary couple, although we know that could be veiling trouble in their personal lives.'

Honor blushed at her own words, and averted her eyes from Harper's. Suddenly her chain of thought was broken and an old pain welled inside her, a dark chasm of grief that threatened to crush her soul from within.

'Question the wife as soon as you can,' Harper said, noting Honor's sudden silence but choosing to ignore it. 'We need to figure out why Sebastian was put up there. When's the autopsy due?'

'By tomorrow,' Honor replied. 'Pathologist will run toxicology as a priority to see if the victim was under the influence at the time. Given that we know Sebastian Dukas was terrified of heights, it's quite possible.'

'Terrified of heights?'

'The wife told us that Sebastian couldn't have hanged himself, that he was sufficiently scared of heights that he wouldn't have been able to get up there at all.'

Harper leaned back in her chair for a moment. Honor silently stomped down on the blackness still swelling within, battered it back into some deep neural tract where it would no longer bother her. Denial. Distraction. She managed to get her eyes up to meet Harper's, and the DI nodded.

'Okay, I'll assign the case to your team. We'll have a meeting with the Borough Commander at sixteen hundred to update him, so you'll all need to be there with everything you know at that time. Sebastian Dukas didn't float up onto that steeple on his own, so use the CCTV to establish a timeline and we'll go from there. I'll send the HAT car to MIT 4 and have them on call for whatever else comes in. Right now, I've got a meeting with the DCI and a capacity meeting right after that: we're woefully short of hands right now, and the MET's suffering just the same. Can you handle this with Green and Raaya for the moment?'

'No problem,' Honor lied. 'What about Hansen, he's got a stick shoved where the sun doesn't shine about me coming back.'

'Hansen's back to MIT 4,' Harper replied, unconcerned. 'We'll catch up at sixteen hundred.'

Honor headed out of the office, cursing herself for letting her wayward emotions fly out of control, even for a moment. Samir and Danny were at their respective desks but joined her in her office as soon as they saw her.

'Team of three?' Danny asked after she filled them in. 'It'll take us days to sift through all the CCTV.'

Honor focused on the crime scene and pushed it to the front of her thoughts. 'Assuming the suspect used the fog to conceal his movements, we can work backwards from oh-seven-thirty this morning. He won't have positioned the body before the fog descended, which was probably sometime in the early hours if the news I saw this morning was correct?'

'Came in off the water,' Samir confirmed. 'Probably one, maybe two this morning.' 'Okay, so let's go from midnight last night until the time of the call this morning, that's seven hours or so of footage, probably six or maybe eight cameras to start with.' She heard their whispered oaths as they dispersed back to their desks. Honor knew that they were in for a marathon viewing session as she started up the PC at her desk and ordered her thoughts: the frontline investigation toolkit. She sat at the keyboard, but her guts churned with nausea as she thought of how she'd almost cracked right in front of the DI. She'd only been back a few hours and her nerves were already shredded. She couldn't bear to think about the possibility of media questioning, the barrage of the public's right to know, the crushing sense of failure if they could not apprehend a suspect. Stress was part and parcel of any detective's life, and she had shouldered that stress successfully, deftly even, for years, right up until…

Nobody is looking at you. Nobody cares. Focus on you, and you alone.

She breathed deeply. In through the nose, out through the mouth. *Get a grip and get to work.*

The crime scene had been secured, and CAD updated with all attending officers, with the EAB updated to contain anything that might later be used as evidence, including Sebastian Dukas's details as found on his belongings. The fact that he was still in possession of his wallet, money, keys and mobile phone ruled out theft as a proximal cause. ICEFLO camera images of the scene were put into a MG11 document and CRIS updated, along with her encounter with Katarina Dukas at the crime scene. The task was laborious, but absolutely essential in recording every tiny detail of the crime scene, to later be referenced when presenting to the Crown Prosecution Service. Honor wasn't ready to start sifting through CCTV when she knew that Katarina Dukas might be able to reveal further information about her husband's whereabouts, so

as soon as she had updated CRIS she headed down to the custody suite.

Katarina Dukas was sitting in a small but tastefully decorated suite, strategically positioned as far away from the "bin" as possible, so that grieving families were not disturbed by cries of protest from the recently arrested as they were processed. Alongside her was the Family Liaison Officer, in this case Officer Charlotte Hammond, a former dental assistant who had joined up four years' previously and was a familiar face around the borough. A fearless beat officer, Hammond looked up as Honor entered the room. Hammond offered Honor the tiniest of winks and nods that Katarina could not see: *you're good to talk to her, but go easy.*

'Katarina,' Honor said as she sat down on an armchair opposite the bereaved wife. 'On behalf of us all, I'm so sorry for your loss.'

Katarina nodded through a stream of silent tears, dark eyes still smudged with mascara that now traced the lines of her pain. She did not speak, merely clutched tissues in one tightly balled hand, enveloped in catatonic misery.

'I need to ask you some questions,' Honor said gently, 'to help us with our investigation.'

Again, Katarina nodded but said nothing.

'When did you last see your husband?'

Katarina's voice was meek in reply, a far cry from her outrage outside the church. 'Yesterday afternoon,' she whispered. 'He finished work and met me briefly for coffee, then headed off to a pub to meet with some friends.'

Honor eased out her notebook and scribbled quickly. 'Do you know which pub?' 'All Bar One,' she said, 'Liverpool Street.'

'Okay, and that was your last contact with Sebastian?'

Katarina nodded, but then she shook her head. 'No, he texted me at about nine o'clock, said he'd be later than planned.'

'Okay, did he say what time he'd be home?'

'No,' Katarina replied, 'but he's never home later than about eleven during the week, because of work. Seb isn't a big drinker.'

Honor made a mental note of that. 'Why was he out? Did he go out much during the week?'

'Not often, no. It was a leaving do for one of the staff, just a few drinks. Seb told me that about eight of them were going. I normally go to bed about nine in the evening, so Seb came to meet me for coffee after work so that we'd see each other for a bit.' She smiled. 'He likes doing things like that.'

Denial. The reality of her husband's death had not hit Katarina yet. A few more hours and suddenly it would knock her to the floor. A few days or weeks later would come the anger, the rage. Honor kept her voice gentle, matching Katarina's timbre as she sat with one leg over the other, crossed toward Katarina in a subtle gesture of acceptance, a simple psychological trick to engender trust in a stranger.

'So, the drinks went on for longer than planned. How did Seb normally get home?' 'He walked,' Katarina replied. 'He likes walking.'

Honor reckoned that Seb's walk home would not have taken more than maybe thirty minutes, down Liverpool Street, south across London Bridge and into Southwark, Vauxhall and then Clapham. A fair stride, but nothing to a healthy thirty-two-year old.

'Any chance that he could have been drunk?'

'No,' Katarina said. 'Tipsy, yes, but never drunk. He hates hangovers with a passion. Two pints, maybe a coke or something between them. I've never seen him drunk in ten years together, and we've had some big nights out.'

Honor nodded as she wrote the details down. A two-pint man could easily be drunk on four if they lost track of what they'd had.

'Were there any issues that you know of, no matter how small, that might lead Sebastian to take his own life in this way, or be the victim of a crime of any kind?'

Katarina's dark, smudged eyes lifted to look into Honor's. 'Crime?' Honor chose her words with care.

'It's possible that Sebastian took his own life, but it's also possible that he was a victim of a homicide. That's what we're trying to work out, so anything at all that you can tell us might help us to understand what happened to your husband last night, and get you the answers you need.'

Katarina shook her head vigorously.

'There's nothing,' she insisted. 'Seb has a good job, we're happy…'

Katarina's grief swelled up inside her, her body crouching over the crushing blows as the realisation started to dawn on her that their family was going to be one short for all time. Honor felt her guts twist as she witnessed a woman's dreams being forcefully ripped from her forever, saw Charlotte's arm squeeze Katarina's shoulders.

Katarina somehow got a hold of herself, eyes wide and imploring. 'You think that somebody murdered Sebastian?'

There it was. The moment, the threshold of altered awareness, that life was now different than it had been yesterday, irreparably damaged for all time. Honor knew that pain, felt it scald like acid through her veins with every beat of her heart, and she couldn't bring herself to lie to this poor woman any longer. 'We believe so,' she replied.

Katarina stared without seeing, eyes as black as night, her features twisted with agony as she processed the knowledge that her husband had not taken himself from her, had not been the victim of some tragic accident. Someone else had taken him, someone out there who was still alive. Katarina's voice surged from wrenched vocal cords to fill the room.

'He hated heights,' she repeated between sobbed breaths. 'He would never have willingly climbed that church. Never!'

Katarina's words trailed off and Honor could bear it no longer. She briefly took and squeezed Katarina's hand, then stood and shot Charlotte an urgent look before she turned and left the room.

The air outside the room seemed cold as she closed the door behind her. A deep breath escaped like a released prisoner from her chest as she leaned back against the wall and closed her eyes for a moment.

'You okay?'

A passing uniformed constable hesitated alongside her. She nodded. 'This shit never gets easy.'

The officer glanced at the suite, knew instantly to what she was referring. 'Keep your chin up.'

The constable went on her way. Honor waited for a moment longer, wondering why the hell she'd returned to work so soon. Beside her, the suite door opened and she heard Charlotte telling Katarina she'd be right back before she closed the door behind her.

'Anything?' Honor asked.

'Nothing more than what you have,' Charlotte replied. 'Same story, no deviation in detail. She's off the planet. If it's an act and she's covering, she's got an Oscar with her name on it.'

Honor nodded. Pretty much the same conclusion she'd reached.

'Can you get an alibi from her? We'll check it out from there, and come back with a time of death once the pathologist has conducted the autopsy.'

'Leave it with me. If she alibis out, I'll call you.'

3

The clock on Honor's office wall told her it was already quarter past one in the afternoon, and she hadn't eaten a thing yet. Her office, a rare luxury for a sergeant in a modern police force, looked out onto a modern glass and metal office block that towered over Bishopsgate, the windows reflecting the sunlight now peeking through the mist dispersing against the blue sky over the city. Just south of the station was a conveniently placed *KFC*, the junk-cuisine of choice for City detectives swamped with too much work to even think about eating healthily. Traffic passed by several floors below on the A10, clattering over a loose manhole cover as they headed south toward Leadenhall and the Thames.

Right now, her MIT had nearly thirty ongoing cases that had spilled over from the MET, with just three detectives to handle them all. Honor was in the process of reviewing the case of Ali-Jahim Mohammad, a twenty-nine-year old whose trial at the Old Bailey the previous week had resulted in a nineteen-year sentence for the murder of a gang rival, who had been stabbed in the neck during an altercation near Tower Hill. There was also the disappearance of seventeen-year-old Tamara Hicks, a vulnerable girl who had last been seen walking alone near Aldgate a month before. The MET were understaffed and overwhelmed with cases, and had called in City of London detectives to help solve the disappearance, so far to no avail. Seven more cases, two of them homicides, were on her desk, all of which had been handed over to her the previous week during a meeting with DCI Mitchell. The briefing had been exhaustingly comprehensive, four hours long, and Honor had returned home to enjoy her first sleepless night in four months.

Danny Green leaned around the edge of her office door.

'Sebastian Dukas's autopsy's been moved up due to paperwork issues with an unidentified male found near Spitalfields, thought to be a homeless man who perished overnight. He's not thought to have died under suspicious circumstances, so Sebastian's next on the list. We should get a preliminary report by this evening and toxicology by the morning if we're lucky.'

'Thanks, Danny.'

Honor walked out of her office and made her way to Samir's desk, where she found him trawling through hours of CCTV footage from sites east of St Magnus the Martyr's church.

'Don't check anything before about 9pm last night,' she informed him. 'The wife says that Sebastian texted her from *All Bar One* over in Liverpool Street at about that time, so he was still alive. I'll update CRIS with her information.'

Samir grinned with delight as he began clicking folders on his screen and archiving them.

'Great,' he said. 'Shouldn't we be tracking his movements prior to the bar to see if he was being followed or anything?'

Samir might be new, but he was eager and had good ideas to put forward.

'We'll hold on to all the footage we have,' she replied. 'That way, if the investigation requires it, we can backtrack and see what was happening to Sebastian when he left work, when he arrived, that sort of thing. Right now, we'll get the bar's CCTV and review it from 9pm onwards because that's where the action is most likely to be.'

Samir nodded, but kept watching her. 'Are you okay?' 'What?'

'After you saw the DI, you seemed a bit upset.' Honor swallowed thickly.

'Murders get to us that way,' she said quickly, not lying but not exactly revealing the truth either. 'You'll see. There's only so many times you can watch a family member's grief and not be moved by it. If it doesn't happen to you, you're a psychopath and we'll probably end up arresting you.'

'Which I'll enjoy immensely,' DC Hansen chirped from his desk, further down the office. 'Dummy recruit joins police and gets himself arrested.'

'You'll have to catch me first.'

'Doesn't sound too hard,' Danny replied, leaning back in his chair and twirling a pen in his fingers. 'That degree in electronics will come in real handy when I'm chasing your arse through the city, mate.'

'Are you covering the west, or just here to provoke?' Honor demanded.

'Running as we speak,' Danny replied with a casual gesture to his screen, his seat swaying back and forth as he kept one eye on the footage. 'Nothin' of note yet.'

Danny's desk was overflowing with case files, but it was also home to scattered pictures of his family perched between the teetering piles, a touching display of affection amid the public record of pain and grief. Danny had divorced from his wife two years previously, but had two young daughters to show for the marriage.

Honor headed back to her office and sat down in front of the screen. She logged into her user account and again updated CRIS with Katarina's new information before taking a look at what CCTV footage she had to review. She had folders containing video files from Monument Street, the same route she'd taken herself that morning to the crime scene. Four cameras had been in operation, and a phone call from Danny earlier that morning had secured footage from all of them, each looking in various directions. With Samir and Danny covering Lower Thames Street, they had all approaches covered but for London Bridge itself and a public walkway that passed beneath it on the north shore of the Thames, which allowed access to the church from the south through a small alleyway and courtyard.

The next three hours were spent fielding phone calls and sifting through volumes of grainy black and white camera footage. Honor was fortunate enough to be treated to a KFC bucket by Danny around three o'clock, both herself and Samir having become sufficiently absorbed in their work to forget to eat.

'I've got nothing so far,' Danny mumbled around a chicken leg as he stuffed fries into his mouth. 'Nobody who's carrying a body over their shoulder, anyway.'

'Nothing on mine either,' Samir added. 'I'm getting through it faster than I thought I would, there's not much traffic on the roads and even less pedestrians.

The fog's dropping, though, so it's harder to pick things out.'

Honor nodded. There were only around eight thousand residents in the square mile, most of which was occupied by office space for the financial district.

'Same here,' she said, using a handful of fries to scoop barbeque sauce out of a little plastic container. 'Fog's concealing a lot but the cameras are covering every angle so one way or another this guy's got to show eventually.'

Honor's phone rang, and she hurriedly swallowed the rest of her food and answered it. She listened for a few moments, asked a couple of questions, then rang off.

'That was the rector of the church,' she said. 'He's there right now with Gary Wheeler and the site manager, Jenson Cooper. Let's head back over and see what they have to say.'

'Gary Wheeler alibied out,' Danny told her as he got up, wiping his mouth and grabbing his coke, 'asleep at home with his wife before Sebastian left *All Bar One*, which she and their children confirmed. Not sure about the site manager.'

'Want me to come with you?' Samir asked.

Honor had actually fancied going on her own, but she could see the keen gleam in Samir's eye, and there was no way she was going to deny a new detective what he wanted: they were in far too short supply.

'She'll hold your hand for you if you like,' Hansen offered.

'Let's go,' Honor said, grabbing her bag and looking at Danny. 'All of us.'

One of the big advantages of working with City of London Police was that virtually every crime scene was within walking distance. The force's territorial boundaries extended from the Two Temples to the Tower, north up to Finsbury Square and were exclusively north of the water. Quite literally a square mile, the territory was densely packed with financial buildings, the skyline dominated by architectural icons such as St Paul's Cathedral and the Tower of London. The City of London Police were renowned for running immense anti-corruption operations within the financial district, bringing down companies for multi-million-pound investment fraud and other white- collar crimes, a far cry from the gritty reality of a brutal homicide down in the city's darkened streets.

St Magnus the Martyr's ancient walls looked out of place amid the high-rise office blocks, its foundation stones at an odd angle compared to the arrow-straight placement of the buildings around it. Honor led the way through the entrance arch, glanced up only briefly to the soaring heights of the spire glinting in the sunlight above.

The sepulchral interior of the church greeted them, several of Gary Wheeler's contractors working inside the building attaching cables to the walls. Two men stood whispering beside the wooden door that led up into the belfry. One was dressed in black and quite elderly, obviously the rector, while the other was wearing a hard-hat and fluorescent jacket. Both turned as Honor approached and presented her warrant card.

'Reverend Gregory Thomas,' the rector greeted them with a friendly handshake. 'I'm the rector. This is Jenson Cooper, the site manager responsible for the day to day running of the renovations.'

Cooper was a robust-looking man with salt-and-pepper hair and a thickly forested jaw, who shook Honor's hand gently.

'You're responsible for site security here?' Honor asked Cooper.

'At this site and a few others north of the water,' Cooper confirmed with a soft South London accent, 'all run by Wheeler Construction. We handle contracts for Hamlets ward.'

'And you were here last night?' Danny asked.

'No,' Cooper replied. 'I'm running a site up near Aldgate. I helped set up the work here and handle the security, but it's Gary's team that are replacing the tiles up on the steeple.'

'Can you account for your whereabouts last night between about nine pm and seven thirty am this morning?' Honor asked, going for the kill right away.

Cooper thought for a moment. 'We closed up here at about five, I then went with the lads to the pub.'

'Which pub?' Samir asked.

'Er, Brewdog, on Tower Hill,' Cooper replied, unperturbed. 'I was there until about ten, then went home.'

'Can anybody verify that you were at home?' Honor asked.

Again, Cooper thought about it for a moment. 'I live near Ford Square, but there's a camera at one end. I'll be on it.'

Honor glanced at Samir, who was dutifully taking notes. Danny saw Samir's frantic scribbling and smiled, but she could see that he was impressed with Samir's attention to detail.

'Reverend,' she said, 'you understand that I have to also ask you the same questions?'

'Of course,' the rector replied. 'My work here at the church kept me late, until about nine I think, upon which I retired for the night. I live in the church annexe.'

Honor raised an eyebrow. 'So, you were here the entire night?'

'I always am,' the rector replied with a kindly smile. 'St Magnus is my ministry and my calling, so unless there are duties that take me further afield, I am always here.'

Samir continued making notes, focusing studiously on the conversation. 'Did you hear or see anything at all suspicious?'

'Nothing,' the reverend shrugged. 'It was unusually quiet for that matter, perhaps the fog kept everybody indoors.'

The square mile was often mostly deserted during the small hours, unlike the rest of the city, which never slept. It was interesting to Honor to think that the city of London had been actively busy for literally thousands of years, never once ever being truly quiet.

'Okay,' she said. 'So, the church was locked, the site secured, and by nine o'clock or so everyone's either asleep or absent. Do we have anything to show us how the perpetrator of the crime managed to get into the church?'

'We do,' Cooper said. 'It's this way.'

Cooper led them back outside to the church's main doors, which were located inside an archway beneath the spire. They were big and made from thick, dark wood, the kind of doors people built when she assumed knights were still wearing armour and riding about on gigantic horses.

'The locks were forced,' Cooper said as he gestured to the doors. 'These are eighteenth-century locks. This archway was the medieval entrance to the city for all people crossing the Thames on the old London Bridge. There are parts of old Roman wharfs still attached to the stonework here that are nearly two thousand years old. Point is, somebody would have to know something of how these doors work in order to gain access to the church interior.'

Honor looked at the big doors, heavy ironwork locks secured with thick bolts in the ancient wood.

'So, you think they knew how to pick the locks, or did they have some kind of pass key?' Danny asked.

'Could be either,' Cooper shrugged. 'Hard to tell, but the doors were closed and locked when Gary Wheeler got here.'

'Then how would you know they'd been forced?' Honor challenged.

'The iron's dented,' Cooper explained. 'You can see inside the barrel with a torch. Whatever tool they used, it's made of something harder than iron and it left impressions inside the barrel. The original keys are made of the same iron as the locks and don't leave impressions when they're used, or if they do, over time those impressions are uniform and easily recognisable as wear and tear.

These marks are scratches, and they're fresh.'

Honor nodded, understanding as she then walked through the doors and into the church interior.

'So, they come through here. Then what?'

'Then nothing,' the rector said, having followed them outside. 'The church interior has no further locked doors, other than those on the ground floor. The intruder would have had access to the rest of the building, the steeple included. There was nothing to stop them moving about in here.'

Honor looked back over her shoulder to where the church entrance was shut off by fences erected by Wheeler Construction.

'Do you have security cameras covering the church?'

'We're setting them up as part of the contract,' Cooper confirmed, and gestured to some wires tacked to the church walls where his men were working, Nexus Cables Ltd imprinted on the surface. 'It's all state of the art, but they're not active yet. Gary's getting the footage from the site security cameras downloaded for you, which might have something on them. If he doesn't send it soon, give me a call and I'll sort it out.'

'And the security gates were closed and locked when Gary arrived?'

'Yeah,' Cooper replied thoughtfully, then turned to one of the workmen attaching cables to the church walls. 'Kieran, the gates were closed when that body was found, right, before Gary got in here?'

Kieran strolled over, Honor noting the name-tag on his hi-viz vest –

O'Rourke. 'Yeah, security cameras were running, he had to shut them off to get in here.'

Honor frowned. 'Well, if they were running then the trespasser should show up on them, shouldn't he?'

O'Rourke nodded. 'Weird though, right? Someone goes to the trouble of hacking the church locks on the main doors, but doesn't bother with the security cameras or gates. Why not just cover the cameras up or something, help conceal themselves?'

'Anything else?' Honor asked Cooper.

'The guy must have headed up to the belfry, and then set up some of the spare planks to hang from. Nothing from the moment they got in here is rocket science, and with nobody about, he could have taken his time. None of us get in here any earlier than about seven-thirty in the morning.'

Honor looked around her at the old church for a moment, then the outside porch area. She glanced at Danny, then made a polite excuse to the rector, O'Rourke and Cooper before leading Danny outside into the courtyard, just behind the church itself. Ancient stone flags were worn smooth by the passing of millions of feet through time immemorial, and littered with the first fallen leaves of autumn. An old manhole cover tilted slightly as she walked over it to stand in front of the church.

'What do you make of it?' Danny asked. 'The guy didn't fly in here, and Wheeler's people seem straight up.'

'We'll check the site security cameras as a priority,' she replied. 'Somebody must have come through.'

'They also had to coerce a presumably resistant victim up into the bell tower and murder them, or at the very least carry a body up there,' Danny added. 'No easy task.'

She checked her watch: ten to four.

'We'd better get back,' she said. 'Group Commander meeting.'

Samir joined them as they left the church, the rector promising to let them know if he recalled or noticed anything unusual in the church. Honor didn't expect to hear from either of them – neither man showed any concern about her questions, and both acted like most people did when they found themselves unexpectedly caught up in a murder investigation: cautious and nervous at first, but increasingly interested as they realised that they were easily able to alibi themselves out of suspicion.

They walked back to Bishopsgate in silence, arriving just in time for the meeting. DI Katy Harper was present, as was Detective Chief Inspector Tom Mitchell, a tall, powerfully built man who had served as a Royal Marines Commando before joining the force as an Armed Response Officer. Mitchell was Harper's direct boss and ruled the Major Incident Teams with a firm but fair hand, the rock at the centre of City CID. Held in a conference room on the second floor, the briefing was led by Detective Chief Superintendent Andy Leeson, a former beat officer who had made his way up through the ranks during a twenty-four-year career with the City of London Police. Young-looking for his age, Leeson cut a dashing figure and didn't waste any time on getting down to business as the door to the room was closed.

'Firstly, good news on the Brendan Flint extradition,' he began, gesturing to a white board covered with photographs of various suspects in the department's on-going cases. 'He's been arrested in the Netherlands and will be returned to custody in the UK by next week.'

There was a commingled exhalation of relief and a few smiles from the team on MIT 2. Flint was a convicted murderer who, during a burglary on Cheapside, had used a leather belt to throttle to death an eighty-seven-year old war veteran. Flint had somehow managed to slip through customs and out of the country two years previously, and the team had been liaising with Interpol the entire time to locate and apprehend him.

'A little more cheer also for MIT 1,' Leeson added. 'Alan Pike was today successfully convicted at the Old Bailey of the homicide of his wife, aggravated assault of their son, battery and several other lesser charges. He's remanded in custody and we're recommending a life sentence, at least fifteen years.'

More smiles, a couple of pats on the backs of detectives who had worked tirelessly for weeks to secure the convictions. One, a veteran DS named Moore, had spent the past four weeks giving evidence at the trial and sleeping in the office to ensure he never missed a moment.

'As most of you will by now know,' Leeson went on, 'we have a new case. MIT 2 are working on the suspected homicide of Sebastian Dukas, who was found hanged this morning from the steeple of St Magnus. Where are we with that right now?'

DI Katy Harper spoke without hesitation.

'DS McVey is working the case, with DCs Green and Raaya. We're gathering and assessing evidence and should have some firm conclusions by the morning. The wife and the construction company owner have alibied out so far. The media's been on the phone but we're staying tight-lipped for now, at least until we have something concrete to say.'

Leeson nodded, and glanced briefly at Honor. 'Welcome back.'

Honor smiled and hoped to hell her skin wasn't colouring up, but she could feel the eyes of the rest of the team on her and prickly heat antagonised the skin at the back of her neck. A few faces caught her eye, smiles, nods of recognition on some, caution and perhaps even concern on others.

'Okay, the Henderson disappearance, where are we on that?'

The DI began recounting yet another on-going case as Honor stood in catatonic silence and waited for the wave of panic looming around her to subside. *Nobody is looking at you.* For once, this was demonstrably true as the rest of the room was listening to DI Harper and paying Honor absolutely no attention whatsoever. Except Samir. She caught him glancing at her a time or two and wondered what the hell he was looking at. Maybe he could see through her thin veil? Maybe he fancied her? No, too young. He was attractive enough to do far better than her, and besides, he could…

'Honor?'

DCS Leeson was looking at her expectantly, as was the entire room. Honor blinked and zapped to the present as her mind performed a rapid calculation, reviewing the words that had been echoing around the room during her brief reverie.

'We don't need the HAT car right now, so it can stay with the on-call team,' she replied. 'The Dukas case *seems* to be singular in nature, at least for now.'

'You think it's connected to other crimes?'

Another brief pause as Honor's panicked neurons realigned themselves.

'The killing appears random, with nothing in the victim's life history to support a notion of motive. What bothers me is the almost ritualistic way in which the body was presented. Had somebody simply wanted Dukas dead, they could have killed him and hidden the remains and we might have never been the wiser. Yet, they put him on display in a *very* visible manner. It worries me that a killer would go to these lengths, take such risks, make such an effort for no apparent motive whatsoever.'

There was a long silence in the conference room as everybody digested what she had said.

'You think that this was not a one off?' Leeson asked her.

In for a penny...

'It's too elaborate,' she said. 'I think that they wanted to be seen, to show off what they can do. I'd put money on there being another murder, assuming we don't find a motive. Somebody's trying to get our attention.'

A few barely concealed smirks appeared on faces around the room. The prickly heat returned to Honor's neck and she felt her cheeks flush red. DC Hansen piped up, leaning against one wall of the room with his arms folded and an expression of weariness on his features.

'More likely a Mafia hit or something similar, yardies on the rampage. They like to advertise their kills.'

'That would have clear motive,' Honor replied in defence. 'There's nothing yet to suggest Sebastian Dukas had any involvement with organised crime.'

'You think that the city has a serial killer on the loose?' Leeson pressed.

The DCS was not mocking her. In fact, his features were as hard as stone. The smirks around the room withered away.

'I can't say, sir,' Honor replied, grateful that Leeson was at least giving her the time of day. 'I just don't see any reason why a body would be displayed in the way that Sebastian Dukas's was, unless somebody *really* wanted it to be seen. There was no way that we could conceal the body before the fog lifted. Everybody knows about it, and by now the rumour mill will be alive across the city. Tomorrow's papers will have images of that man's remains on their front covers, which will be immensely painful to witness for the victim's family. Murderers generally do everything they can to conceal their crimes. They don't normally go for front-page coverage.'

More silence from around the room.

'Maybe he lowered himself off those planks slowly, climbed down on the rope with the end of it around his neck, then let go at the bottom,' said DI

Harper. 'A suicide to look like a murder. It's rare, but it's been known.'

Honor nodded, not reacting adversely to the assault on her theory. Critical analysis of a crime scene was part and parcel of their work, and often revealed insights into a crime that a detective working alone would not have noticed.

'The victim was terrified of heights,' Honor said. 'We have it on record that the guy got dizzy standing on a thick rug, never mind climbing two hundred feet up a church steeple. To then walk out on an eight-inch wide plank and lower himself to his death? It's a bigger reach than to suggest he was murdered.'

The conference room hummed with silence, but the faces around Honor were interested now.

'Autopsy?' Leeson asked.

'Results should be with us first thing tomorrow,' Honor replied. 'Toxicology too, if we're lucky.'

DCS Leeson looked at DI Harper. 'Set up an incident room here at B-Gate, not at Wood Street, if the results confirm suspicious circumstances. I'll field the media, but we're going to need something to say if this starts gathering pace. If we go with suspected suicide, but Honor is right, it could goad a killer into striking again if they think we're not getting the message they want to send.'

Honor's nerves jangled with a heady fusion of delight and anxiety as she saw her assessment officially vindicated. She intercepted a dark glance from Hansen as the rest of the briefing played out. By five o'clock they were out of the conference room. A firm hand squeezed her shoulder as she walked.

'Nice work, boss,' Danny Green said. 'Not a bad first day back.'

Honor returned the compliment with a smile but said nothing as she returned to her office and sat down. The sky was rapidly darkening outside, the pale blue vault of the heavens laden with thunderheads, their heights bathed in orange light from the setting sun that reflected off windows on the tower blocks.

'Honor?' She turned and saw Samir at her office door. 'We're heading over to The Bull. You in?'

The Bull was a traditional pub, tucked away in a tiny side street called Devonshire Row, where many of the local officers and detectives descended for drinks when their shifts were up, or meals when they were late in the office and needed to get out from behind their desks for an hour or so. Honor shook her head.

'Not tonight.'

'They're serving roast,' Samir teased with a smile, 'and I could pick your brains about all sorts.'

Honor forced a smile onto her features. 'No thanks, I've got a full plate here and I'm pretty tired. Busy first day and all that.'

Samir hesitated for a moment, then he nodded in understanding and left. Honor watched the empty space where he had been standing. She knew that she should just get up and go. Her shift was over, although on an active case there was rarely anything known as a "standard" shift. Everybody worked overtime, and leave was often cancelled when things got really intense, not that anybody wanted time off at those moments anyway. But the Dukas case was not yet a truly active homicide investigation, and the media would not take much notice of the team having a meal in the pub. Give it another couple of days, or, heaven forbid, another similar killing, and nobody in MIT 2 would be able to pass wind without journalists knowing about it. Eating in a pub would be used as "evidence" for low-blow journalism pieces accusing police of not working hard enough, or that they somehow didn't care about finding the perpetrator.

Honor leaned back in her seat as she accessed the latest church CCTV footage, sent to her by Gary Wheeler's construction company. Jenson Cooper had come through and e-mailed it to her while she had been in the meeting. Within minutes of beginning to review the footage, she had forgotten about Samir and the pub meal.

4

'Bollocks! I don't believe it!'

The *Crosse Keys* pub was overflowing with people around its central oval bar, where milling crowds fought for space and the attention of the staff

Amber Carson shook her head, giggling over her wine as she sat with friends at one of the many tables that surrounded the bar.

'I'm telling you; it was Sean Bean! He signed my bra!'

There were four of them, Amber sitting with her friend Rachel to one side of the table, Julie and Michelle opposite. All were on their fourth drink, or maybe it was the fifth, and nobody was in the mood to stop despite everybody having to go to work the next day.

'I want to see that bra!' Rachel yelped.

'I'm going to get it framed,' Amber replied. 'Signed by Ned Stark, *aka* Sean Bean.'

'Did he look like he does on the telly?' Julie enquired.

'He's a bit older now,' Amber admitted, 'but like all men, he's better in the flesh.'

'In your flesh, or just generally?' Michelle purred.

'Will you leave it out?'

They had been in the pub since finishing work, and Amber glanced out of the tall windows nearby to see the night sky dark, car headlights flickering past. She glanced at her watch: 8.59pm. Her vision was blurring slightly and she realised that the drinks were going to her head quicker than they normally would. *That's what you get for skipping dinner.*

'I'd better go,' she said.

'Are you kidding?' Rachel said. 'We only just got started!'

'We got started about eight years ago,' Michelle replied, 'and haven't dried out since. Amber's right, I need to go now too or we'll still be here at midnight.'

'That's the idea!' Rachel chortled, but Amber could see the disappointment in her friend's eyes. They weren't twenty-years-olds now, and it was starting to show.

The four friends stood up and put on their coats and jackets before hugging each other goodbye. Amber had only a fairly short walk up to Hackney, while her three friends all lived south of the water.

'You want us to call you a taxi?' Julie asked.

Amber smiled. She would have liked a ride home, but money was tight since she'd split up with her boyfriend, so throwing a tenner on a cab wasn't an option, especially when she could walk the route in less than twenty minutes.

'Thanks, but it's fine, it's still busy out there.' 'Okay, call me when you get home, okay?' 'Will do!'

The foursome made their way out of the cosy warmth of the pub. Amber could still see a hint of dark blue sky above, but black clouds were scudding across the heavens and she could feel tiny spots of rain spiralling down toward them. She reached up to her collar and pulled her hood over her head as she waved goodbye to her friends and set off north.

She walked past the chambers and the amusingly named *Dirty Dicks* pub, heading toward Old Spitalfields. The darkened streets were now the domain of city suits hurrying home from their offices and the trading floors, the skyline around her a glittering array of towering office blocks filled with soft lighting. The suits rushed by without a glance, broadsheets tucked under their arms, umbrellas in their hands as they raced the forthcoming storm for home. The wind whipped between the huge office blocks, tugging at her raincoat as Amber forged her way north.

Her home was a tiny, one-bedroom apartment above a little cafe on Scrutton Street, right opposite the *Old King's Head* pub. Compact, to say the least, and with a monthly rent that could have bought her a small country in other parts of the world, Amber had remained there after her last boyfriend had ditched her for a younger version, or so she'd later been told. The sting of that hadn't been as bad as she'd assumed – better now than later, when kids and mortgages and messy divorces were involved. At least she'd kept his half of the apartment deposit, which she assumed the bloody idiot had forgotten about in his haste to dip his wick into whatever floozy he'd presumably picked up somewhere along the line.

Amber buried her head into her hood and walked faster. She was leaving the edge of the financial district now, the glossy tower blocks behind her, a few more under construction partially concealed behind security sites. She could see towering cranes reaching up into the darkness of the night, red lights slowly flashing on top to warn low-flying helicopters of their presence above the city.

The suits were gone now, replaced by ordinary folk going about their business. People talked on mobile phones as they walked, others smoked e-cigarettes or real ones. Corrugated iron fences concealed building projects, their rusting metal surfaces inked with a kaleidoscopic array of graffiti and gang tags.

She cut left onto Worship Street, swallowed by the darkness between two massive office blocks. There bustle of the main road disappeared behind her, until she could hear her heels clicking once more on the pavement. This was the part she hated the most, and despite the somewhat comforting presence of CCTV cameras on the buildings she could not help but feel vulnerable. She felt dizzy and nauseous, far more so than she really should have done on three glasses of Pinot. All she could think about was getting home and throwing herself into bed to sleep it off. It had been a long day at work beforehand, and she felt incredibly fatigued. Maybe Robbie's decision to leave her had affected her more than she thought. She hadn't gone out as much while they'd lived together, enjoying their little life of watching television and having take-aways when they could afford it. Now she was alone and craved the company of her friends, even if it meant drinking a little more than she was used to.

She turned right into the narrow confines of Holywell Row, and was truly alone. Hemmed in by the backs of anonymous offices and commercial properties, the alley was a through-fare and little else. She could only just about hear the sounds of occasional traffic from distant streets.

She walked as fast as she could without looking desperate, breathing deeply to clear her mind. Her footsteps were uneasy, as though she was losing her coordination, and she wondered if she was coming down with something. A couple of the guys in her office had recently been off sick with the flu. What she really didn't need right now was two weeks in bed, her sick pay nothing like what she needed to pay the rent.

A figure appeared ahead, walking down the alley in the opposite direction. Amber's grip on her cell phone tightened in one hand, her grip on her apartment keys tightening in the other. Simple tricks; a phone to call for help, the key a weapon to strike an attacker's face should she be unlucky enough to be confronted.

The figure was male, tall, his hood up against the light drizzle now gusting down from the turbulent skies above. He walked in the centre of the road, dominating the street, his head down and his hands tucked in his pockets. As the man closed in on her, Amber began to wish she had taken the offer of a taxi. She stayed on the pavement, but her heart began to pound in her chest as the man veered toward her, closer now, enough to see a bull-neck and thick shoulders. A big man, far too powerful for her to fight off. She opened her mouth, ready to scream bloody murder if the man made a move for her, her hand gripping her apartment key tightly enough that pain throbbed through her fingers.

The man was almost upon her. He looked up, his features shadowy within his hood, and a look of surprise flashed across his features as she heard the whisper of his iPod playing music through his Bluetooth earphone. The man veered away from her, lost in his music, and Amber passed by. She walked ten paces and glanced over her shoulder to see the man still walking away from her, his head down as he disappeared around the corner of Holywell.

Christ, you need some rest, girl.

The lights of the *Old King's Head* and the sound of laughter and people talking outside calmed her nerves as she reached Scrutton Street and crossed to her apartment. The front door was in a narrow alley alongside the building, itself protected by a metal-grate security door. Amber unlocked the security door, then the front door, and stepped in before locking both doors behind her.

She slumped against the wall and suddenly a wave of nausea hit her. She felt awful, as though a hangover was already dragging her down. She slowly climbed the narrow stairway to her tiny apartment, her legs weak and untrustworthy. Her world swayed off-balance as she reached the top of the stairs, her stomach in turmoil as she turned right in the darkness and staggered into the bedroom.

Amber kicked off her shoes and slumped face-down onto the bed. *God, she was so tired*. This wasn't like anything she had ever felt before, and she knew that she had to sort herself out before she fell asleep, else she'd still be wearing her work clothes in the morning.

Slowly, with great effort, she pushed herself up into a sitting position and reached out for the bedside lamp. The light switched on, and she turned to stand in time to see the man rush upon her from the living room. He moved so fast that she could only make out a bulky, heavy-set frame dressed all in black, his face concealed behind a balaclava, gloves on his hands and two fearsome eyes glaring at her as he filled her vision.

Amber opened her mouth to suck in air with which to scream, but the man ploughed into her and she toppled backwards onto her bed as though she'd been hit by a train. A gloved hand covered her mouth, the man's eyes staring into hers from inches away as she fought with what little strength she had left. To her horror, she felt him gently stroking her hair as he pinned her beneath his weight. She tried to squirm away, but her body was now so utterly bereft of energy that it was all she could do to keep her eyes open.

Moments later, she could not even do that, and her consciousness slipped away into a deep blackness, the man's eyes the last thing on her terrified mind.

Beautiful.

That was what he thought of her. So many of them were these days, too many to choose from it seemed. But this one, like the others, was special. Some girls just had that *magic*, a vibrance that made them stand out. It wasn't that they were supermodels, it was something more subtle and unique: the way they giggled, the way that their lips curled as they smiled, the shape and set of their eyes. Sometimes, it was just the way their hair curled over tiny, pixie-like ears, just as Amber's was doing now.

Power.

The power was intoxicating, like nothing else he had ever experienced in his life. The power not just of life over death, but the power of time, power over the moment itself. This moment, and those that would soon follow. The crucible of life was a painful, laborious affair laden with strife and disappointments. Thus, few people ever got to experience moments of power such as this, although he knew that many dreamed of it, fantasised about it, some for their entire lives. They attempted to quench their thirst for power through violent video games, or by hiring women, or joining fetish clubs and other bizarre pursuits, but all of it was just to avoid the truth that all men carried in their black hearts, that absolute power over a woman was a drug in itself, a virus sought by all yet avoided by most, who lacked the courage to surrender to their true convictions.

He looked down at her now. Amber Carson. Even her name, Amber, was perfect, matched her features, her personality, her smile. He stroked her hair some more, marvelling at how soft it felt. Her face was serene, her sculptured lips soft and inviting. He could smell her perfume, but more than that he could smell the scent of her, a primal elixir that sent spasms of heat pulsing through his groin.

Not this one. This one is special.

He closed his eyes and forced himself to step back from the brink. He'd violated the last one, and had as a result been forced to wait over two months before the right opportunity had again presented itself. Time was of the essence.

The first victim had been the bait, and it had been a tortuous task to suspend the body from such great height, but now it was done. A question arose unbidden into his mind; *do I leave them floundering, wondering what happened to Sebastian Dukas? Or do I start now, and bring forth the hell that is waiting?*

Power, again, adrenaline lacing his veins, thundering like a freight train through his nervous system. Anticipation surged with every heartbeat. He could wait, use Amber for his pleasure before disposing of her, but he knew in his heart of hearts that he did not want to wait any longer. Now was the right time, and the conditions of yesterday had been perfect. It was time, his time.

He needed to leave his mark on her though. Slowly, he reared up, kneeling over Amber as he reached down and unbuttoned her blouse. He took his time, slowly easing the fabric aside before gently lifting up her bra to reveal large, soft breasts. He leaned down and slowly ran his tongue across them, tasted them one at a time. The temptation to use her was almost overwhelming but he refrained, driven by a greater purpose. He sat up again and gently placed her bra back in place as he savoured the taste of her skin, soft and clean, so *alive*. Then, he removed her blouse, leaving her underwear and jeans in place as he carefully folded the clothes and slipped them into a leather shoulder bag. He stood up, watched her for a moment longer, and then he reached down and slipped her earrings from her. He put them in his pocket and checked his watch. Too early. He would have to wait. He sat on the edge of the bed, and in the darkness silently watched Amber sleeping.

There was no need for him to restrain her, for she would not awake for at least four hours. That would be enough time to do what he needed to do. She was smaller than Sebastian had been, so the dose had been lighter. Then again, Sebastian had fought with surprising gusto before being overwhelmed, to the extent that he had been forced to squeeze the life out of him before the time was right.

He hadn't been able to watch Sebastian die on the end of the rope. He wouldn't make that mistake again. This one had to be just *perfect*.

5

Living alone in London was both a comforting and contradictory experience for Honor. The city, so large, so vibrant, and yet as soon as she closed the door to her apartment, she occupied a world of near-permanent silence. She had been fortunate, if that was the word, to buy the property using a settlement she had received the previous year. She had not been able to afford to buy outright in one of the most expensive cities on earth, but at least she was on the property ladder, something out of reach for a large number of people her age in London.

The apartment in Cornwall Road was one of several built when a row of three- bedroom homes had been converted into apartments, a stone's throw from Waterloo Station and the water. Honor had chosen it because the road was quiet, and the top floor apartment offered greater separation from the streets below. With London Bridge and Southwark station minutes away, she was never far from work, essential when she could be called at any time of the day or night should something kick off in the square mile.

The walls were mostly bare, painted in warm but neutral colours. Honor walked past the bathroom and kitchen to a living room that looked out toward St John's church, the glittering tower blocks of the South Bank beyond. The sight of the church tower bathed in the glow of spotlights reminded her of Sebastian Dukas, now lying in a nearby morgue. Katarina's grieving face filled

Honor's thoughts as she saw her own reflection in the apartment's blackened windows, the night outside blustery, rivulets of rain pouring like tears down the panes and her face in the reflection.

Honor turned and walked into the kitchen, switching on the light. People sometimes said that a room was so small, one couldn't swing a cat in it. Honor would never know because her cat couldn't fit in the kitchen with her anyway. Everything was compacted as much as possible into what she suspected had once been a small bathroom or similar. She opened her fridge with one hand, while the other opened a cupboard on the opposite side of the room and pulled out a wineglass.

Her cat, Bailey, strolled out of the bedroom on cue, stretching and scraping his claws anywhere but the scratch post she'd bought for the purpose. She put fresh food on a plate for him, wandered back into the living room with a glass of chilled wine, and finally slumped onto her sofa. She checked her watch.

9.47pm.

A fourteen-hour shift, not too bad for her first day back and an active homicide investigation. At least she wasn't asleep at her desk, not unknown in the past. She glanced at a picture frame on one wall, her parents smiling back at her, herself pinned between them, aged twelve or so. Family holiday, Menorca, her brother larking about somewhere in the background, probably hurling himself into the pool or something. Standard for Billy McVey, always messing about. Her parents had recently retired to Eastbourne, the mecca of the elderly. Billy was working as a plumber in Kent, which was a worry for everyone concerned as the idea of Bill playing with gas pipes was akin to asking Oliver Reed to run a brewery. Still, he was married and happy, with one son whom it seemed destined to be a chip off the old deranged block.

Honor's eyes drifted to the right, past the television, to where a small framed picture of an ultrasound scan graced an otherwise bare wall. She stared at the little image for a moment, the ghostly shape of an infant body against darkness, then closed her eyes and took a sip of her wine.

Nobody cares. Nobody's watching.

The wine hit her sensorium to soothe the turmoil inside as she sank back into the sofa. Bailey appeared, licking his fur before jumping up and settling in on her lap. The tortoiseshell male with a calm temperament and a teeny-tiny little voice was the only company she kept these days outside of work. There were three lively pubs within walking distance of the apartment, but she had visited none of them since moving in late the previous year.

The silence was deafening, and she revelled in it. Neighbours here were not noisy, the street outside was not busy and the windows were all triple-glazed. She absent-mindedly stroked Bailey, listening to his soft purring as she sipped her wine and stared out of the broad windows into the darkness, across the city streets glittering with tiny lights. She could just see, between the South Bank's tower blocks, the London Eye and beyond it, Big Ben and Parliament, and the moving lights of vehicles on the Embankment. Life, on-going, where elsewhere there was only the ending of life.

She couldn't get Sebastian Dukas out of her mind. No, perhaps more appropriately, she couldn't get his wife and family out of her mind. She knew too well what they were going through. The human condition was not well adapted to adjusting to a sudden loss of life, something so vibrant suddenly silent and cold, lost forever. The pain was something for which there was no cure - a life-long, terminal condition that haunted the soul.

Honor knew that she should get up and eat something, but sitting here on the sofa was the one contemplative place where she could visualise her quarry, could think clearly, separated in catatonic silence from the rest of London. Somewhere, out there in that city, a killer was on the loose, and she felt certain with every fibre in her body that he or she was going to kill again. What stood in her way was what had always stood in her way: a toxic dish of chronic anxiety sprinkled with a dash of Obsessive-Compulsive-Disorder.

Most people assumed that OCD meant stacking things in perfect order or whistling a tune every hour, on the hour, to get through the day. Honor had a fair dose of these afflictions, the apartment a miasma of duties. The mirror must always be clean, because she didn't like marks on the surface. She didn't like clutter: things needed to be orderly and aligned, although she wasn't *so* far gone that all lines needed to be parallel or perpendicular. She never left the apartment with the bed unmade or the sink full of incomplete washing-up. Door locks would be checked, at least twice, probably three times – it wasn't hard to do on the way to or from the kitchen. Lights always off, no cell phones or laptops or e-readers left on charge or chargers left plugged in. Nothing left on stand-by.

But such habits were as much born of natural caution and common sense as the dark fruit of OCD. The true condition was veiled with further complex afflictions: random and unconnected thoughts of violence or shame, the signatures of anxiety and loneliness, of reduced self-worth and self-confidence. Honor fought them every day, but she had come to realise that her work as a police officer had somewhat veiled her condition, silenced the unwanted voices in her mind behind a wall of real suffering, the true grief of countless lost souls.

Such sights were not unusual for a serving police officer, although it wasn't often the blood and gore of the movies, even when working for CID. More, it was the unusual, the bizarre, the way people live that she would never before have thought possible; the fetid squalor of the poor and the addicted; the confused mess of the hoarder; the lonely darkness of the social recluse; the frantic, deranged ranting of the addicted; worlds different and yet on the doorstep, perhaps just yards away. There was never any time for her to focus on her own demons, which often seemed so trivial compared to the trials suffered by others less fortunate.

But the voices had come back during her sick-leave. As the stress of her job had eased, so her mind had wandered, and whenever her mind wandered, it reached into places that she didn't want to think about. She took her maudlin thoughts and crammed them into a box in her mind, buried them away. Distraction. Denial.

Instead, she focused on the glittering lights of the city and wondered whether their quarry was about to strike again.

I'm going to be late for work.

The thought emerged from a deep darkness as Amber's senses began reconnecting themselves. Random thoughts tumbled through the field of her awareness, only to fade away again into the blackness. She still had a hangover, still felt rough. Memories fluttered through her mind: the bar, her friends, the walk home and how terrible she'd felt, and then…. Then…

Amber's eyes flicked open and she tried to scream.

Despite her eyes being open, she realised that she remained in utter darkness. Panic ripped through her as she realised that she was confined within a tiny space, and that her wrists and ankles were firmly bound and her mouth was tightly gagged.

Oh God, no, what's happening? She looked down, felt cold stone against her skin, but she could also feel that she was wearing her underwear. Thoughts of rape crept like demons through her mind, but she did not have the sense that she had been violated in any way. The darkness was intense, deep, terrifying. Her heart began to beat against the walls of her chest as she tried to see something, anything around her.

There was a scent that made her cough and then almost gag. It was damp, cold, laden with something that sent primal terror coursing through her mind as she shivered in the silence. She thought that she could hear water gurgling somewhere nearby, the air stale.

Escape.

Amber tried to get to her feet, then realised that she was bound to an iron ring that itself was bolted into the stone. *Jesus, what the hell is going on?* A splashing sound reached her, and she sensed rather than saw somebody coming towards her out of the darkness. Amber reared back in terror as a figure loomed over her, and silently unfastened the rope binding her to the iron ring. Before she could move, the figure gripped her tightly and lifted her onto his shoulder as though she weighed little more than a newborn.

Amber thrashed and squirmed, but it was little use as she was carried through the darkness. The man stopped, and then she felt herself being carried up a ladder, the thump of boots on metal rungs. A waft of fresh air reached her, and moments later she was carefully, but with great strength, pushed up and out of the passage and onto soft grass that was damp and cold.

Amber saw the sky above her as she flopped onto her back, and to her right a great cathedral that was bathed in the glow of countless spotlights. She tried again to scream but no sound came forth, her gag silencing her and her vocal cords strangely subdued. The man climbed up alongside her, and she was again lifted physically from the ground and carried toward the cathedral. Amber had absolutely no idea who her captor was or what he wanted with her. If he had not raped her, and had not already killed her, then what the hell was he doing bringing her here?

The man set her down alongside the cathedral walls, where deep shadows concealed them from the security cameras she presumed were watching. She'd once heard that nobody could walk anywhere in the city without being seen by at least four cameras in any given place, but she wasn't sure that she believed that right now. The man walked away toward some large plastic sheets that were spread across the ground under the cathedral walls.

Amber tried to move but her limbs remained too weak. Then, she tried to roll. With a heave of effort, she rolled over onto her front on the damp grass. She glanced at the man, but he remained engrossed in his work. Amber heaved herself over again. The cathedral lawns were beneath the level of the traffic on the nearby A3 that led to London Bridge, but she could see that the traffic was light and that there were no pedestrians in sight even if she could call for help.

She rolled again, hoping that she could reach the steps that led up to the main road and perhaps pull the gag from her mouth, hook it over something and wrench it free. She was on her fifth laborious roll when the man caught up with her and hauled her upright. Amber was powerless to prevent him from lifting her off the ground, and he carried her back to the cathedral walls.

The man sat her down on the grass, and then drew back one of the large plastic sheets. Amber was unable to contain her curiosity as she looked inside and saw that a series of stone flags had been lifted, revealing cavities beneath the huge walls. Three of the cavities had been filled with cement. Two were still empty, deep, and beside one of them she could see a mound of earth where it had been dug deeper than the others.

The man lifted her gently, as though she were the most important thing in the world, and he carried her to the edge of the pit. As Amber looked down and saw what was in the pit, so raw terror pulsed through her nervous system and with every ounce of her strength she tried to squirm free from his grasp. She wrenched her head to one side, opened her mouth and tried to bite the man's face, but he drew back from her, and she saw in his eyes a delighted amusement, an excitement that only increased her horror and disgust.

Slowly, with reverential care, the man stepped down into the cavity and lowered her into the coffin that lay within its depths.

'Ssshhhh,' he murmured.

Amber saw the sides of a coffin rise up on either side of her, her wrists still bound, her ankles too, her mouth gagged. She could not move, and she stared up at the man with pleading eyes as he towered over her, the cathedral's magnificent walls soaring above him, the stained-glass windows glistening with colour from the streetlights as he watched her for a long moment.

'You will not be alone,' he murmured. 'More will follow.'

Amber tried again to free herself, but it was of no use. She was bound far too tightly, and now her breathing was coming in hard snorts of terror as the man clambered out of the pit. He turned, crouched, and reached out for the edge of the coffin's lid.

Amber's body began to convulse, not enough air getting into her lungs. *What have I done to deserve this? Who is this man? Why is he doing this to me? Doesn't he know I suffer from terrible claustrophobia?*

'There's nothing to be afraid of,' he said, his face still concealed behind the balaclava. 'All things come to this, eventually. I will be watching.'

Amber found her voice and emitted a scream that was heavily muted by the tight gag. Tears streamed down her face as she saw the casket lid close, and with a thud she was suddenly sealed into the coffin and in complete and utter darkness.

Amber felt herself going into shock and tried to control her breathing as a thousand thoughts rushed through her mind. *Don't breathe too fast, the air will run out. Somebody will find you in the morning. Try to find a way of making noise. Do something, but don't let him know you can do it. You must wait until he's gone.*

The coffin was eerily silent for a long moment, and then a tiny blue light flickered into life just inches from her face. It peered down at her and provided meagre illumination within her grim prison. For a moment Amber hoped that this was all some elaborate prank, a joke played on her by friends, for which she would absolutely be taking legal action. Then she realised that it was a tiny camera, glowing on the end of what she took to be some kind of optical fibre. Alongside it appeared another tube, this one empty, and she guessed that it was some kind of breathing tube.

Then she heard soil falling outside the coffin.

Oh God, please no.

The rhythmic thump of soil outside hammered the coffin lid, and Amber knew that the man was filling the cavity back in, concealing her beneath the ground. For a moment, she could not believe that this was happening to her, could not understand that this was a reality, that she was going to die here buried under a foot or more of soil and....

The concrete.

Amber's panic rose up within her like something alive, her heart hammering in her chest as she heard more soil being dumped on the coffin. The sounds became more muted after a few minutes, and with terminal certainty she knew that she was already buried and that he would be filling in the rest before stamping it down. He would then leave, would remove all trace of his presence. Then, in the morning, the cavity above would be filled with cement.

The air became hot, no room to move, no room to breathe. Amber felt prickly heat stinging her forehead and the back of her neck. Even with the breathing tube, she would suffocate in here long before anybody would ever find her. The thought provoked another, terrible realisation.

Was the tube long enough to reach through the cement?

Her choked sobs broke out around the gag as she fought to free herself. Her hands were pinned behind her back, but if she could get them free then maybe she could escape somehow? The concrete wouldn't be laid until tomorrow at the earliest, so she had the rest of the night to figure something out.

Amber, her anxiety soaring, tried to think. There *had* to be some way out of this. She could see the interior of the coffin as she lay in the near blackness: cheap wood, thin, weak. Shit, the bloody thing wouldn't hold up against the weight of the soil *and* the concrete, would it? What if the thing collapsed, then she would be…

Oh Jesus, please no, not like this.

Amber's hands rubbed against her leather belt, and she had a thought. Her jeans had little metal buttons, and her belt had a buckle. If she could free her hands and then remove the belt, she could maybe hack or prize her way out of the crude coffin and dig herself free. There was only about a foot of soil above her, she guessed, maybe even less. If she could push hard enough on the coffin lid, she might be able to open it. It was all she had, the only chance to get the hell out of here before she was sealed in, forever. Amber shifted her hands slightly as she searched for one of the little metal buttons on her jeans. She was bound with rope or plastic of some kind, and both were weaker than metal. If she could rub the bonds against the edges of the metal buttons, she could possibly break free of them, and that would free her hands and let her remove her gag.

She had no idea what time it was, but she knew she had only hours to get the hell out of here before she became just another tomb beneath the cathedral.

6

Honor walked into Bishopsgate Station at a little after seven in the morning, the sky above laden with heavy clouds scudding low over the city. Streetlights, headlights, the glittering tower blocks and the "Gherkin" glowed in the morning gloom, fine autumnal drizzle spiralling through the city streets on the blustering wind as she hurried inside.

She headed up to her office on the second floor, switched on her computer and began to think about updating the CRIS database. Danny and Samir would almost certainly have new information to add. She didn't know until what time their evening gathering had lasted, but she was sure that they were professional enough to know not to get drunk when there was a major investigation in the offing.

Both men arrived within ten minutes of her, and to her satisfaction both were looking fresh as a daisy.

'Morning, boss,' Danny said as he sauntered in, a coffee in his hand. 'Any news?' Honor asked.

'The beef steak was good, and they serve a great pint of London Pride,' he grinned. 'I just called the pathologist, and she's asked us to pop over.'

Honor felt a pulse of excitement flutter through her as she picked up her bag again and headed out of the office. The pathologist would normally just call with information, even important information, but a visit meant that there was more to the case than just the final report from the autopsy. Samir walked at her side as Danny led the way, and they were intercepted by DCI Mitchell as he barrelled his way through the corridors with a fat wad of court papers under one arm and a mug of coffee grasped in his bear-like hand.

'You've got your incident room,' he said to her as he passed them by. 'Pathologist has something for you that confirms homicide.'

Honor nodded. 'We're heading down there now.'

'Fill me in as soon as you get back, I want it in the morning briefing.'

Danny drove, Honor alongside him in the front and Samir in the back as they headed south over the water at London Bridge, then turned left for St Thomas Street and Guy's Hospital. The building, famous across the world for its pioneering work with sick children, was located right opposite the Shard, a towering icon of metal and glass that soared a thousand feet into the turbulent London sky.

Dr Willow Coulter was a brunette in her late thirties, who seemed too softly-spoken to have spent a career carving up over ten thousand dead bodies. The forensic pathologist had worked first at St George's in Tooting before running her own department at Guy's, which was registered specifically to work with homicide detectives.

'Honor,' Michelle greeted her with a smile. 'Good to see you back.'

It was somewhat ironic that Honor's warmest welcome would come from coldest of environments. Michelle's office was alongside the morgue, an entire department supposedly devoted to the study of the cause of death. Despite what people saw on television, most pathologists rarely saw a cadaver or even body organs, their work instead involving the study of life, not death: toxicology, cytology, clinical embryology and countless other fields within nineteen separate disciplines.

'You have something for us on the Sebastian Dukas case?' Danny asked as they gathered in Michelle's tiny office.

'Yes,' she replied, picking up a slim folder and opening it to a toxicology report. 'You struck lucky, or rather, we did. As you know, wide-spectrum toxicology will take longer to come back, but we went in with the usual suspects and added a few randoms, given the unusual nature of the case. I wondered whether the victim was under the influence of anything when they apparently chose to take their life in such a way. What came up was somewhat unexpected.'

Michelle handed Honor a list of contaminants found in Sebastian's blood toxicology. In truth, the pathologist might just as well have handed Honor a sushi recipe written in Japanese, as most of the report meant little to her, but as Samir and Danny gathered to peer at the page, Michelle explained its contents.

'Minimal alcohol, no common drugs, nothing out of the ordinary at all except for one: Gamma-hydroxybutyrate.'

The name was familiar to Honor from previous cases. 'The date-rape drug,' she identified the chemical.

'The same,' Dr Coulter agreed. 'It must have been in his body in volumes sufficient to floor a grown man for maybe a few hours. Much of it was processed out by the time of death, so I'm pretty certain he was conscious when he was murdered. Tracking back from that time, it's hard to tell just how much might have been there, but it's of no doubt that Sebastian was unable to defend himself.'

'Cause of death?' Samir asked. 'Asphyxiation,' Michelle replied. 'So, he *was* hanged?'

'He was hanged,' she agreed, 'but that wasn't what killed him. The bruising around the victim's neck was consistent with being strangled, but inconsistent with being hanged. The rope marks distorted the flesh and helped to conceal the proximal cause of death. Sebastian Dukas was murdered, and then hanged in an attempt to conceal the original crime as a suicide.'

Honor stared at the printout in her hands, but she was no longer reading it. Now, she was staring in her mind's eye at Sebastian's body, hanged from the towering spire of St Magnus' Church, veiled by the fog. The killer had intended to conceal his crime with the act of a supposed hanging, but had then simultaneously decided to place his victim in a highly-visible manner, thus both concealing and displaying the crime simultaneously.

'Doesn't make sense,' Danny said, evidently following the same train of thought. 'The guy tries to hide the murder, yet puts it on display at the same time? Why not hang him somewhere he might not be found?'

If there was one thing that Honor had learned in her career, both as a police constable and as a CID detective, it was that a sane person could not begin to fathom the inner workings of the insane mind. It was analogous to a dolphin trying to figure out the ramblings of a drunk gorilla. Sure, even very disturbed people had patterns of thought, strange ebbs and flows, impulses that could be detected in the confused tides of their minds, but trying to deduce their next move was all but impossible. A deranged person could hold a perfectly normal conversation with a friend in a bar, and an hour later be standing over the corpse of a child with a bloodied knife in their hands.

'Honor?'

She blinked herself back into the moment.

'We can't make any judgements yet,' she said finally. 'Somebody went to great lengths to both display the body and conceal their crime, but we don't have motive and we certainly don't have a suspect. Is there anything new from the victim's family?'

'Nothing as of this morning,' Samir replied. 'We're still looking at CCTV but nothing's popped. How the hell they got in and out of Lower Thames Street without showing up is beyond me. I'm at four-thirty in the morning and nobody's gone in or out of that church.'

'Same for me,' Danny admitted. 'Nothing west of the bridge.'

Honor's own efforts had also been fruitless, and she was almost at dawn on her footage. The fog was thick in the videos, and she was certain that the body was already dangling out of sight somewhere above the shot.

'Michelle,' she asked the pathologist, 'any idea of the size of the individual who strangled Sebastian Dukas?'

Dr Coulter replied without hesitation.

'Male, large hands, enough so to wrap around Sebastian's throat almost completely. The initial bruising pattern says it all. It's likely Sebastian would not have been able to put up much of a fight even if he were not hindered. In his drugged state, he would have been completely unable to resist.'

Honor nodded.

'Thanks for your time, Doctor,' she said. 'You'll send us the rest of the reports when they come in?'

'Should be with us in a couple of days.'

Honor turned to leave the office, when her mobile phone rang in her pocket. Before she could even reach for it, Danny's and Samir's phones also rang. The three of them exchanged a glance, Honor's guts plunging with the certainty that something new and terrible had happened.

She looked at her phone screen, and saw DI Harper's name there as she answered. 'What's up?'

'Get back here right now, as fast as you can,' Katy Harper ordered. *'There's been a development.'*

DI Harper had set up the Incident Room in one of the main conference rooms at Bishopsgate. Honor walked in with Danny and Samir to see a dry-wipe board erected at one end of the room, a wall-mounted television switched on nearby and clearly displaying a video that was on pause. A number of desks had been set up, hurriedly connected to phone lines and Internet routers by the IT team, so that calls pertaining to the investigation could be directed straight to the IR and avoid clogging up the lines on Bishopsgate's main desk.

The room was filled with several detectives and a number of police constables, DCI Mitchell holding court near the wipe board. Beside him was DI Harper, her small frame dwarfed by the former soldier.

'Close the door,' Mitchell said to Samir Raaya as they walked inside.

DC Raaya obeyed, and as soon as the door was shut, DI Harper wrote with a red marker across the top of the wipe board in large capital letters.

OPERATION BOLD FRONT

'As of now,' she said, as she put a cap back on her pen, 'this is an official homicide investigation into the murder of Sebastian Dukas, aged thirty-two, who was found hanged from St Magnus church yesterday morning. DS McVey is running the investigation, having deduced the murder before the pathologist had completed her examination.'

Honor's stomach tingled as she intercepted a few admiring glances from the younger PCs around her, DI Harper's unabashed plug boosting her confidence. Honor kept her features composed though – *don't count your chickens, love, you know it could all come crashing down real fast*. She just hoped that her skin was not flushing red.

'The pathologist has confirmed homicide as the cause of death, via strangulation,' Harper went on, 'with the elaborate hanging thought to be designed to conceal the murder. We have very little to go on, as house to house enquiries have yielded no leads. This is about as fresh as a case gets and it would already be stone-cold, were it not for the video you're all about to see.'

Honor's skin tingled again and she glanced at Danny. He shrugged back at her, and she wondered whether somebody had come forward with some CCTV of the hanging, or some other piece of evidence that might lead them toward new avenues of investigation.

DCI Mitchell's next words quashed that fervent hope like an insect between forefinger and thumb, his voice sombre.

'This video footage was this morning sent to the family of one Amber Carson, a twenty-four-year old office worker from Hackney. We've called her place of work, and they have confirmed that she has not shown up this morning and she's not answering her phone at home.' Mitchell paused. 'Some of you may find this footage quite distressing.'

Every pair of eyes in the room locked onto the television on the wall as DI Harper pointed a remote at it.

The screen appeared perfectly black for a moment, and then Honor heard the sound of laboured breathing. The sound was intense, amplified, and then she saw why. An image slowly faded in from the blackness, and they could all see the face of a young woman filling the screen. Her mouth was gagged, her eyes puffy and red, the skin around them and on her cheeks glistening with tears as she squirmed and fought for movement. A faint glow illuminated her, and the soft padding of some kind of bed beneath her. It also illuminated wooden walls close by on either side of her body, hemming her in, pinning her in place.

Honor stared in silence at the footage for a moment, and then an image of Sebastian Dukas's body hanging from the church spire flashed once more through her mind. Katarina Dukas's words echoed through her thoughts, as though coming from the confines of Amber Carson's horrendous prison. *He couldn't have hanged himself from up there. He was terrified of heights!*

The surrounding darkness, and the strangely amplified noise of the victim's breathing, left Honor in absolutely no doubt about what had happened to Amber Carson.

'She's been buried alive.'

Honor spoke the words without conscious thought. They were not loud but they carried throughout the room, accompanied by Amber's terrified, laboured breathing.

DI Harper paused the video and peered at her. 'Explain.'

Honor felt a growing pressure as she sensed the other detectives watching her, but then she saw Amber's horrific suffering and knew that her own anxiety was as nothing compared to what that poor girl was going through.

'Sebastian Dukas was terrified of heights,' Honor said. 'His wife, and his family, all insisted that he could never have got up on that church, let alone hang himself from eight-inch-wide scaffolding boards. He had to have been drugged to have ended up on that spire, and the pathologist's toxicology report found traces of Gamma- hydroxybutyrate in his system, supporting the notion. The pathologist believes that he died from strangulation. This is only speculation, but if he woke up from the drugs too soon, the killer would have been *forced* to murder him before hanging him.'

There was a deep silence as the officers in the room considered her words.

'What do you mean *before* hanging him?' DCI Mitchell demanded. 'You think the killer wanted to murder Sebastian Dukas twice?'

Honor shook her head as she stared at Amber's features, twisted in a paroxysm of terror; eyes wide, pupils dilated, the sound of her breathing echoing through the lonely vaults of Honor's mind, slipping away, doomed to die in abstract terror.

'No,' she replied, her voice almost a whisper. 'I think that he wants them to die from their greatest fears. I think that he's killing people based on their phobias.'

DCI Mitchell stared at her for a long beat, and then his gaze snapped to a uniformed officer close to him.

'Harris, get on the phone to the family, find out if Amber suffers from claustrophobia or any similar affliction.'

Constable Harris darted from the room as DCI Mitchell looked to Honor.

'What do you make of this video?'

'Play it further.'

DI Harper complied and the video played on. Honor could see that it was only a minute and four seconds long, but that minute and four seconds seemed to last for an eternity as they watched Amber writhe and thrash. The camera vibrated a little with her movements, shuddering as her head hit the side of the box in which she was trapped.

'The camera moved,' Honor said, the footage only having a few seconds left. 'Play that last bit back again.'

DI Harper backed up the footage a few seconds. Honor saw the camera quiver as Amber's head hit the side of the coffin. Honor's mind raced as the final seconds of the footage played out and the screen faded slowly to black. The video ended and DI Harper looked at her.

On the fringes of her awareness, Honor realised that everybody in the room was watching her now, but this time it barely had an effect. She was transfixed by her thoughts, subconsciously moving closer to the screen as she spoke, partly to herself, partly to her fellow officers.

'The video faded in and out,' she said, her eyes almost vacant, seeing the room and yet seeing in her mind's eye their killer at work somewhere in the city. 'He's *planned* this. He's taken care over this footage.'

The quivering camera, shuddering at Amber's movements.

'The camera moved, so that coffin must have moved,' Honor said, letting her mind run with her thoughts, letting it probe the impossible and allow the scene to speak to her. 'She's in a shallow grave, the earth not packed deeply enough to render the coffin totally stable.'

Honor saw Amber's face, squirming, twisting, yearning to be free.

'She's trying to escape, but her hands are out of sight and the gag's still on, so she's bound by the wrists and probably by the ankles.'

Honor closed her eyes, the video playing back in her mind, momentarily oblivious to the room around her.

'The video is recorded but it had to have been shot recently,' she said out loud. 'She's buried alive, but the killer obviously isn't nearby.' Honor's eyes jerked open and she whirled to DI Harper. 'The footage must be remotely gathered. The killer must be using some kind of Internet or phone connection to keep him separate from the scene of the crime.'

DI Harper turned to Detective Constable Tom Cattini, a CID officer assigned to the fraud units.

'You think that you can source the e-mail this was sent from, maybe back-trace it to a location?'

Tom was moving for the door before the DI had finished her sentence. 'I'll get the Cyber Griffin team onto it, and get back to you as soon as I can.'

As DC Cattini exited the room, Honor saw again an image of Sebastian Dukas flash through her mind, dangling from the heights of the church spire. He had already been dead when he had been hanged, but that must not have been the original plan. Had the killer wanted to watch Sebastian die too, suspended from great height and unable to free himself from the noose, to film his demise?

'Amber could still be alive.'

Danny Green's statement filled the room and Honor knew that he was right. Worse, she knew that being buried alive was not enough for this killer, whoever they were. The human body could survive for a few days without food and water at most, but a few days might be enough for Amber to free her bonds, remove her gag and start screaming for help.

'She won't be for long.'

Honor felt certain, with every fibre in her body, that there was something else that their killer had lined up for Amber Carson.

'We don't have a timeline yet,' DI Harper said. 'Amber Carson's whereabouts are not known, but we have an FLO with her family right now. Once we get a timeline, we'll have some idea of how long she might have left.'

'Days, if she's left undisturbed,' Honor said, 'but it's my guess that whoever put her there won't want to wait long to see her demise. It's bloody awful, but I think our killer might be getting his rocks off watching people at their moment of death.'

'I agree,' Danny Green said alongside her. 'Both crimes are too elaborate to be just coincidence. Whoever's behind this wants people to suffer their worst nightmares, to die while doing so.' Danny peered at the screen. 'He's literally scaring them to death.'

Constable Harris hurried back into the IR, a mobile phone to his ear, which he covered with one hand as he sought out Honor.

'You're right,' he said, 'Amber Carson is highly claustrophobic, ever since a childhood accident when she was partially buried by a landslide near her parent's home in Cornwall.'

A rush of whispered exclamations rippled through the crowd of officers.

'Get her family down here as soon as possible,' DI Harper ordered. 'I want to know where Amber was last night, who she was with, everything. If the person who did this to her knew about her phobia, then he must know her well enough that the family might know him too.'

'Will do,' Harris replied as he hurried back out of the room.

DCI Mitchell took one last look at the television screen before he turned to Honor. 'What do you need?'

There was a moment when Honor again felt the eyes of the room upon her, but now things were different. Now, she had not only been vindicated, but the DCI was clearly handing her control of the investigation in a public manner. There was to be no more bickering or whispering behind the scenes: Honor was back, and the onus was being placed on her to track down and apprehend this killer before he could strike again.

'As soon as we find out where Amber was last night, I'm going to need officers trawling through all and any CCTV we can find. Somebody, somewhere, must have seen *something*. We're going to need a canine unit,' Honor added, 'as soon as we figure out where Amber was taken from. It hasn't rained hard yet, but the forecast isn't good over the next couple of days so we risk losing what trail our killer might have left.'

The thought of the weather crept into Honor's mind again. The fog had hidden Sebastian Dukas's murder from view until it was too late to conceal the crime from the media. There were storms forecast for the following day, great downpours as a violent weather front rushed in from the Atlantic.

Water.

'She could be near a river,' Honor suggested. 'There are floods forecast within the next forty-eight hours. If she's buried beneath the water table…'

Nobody needed to ask what that meant. London was a low-lying city, and the government had built the enormous Thames Barrier out near Woolwich to protect the city from storm surges and weather depressions that would otherwise flood the entire square mile and the length of the Thames.

'Get on it,' DI Harper urged. 'Report back the moment you find anything.'

7

The heat was stifling.

Amber's skin was slick with sweat. Her wrists were still pinned behind her back, the plastic stubbornly refusing to snap despite the hours she had spent rubbing it against a metal stud on her back pocket. The loathsome pain that throbbed through her wrists told her that she was bleeding, but right now she couldn't tell the blood from the sweat. Her heart was hurting in her chest, her breath coming in laboured gasps through her dry throat, trying to suck in enough oxygen to stay conscious. The stale air in the coffin was heavy around her, pressing in even more than the walls that touched her shoulders
and the lid that was inches above her nose.

She had long ago lost her sense of balance, the coffin seeming to move and sway around her in the pitch darkness. Amber knew that she was slowly suffocating, the amount of air getting to her through the miniscule breathing tube insufficient to keep her alive. No doubt the bastard who had put her in here had done this intentionally, and somehow, she knew that he was watching her through the optical fibre tacked to the lid of the coffin.

She had stared into that soulless blue light as she fought to free her hands from the bonds. Her captor was obviously seriously ill, an unstable psychopath who wanted to watch her die here in this horrendous coffin. Maybe that was what excited him? Weren't there people who got their kicks out of watching other people die? *Snuff movies*, they were called, or something similar.

Amber tried to look down the coffin at her feet, her eyeballs aching as she did so. A headache was raging through her skull, adding to her misery, but she knew that she had to keep fighting. *Keep trying.*

Amber turned her wrists to one side again, pain searing her skin as it tore, trying to pull the plastic ties across the edge of the metal stud. Every now and again the plastic would catch, suggesting that she had managed to tear it a little. Now, she had to split it and finally get the damned thing off.

She shifted position and pushed her wrists into the small of her back. She felt the plastic cable catch on the stud and she pulled, writhing this way and that, the muscles in her back exhausted from endless hours of squirming within the confined space. The plastic caught and then slipped over the stud, and she was forced to try again.

Amber's frustrated tears flowed with the grimy sweat now caking her cheeks, exhaustion and defeat crowding in on her like the walls of the coffin. She twisted her hips to the opposite side and pulled her wrists up to try to find the stud on the other side of her jeans, and then she heard the noise from outside.

She froze in the hot darkness, listening. The sound was muted, something like stones falling on a tin roof. For one dreadful moment she thought that it might be the concrete falling on the lid of the coffin, but then she recalled that her abductor had shovelled soil onto that already, so she wouldn't hear the same kind of noise again.

She closed her eyes, listening, and then she realised that it was the sound of metal chains being pulled through security gates at the entrance to the cathedral. Panic ripped through her as she heard the distant sound of voices, and then a rhythmic beeping sound that seemed to come from even further away.

Then a voice spoke, soft, distant, repeating a monosyllabic sentence over and over again.

CAUTION: THIS VEHICLE IS REVERSING

No!

It was morning already. In the darkness she'd lost track of the passing of time. Amber writhed and yanked her wrists up against the stud in her jeans, felt the plastic catch against it. This time, she pulled harder, pain tearing at her skin, and she began frantically rubbing her wrists from side to side as she fought to escape the bonds.

The sound of the reversing truck grew steadily louder through the coffin and the soil concealing it below the foundation pit. The metal studs of her jeans tore at the plastic and the flesh around her wrists. She knew that she was bleeding badly now but she had no choice, her heart thundering within her chest as though it were trying to beat its way past the bars of her ribcage.

The recorded voice-warning suddenly cut out, but she could hear the cement truck's engine still toiling, making it hard to hear other voices. If she could just break free now, yank the gag from her parched mouth and scream loud enough for the rest of the universe to hear her, she might, *just might,* get out of this alive.

The plastic bonds caught on her stud again and she arched her back and hauled with all of her might. The skin on her wrists tore on a wave of white pain that soared up her forearms and she screamed through the gag, sweat blinding her eyes, waves of heat washing over her body as she thrashed back and forth.

The plastic cable ties suddenly parted and her fists slammed into the walls of the coffin either side of her. Amber twisted her arms up over her body and clawed at the gag in her mouth, pulling it aside. In the light of the camera she could see blood streaming from raw wounds up and down her wrists, her flesh on fire with pain as she sucked in a breath and screamed out loud for the first time in hours.

'Okay mate, bring it over here!'

Ian Jenkins grabbed the end of the metal chute that swung out from the rear of the cement truck and guided it over the pit, one eye on the site manager as he prepared to open the mixer and dump the cement. The towering walls of the cathedral soared above him, replete with stained glass windows and scowling carved gargoyles.

The weather was shit, grey clouds scudding low across the city, obscuring the Gherkin's angular glass and steel. The wind gusted in off the river in squalls,

Ian already damp, cold and miserable. He'd known that it was going to be a hell of a day - multiple drops across the city, lousy traffic, and he'd had one beer too many last night after a tough day filled with breakdowns and pissy customers, who acted as though the world revolved around their contract alone.

He heard kids screaming and shouting on their way to school somewhere nearby, and wondered briefly how anybody could feel so energetic on such a shitty day.

'How's that?' he called above the truck's engine noise to the site manager. 'Two ton, yeah?'

The site manager, a rotund man with thick forearms and a florid complexion that suggested too many takeaways and nights out with the lads, nodded from beneath his hard hat as he signed off on the delivery. Two tons of wet cement, to be covered before the forecast storms blew in from the Atlantic. Ian could see large boards leaning up against nearby walls, ready to lay over the pit, and tarpaulin sheets that would be tied down over it protect the drying cement from the downpour. Underpinning the cathedral's immense walls, section by section, was a major operation.

'Let her go!' the manager called, standing back to watch.

Ian turned to the controls at the rear of the truck. He yanked a lever to spin up the engine revolutions, which powered the slowly rotating cement container mounted on the rear of the truck. The engine's growl rose to a level suitable for Ian to pull his ear-protectors down as he waited for the cement to mix a little more before opening the valves.

Her time has come.

He sat in front of a monitor and watched, pensive, as he saw Amber thrash and scream. She had done well, very well, to break free of her bonds, but he could also hear the sound of the vehicles above her and he knew that she had only seconds to live.

Now, he watched her closely, her face twisted with terror, frantic, desperate.

He waited, for that final moment, that last instant of existence. He squirmed in his seat, the leather smooth beneath his naked body as he watched Amber's face and her panicked eyes. His gaze was transfixed, as though he were there with her in her grotesque prison, facing that exquisite moment of realisation that life, *her* life, was going to be extinguished in the way that she feared the most.

One hand formed a hollowed fist and reached down to his crotch, moved in slow rhythm as he stared, eyes wide and dry, waiting for the moment when Amber would die. The other hand reached out to a mobile phone that was lying on the bed beside him, and he barely glanced at it as he lightly touched one finger to a button. The mobile phone beeped and data began to flow as he returned to watching Amber Carson's final moments.

Honor McVey rushed to her office, sat down in front of her monitor and began playing back the footage of Amber's desperate plight as she started dialling numbers across the city, begging for access to CCTV from around the area of both the pub where Amber was last known to have been, the *Crosse Keys*, and her apartment in Hackney. Samir hurried into her office, right behind her.

'I've got some images on the way from the pub,' he said. 'Danny says he's got some from about the half-way point between there and Amber's home.'

Honor nodded, one hand over her phone's receiver.

'He's got to have grabbed her somewhere along the way, or maybe even at her home. I'll take Hackney itself and work backwards. If people can't get the footage to us, beg them to check it where they are for any sign of Amber.'

Samir whirled and hurried out of the office again, Honor finishing her call and setting the phone down as she stared at an image of Amber, her face wrought with terror. *Jesus, who the hell would do something like this?* The more she thought about it, the more appalled she was.

'Why the hell would somebody go to such lengths to murder innocent people in such an appalling way?'

The question slipped past her lips without her really realising it. If the killer hated these people so much, then they must have some kind of connection to each other. But, so far, there was nothing to suggest that Amber Carson and Sebastian Dukas had ever heard of each other, let alone met. The only thing that they did have in common was their…

'Phobias,' Danny Green said as he hurried into her office and tossed three pages of printed A4 right in front of her. 'Sebastian and Amber were both members of an on-line forum called *"Face Fear"*, dedicated to sufferers of extreme phobias.'

Honor picked up the sheets of paper, saw on them comments from a forum post about fear of spiders, *Arachnophobia*. A scattering of people was offering comments in support of a woman who had just spent three hours standing on a chair in her kitchen, while a common house spider casually made its way across the floor. Honor realised guiltily that even she would have found the story vaguely amusing, were it not for the terrible situation faced by Amber right now. And there, commenting in the threads, were both Sebastian and Amber.

'Could be a source for the killer to target victims,' she agreed. 'And that means that anybody on that forum could be a target.'

Danny nodded.

'I've sent an e-mail to the site warning them of our concerns, but they haven't got back to me yet. It also means that our killer could be on the site. It's not something that you can view from outside, publicly, if you know what I mean? You have to be signed up to get in there, because many of the members are ashamed of their phobias.'

Honor was surprised to hear that, but she couldn't think about anything other than finding Amber Carson before it was too late.

'They won't be keen to send us their data without a warrant,' she replied. 'Get DI Harper onto that, we need to stay with the CCTV and try to find Amber.'

Danny Green hurried back out of the office as Honor ran a hand through her hair and tried to put her thoughts in order. Amber Carson had been out drinking, and after some calls to people identified as having been with her that night, her friends had said that she'd headed off sometime just after nine-thirty. Hackney was a twenty-minute walk from the *Crosse Keys* pub, and her friends were sure that she'd walked and had not got a taxi. Twenty minutes. Somewhere on that journey she'd been abducted, and she would have had to have been restrained too, most likely – not something that was easy to do on a busy street, even at night.

Honor turned her attention to the narrow streets near Amber's home. She could more easily have been snatched from those areas, with poor CCTV coverage and few pedestrians at that time of night. Likewise, a quick glance at Google Earth gave her the location of Amber's flat, and it was clear that although it was in a well-trodden part of the city, there were numerous alleys and through fares where anybody could have been waiting to grab her and…

'Honor!'

The call came from the Incident Room, Samir's voice pitched high with alarm. Honor bolted out of her office and ran down the hall to see several people gathered around a computer monitor. DCI Mitchell lumbered into the room right behind her as Danny called out.

'It's live!'

Honor's heart skipped a beat as she saw a grainy image of Amber Carson. The sound came through a moment later, and her screams pierced Honor's ears and made several of the team flinch. Amber's terror was alive within that cry - slithering, evil, the sound of a person facing their utmost fear with no hope of escape.

Amber heard the truck's engine wind up and she screamed again. The air inside the coffin was so thick and hot that she could barely breathe, stars flashing in front of her eyes as she tried to suck in more air. She felt as though her head was wrapped in clingfilm, the heat a physical thing pressing against every inch of her skin, pushing into her, crushing her in the humid darkness.

The concrete would flow into the pit within moments, so she clawed at the lid of the coffin, began to push against it, picked her legs up and pinned her knees against it as she tried to push against the weight of the soil above and lift the lid. The soil above her was damp and heavy, but she pushed anyway, strained with the last of her strength to free herself before it was too late. With a final scream of effort, she pushed one last time, and the coffin lid shifted upward an inch.

A sudden rumbling noise filled the darkened space and she felt the coffin shudder, vibrations rippling through it from top to bottom, and the coffin lid slammed shut. With a terrible certainty Amber knew that the concrete was tumbling onto the soil above her. She let out one final, defeated cry, and then she stopped pushing.

The heat around her clogged her skin just as anxiety now clogged her arteries, labouring her heart. *I'm going to die.* There was nothing that anybody could do for her, nobody that could save her; no shining knight, no last-moment miracle. Suddenly, there was no longer a reason to fight. An image flashed unbidden through her mind in the darkness, that of a broad blue sky, flecked with white summer clouds. A meadow, open and airy, warm sunlight on her face, a cool breeze caressing her skin with nature's gentle touch. A place from her childhood, far away, when she was younger, when summers were longer, when life was safer.

The sound of tumbling concrete faded away, Amber uncertain of just how much was being poured onto the coffin. Then, something landed on her chest. In the dim light of the camera, she looked down and saw a lump of damp concrete. Then, more followed, spluttering through the breathing tube.

Terror rose through her like a black wave and she looked at the camera as she screamed.

'There's something on her!'

Samir spotted the grey ooze falling into the coffin, and for a moment nobody knew what it could be. Then Honor thought about all the horror stories of mafioso killings, of bodies buried beneath the foundations of large buildings, back in the day when organised crime had controlled much of London's building trade.

'Concrete,' she gasped. 'She's being buried under concrete! Get on the phone to every building site in the city, shut them down right now, no matter what!'

Before anybody could move, they heard Amber Carson's horrific shriek of terror that soared out of the television set and through the corridors outside. Honor's hand flew to her chest in terrible empathy as she heard the poor girl screaming at the top of her lungs.

'The cathedral!' Amber shrieked with terminal desperation. *'Somebody please, Southwark Cathedral!'*

Honor's heart leaped and she dashed to one side to the nearest phone. She grabbed it even as Danny was scrambling to get the phone number of the cathedral on his mobile. He read it out to her and she punched in the numbers, while beside her MIT 4 poured from the Incident Room and sprinted for the HAT car. Katy Harper got onto local police vehicles patrolling the city, while Danny began dialling the fire brigade to dispatch them to Southwark Cathedral.

In Honor's ear, the cathedral's phone began ringing, but nobody was answering. 'Pick up the fucking phone!' Honor yelled, her gaze fixed on Amber, trapped beneath tons of concrete.

The air was getting hotter.

Amber could shout no longer, could scream no more, her lungs heaving in her chest, filling with nothing but the carbon dioxide now building up all around her. *Typical.* She'd feared being buried alive, but now her greatest threat was asphyxiation. Better than the alternative, slowly starving to death or rotting down here. With a bit of luck, she'd pass out in a minute or two. *Luck*.

Amber snorted, and was immediately struck by how bizarre it was that she would find amusement in her moment of death. Her rational brain briefly snapped back into gear. Hypoxia. She wouldn't last long.

Above her, the sounds of concrete were long gone, but now there was another sound. Something on the lid of the coffin, the sound of something moving. Amber's mind was too weary to focus on it, drained to the point of exhaustion, but she listened for a moment longer and her heart lifted as she thought that she heard the sound of people scrambling to free her. Hands and shovels were digging her out of the coffin, weren't they? She tried again.

'Hello? Can you hear me? I'm in here!'

Her voice was meek, her breathing coming in shallow rasps. Another sound, louder this time, right in the centre of the lid.

Amber looked down, and she saw the lid bowing down toward her. A fracture line split with a sharp crack, the lid's curved inner surface bulging downward. She was too exhausted to scream again, but she felt tears fall once more from her eyes as she weakly shook her head.

'Please, no.'

'Please, no.'

Honor heard Amber's weary, terminal plea from the television as she held the phone to her ear, still ringing inside the cathedral at the other end. She saw something then, in the girl's eyes, something that she had never seen before. Amber was not looking at anything, her eyes wide and yet somehow dead already, devoid of the glow of a living being. They stared up into the darkness, blank discs of pale green.

Honor flinched as a sharp crack as loud as a gunshot split the air in the room, saw something spill onto Amber's body, and then Amber emitted one last horrendous, tortured scream.

The coffin lid suddenly plunged down and the feed was brutally cut off.

Honor felt nausea churn her guts as the phone slipped from her hand and clattered to the office floor. There were several other officers with her in the room but none of them moved, all staring in comatose silence at the television screen as it hissed back at them with white noise.

'Jesus,' somebody whispered.

Honor closed her eyes and slumped against the desk beside her, unable to comprehend what she had just witnessed. In her career, she had seen many dead bodies: mutilated corpses, mangled road-crash victims, deceased children; those who had been raped, those who'd had their faces dashed with acid, or new-born infants abandoned to the brutal cold of a winter's night, found rigid as a board. But never, not once, had she ever witnessed the final moment of life, when life became death, when somebody for the first and last time witnessed their own mortality written starkly before them. Now, right this very instant, Amber Carson was being crushed and suffocated under several tons of wet concrete, and there was nothing that she could do to stop it.

'You sick bastard,' she muttered.

'What?' DI Harper asked finally, looking at her, her own eyes brimming.

Honor sucked in a ragged breath of stale office air, surprised at how emotional she suddenly felt.

'He's watching them die,' she said. 'That's what he's looking for. He wants to see their last moments play out, to see the point of death without having to be there.'

'Amber's not dead yet,' DCI Mitchell pointed out, refusing to succumb to the horror they had all witnessed. 'The cars are on their way.'

'They won't make it,' Honor replied. 'We all know that. If she's been in that thing all night, and they've just dumped a few tons of concrete on her, we'll never get her out in time.' Honor turned away, winced as she felt needles poking at the corners of her eyes. 'She's dying as we speak.'

The silence in the Incident Room felt briefly as oppressive as the confines of Amber Carson's tomb.

'There were no cameras at Sebastian Dukas's death,' DC Hansen pointed out. Honor shook her head.

'We know that Dukas showed signs of having fought back,' she replied. 'He didn't die the way his killer wanted him to, in utter fear. That's what he's seeking, the sight of someone dying from their greatest phobia, the actual moment of death. He's obsessed with it.'

The silence deepened, only the hiss of the television filling the room. Katy

Harper had been stunned into silence, and no other officer seemed able to break themselves from their horrified lethargy. DCI Mitchell grabbed a file and slapped it down on a desk with a loud crack, pointing one arm like a shotgun at each of them as he gave orders.

'Get in touch with every supplier of coffins in the city. I want to know where the killer got that coffin and any CCTV there might of him. If we find Amber at Southwark Cathedral, I want every last inch of surveillance we have of the area, every witness questioned, no stone unturned. I want the MET informed of what's happening and all other police forces bordering the city. I'll call MI5 and SO15: the more forces that are aware of it, the more chance we have of bringing this to an end.' He turned and pointed to the status board. 'I want a progress meeting in two hours' time. Get me everything, all of it, every grainy traffic camera image, question every resident and interrogate every last bloody pigeon in the city if you have to. I don't care if you have to go to fucking NASA, I want this bastard found and I want him in custody!'

8

The room was silent, dark, the air stained with a potent aroma of loose hormones and sweat. He lay on his back, stomach heaving, bare skin glistening. He was at peace. The boil had been lanced, the pressure relieved on the seething cauldron of hatred that simmered deep within the recesses of his soul. It wouldn't last, but for now it was enough for him just to lay here, his manhood flaccid and spent, the air cool on his skin and his breathing slow as he stared at the sight of Amber Carson's face, caught forever in time just before she was crushed to death, deep below ground.

The room was small, his home in a backstreet between Spitalfields and Whitechapel. It was his favourite part of the city, a dense warren of back alleys and narrow streets, of strange scents and dark histories that haunted the city nights. The lair of the Ripper. He heard the sounds of the city return slowly to him as he emerged from his reverie, one hand gently brushing his stomach. His mother used to do that, many years ago, to calm him when he'd swung up into a manic phase. It was the only thing that he could remember about her with any real clarity; her gentle smile, her gaze so full of compassion, the centre of his world. There had been no other who could provide surcease when wayward neurons rampaged through his brain, and now there was nobody left in the world who could assuage the demons stalking the darkened vaults of his mind.

A shout from the street below yanked him irritably back into the present. He lay for a few moments longer, but youths outside were trading banter and insults, an unwelcome reminder of the realities of life. The surcease was always brief. He slowly rose from the bed and saw again the image on the television before him, captured just an hour before, of Amber Carson, frozen in time a split second before the lid of the coffin had caved in. The look on her face.

That look. The "dead-zone", he called it. That last moment before life became death, the last expression a person would ever have, the last thought in their mind, the last breath that they would take. It wasn't easy to capture that look – God knows, he'd tried enough times. But now, now he could see it, a dread unmatched by any other emotion that life could offer. The last moment. *The last moment.* He smiled. It had been the perfect start to his day.

Sadly, he could not afford to dwell long on his victory, for there was more work to be done. He swung his legs off the bed and cleaned himself before dressing and switching off the television. He was careful to back-up the footage of his victim's last moment, placing it on an SSD drive that he put in a metal lock box. He reached up to an old ceiling joist and carefully removed a panel, slotted the SSD inside and then covered it up. Then, he deleted all other traces of the footage from his laptop computer. It took him only moments to deactivate the mobile phone that he'd used to carry the signals from the camera inside Amber's coffin. He knew, of course, that the police would search for the source of the feed, and he knew that they would quickly pin-point the cell towers used by the phone, which would direct them to Whitechapel and Spitalfields as the likely location of the killer they would by now so desperately be hunting. Still, the area was densely populated and it was easy for him to evade their CCTV and other surveillance devices, the routing for the Internet feed he used repeatedly bounced off servers all over the world. As for the phone, before the end of the day it would be sinking in sediment at the bottom of the River Thames, its signal never to be heard again.

Satisfied, he turned and walked from the bedroom onto the landing. The home was small, one in a row of three-storey terraced houses built just after World War Two. He had inherited the home from his parents, the only reason he could afford to live in the city at all. Well, perhaps *inherited* wasn't quite the word.

He walked down the staircase, which wound to the left through ninety degrees into the entrance hall. The front door opened onto the narrow street outside, but he turned instead and walked to a small door under the stairs. He unlocked it, and stepped inside. The walls here were of cool stone and it was dark, a series of stone steps heading down into a small basement that ran the length of about half of the house. Built back in the days when all homes needed a coal cellar, this one had been converted into a living space.

He made his way down the steps and flicked on the light.

A small room, devoid of furniture but for a bed beneath the harsh glow of a bare lightbulb. Partition walls created three such rooms, one at the rear, this one, and a further room at the front of the home. He walked off the steps and turned right, to a door that led into the front room of the basement. He stood at the door and listened for a moment to the sounds coming from within.

It was faint, a distant, keening sound that whistled through aged vocal cords. The sound was too weak to travel far, so it didn't bother him much. Still, he would have to deal with it eventually. Saving the best until last was what he was all about.

'It worked,' he whispered through the door. 'Perfectly.'

The sounds intensified a little, became more desperate, pleading. He smiled, and then switched off the light.

The patrol car screamed south through the city, heading for the Thames as Honor grimly held onto her door handle. Danny drove, the car's blues lighting up the city streets as the sirens screeched, the piercing whine echoing off the Georgian buildings and glassy tower blocks lining Bishopsgate as they rushed toward London Bridge.

Though Honor knew in her heart of hearts that they must be too late, she was still holding out for a miracle. Maybe an air pocket, something, *anything* that might keep Amber Carson alive for long enough that the fire brigade could get her out of her macabre tomb and revive her, to deny a sadistic killer the satisfaction of knowing that she was dead.

The Shard loomed into view on the south bank to their left as they raced across London Bridge, the flecked green waters of the Thames churning past below, while to the right the four spires of Southwark Cathedral poked up into a slate grey sky. They hit the other side of the river, and beneath the London Bridge rail overpass Honor could see the entrance to Green Dragon Court, the whole area swamped with police vehicles and two fire engines, a sea of hazard lights flickering vivid blue and red against dark Victorian brick and ironwork.

Danny pulled up alongside a police cordon guarded by two MET constables, while other uniforms were busily keeping pedestrians at bay. Honor hurried with Danny toward the cordon, Samir joining them as she pulled out her warrant card. The officers let them through, one of them pointing to a courtyard down below the level of the main road, inside the cathedral grounds.

'Down there, turn right.'

Honor didn't break her stride as she descended into the courtyard, where rows of tables were positioned outside a cafeteria, the immense cathedral looming over them. The spires reached up toward the clouds scudding low across a threatening sky, a faint drizzle gusting on the buffeting wind as they hurried toward a cement truck parked alongside the cathedral grounds.

Two ambulances were parked to the left of the truck, a fire engine to the right of it, and Honor could see firefighters scrambling to get into what looked like some kind of pit right under the cathedral walls. As they reached the fire engine, so they were waved back by the officer who was overseeing the operation.

'Stay back, if this stuff blows out it'll burn your skin off!'

Honor stopped where she was and watched as the fireteams frantically dug out lumps of thick cement and hurled them onto the grass all around the pit, while others reached down into the heavy grey mess, trying to get hold of something deep inside. From her vantage point, Honor could see that the pit was around four feet deep beneath the walls of the great cathedral, and that Amber Carson was somewhere at the bottom of it. The firefighters were lying on the grass as they reached down and groped about in the thick gloop, their arms slotted into long, thick gloves that reached almost to their shoulders.

The fire engine was roaring as a suction hose drew cement out of the pit, spluttering it out of a vent on the side of the truck onto the grass nearby. The level of cement in the pit was reducing only slowly, but it allowed the firefighters to reach deeper into the pit.

'I've got something!'

A firefighter at the head of the pit craned his neck back and stared up at the walls as he sank to his throat in the cement, craning his head back to keep it clear of the mess, and then he began to pull. Two other men moved to his side, reaching down as he was and trying to get their hands on whatever they were hauling up through the muck all around them.

Honor's heart seemed to stop beating as she watched the men haul from the pit a large mass of concrete slurry and soil, from which protruded limbs thickly coated in the congealing grey mess. The firefighters strained with the effort of fighting against the weight of the concrete trying to keep the body in place.

The paramedics rushed in, likewise wearing protective plastic gloves as the grey mass was dragged out of the pit and onto the grass nearby. Honor felt sick as she saw the vague shape of the human body entombed within the sludge. The paramedics held back as two fire officers turned their hoses on the body and blasts of water splattered concrete across the lawns.

Honor felt her heart breaking as Amber Carson's tiny form was battered by the water, her limbs flailing lifelessly, but she knew that there was no time left for anything other than drastic measures. The water revealed her bare skin glowing bright red from the burning effects of the concrete, her blonde hair thick with grey mess and wet soil, and then her face, twisted into a grimace of terror, her mouth open and filled with soil, her eyes packed with it, her nose, her ears, everything.

Honor turned away as nausea twisted her stomach, barely able to conceal the horror now ripping at her soul as the water hoses were switched off and the paramedics rushed in with a defibrillator and oxygen mask. The fire crews stood back, sweating from exertion, others stone-faced as they watched the paramedics frantically try to revive Amber Carson.

Honor looked up to the main road above them, scanned the crowd that had gathered there, mobile phones in hand to take snapshots of the ongoing crisis. She wanted to see who was in the crowd. It was not unknown for killers to visit the sites of their handiwork, often multiple times, reliving their gruesome conquests and killings in macabre pilgrimage. The onlookers stared back down at her, and she quietly moved her gaze from one to the next, taking the time to mentally note details of their faces and… A mobile phone clicked beside her head, and she turned to see Samir taking an image of the onlookers. He offered her a faint smile. 'A bit easier to remember, this way.'

Honor would have smiled back at him, but her mood was as dark and foreboding as the turbulent skies overhead as she turned back to the crime scene. She flinched as Amber Carson's body jack-knifed as the defibrillator jolted her with current, then landed with a splat amid wet concrete, limp and unresponsive. The paramedics tried twice more, but then they leaned back and one of them looked across at her and slowly shook his head.

'Fuck's sake.'

Danny Green turned away, stalked off, his shoulders hunched and his head down as he pulled out a packet of cigarettes. Danny had two daughters not far off Amber's age. Seeing scenes like this required nerves, but detectives and police officers were not machines.

'I'll talk to the driver,' Honor uttered to Samir as she fought to contain violent emotions churning within. 'Can you get the uniforms on witness reports?'

'Done,' Samir replied, glanced at his notes. 'The driver's name is Ian.'

Honor made her way to the ambulances, where the cement truck driver was sitting with a coffee in one hand and a cigarette smouldering in the other. He looked to be about fifty, perhaps a little more, a yellow hard-hat perched on his head, his features ruddy, thick stubble foresting his jaw. Despite the drizzle he wore only a T-shirt beneath his Hi-Viz vest, his forearms thick, his boots and jeans encrusted with cement dust and grime.

Honor could tell a lot about a person just by the way they looked. The driver was working class, salt-of-the-earth, not a man easily shaken. But she could see his hands trembling, the cigarette stub about to scorch the skin of his left hand. He was staring at his boots, eyes vacant.

'You okay?' she asked as she approached.

The driver looked up at her and nodded. Tears wobbled precariously above dark sclera.

'Is she…, she gonna be okay?'

Honor took a breath. 'I'm afraid she's been pronounced dead at the scene.'

The man stared into Honor's eyes for a moment longer, and then she watched him start to come apart. The mug dropped from his hand and shattered on the pavement, his body shuddering as convulsive sobs began to wrack his big shoulders.

'I heard her!' he gasped, choking back his tears. '*I heard her*! Thought it was kids on the main road, I didn't know she was…'

'We know,' Honor said, although instantly she realised that she didn't actually know if the driver was telling the truth. Still, it was tough to put on an act like this and she didn't doubt the driver would alibi out. 'Can you tell me what happened?'

The driver's cigarette dropped from his hand and he crushed it with one angry boot. 'Nothin' unusual,' he replied. 'Site manager unlocked for me, and we set up to pour the concrete. Standard job. Didn't know anything about somebody being in there until the police came tearing in here screaming at us to shut off the flow.' The driver looked up at her again. 'I had a hangover this morning, not a bad one but I wasn't quite with it. If I'd have heard her then, I might have been able to stop the flow, might have been

able to do something to…'

'You didn't put her there,' Honor cut him off with a stern finger pointed at him, determined not to let an innocent man shoulder responsibility for the murder of Amber Carson. 'Her death is down to whoever put her there, nobody else, is that clear?'

'But if I'd just…'

'If you'd been a lazy bastard and taken the day off you wouldn't have saved her life, because somebody else would have come here and maybe they wouldn't have heard Amber's cries either. It's not on you.'

The man sat for a moment and whispered her name, tears streaming down his reddened cheeks. 'Amber.'

Shit. Honor reigned herself in. Her job wasn't to console the innocent, it was to find the guilty. The FLO would have to take over here, before she got herself in too deep.

'Ian, right?' she asked, and was rewarded with a nod.

'Okay, Ian, you're going to be questioned about this morning's events. You won't be under caution, and as long as you have a secure alibi, everything will be fine. I just want to ask you whether you saw anyone or anything that might help us understand how this killing occurred? Was there anything at all that you thought was wrong or unusual about the site this morning?'

Ian frowned, concentrating, but he shook his head.

'I don't remember anything unusual at all, other than it being a lousy day and me having a headache. I'm sorry, I want to help but I can't think straight.'

Honor nodded, and pulled from her pocket a card with her details on it. 'Call me at any time, if you think of anything, okay?'

Ian nodded, barely looking at the card as he took it. Honor turned and crossed to where Amber Carson was lying on her back on the grass, surrounded by cold concrete, her corpse laced with dirt and other debris that marred her once vibrant youth. Honor had seen many dead bodies, but none with such an expression of horror forged into their dying features, an eternal rictus that twisted the once-beautiful face into a stone gargoyle not dissimilar to the ones looking down upon the grisly scene from the heights of the cathedral walls. Amber's features were now a skull-like shell, the weight of the compressed concrete having punctured her eyeballs, her mouth hanging open, her limp tongue coated with concrete mess.

'Got to be a link here.'

She turned to see that Danny Green had returned and was staring up at the cathedral. His eyes looked sore, and there was a slouch in his shoulders that reminded her of her father, when he had lost his mother to old age.

'One church, one cathedral,' Honor nodded, sensing his train of thought.

'Could be the building sites, construction works on both premises.'

'Gary Wheeler?'

Honor shook her head, glancing at site boards mounted on the temporary walls surrounding the works site. 'Different company, but they could be connected. Can you look into that, see if anybody works for both companies? Could be a useful place to start.'

'What about the other guy, Cooper, the site manager?' Danny asked.

'He alibied out,' Samir said. 'CCTV's got him going home when he said he did. Doesn't appear again until the following morning. Same goes for Kieran O'Rourke and all other workers contracted on the site.'

Danny nodded, but his eyes were still casting across the cathedral's immense Gothic façade.

'Kind of grim, when you think about it,' he said, almost absent-mindedly. 'Celebrated architecture, but it's covered in carvings of demons and gargoyles and all that kind of stuff. Not exactly welcoming.'

Honor nodded, but said nothing. Maybe Danny was just distracting himself. He hadn't looked at Amber's corpse since he'd returned.

'Get onto Gary Wheeler,' she repeated, sensing that he would be better employed elsewhere. 'I'll work with forensics here.'

Danny nodded and walked away from the gruesome scene. Honor watched him go for a moment, then turned to Samir, who gestured to the scene.

'Forensics are on the way, but with two tons of concrete on her, I don't think we're gonna get much.'

Honor disagreed, although she didn't say as such. The concrete would indeed have removed much physical and genetic traces of a second party, and their killer appeared to have an almost supernatural ability to conceal himself from detection, but they only needed a single hair.

'She's only got her bra and jeans on,' Honor pointed out as she examined the body without straying too close. 'Last footage we have of her, she had a blouse on.'

'She made it home,' Samir guessed as he looked down at the corpse. For a moment he was detached, clinical, but then he seemed to see Amber for who she had been and he turned away briefly. Honor said nothing, waited for a moment until Samir got himself back under control. A few deep breaths. A cough. She pretended not to notice the waver in his voice as he continued.

'Either she undressed herself, or the killer dressed her this way, maybe as some ritualistic device.'

'Could be either,' Honor agreed. 'Sebastian was found wearing the same suit he'd left work in, so it doesn't quite fit the profile of a ritual killer.'

Samir nodded, staring at Amber's remains but thinking more clearly now. The hunt was on. She could see it in his eyes and in his posture - his back straightening, his chin rising. The anger was coming, the hunger was there, and despite the appalling scene they were witnessing she felt a little spark of joy to see the predator in Samir assert itself, the desire to catch a killer sparking into life like a pale flame in an immense darkness.

'He has to be on CCTV somewhere around her home,' he said. 'The guy had to make his way there and either lay in wait for her outside the home, or break in and wait.'

'Get back to the office, watch anything we have from the pub opposite Amber's apartment or on any of the approaches. There's an alleyway down the side of her home so he could have come in from another street to the east.'

'Got it.'

'Ma'am?'

One of the fire crews called for her, and Honor walked onto the grass, carefully avoiding the thick cement residue caking the ground as she picked her way toward where the fireman was standing in waders in the deep pit. He held something in his gloved hands, and as Honor got closer she realised that it was a mobile phone, connected to a thin wire, from which drooped globules of cement.

'Don't move,' she snapped as she fumbled in her pocket for an evidence bag.

She could see the forensic team arriving nearby, but she wanted the mobile phone inside an evidence bag and protected before it could be contaminated by anybody on the scene. The fireman dropped the phone into the bag, and then carefully began easing up the thin wire that led down into the grim grey mess in which he stood. Honor watched as he slowly brought the thin cable up, and it finally broke free from the surface of the concrete to reveal a small camera attached to one end.

'It's a fibre-optic cable,' Samir said as he watched the fireman guide the cable into the evidence bag. 'The video link we watched.'

Honor sealed the bag as the forensics teams arrived, and she handed it promptly to the scene examiner with a brief about where it was found.

'What about the video? He must have used some means of broadcasting it. There has to be a source, an IP address or whatever?'

'I'll contact the Cyber Griffin team and see what they can do for us,' Honor said, referring to the City of London Police unit dedicated to digital crimes. 'We've got people who can track IPs down, and the e-mails that he sent the family.'

Samir hesitated, and Honor instantly realised that the duty to inform the family of their daughter's horrific death would now fall upon her shoulders. Even with DI Katy Harper alongside her, it was a task that all officers dreaded. They had failed to protect Amber, had been unable to derail the plans of a killer deranged and sadistic enough to orchestrate both this murder and perhaps that of Sebastian Dukas. No matter how much she told herself and others that this was nobody's fault but that of the perpetrator, it still felt as though they were letting people down.

'I'll take care of the family,' Honor said, knowing what Samir was thinking. 'You focus on spotting the perpetrator - hopefully we can identify him before he tries something like this again.'

'You think he will?' Samir asked. 'Do you think this is the work of an actual serial killer?'

Honor looked down at Amber's pitiful remains, and she knew damned well that this wouldn't be their quarry's last kill.

'I think he's only just got started,' she said softly, and then a new and worrisome thought crossed her mind. 'These may not even have been his first.'

9

Honor made it back to Bishopsgate just after eleven, as City Police began mobilising in the wake of the double-killing, but her first port of call had been the custody suite and Amber Carson's family. With DI Katy Harper, they had broken the news of Amber's passing before questioning them as gently as they could in the presence of an FLO.

Honor headed quickly past the commotion in the Incident Room and slipped into her office, closed the door behind her. She had to do this, or the events of the past few hours were going to overwhelm her and she'd be no damned good to anybody.

Amber Carson's parents had been utterly bereft, the mother hitting the verge of a nervous breakdown right there and then as Honor and DI Harper delivered the awful news. The father had worn the same blank stare his daughter had right before her grisly demise, as a part of him withered and died within. One brother, one sister, all four of them huddled together as grief spilled from their hearts, forever to shadow their futures. It had been all that Honor could do to maintain some degree of professional detachment from their pain.

Then the anxiety attack had come, the first in months.

The loss of balance got her first, the world seeming to become two dimensional around her. She realised that she had not taken a breath for some time, and sucked air in only to slump against the wall outside the suite. Her throat felt as though somebody was crushing it, air whistling through a narrow gap as steel bands squeezed her chest. She couldn't get a full breath in, she just fucking couldn't. Stars whorled in her eyes, her legs rubbery as the ground shifted beneath her feet. *Get a grip.*

She had managed to get control of herself again before the FLO and DI Harper returned from the suite, but Honor said nothing, entrapped within a crucible of panic as the black chasm of anxiety threatened to rush up and consume her whole. She needed to get control of herself, right now.

Just a few moments.

The building opposite Bishopsgate Station was a tower block that she shut out with a twitch of her window blinds. Then she sat down at her desk, closed her eyes and began trying to control her breathing. Cognitive Behavioural Therapy. *Nobody is looking at you. Nobody thinks the worst of you. People are only going about their business, just like you are.* Honor began to control her breathing, in through the nose, out through the mouth, smooth, calm. *Find your happy place.*

She couldn't remember precisely where she had been, but an image of a beach flashed into her mind: white sand, blue water, laughter, happiness. Her parents close by, Billy splashing manically in the water, ice creams, the excitement of staying somewhere that wasn't home. *Focus in on it. Ignore the images, capture the feelings.* Honor leaned back in her seat, breathing in slow rhythm to the waves of the tide washing onto the immaculate beach. Her mind began to clear, the tension in her shoulders leaking away, leaving her to roam blissfully alone in the darkened vault of her mind.

She knew that she would only have a few minutes, so Honor sat in silence until she felt calm enough to consider something beyond her own state of mind. Slowly, furtively, she allowed an image of Sebastian Dukas to materialise within the serene blackness. She saw him from a clinical viewpoint, her emotions no longer a barrier to her perception. He was hanging from the rope. There was no camera watching him. No moment of death, nothing for the killer to take away. *Why?* Dukas had died from asphyxiation, had been throttled to death. Did the killer want to witness that death personally? Was that his normal MO, to kill while looking into his victim's eyes? If so, why use the GHB drug on him? Was the killer a coward, afraid to take on a man without first incapacitating him? There was nothing sexual noted in either of the murders, so that was not his goal, or at least didn't appear to be at this stage.

Something nagged at her. She allowed herself to picture Amber Carson, not the grim visage of her death but vibrant in life. Amber was smaller, younger, more vulnerable that Sebastian Dukas had been. Both victims frequented a website, *Face Fear*, that allowed sufferers of extreme phobias to communicate. Beyond that they were unconnected, and had likely never heard of each other or met. Their phobias were the only connection. One male, one female.

A killer like the one they sought would need to have found a way to drug both victims, assuming that Amber was also under the influence of GHB. The first thing that came into Honor's mind was drink-spiking. The second thing that she thought of was the fact that both victims were present in bars or clubs before they disappeared, presenting an opportunity for the killer to spike their drinks at some point in the evening and make his attack as the victims headed home. But how would he know their mode of transport, or their plans? What if a victim got a lift, or had somebody at home waiting for them? The killer's scheme would come to nothing if he was challenged or outnumbered, and his position would be considerably worse if he was identified and reported to the police. He would instantly become a person of interest.

The answer came to her in an instant, a confirmation of her earlier instincts. He had to have planned this. Not just the first killing, not the second, but *all* of the killings. This wasn't a random attack on anybody he could find, but a specifically targeted campaign. It wasn't just the phobias. The killer would have to *know* the person in some way, would have researched how they moved, where they lived, who they knew, in order to coordinate his attacks to precisely locate and entrap the unwitting victim when they were both most vulnerable *and* had been successfully drugged.

Honor sat for a moment in silence, basked in the aura of peace surrounding her. The black chasm receded, cringing away from the immense power of a focused mind. She opened her eyes. Danny Green stood on the other side of her desk.

'Sorry, boss, I knocked but you didn't answer.'

Bugger. Honor stared at him blankly, her recently erected shield of karma-armour threatened with imminent collapse.

'CBT,' he said, and she nodded furtively in response. 'Bloody love it, I should do it more often.'

Honor blinked. 'You did CBT?'

Danny glanced over his shoulder at the office door, tapped it closed with his heel and then slipped into a seat opposite.

'Time to time,' he admitted. 'I got help a few years back. There's only so many car- crash victims covered in claret that you can see, y'know?'

Honor felt her heart warm as though touched by the sun's rays, and the yawning black chasm slipped away into obscurity. Honor realised that she was smiling, tried to stop it, and then wondered why.

'Guess we're all being frazzled by this one.'

Danny nodded, his own eyes still haunted by grim shadows from the scene at the cathedral.

'Forensics have got the phone, the coffin and a few other bits and pieces out of the pit,' Danny said, changing the subject. 'The pathologist is prioritising Amber Carson's autopsy, but we won't know until tomorrow about anything in her system.'

'Ask Michelle to draw fluids now,' Honor said. 'GHB can disappear from a victim's body within a few hours, we don't want to risk losing a link with Sebastian Dukas's killer. Being members of the same phobia website on its own isn't going to be enough to convince CPS that this is a campaign.'

'Fraud squad are going to use their wizardry to check out the IP addresses used by both the phone and the sender of the e-mail that went to Amber's family,' Danny added. 'Same goes for the video link, but given how careful this guy's been up to now, chances are they'll trace back to other countries, remote servers, that kind of thing.'

Honor nodded.

'I think he's following his targets, learning about them before he strikes.' 'The phobias?'

'Everything,' she replied. 'Makes sense that he could identify targets from the website, but what about their friends, families, loved ones, other people getting in the way and spotting him? He needs to work in private, to catch his targets when they're alone. I think this is a campaign, one he's been planning for a long time.'

Danny nodded thoughtfully.

'That would mean his next target is either already abducted, or is about to be.'

'Get us a list of all persons reported missing within, say, the past forty-eight hours. If anybody on that list is also a member of the phobia forum that Sebastian and Amber visited, there's a good chance they're in this killer's hands.' Danny stood up.

'Status meeting in ten minutes,' he said. 'Let's bring this with us, see if it sheds any light on this guy's next move before he makes it.'

Honor took a breath and followed Danny out of her office to the Incident Room. Within, more desks had been added, extra phones installed, and there was a buzz of quiet activity as more officers were drawn into the investigation.

'DI Harper's in a meeting with DCI Mitchell and the borough commander,' Danny said as they walked into the room. 'Looks like they're going to push this up.'

Honor nodded. 'Have the media been in touch?'

Danny gestured to the television screen, which was playing BBC News, and Honor got her answer right there as she listened to a broadcast playing out with a shot of Southwark Cathedral in the background. A reporter's black hair was being whipped around by the wind as she stood on the A3 alongside the cathedral grounds.

'... as what can only be described as a scene of chaos just south of London Bridge. Several ambulances, fire trucks and police vehicles were called here at dawn, and I understand that at least one body was removed from the scene. There are forensics officers at work now, concealed within tents so we can't tell quite what they're doing, but local witnesses reported that there were workmen here prior to the incident, and that they were either digging or filling foundation works around the cathedral as part of ongoing renovations.'

The broadcast snapped back to a well-known presenter in the studio.

'Can you tell us anything about the victim, or victims, Rebecca, or anything about how they were found?'

Rebecca, her hair vigorously trying to leave the scene, shook her head as she swiped strands from her face with one hand.

'The police are not sharing information at this stage, but what we do know is that one body was extracted from a pit filled with concrete, and that paramedics attempted to resuscitate the

victim but were apparently unsuccessful. What is interesting about this is that it's the second morning in a row that police have been called to a scene of a bizarre death. Yesterday it was the body of an apparent suicide victim seen hanging from St Magnus church, just over the water near London Bridge. Now, it's one or more victims possibly buried alive in Southwark Cathedral grounds. Whether the two murders are connected is as yet unknown, but it's clear that the City of London Police are acting on information that even the workers here on the grounds were not aware of, as witnesses say the police came in here at dawn with all sirens blazing, closely followed by ambulances, just moments after the cement had been poured. What that tells us is that they learned that there were people inside that pit before it was filled with concrete, and that in itself tells us that they know more than they're telling the public. Rebecca Tillbourne, London Bridge.'

Danny and Honor stared at the screen for a moment, and then glanced at each other. Moments later, the phones in the Incident Room started ringing, one after another.

'Here we go,' Danny said.

As officers started answering the phones, DI Harper strode into the Incident Room. Seeing that the entire team was assembled and either answering the phones or collating evidence, she closed the door behind her and gestured for the detectives to prepare for the briefing.

It took another five or six minutes for the first wave of calls to stop coming in, and it was evident from what Honor could hear that most of the calls were from journalists and television crews eager for the latest pick-up on what was happening in Southwark. Each of the calls was coming in through the

Bishopsgate front desk and being routed to the Incident Room to avoid clogging up the lines, but that would all change as soon as DI Harper decided to set up a direct link to the room, a move which would require a public announcement and the cooperation of the media itself.

'All right,' Harper snapped as soon as the last phone call had ended, 'where are we at? Honor, what's the status of the investigation?'

Honor replied smoothly, her recently renewed karma-armour doing its job.

'The victim in Southwark has been confirmed as Amber Carson, thirty-two. We have confirmed that Amber was also a member of the phobia forum *Face Fear* along with Sebastian Dukas, and that her greatest fear was claustrophobia, caused by a childhood accident. Autopsy is due in the morning, but I'll ask the pathologist to draw blood and fluids for testing in case any trace of GHB, which we suspect may be in her system, becomes too diluted to detect.'

Harper nodded. 'CCTV and surveillance?'

'We're reviewing footage from all pertinent locations,' Samir Raaya replied. 'Focusing on her home now, but it's located in Hackney alongside a narrow alley so her abductor may have been able to access her home undetected. I'm working on likely routes in, and waiting for CCTV from the bars the victims both frequented before they were killed, looking for places their drinks might have been spiked and who might have been able to do it.'

'Okay,' Harper replied, 'what about this smart arse's data and IP addresses?'

'Fraud and cyber are both working the addresses and the phone recovered from the Southwark crime scene,' Danny replied. 'It's gonna take some time, but we're hopeful that there might be a link back to an account here in the UK that we can raid.'

Nobody said anything in reply, mainly because everyone knew that there was only a slim chance that their killer would leave such an obvious and easy route to arrest open for the police.

'Motivations?' Harper demanded, and although she didn't say her name, she looked directly at Honor.

'He's not seeking sexual assault,' Honor replied, 'and although we will have to wait for autopsy to confirm any sexual assault on Amber Carson, I don't think we'll find it. The video piece says it all: he wants to watch them suffer, to watch them die. This is sadism, some kind of ritualistic rite-of-passage from which he may gain sexual gratification. I can't say what's driving that need, but I can say that if I'm right, it won't end here. These attacks are carried out too cleanly to be opportunistic.'

'You think it's a campaign, that it's been thought out?' Honor nodded.

'You can't just walk into people's lives like this and pluck them from their families, and he needs time to drug them in advance. GHB is a tricky substance to work with, it's tough to get the right measure into someone so they're compliant yet not comatose. Watching them die is important to him, it's a major part of what he's trying to do. If they're out cold when he kills them, then there is no gratification, he's denied what he most needs.'

DS Hansen's voice reached her from across the room. 'He didn't attach cameras to Sebastian Dukas.'

'I know,' Honor said, 'and Sebastian didn't die from being hanged, either. Something went wrong there. It's my guess that our killer didn't get the GHB dosage quite right and Sebastian came around too early, started fighting back, and so he had to be throttled to death. That would have allowed our killer to witness Sebastian's final moment of life, but it would not have been enough to fulfil his needs. He wants to watch that moment, but not while struggling to kill someone. He wants to enjoy it on his own terms, somewhere else, safe from the event itself.' Honor thought of something on the spot. 'Without risk to his *own* safety.'

For a moment Honor was lost, visualising their killer, enjoying the suffering and fear of others but keen to distance himself from any danger of suffering the same ordeal. It felt important, a glimpse into the mind of a killer more deranged than any she had encountered before.

'Honor?'

She blinked herself back into the room as she realised the DI was talking to her again. 'Sorry, I was considering the killer's motives.'

'Next targets? Can we beat him to them?'

'Danny's looking into missing persons reports and will match them against users of the phobia forum that Sebastian and Amber both frequented. If we get a match then we'll know there's a decent chance our guy has abducted his next victim. However, there are countless on-line forums out there dedicated to phobias, so he could in theory pluck targets from any one of them.'

Harper looked down at her notes. 'What about the media angle, what are they asking for?'

Detective Constable Zara Flint, a new officer on the team who had made her way up from the beat the year prior, answered with her customary keen-as-mustard enthusiasm. 'Everything and anything,' she said. 'They know something's going on and people are talking about this on social media. It'll be trending by rush hour. BBC and ITV are both connecting Sebastian Dukas and Amber Carson as the work of the same killer, even though on the outside there's nothing yet to say they're related. We need to tread carefully with this one. We can't hide too much, they already know we're working the case in both instances, but we can't tip our hand too early or it'll risk giving the killer an idea of how close we are to apprehending him.'

DI Harper grinned, clearly enjoying Flint's enthusiasm.

'The media are a double-edged sword,' she replied. 'You can't always catch a killer without them, but sometimes they reveal so much that the killer escapes before they can be brought to justice. For now, we hold out. That said, a press release is going to be essential before too long, especially if we get another incident.' She turned to Honor. 'When the time comes, I want you to hold the press briefing. You're closest to the investigation and you're already on the news.'

Honor's train of thought slammed to a halt. 'I am?'

Samir spoke to her softly from one side. 'Onlooker mobile phones,' he explained, 'they captured us both looking up at them from the crime scene in Southwark, and some other shots I think from St Magnus church.'

Oh shit. Honor's anxiety swelled again, the black chasm churning in the depths of her neural cortex. *Nobody's looking at you, except for a few million people watching breakfast television every morning.*

'You okay with that?'

DI Harper was looking at her for a reply, along with every other detective in the room.

'Sure,' Honor managed to utter, a breath of a word that barely made it past her lips and then seemed to try to scramble back from where it came.

'Press won't be held at bay forever,' Harper announced to the room,' so sooner or later this is going to get out, and when it does, we can't hold anything back. We have a serial killer on the loose in the city and he's targeting people based on what they're most afraid of, which is quite the bloody headline. The hacks will have a field day with it. I want something concrete…' Harper hesitated, regretting her choice of words, '… something solid to give them, when the time comes. A name, a face, something to show for the time we're spending on this. Get to it.'

The meeting broke up, Honor making her way back to her desk with a new shadow of doubt weighing her down. A press briefing, and she'd only been back two bloody days. The thought of her being on the television was bad enough, made worse now by the fact that she was already the face of an investigation that the media were stalking, like wolves hunting a wounded elk. Soon, their prey would tire and they would start nipping bits of flesh from its flanks, drawing ever more blood.

Danny and Samir followed her into her office, instinctively aware that she would need to talk to them before getting back to work. Honor glanced out of her window and saw that the sky was looking more threatening than ever, heavily bruised clouds tumbling through darkening skies.

'Where are we with CCTV on both cases?' she asked.

'It's a bust from me on St Magnus,' Samir replied. 'Nothing coming in on any of the cameras.'

'Same for me,' Danny replied. 'There's no evidence of anybody trying to break into the church grounds, or out of them for that matter. The first people of interest I saw on the footage was the police arriving at the scene, at about seven-thirty in the morning.'

Honor placed her hands on her desk, breathing calmly for a moment to clear her thoughts.

'I've only got an hour of footage left to watch,' she replied, 'and I haven't seen anything suspicious either. The only conclusion I can reach from this is that our suspect did not reach the scene by road, which must mean he used the river.'

The Thames was of course one way in which a suspect could move about the city without being detected by CCTV, but the river had its own patrol force and they would have noticed an unregistered vessel or suspicious activity.

'Get in touch with the MET Marine Policing Unit,' she said to Danny, 'find out if they've got anything on record for the London Bridge and Southwark area that might fit the estimated movements of our suspect.'

'Will do.'

'What about the IT guys, anything there?'

Samir shook his head. 'They're working on it, but it'll take time.'

Honor mentally kicked herself. Danny had mentioned that only a moment ago. She was losing her grip and she needed to stay on top of this: lives were at stake.

'Right,' she replied. 'I'll review what CCTV I have left of St Magnus, then pick up the threads of the Southwark footage with both of you. Either way, we've got a real mystery here – if this guy turns out not to be using the river, how the hell did he gain access to the church and the cathedral without being noticed by anybody?'

Neither Samir or Danny had an immediate answer.

'Okay, let's finish clearing what we can of the surveillance footage and then switch to other means of transport. I need you both back in here by the end of play today to collate what we know.'

Samir and Danny left the office for the IR, and Honor was about to update the CRIS database when Danny again poked his head around the corner of her door. 'You got a minute?'

Danny walked in and shut the door, glancing into the corridor before he did so. He moved across to her desk and perched himself on the corner.

'How you holdin' up?'

Honor kept her features impassive. 'I'm fine.'

Danny grinned, something between sympathy and bemusement. 'You coloured up when Harper put you on the spot about the press conference.'

Honor felt patches of heat touch her cheeks, a vague dizziness swaying her seat. 'I can handle it.'

'You sure? I can stand in for you if you'd rather stay off the six o'clock news.'

'I'll be fine.'

Danny hesitated, chose his words with care. 'I get it, remember? I know how it feels. There's no sense in pushing yourself into a corner and then realising that you can't fight your way out of it. This case, it's one of those once-in-ten-years cases, one that the media will really get their teeth into. It's unique, unusual, and you've just been dropped right into the middle of it.'

Danny said nothing more. Honor stared at him, wanting to retaliate, wanting to say *something*, but her brain had turned to mush and couldn't come up with a single bloody word in response. The hum of her computer's hard drive was the only sound. She opened her mouth to try to say something, but there was nothing to say.

Danny stood up, watched her for a moment.

'That's what I mean,' he said. 'Don't take this on if you're going to dry up like that in front of a few million viewers.'

The silence in her mind broke and she shot up out of her chair. 'Well, what the fuck would you like me to do?'

Danny grinned as he gestured airily toward her. 'Something like that.' Honor realised she'd been baited. She rolled her eyes. 'It's not that easy.'

'It's not that hard, either,' Danny pointed out as he turned to leave. 'Be yourself. You've got this, don't let your anxiety hold you back, okay?'

Honor watched him go, then slumped back down into her chair and watched the world going by outside her office window, worrying about how many of them had seen her on the television that morning.

10

There was no going back now.

This was where the anticipation began to build, where the excitement was, swelling within, an unstoppable wave of lust. No, not lust, an unworthy choice of word. Desire, yearning. Primitive cravings churned within him, tingling on his skin and filling his mind with thoughts that he would once have considered taboo.

He stared at himself in the mirror, and wondered whether anybody else out there ever had these thoughts. He doubted it. Most people were entrapped within the bubble of their own existence, oblivious to a world beyond the prison of their lives. Work, eat, sleep, raise kids, pay mortgage, watch the government rip off generation after generation but doing nothing to rectify it, retire, fall ill, lose mind, die. The whole circus appalled him, as though he alone could see its unjust flaws.

He had long ago chosen a different path.

He had showered, and now he shaved carefully as he considered that greater world, the one into which he had chosen to travel, one in which most feared to tread. He had broken free of the constraints of society, slipped the moorings of what was blithely considered acceptable, *normal*, and voyaged into the wild, uncharted waters of undiluted hedonism. And all of that had happened years ago. He recalled fetish clubs, where grown men and women chose to whip each other, to humiliate, to cause pain. He had been shocked to find people who actually *wanted* to be abused, to be struck, to be chained and whipped and even to have consensual sex as a part of the experience. It amazed him that any man would risk arrest and prison for crimes such as rape or assault, when, were they to look in the right places, they could live out their fantasies with like- minded souls. Some wanted to control, others still wanted to be controlled, pliant and submissive.

But that had not been enough.

There had been those who wished to be brought to the edge of death as part of their fantasies, and, occasionally, those who accidentally went too far in their pursuit of the sordid line between pleasure and death itself. And at one such event, he had witnessed it for himself.

The woman had not wanted to die. She had been suspended by the neck with a belt from a door that was ajar, while being taken from behind by a man in a mask. He had watched with others, the woman groaning, her tongue rolling around her lips as though in pleasure, not the throes of death. Nobody had noticed when she fell silent, her body shuddering with each vigorous thrust. Nobody noticed that her eyes briefly filled with panic, her tongue bulging. Nobody except him.

He had watched, enraptured, as the spark of life in her eyes faded, that last moment as she stared, unseeing, into the void of her own mortality. Then she died, the grimacing man behind her reaching a loud and violent climax.

Only when she voided herself a moment later did anybody realise that she was in danger. He had watched as the other men in the room frantically tried to revive her before calling an ambulance. He himself had done nothing wrong, and every other person in the room was a stranger, so he had simply dressed and left the scene with images of the woman's last, desperate moment of life imprinted on his mind. It was then that he had realised that the sex was not what he craved. Carnal pleasure was as transient as the feeble relationships he had forged with others in the BDSM community. Mortal pleasure, on the other hand, was literally for life.

He combed his hair in front of the mirror, then pulled on a comfortable shirt. He dabbed a touch of aftershave onto his jaw, preparing himself for the night's exertions. This would not be an easy or pleasant experience for the subject, but he knew that it would be worth it for all concerned, for this was the night when he would come out of his shell for all to see. This was the moment that he had been waiting for, planning for, all these years.

He walked downstairs and checked his watch: *6.12pm*. He then opened a small notebook that he kept on a mantelpiece in the living room. He opened the notebook with care and sat down, switching the television on as he turned to a page with a list of names. Slowly, carefully, as he watched a BBC newscast about the body found in Southwark cathedral grounds, he drew a line through a name on the list.

Amber Carson.

Above the name was another, with a line already drawn through it: Sebastian

Dukas. Slowly, with a delighted relish, he turned back to the previous page, and cast his eye over the names therein, each with a thin line through the middle. Why had he not thought of this before? Why had he killed without being known? Such things were to be shared, to be marvelled at, to be shown to others. All work and no play…

The media were aware of the deaths and were circling the scene for the next revelation, wolves around a decaying carcass. The police were scrambling, unsuccessfully, to catch a killer. Everything was in place for the game to begin. Timing was essential: too early, and his victim would recover consciousness too soon; too late, and they would not be conscious in time. He slipped on his jacket, and tucked a compact umbrella into an inside pocket, for he knew well that rain was on the way. Lots of rain. Autumnal storms were sweeping in from the Atlantic, threatening the city with torrential downpours. The foggy mornings were already gone, replaced with the squalls and gales of what was promising to be a turbulent September. He would have to hurry to make sure he was in just the right place, at just the right time, for his date with another victim's destiny.

Carefully, he put the notebook back on the mantlepiece, and was about to switch off the television when a reporter's broadcast caught his eye.

'… *when onlookers were able to take some brief images of the Southwark crime scene before forensic teams were able to put up tents. While we were unable to see anything of the victim or victims, we were able to identify several City detectives at the scene who appear to be running the case, although at this time there has been no response to our enquiries with the force and…*'

He was no longer listening to the broadcast, and he hit the pause button on his remote as he saw an image of two detectives staring up at the onlookers, who must have been trying to take photographs of the crime scene from up on the A3. Slowly, he crouched down in front of the television, the high-resolution image easily picking the two faces out.

A woman, tense-looking, shoulder-length blonde hair, small, maybe early-thirties. Alongside her, a younger, taller Asian man with black hair, a camera in his hand as he snapped an image of the onlookers.

He smiled.

'Hello, Detectives. Welcome to the game.'

DI Katy Harper held a second briefing that evening, just as the sun was going down outside Honor's office. The tower block opposite was bathed in golden light from the low sun that contrasted sharply with the dark, lumbering clouds unfolding across a brutal sky. Gusts of drizzle blasted the windows in random squalls that came as fast as they went.

'We've lost one detective as of tomorrow morning,' DI Harper announced. 'DC Jim Broadbent is at the Old Bailey for the Abdul Mohammad trial, and won't be back for at least two weeks. I've asked the MET for support but their hands are full, so all leave is cancelled until we can get a handle on the Dukas and Carson cases.'

Nobody complained. This was what detectives did: when a major case broke, pretty much everybody gave up the idea of family or social lives for the duration. Honor found that easier than most, as she lived alone and had no dependents, and she imagined that Samir also coped well with such hardships. It was a tough call though for Danny, who might go several days without seeing his family.

'Where are we on CCTV with either case?' Harper asked.

'It's a bust at St Magnus,' Danny reported, 'absolutely nothing on any cameras that we have access to. He didn't get there by road. Thames River Police are reviewing their records to see if this guy somehow got into the site via the river.'

'Same from us,' Honor said, gesturing to Samir. 'All footage of St Magnus is in and it's clear. Southwark Cathedral is in progress, but we're expecting the same. This guy is moving about in some other way.'

'He's not a bloody genie,' Harper snapped. 'Stop looking at monitors, get back down there and start investigating, that's what we're supposed to do, isn't it?'

'It's not like we're sitting here with our thumbs up our arses, boss,' Danny shot back. 'The sites didn't reveal anything about our suspect's movements, he hasn't so far left a trail, and the scene at Southwark was wrecked by people trying to save Amber's life.'

'I understand that,' Harper acknowledged, a little softer in tone. 'Just try again to see if you can figure out how he's pulling this off, and we might find a way to catch him in the act.'

Honor had been thinking the same thing. 'I'll head to Amber Carson's flat in the morning, see what I can see. The landlord has given us access to the property. It's possible the perpetrator might have been there, even though the site seemed secure when local police arrived.'

'Good. What about the IT side?'

'Nothing solid yet,' Danny replied. 'The phone used in the coffin to relay the signals was badly damaged, but the Cyber Griffin team think they can get the data out of it. That'll allow us to identify the general area that the phone was sending signals to, once we contact the provider, but I don't think we'll have that until the morning.'

'And the phobia sites, the ones the victims were using?'

'We're tracking down *Face Fear* users at the moment,' Samir said. 'So far, twelve people who live in the vicinity of the square mile have been identified as safe and well, but there are hundreds more on the site and countless other similar sites on the Internet who live in the city. It could take months to identify all of them.'

DI Harper nodded, well aware of the scope of the issue.

'If this gets any worse, we'll have to use the media to get the message out,' she said. 'Spreading panic is the last thing I want to do, but if we're not able to reach anybody who might be a victim of this killer, then it's our only option. Twenty-four hours, folks, we can't sit on this any longer than that. If we don't get a major break in the case by tomorrow afternoon, I'll contact the families of the victims for permission to take what we have to the media and officially announce the investigation.'

'He's going to strike again,' Honor said, 'there's no doubt about it. That's two now, and I'm willing to bet that he's already hunting the third.'

'Anything on missing persons to support that?' The DI was answered by silence from the detectives. 'So, *theoretically*, the Dukas and Carson cases could just be coincidental?'

Honor shook her head.

'I doubt that, there's too much similarity between them. I still think that Sebastian Dukas's murder went wrong, he wasn't killed the way he was supposed to be.'

She could tell that the DI still wasn't buying her hypothesis in full, but neither could she deny that the facts they did possess supported the idea that one killer was responsible for both crimes. As though on cue, the door to the Incident Room opened and a uniformed officer hurried in with an urgent look on her face.

'Apologies, but I thought that you should all know: the pathologist conducting the autopsy on Amber McVey got a baseline toxicology report back. She searched for GHB and found it in Amber's blood, confirming that she was drugged prior to her murder. Is that relevant to the case?'

'Yes, it is,' DI Harper replied, and then looked at Honor. 'The CCTV, from the bar she was in.'

'Understood, I'll take it home with me and check it tonight,' Honor replied.

'I'm halfway through it,' Samir added, 'nothing yet but I'll do the same. If he's there, we'll spot him.'

'Good,' Harper said. 'We need this guy in custody before he can attack his next victim. I want everybody in here at seven-thirty sharp tomorrow morning, and make sure the CRIS database is fully updated in case the MET or river police pick anything up overnight.'

Honor glanced at the clock and saw that it was already nearly eight o'clock. Thirteen hours in on day two, two bodies in the morgue and they still didn't have a clue how their killer was making his way around the city without being seen.

11

Honor's flat seemed somehow less inviting as she locked her front door behind her and switched on the hall light. Wherever she walked, all she could see in front of her was Amber Carson's face, caked in cement, her skin sloughing off, her hair thick with congealed concrete: and behind it all, her features twisted into that hellish mask, her terminal scream of terror. The interview with her family had been overwhelming, their grief crushing Honor as though it were her child that had been lost…

She leaned against the wall, suddenly fatigued beyond all comprehension, anxiety churning like black oil in the pit of her stomach. From the living room, Bailey strolled slowly around the corner of the door and looked at her before stretching expectantly. He wandered over and rubbed his body against her leg, wrapped his tail around it.

Honor prepared some food for him, set it down on the kitchen floor before shoving a ready meal into the microwave and pouring herself a glass of chilled wine. She headed into the living room and switched on the news, keen to keep an eye on it while she scanned through the CCTV from the pubs that Amber and Sebastian had frequented before their untimely deaths.

The footage from inside the *Crosse Keys* pub where Amber had spent her last night was of reasonably good quality, and she could see easily the group of four girls occupying one of the tables near the pub's central, circular bar. The footage was in black and white, and only showed a frame every four seconds in order to save storage capacity on its solid-state drive. Still, that was enough to catch most people who were in the bar that night, and her eyes were particularly focused on the table where the girls were sitting.

Bailey joined her on the sofa as she watched the footage play out. The girls were enjoying a few drinks and some food, Honor eating her own nuked meal as she watched. They were laughing, enjoying themselves, occasionally glancing at attractive young men entering the pub. The girls were probably single, then, or willing to play out of school – possibly something that a killer could take advantage of. Honor watched as the footage played out in staccato monochrome, fifteen seconds to each minute, fifteen minutes to each hour: she guessed that she would be done in forty-five minutes or so if…

'… *reports of a connection between the two recent murders in the capital, after an anonymous tip off from the public revealed that the victims were one Sebastian Dukas, thirty-two, from Camberwell, and Amber Carson, thirty-two, from Hackney.*'

Honor hit the pause button on her laptop and stopped chewing, her eyes fixed on the television as a sensation of dread gripped her. A woman was reporting from a location in Southwark, right alongside the cathedral, the building illuminated in a grand display against the night sky and the twinkling lights of the embankment.

'*The report revealed that both victims were in fact murdered in a particularly gruesome way,* with both being exposed to their greatest fears. In fact, they were deliberately killed while enduring their greatest phobias.'

'Oh, shit.'

'It has been alleged that Sebastian Dukas was terrified of heights, and was hanged from the steeple of St Magnus the Martyr Church in Bishopsgate, two hundred feet above the ground, while Amber Carson was buried alive in the grounds of Southwark Cathedral, before tons of fresh cement were used to fill in the pit as part of an underpinning renovation on the cathedral's wall. These allegations also confirm that the City of London Police already know that there is a serial killer at work in the city,

and that they have actual footage of the moment of death of at least one of the victims. The witness report stated that the police are expecting more murders and are currently powerless to prevent them.'

Honor heard her mobile phone spring into life on her coffee table, and she answered it immediately.

'McVey.'

'Harper,' came the DI's furious tone down the line, 'what the actual fuck is going on?'

'It's not my boys, boss,' Honor replied, certain that neither Danny nor Samir would have reported this to the media. 'This isn't a leak inside the unit. This came from the man who committed the killings.'

'You can't know that.'

'We're a small team,' Honor shot back. 'Nobody wants to see this killer get away after what happened to Amber Carson. You saw how that affected everyone.'

'Could be the families of either of the victims,' Harper said, cooling somewhat.

'Maybe they're not happy with the lack of results.'

'Too soon,' Honor countered. 'They're still in shock, the anger won't have hit them yet. We need the BBC to reveal their source.'

'They're not going to drop an informer in the can and flush them on our say so,' Harper pointed out. 'Besides, the tip-off was anonymous. This is on us, whether it's a leak or this arsehole pulling our chains. Do we have anything new to tell them?'

'We're reviewing the bar footage now, and should have something to say within an hour or less.'

'Such as? Blurry image of man in bar? And what if we don't have anything to show?'

'I can't say,' Honor replied, knowing that it was both the truth and entirely inadequate.

Then, she heard nothing but the television in the background as she saw her own face on the screen, a pixelated blown-up image of her.

'Detective Sergeant Honor McVey is reported to be leading the team seeking the murderer, a career police officer and detective with over a decade on the force, but who was recently off work for over six months for a stress-related condition. She's partnered with a male detective who is known to have been a direct-entrant to the force with no prior experience. With an apparently sadistic killer on the loose in the city and no known leads at this time, it raises questions about the decision to assign a newbie and a recently recovered stress victim to the *case. Sarah Griffiths, BBC News, Southwark.'*

There was a long silence on the line as Honor stared at the screen, her body numb, her heart battering the walls of her chest as her vision blurred. An image of DC Hansen flickered through her mind, smirking.

'We need to get ahead of this, Honor,' Harper said, breaking the silence with a somewhat more sympathetic tone – she had evidently heard the same broadcast at the same time. *'Press conference, tomorrow, and I need you to lead it. Looks like you've become the face of this investigation. It'll be a good opportunity to put doubting minds to rest. Let me know the moment you find anything on that CCTV footage.'*

DI Harper cut the line off and left Honor sitting comatose in front of the television, staring at an image of her own face where she had paused the transmission, now being broadcast in detail to a few million fellow watchers. For some reason she had the sense that she was being exposed as a villain, rather than a detective stoically hunting a grim assassin. The media would now pin the burden of success upon her shoulders, charging her alone with the task of apprehending a man whose name they did not yet know.

She sighed and leaned back on her sofa, closed her eyes. Breathe slowly, *in through the nose, out through the bloody mouth.* She knew that she had to keep a lid on her wayward thoughts, lest her mind be cast adrift from its moorings and drift helplessly into the turbulent storms beyond her darkened sanctuary.

Focus.

She opened her eyes and focused on her laptop, then opened the *Face Fear* page. The forum was administrated by a UK user, whom Honor had been able to identify from their own profile page. The site had some one thousand, seven hundred followers and a lively timeline. She had been able to identify several members who lived close by, their profile pages revealing photographs of summer barbeques that betrayed their precise location based on the Shard poking up into the sky in the distance and other key reference points. The time of day, the date and the angle of the sun in the sky was all that one needed. Honor had then been able to identify their friends, where those friends lived, where they worked, everything.

She had not used a special gadget to perform this work – there was little need. The average Facebook user had little concept of how easy it was to expose personal information from their pages, even when that information was not explicitly stated. Tiny details could be gleaned from photo albums; locations identified, personal habits and preferences noted, even travel plans. Big companies like Facebook were expert data gatherers, with algorithms based not just upon what a person typed on their profile or what pages they visited, but upon what images they posted and the kind of information they shared.

Honor surfed the page for a while, uncovering a litany of phobias that she was surprised even existed. She had heard of the most common ones, such as arachnophobia, hydrophobia and so on, but *nomophobia* got her attention: the fear of being out of range of one's mobile phone service, or out of credit. Anemophobia was a fear of the wind; Spectrophobia was a fear of seeing one's self in the mirror, which Honor could attest to suffering most days, especially when enduring a hangover. Linonophobia was a fear of string. That made Honor think for a moment, about the nature of fear itself. By a fair margin, a piece of string was not the most hazardous object in the universe, and a fear of falling onto a piece of string and somehow being throttled to death by it seemed a stretch.

'Death by string,' she murmured, and giggled as she shot Bailey a serious expression. 'The string did it, y'onour.'

Bailey blinked, then continued licking his fur.

Ablutophobia: a fear of bathing; chorophobia: a fear of situations involving dancing. Her father should suffer from that, but apparently was unaware of it and had often afflicted her with his own personal form of *thing-shaking* that had embarrassed her in front of family and friends as a child. Allodoxaphobia: a fear of opinions…

'DC Hansen, take note,' she chortled as she sipped her wine.

Optophobia: the fear of opening one's eyes, common knowledge to anybody on a Monday morning. The list went on, Honor scrolling down through some of the weirdest fears that she had ever encountered, until one stopped her in her tracks and made her lean closer to the screen. *Thanatophobia:* a fear of death, or the process of dying, named after the Greek figure of death, Thanatos.

Honor saw the face of Amber Carson, frozen in time a split-second before her life had come to an end; terrified, buried alive beneath tons of wet concrete. The killer had purposefully placed that camera inside the coffin, had purposefully wished to watch the moment of her death, presumably in real time. Honor suspected that the killer had intended for something similar to happen to Sebastian Dukas, but he had fought back too soon, forcing the killer to throttle him to death, to watch his moment of death in real time but not in the way the killer had intended.

'Snuff videos.'

The memory of a spate of "snuff" videos that had entered mainstream consciousness a few years before jolted uncomfortably. The videos were of people dying, whether by choice or not, and had appeared in various dark and sordid forums for years before service providers were able to crack down on them. Honor was aware that they still appeared from time to time on the so-called Dark Web, a sort of mirror-image of the Internet, which she had no idea how to access. The IT guys would know, for that was also where lurked the paedophiles in their miserable hordes, sharing their disgusting images with each other.

Honor leaned back on the sofa again, sipped some more of her wine. Fear of death itself. An *obsession* with death. Obsession was not far removed from fear in many ways, the sufferer unable to deflect their thoughts and attention away from what they perceived as a threat. Sufferers could therefore become afflicted with an obsession, or it could become a part of their killing strategy, something that they wished to observe or somehow take part in, of course without implicating themselves directly in the death itself.

'He *is* obsessed,' she said to Bailey.

Her gaze drifted to the image on the wall, the ghostly shape of a baby's head, gold pixels against the dark cradle of life, like stars shimmering in an infinite cosmos. There had been life there, once, cruelly snatched away, a life that did not yet know that it *was* life. Honor looked away again, pain pinching the corners of her eyes as she focused on the screen for a few moments and kept reading to divert her maudlin thoughts.

Thanatophobia, it was believed, was rooted in the human denial of death itself. Human beings had developed some level of self-awareness and understanding of mortality one hundred and fifty thousand years ago, so the piece said, and had thus been dealing with the concept ever since. It could not be said whether any other animals understood that their lives would come to an end, and even intelligent animals like elephants seemed unable to understand why elderly members of the herd would eventually keel over and never move again. They did show undeniable evidence of grief, however, suggesting that they eventually recognised the moment where a well- known member of the herd was never again coming with them.

The point of the piece, she learned, was that no living human had *ever died*. People were brought back from a state of death, but near-death experiences not-withstanding, they were not conscious during their actual deaths. Hence, death was something that people could not deal with in the normal emotional way as, by definition, they were unable to do so, so they lived their lives in a permanent state of denial, whether they knew it or not: death always happens to the *other* guy.

Honor kept reading down, and then she read something that further caught her attention. Suddenly, she knew what the killer was thinking. Honor grabbed her mobile phone and started dialling.

He sat in the living room and stared at the mirror, watching himself while he waited for the time to leave. It was something that he had learned to do as a child, when he had first wondered about himself and his place in the universe, had first asked: *why am I here?*

He had been about seven, maybe eight years old at the time, young to be thinking such things. It had been at about the same age that he had first realised that he would, one day, die. The awareness, the revelation, had both intrigued and bothered him ever since. What would it feel like to be dead? How could one exist, and yet then simply *not* exist?

He had rationalised this for himself. The universe was nearly fourteen billion years old, and he had not existed for the vast majority of that time. Thus, being dead had not bothered him. He had not existed, and not existing was the very definition of being dead, or at least, not yet alive. Therefore, no problem. Except that, now, he *was* alive. He could no longer not exist, for he had once existed. Descartes, in a roundabout way – *I lived; therefore, I was.* To his young mind the question was of immense importance, but most seemed to avoid it. His own father's words had been typically dismissive.

'You'll know when you get there,' he had uttered with an uninterested shrug of his shoulders, as usual not even looking at his son.

But, if he had once existed, then how could he no longer exist afterward? He had devoured books on the occult, and on experiences of the "afterlife", of near-death encounters and other esoteric and impossible-to-prove witness accounts of heaven, hell and the something in-between called purgatory. For years, he had been obsessed with it all, and at the end, eventually, he had been forced to draw his own conclusions. That moment had been a finality with implications both moral and existential.

'We live only once.'

He reaffirmed his own faith as he watched himself in the mirror. There was no afterlife, no deities, nothing after what mankind knew and understood as life. Life was precious because it only occurred once for the individual, a vanishingly brief flicker of awareness amid the immense antiquity of an endless, lonely universe. He had realised that, as a baby, neither he nor any other human being had any recollections. Those came later, at the age of two years or so, when he could recall events, faces, simple memories in his mind that suggested he had become aware of his surroundings. Before that, he had been alive but clueless about it. Others still, in old age, lost their awareness, their sense of self, through Alzheimer's and other illnesses that robbed them of their entire being. They were alive, but their true selves were present no longer. Thus, existence itself was a product of the mind, of squabbling neurons and writhing electrical currents, and when the brain was too young to form the connections necessary for self-awareness, or so old that it decayed and those once-firm connections were loosened, life itself came to an end and the sense of self was lost. One could be dead or alive, and it wouldn't matter, because they wouldn't know either way.

Nothing matters.

He looked at himself again. He looked younger than his years, no grey hairs marring his head, his skin smooth and untainted by the ravages of hardship or afflictions. He had led a healthy life and he was considered of high intelligence, having once almost got into MENSA, falling short by only a handful of IQ points. At no point had he ever been suspected of being a psychopath.

The word irked him, although he knew that in some ways it applied. It was a word that was bandied about, applied to anybody who broke free of society's so-called "norms" and forged a path of their own. He saw himself more as a pioneer, somebody who was willing to break those bonds, to traverse the taboo and the forbidden just to see what was out there. Had others, more famous, not sallied forth on equally perilous but valiant journeys? Copernicus, Columbus, Armstrong? All had faced the unknown, confronted it, explored it, and in some cases lost their lives in the pursuit of satisfying their insatiable curiosity.

He sat a little straighter, his confidence buoyed. There was no right or wrong, only what mankind made for itself. There were no consequences, no price to pay other than at the hands of the law, which he feared little. There was nothing in life that could keep him from the crucible of his mind, for there alone he ruled as God, the conqueror of his own existence, and as it was the only existence he would ever have, he intended to use it as he saw fit.

He stood up, his eyes bright with the glow of enlightenment or the radical glitter of fanaticism, depending on how cynical the observer. Dark jeans met brown leather boots, and he slipped on a leather jacket to complete the look he preferred. He was ready to quell the darkness inside, reaching out to consume him. He no longer feared it, the wolf within, although he could admit to himself that he also did not understand it. All he knew was that it must be assuaged, fed, satisfied, before it would return to slumber in some deep conduit of his brain where it would not bother him, at least for a while.

The police would eventually identify him. He stood out in a crowd: tall, handsome, well-built and in good shape for someone his age, a result of never smoking and never being much of a drinker. His timing would have to be perfect. If the *Ripper* could melt away into London's history as the greatest and most brutal serial killer of all time, so could he. His only remorse was that he could not be like the Ripper in every way, but sadism had its limits. He was squeamish around blood, always had been, and he disliked direct confrontations. The idea of carving victims up, dead or alive, appalled him. No, his method was different, even more cruel in many ways, for his victims lived right up until the end: they did not die while unconscious, from shock or massive blood loss, they remained entirely *compos mentis* until the very, *very* last second.

He turned and walked to his laptop computer, the screen displaying the *Face Fear* forum that he so often frequented, using a fake profile. He sat down in front of it, and hovered the mouse over the profile of Jayden Nixx.

He had watched Jayden for almost a year, and in that time, he had gathered a considerable amount of data about her. He knew where she lived, where her family lived, her mobile and home phone numbers, where she worked and with whom. He knew her favourite haunts in the city, how she travelled and, most importantly, where she was travelling tonight.

The *Hoop and Grapes* pub was located in Whitechapel, beneath a block of modern offices, just off Aldgate. It had an outside terrace, although with the rapidly deteriorating weather he knew that all drinkers would be inside. Jayden, he knew, did not smoke, so she would remain inside the pub for the evening.

He had picked up on the planned gathering by simply ensuring he was often in the right place at the right time to overhear conversations. He had in fact spoken to Jayden once or twice in passing, as she had come to recognise him, although they had never been formally introduced. The knowledge that she knew her killer excited him, although he knew not why. He knew only that it intoxicated him, knowing that her death was close, that she was being hunted, and that only *he* knew it.

Jayden would be leaving her house about now. The time to leave was close, and he would need to be extremely careful in how he conducted himself, as he could not really afford to be seen close to Jayden. The police would check CCTV footage of the pub in the wake of her death, and if he was seen in close proximity to her, they would seek to identify him. No, tonight he must stay in the shadows and his visit must be brief. The advantage was that he knew the layout of the pub very well, and he was already planning his strike as he walked out of the living room and headed for the front door.

He was halfway there when he heard a thump from downstairs, in the cellar. He sighed, turned, and unlocked the basement doors before heading down. He hit the light to reveal the spare rooms, and turned right. Another dull thump. He walked to the doors, selected another key, unlocked and opened them.

The darkness was absolute, the heat in the room thick and heavy. A single, bare light bulb cast a sickly light, the room's sole street-level window sealed shut and covered with a veil of black cloth.

The stench hit him, as it always did, the commingled odours of decay, of rotting skin and flesh, of a human body both alive and in a state of semi-death. He stepped inside and looked down at the bed, sagging beneath the emaciated bones of a body that quivered with the last desperate threads of life fluttering weakly within.

The limbs were grey and laced with purple veins, the skin almost translucent. He could see the rib cage poking through the chest, the skin seeming to hang from the body like limp sails from a ghost ship's yards. He let his gaze travel to the skull, shocks of ragged white hair clinging in patches to blotchy skin, eyes dull within sunken pits ringed with bruised sclera. Yellowed teeth peeked between thin lips pulled back in a rictus of near-death. The figure emitted a feeble, high-pitched whistling cry of misery, ragged breath coming in short, soft gasps.

He leaned down, and gently patted the back of one bony hand, its wrist bound with chains just as were the ankles and neck.

'Soon,' he promised, looking into the man's eyes with a smile. 'Soon, Father.'

12

Dread. She felt it every time she closed her eyes. She couldn't sleep for it haunting her every thought.

Honor instead sat in silence on her sofa and watched the city, the twinkling lights blurred and distorted by rain splattering in squalls on her window. She was sitting in darkness, the way she liked to sometimes when she needed to think. Bailey knew the drill and was curled up asleep on the other end of the sofa, dreaming, his paws occasionally twitching as he swiped at birds in some imaginary forest.

She knew. She *knew* what he was thinking, and she was sure that by now he would be at work again, stalking somebody out there in the city.

She had called the station and spoken to Danny, who was still in the office trawling through CCTV footage from *All Bar One*, the location of Sebastian Dukas's last night. He still hadn't seen anything, and the lack of evidence was hugely frustrating for the team. Nobody in the footage from the *Crosse Keys* stood out either, literally nobody, and yet somehow Amber had been incapacitated with GHB before her death. They could only assume for now that the drugging had occurred at her home, but somehow the pieces didn't quite fit well enough for that.

'I'm running footage now of her heading back to Hackney,' Danny said on the phone. 'She looks fine, maybe a little tipsy but nothing too bad. She's alone, the whole way so far.'

That information also bothered Honor, knowing that Amber was neither followed nor being watched in the pub. The evidence suggested that she was targeted randomly, but then her manner of death of course had been anything but random.

'What about Samir?' she asked. 'Is he getting anywhere?'

'He left a couple of hours ago to get showered and eat,' Danny replied. 'He's been trawling through the phobia forums, trying to find a link between the victims beyond their presence on the site. He says he's coming back in to look over some more footage and go over the witness reports at St Magnus the Martyr Church. Something's got to pop on this guy, he can't just vanish into thin air.'

Honor leaned back in her sofa and took a breath. 'I think I know what's driving him.' 'The killer?' Danny asked, cautious. 'We don't know anything about the guy.' 'Hear me out,' Honor replied. 'He's targeting people with phobias, and planning everything meticulously. That suggests he's particularly sadistic and likes to watch his victims suffer for long periods of time.'

Honor could hear Danny munching on a packet of crisps before he replied. 'Nothing unusual for a fully paid-up member of the psychopath club. What's your point?'

'So, I'm starting to think that this guy is acting something out. He's reliving something, something from his past maybe. People don't just decide to go out and start hanging people from church spires – this is something he's been building up to. It may not even have started here.'

'You think he's killed before?'

'It's possible, and if he was successful then so far he's remained undetected. Maybe that isn't enough for him? Maybe he decided that he wanted to start advertising his work, get some notoriety. He's local to the city, we're pretty sure of that, maybe lives right there somewhere in Spitalfields or Whitechapel.'

'Ripper territory,' Danny agreed, 'but this guy's not showing any signs of wanting to tear people up. If anything, the murders are gruesome but clean.'

Honor nodded, thinking about that. Not once had they found blood on their victims.

'It's spectacle,' she said, thinking out loud. 'He wants the scene, he wants the attention, the thrill of the chase, just like a serial killer on a television show. He wants to play cat and mouse, but he's not sadistic in the sense that he wants to bleed his victims. That suggests he's more…'

There was a brief silence. 'More what?'

'More down to earth,' was all that Honor could say, unable to articulate precisely what she meant. 'Look, killers in movies blow people up, hang them from meat hooks, cause all kinds of horrible torture, but we know that most real killers aren't like that. They're shooters and stabbers, definitely, but only crimes of passion tend to be the bloodiest. This isn't about outright rage, the killings are too planned, too controlled for fury, right?'

'Sure,' Danny replied, remaining cautious. 'You want to lead with that tomorrow?'

Honor knew that she was speculating, that DI Harper would not bite on something as tenuous as her instinct, but she could sense a foreboding building within her, that something new was about to happen.

'He's out there, right now,' she said with a conviction that surprised even herself. 'He's going to do this again and he's going to escalate it.'

'We need the media,' Danny replied. 'We're not getting anywhere fast and if you're right, we're going to be in for hell when the story breaks.'

'That's what he wants,' Honor insisted. 'He wants the attention! If we go public with this, we're giving him precisely that.'

There was a long silence before Danny replied. 'And if we don't go public, and the story breaks without us?'

Honor knew that she had nowhere to go. There would be an outcry if they kept a lid on this for too long. But then they couldn't just play into the killer's hands and give him the notoriety that he wanted.

Honor's racing mind got the better of her. 'How many victims did Jack the Ripper kill?'

Now, the silence on the other end of the line was deep. Honor waited, and for a moment she thought that Danny had cut the line off, but then his voice reached out to her from what felt like a universe away.

'We need to stick to what we know.'

'How many?' she asked again. 'I can Google it, but I know you're into all the history stuff. How many?'

Danny sighed softly. 'Five canonical victims, all supposedly East End prostitutes although that's now been pretty much proven false, slashed and dissected with possible surgical or butchery skills, although even that too is now contested. Lots of suspects in the case both then and now, but as everybody knows, Jack the Ripper was never knowingly caught and convicted. Several killers at the time were captured and hanged for murder, and any one of them could in theory have been the Ripper, but we'll never know.'

Five known victims. Sebastian and Amber were dead. Honor felt certain that there would be another tonight.

'Do we have dates, for the murders that the Ripper was known to have committed?' Now, the silence before Danny replied was charged with tension. 'August 31st and November 9th, 1888.'

Honor felt the hairs on the back of her arms and neck rise up, tingling as insects of loathing scuttled beneath her skin.

'This started August 31st,' she said. 'Sebastian Dukas was murdered that night.' Danny said nothing, but Honor was not waiting for a reply. Same time of year, same location, Whitechapel, but a very different method of killing - less bloody, but no less terrifying for the victim and just as deadly. No sexual assault, no known links between murderer and victim, all victims abducted by night, their bodies on display in one way or the other the following day.

'Unique murders,' she said down the line, 'highly visual, something that the press can really get their teeth into. This is a modern-day Ripper, somebody who wants to emulate the Victorian killings for today's audience, and put them on display for all to see.'

She could hear Danny's agitation on the other end of the line, the occasional sound of a ringing phone in the background.

'Let's say you're right,' he replied finally. 'You can't walk into a press conference with that – it'll drive the media wild, for sure, but nobody's going to be able to use it. It doesn't tell us anything about his next move, and if he is somehow attempting to emulate the Ripper then he's probably using some deranged interpretation of history to do so.'

Honor knew enough about the history of the Ripper's killings, and the more recent revelations dispelling many common myths, that basing any modern crime on the historicity of Whitechapel's most famous killer was a fallacy in itself: nobody could do so in any real sense, as there simply wasn't enough known about the person behind the murders.

'Okay, so put that aside for a moment. He's killed a victim using heights, and he's killed another using their fear of being buried alive,' Honor replied. 'What does that leave us with? There are hundreds of phobias out there. I've been reading about them, but most can't kill a person.'

'Christ, I don't know. Snakes?'

'Spiders,' Honor added, 'anything venomous usually has a phobia attached.'

'And any other animals capable of killing a person,' Danny added, 'so maybe we should just label any kind of exotic pet as a possible target.'

'What else?'

'It could be anything.'

Honor closed her eyes. She knew that Danny was right, and that they couldn't afford to waste too much time on what was essentially an exercise in speculation, but right now they had nothing else to damned well go on.

Something rattled the apartment windows and she opened her eyes and looked out over the darkened city. Rain splattered against the glass and fell in rivulets, the colourful city lights twisting and contorting before her.

'Water,' she whispered down the line as she remembered the fog that had consumed Sebastian Dukas's body. 'The weather. There are floods forecast for tomorrow.'

Danny didn't reply right away, but when he did, he shared her conviction. 'The river,' he said, 'he could use the river again.'

'Call the River Police, I want them on high alert for any suspicious boating activity on the water, either tonight or in the morning!'

Danny agreed and shut off the line. Honor set the phone down but she didn't switch the lights on. Instead, she walked to the apartment window and let her gaze drift across the cityscape before her. The foreboding, the dread, it was still there, and she saw in her mind's eye a shadowy figure once again stalking the rain-sodden alleys of Whitechapel, murder on his mind.

The rain was falling, squalls spilling through the glow of streetlights like diamond chips from an inky black sky. The streets reflected glowing windows in colourful halos of light, the splash of cars down nearby Mansell Street echoing through the apartment buildings that surrounded him as he walked with his hood up and his hands tucked into his jacket pockets.

There was nobody around, residents holed up in their homes, gangs hunkered down in flats, running their drug deals out of the rain. Not that he feared them at all. He was big enough that he had never been challenged, despite preferring to stay to the back streets of the city.

The *Duke of Somerset* pub was busy as he walked down a narrow alley that led out onto Little Somerset Street, cutting around the edges of several large office buildings. He liked using the alleys. Although the days of Victorian London were long gone, with the most dangerous thoroughfares long since widened and forgotten, it still gave him a thrill to stalk these darkened recesses, wondering what it would have been like to have hunted there a century or more ago.

He walked the length of the street and came out onto Aldgate, and there to his right was the *Hoop and Grapes* pub. The pub was a timber-and-beam building that had survived the Great Fire of London in 1666, the Year of the Devil, as it had once been known, the conflagration killing surprisingly few but in a single night turning half of the city into a blazing inferno. Just a couple of hundred metres from the Tower of London and the river, Jayden Nixx's choice for her night out was perfect.

There would be little time for him to make his move. Jayden and her friends liked to get to the pub early, to get a table at the back where they could chat without being swamped by people at the bar. He took his time walking to the front of the pub, scanning the windows to see who was sitting inside.

His heart gave a little flip as he saw her, as though she were a new girlfriend awaiting him on a first date. She was sitting with her back to the pub, side-on to the windows and facing slightly away from him. Long, curly black hair, slender, wearing an off-the-shoulder cardigan that exposed tantalising smooth, dark skin. He had admired the images Jayden had posted with delight on her Facebook page, tempted to meet with one or two of her equally attractive friends at some point in the future, but for now he would have to stay the course.

He sauntered up to the pub door, opened it and walked inside, pulling his hood off as he did so but keeping his head down and turned away from the pub's cameras.

The pub was busy, packed with mid-week drinkers elated to have once again passed what was termed "hump day" in the modern vernacular. He shouldered his way gently through the crowd and reached the bar, where he was soon served by a member of the staff.

'Stella, please,' he asked.

'I got a *please!*' the girl reported to her colleagues with a smile as she poured his pint.

That happened a lot. He understood that being polite got people a long way, one of many life lessons that he'd learned from his dear old dad, who had spent most of his life being cruel and rude. He smiled his thanks to the girl as she handed him his change, an image of his father's emaciated remains shuddering with the last pulses of life crawling through his veins causing his smile to widen. He noted the girl's cheeks and throat flush with colour, her eyes wide and filled with light and life, and realised almost belatedly that she was coming on to him without saying a word.

Although his smile didn't slip, he cursed inwardly. He couldn't afford to be too memorable, and so he turned and made his way back through the crowd. As he turned, his gaze swept the bar for security cameras and instantly identified two of them: one above the bar, looking down its length, and another on the beams at the far end, looking down the length of the rest of the pub.

He made his way to a spot where he could stand without being in easy sight of either camera, and watched the crowds. Many people were out with friends, but just as many were alone, reading, working on laptops with a quick pub-grub dinner beside them. He leaned against the wall and pulled out his mobile phone, set his pint on a mantelpiece above an old fireplace, and began messing about with the phone while watching Jayden and her friends at the far end of the pub.

It would not take long. They were laughing and joking, four girls and two guys, work friends if he recalled correctly: Jason and Kyle, maybe Karl, he couldn't remember for sure. The drinks were flowing, and he made a mental note to check that Jayden went home alone. He knew that she was single, but there was the chance that their night out could result in one of the young men returning with her, and that was something that he couldn't allow, not on Jayden's special night.

He drank his pint carefully, timing it to roughly match that of Jason and Kyle, while also trying to see how far Jayden was through her own drink. This part of the game was luck and timing, and he waited for almost twenty minutes before Jason, the taller of the two men accompanying Jayden, stood and got his wallet out.

As he watched, Jayden raised her glass at him. Although her back was turned, Jason was standing to her right, and as she spoke, he saw Jason repeat her request.

'Pinot spritzer.'

He drained his pint and moved only when Jason had almost reached the bar, sidling in nearby and making sure that Jason got served first. Then, he waited. Jason was a few inches shorter, making it easy to watch the order being placed and the drinks fetched. As soon as a space was available, he slid in alongside Jason at the bar and waited for a member of staff to catch his eye.

Jason ordered two pints of Peroni, two dry Chardonnays and a Pinot spritzer with tonic water. As expected, the pints came first.

'What can I getcha?'

He turned to see his favourite bar girl waiting for him, her big brown eyes wide as he got his wallet out.

'Another Stella, please.' 'Hey, I got another *please*!'

He smiled, glanced to his left and saw Jason grinning. 'I think she likes you, mate.'

He smiled back, not wanting to keep the conversation going for too long. 'I'm already taken,' he answered, then his grin widened, 'although I wouldn't mind trying for that one.'

Jason nodded his agreement as he turned to check out the other bar girl, with an enviable figure and long dark hair who was working down the far end of the bar. With Jason distracted, he flipped a tiny, clear crystal from his wallet into the throat of Jayden's Pinot, the crystal vanishing amid spiralling bubbles as it dissolved.

'I know what you mean,' Jason murmured in reply.

Within moments, Jason had turned with his tray of drinks and was heading back through the crowds to Jayden's table. He turned with his own pint and resumed his watchful post, staying long enough to see Jayden begin drinking her wine, and then made a show of checking his watch before he drained his pint and headed for the door.

He pulled his hood up against the rain and stepped outside, and moments later he was walking back down Little Somerset Street and vanishing into the rain-swept night.

Now, it was time to enact the second part of his strategy.

'Are you okay?'

Jayden Nixx barely heard her friend's question above the busy noise of the pub, but she turned and nodded, saying nothing. Everything had been fine before her second drink, but now she felt nauseous and weary, suddenly able to think about nothing but her bed and the chance to get some sleep.

'You sure?' Amanda asked. 'You look pale.'

'I don't feel great,' Jayden replied, glancing at her now half-empty spritzer. 'I think I'm going to head home.'

Jason overheard the conversation and downed the rest of his pint.

'I'll walk you back if you like,' he offered. 'I need to get home too. It's been a long day and I'm up at seven tomorrow.'

Jayden nodded vacantly, certain that she was going to be sick at any moment. Normally, she wouldn't have accepted the offer of a walk home from Jason – she had known for some time that he held a candle for her, but she had only ever seen him as a friend and didn't want to encourage him. But she could also see that Kyle still had most of his drink left and the girls wouldn't be leaving for another hour at least.

She reached for her coat and umbrella, slid into the coat as she stood. The world tilted a little around her and she swayed, this time her friends standing up to support her.

'Wow, that came on fast Jayden, you sure you're okay?'

She nodded, took a deep breath, and her head cleared a little. 'Yeah, I think so, just really tired. I'll see you all tomorrow, okay?'

Jayden hugged each of her friends as Jason put a hooded jacket on, and then they left, Jason easing his way through the crowds to the exit with Jayden just behind. They walked out of the pub into the darkness, the door swinging shut behind them to mute the noise and allow her to hear the rain falling all around. The cool air cleared Jayden's head and she felt a little better as they set off for her apartment, which was only a couple of streets away.

'You feeling better?' Jason asked as he pulled his hood up.

Jayden nodded as she extended her umbrella. 'Yeah, must've been the heat or something.'

Jason shrugged as they walked, his features concealed behind the hood. Normally, Jayden would have avoided a man walking with his hood up like that, but she knew Jason from work and he was one of the kindest souls out there. Funny, how deceiving appearances could be – had she not known him, she would have taken him for a drug dealer or something.

'Good night's sleep will clear your head,' he said as they walked. 'You didn't have much though, I've seen you tank down enough booze to sink an ocean liner before now and still walk home.'

Jayden wasn't sure if that was a compliment or not, but she decided to take it as one. 'Getting older.'

'Yeah, I know what you mean.'

The conversation was stilted, awkward, and she knew why. Jason was working his way up to something, and instead of just being himself, he was struggling. She didn't know why guys got like that, all tongue-tied and self-conscious. Most times, even if a girl wasn't interested, being asked out nicely was always a huge boost to morale and confidence, especially these days, when anything more than a twenty-inch waist and an arse the size of two grapes was considered obese. She thought about letting him know in some gentle way that she wasn't interested, but then the nausea returned from nowhere and she began to sway as she walked.

'Jesus.'

She almost tripped and toppled sideways. Jason jumped into motion and caught her as she slumped into him.

'Jayden,' he murmured as they stopped in the rain, Jayden's umbrella pinned between them at an awkward angle. 'You can't be drunk; you haven't had enough.'

Jason was propping her upright on legs that felt as though they had turned to mush. 'I know, I only had one and a half glasses.'

Jason looked at her for a moment, peering into her eyes. 'I reckon your drink's been spiked or something. Come on, you just need to get your head down and sleep it off.'

Jayden allowed Jason to lead her along, but her mind was racing as fast as its lethargy would allow. Could somebody have spiked her wine? Why? It wasn't like she was on her own or anything, how could anybody have thought that they would end up alone with her and...

Jason bought the round.

The thought hit her hard, and she peered sideways at him. She couldn't see his face behind the hood. He wasn't like that, was he? Would he really do something like this? They worked in the same office for God's sake, it wasn't like he wouldn't be under suspicion if he tried anything. He'd be the last person to see her before...

'I think I'm alright from here,' she said, and gently pushed away from him.

Jason reluctantly released her, but she could see concern in his eyes. 'Are you kidding? You can barely stand. If somebody spiked your drink, you're gonna be a lot worse soon.'

Jayden sucked in a deep breath of cool, damp air, smelled the scent of unwashed roads as cars splashed past nearby on the Aldgate Road.

'I'll be fine,' she promised, 'I can see my place from here.'

Jason glanced at the small block maybe a couple of hundred metres away, and shrugged.

'Okay,' he said, 'you sure you don't want me to get you at least to the block? You look really unsteady.'

She shook her head, both cautious of the offer and surprised he was folding so easily. 'I can make it,' she said with a bright smile, 'have a good night. I'll see you tomorrow.'

Jayden turned and began walking. Within two paces the whole world tilted crazily and she stumbled, staggered to her left and was lucky to reach the grass before she crashed down onto her knees. The umbrella fell from her grasp and she struggled to keep her eyes open.

Jason leapt to her side.

'Okay, that's it, I'm getting you home even if you scream the whole bloody way.

Get up.'

Jason helped her to her feet, grabbed both of her shoulders and forced her to look at him.

'I know what you're thinking: you think that I might have spiked your drink, and you're worried about it, right?'

Jayden's mind was fuzzy, as though she'd drunk ten bottles of wine, not two glasses.

She nodded vacantly.

'I wouldn't do that,' Jason said as he reached down with one hand, picked up her umbrella and handed it to her. 'If I wanted to date you, I'd just bloody ask. As a matter of fact, I was thinking about doing just that, but not now, not while you're like this.'

Jason slipped her arm through his and walked with her as he pulled out his mobile phone and dialled a number. Moments later, Jayden heard the noisy pub and Kyle's voice answer on the other end of the line.

'Kyle, mate, it's Jason. Jayden's not in good shape. I'm going to get her home but I want the girls to check in on her when they head back, can you ask them for me?'

'Sure thing mate, they'll be there.' 'Ta.'

Jason shut the line off and tucked the phone back in his pocket.

'I'm sorry,' Jayden mumbled, regretting her suspicions. 'I just thought that…'

'Doesn't matter,' Jason replied. 'Let's just get you home, you can apologise to me tomorrow night when you buy me a drink for being such a noble hero.'

Jayden smiled through her crippling fatigue, glad now that she was with somebody who could chaperone her to her door. They walked the last hundred meters in companionable silence until they reached the apartment doors, which were protected with a security lock and a number pad.

'Alright,' Jason said. 'Can you make it from here, or do you need a hand inside?' Jayden steadied herself. *Get a grip.*

'I'm good,' she said, 'I can make it to my bed.'

'Okay,' Jason replied. 'Get your head down, and don't come in tomorrow if you're not feeling up to it. The girls will swing by in a bit to check on you.'

'Thanks, Jason,' she said, and gave him a hug. 'No worries, see you later.'

Jason turned and walked away with his hands tucked in his pockets and his hood up against the rain. Jayden turned, focused on the security pad, then tapped in her number. The locks clicked as they unlatched, and she walked into the block and heard the doors close and lock again safely behind her.

Jayden staggered up to the first floor, and eventually made it to her door. She reached into her handbag for her keys, opened the door and almost fell through it into the hall. She hit the light switch, closed the front door behind her and managed to drape the security latch into place with the last of her strength before she staggered into her bedroom and collapsed onto her bed, every limb feeling as heavy as all the earth.

She closed her eyes, falling asleep, hypnogogic imagery flashing before her eyes as she passed through the murky realm between wakefulness and dreams. It was only then that she felt the hands press on her. Panic lurched through her and she tried to move, but her limbs were unresponsive, her breathing shallow. She felt the weight of a man press down upon her, felt his breath in her ear and smelled a hint of aftershave on his skin, and as the terrible lethargy overpowered her and her consciousness slipped away, she heard his voice whisper in her ear.

'Your time has come.'

13

Grey clouds tumbled in disarray across the dawn sky, patches of pale blue visible between them and the scent of rain on the air. From Honor's vantage point, the city skyline to the west was lit with stark, low sunlight against a backdrop of deeply bruised clouds.

The apartment that Amber Carson rented in Hackney was tucked alongside a narrow alley opposite waste ground, the entrance deeply sheltered from any security cameras outside the nearby King's Head pub. Honor surveyed the flat, which was above a small café, from the street outside.

A constable made way for her through the police cordon when she showed him her warrant card. There had been a media presence ever since the news broadcast which had named the victims in the case so far, but at this early hour none of the journalists were present. Honor had already called in the crime scene examiner and forensic teams, but they were on their way and she needed to see the scene for herself.

'Easy to hide,' Danny said beside her as he looked at the alley where the apartment entrance was located. 'Real dark here at night, and no camera coverage.'

Honor made her way to the open door, which was of the double-security type, metal bars across a standard front door. Her first thought was that the killer, whomever he was, would have been required to make his way past these double doors if he was intending to strike at Amber from within her home. The chances of him being able to do so, to get ahead of her and break in through both doors, seemed highly unlikely.

The apartment was scented with damp at the bottom of the stairs, which led up a staircase so narrow that even Honor's narrow shoulders almost touched the sides. At the top, a small landing branched off into a kitchen and bathroom to the left, living room and bedroom to the right. Honor walked into the living room, as she always did when first visiting the scene of any domestic incident. Say nothing. Do nothing. Just *look*.

A small two-seat sofa sat opposite a wall-mounted television, a scattering of magazines on a tiny coffee table between them. Polished wood floors, originals by the look of them, stained mahogany brown in contrast to the pale walls and ceiling. Amber was a woman who knew how to use light to make the tiny apartment feel just that little bit bigger and brighter.

The walls were adorned with colourful paintings of sailing vessels on blue seas, golden beaches shimmering in abstract brush strokes. Honor spotted photographs in frames on a narrow mantlepiece below the television: Amber's parents, her brother, what might be cousins too, all taken on various holidays to sun-drenched coasts.

'She travelled,' Danny noted.

'Always with family. No sign of a boyfriend,' Samir added as he joined them.

Good, Honor thought to herself, Samir's coming along nicely. He too was standing still, just looking, perhaps mimicking her style.

'Homely,' she replied, 'looks after the place, no mess. Conscientious, seeing as she doesn't own it.'

Danny turned and walked to the bedroom door, performing the same ritual.

'Look at this.'

Honor squeezed in alongside him so that she could see the room. The bed was made, but there was a depression upon it, the sheets slightly ruffled. A crime scene photographer was taking shots of the bed.

'She might have sat down,' Honor said.

'Lain down, the depression's too long, but that's not what bothers me the most.'

Honor then spotted the bag and phone on Amber's bedside table as Danny gestured to them.

'He was here,' she said, her voice almost a whisper. 'Damn me, he was in the flat.'

'Which means that she must have known him, right?' Samir added. 'He can't have got through those double doors.'

Honor didn't say anything for a moment. She knew, or rather was certain, that their killer had planned everything that was happening. But to what lengths had he gone to in order to abduct and detain his victims?

'We know that Amber was with her friends in the pub,' she said, her voice somewhat amplified in the confines of the apartment. 'There was no sign of a man at their table.'

'None that we've seen,' Danny confirmed.

'Yet she *was* drugged at some point. Could it have happened here? Could she have been abducted from home, her killer lying in wait?'

'But then how would he have drugged her?'

Honor could only think of one answer. 'An accomplice.'

Danny shook his head, but then she saw him think about it for a moment.

'Both victims were in pubs at the time they were presumably drugged,' he said, thinking out loud. 'Both were in large groups.'

Honor realised that it didn't make sense.

'The killer couldn't have ingratiated himself into both groups of friends – Sebastian was on a work do, right? Amber was just out with friends. Neither group shows any sign of a connection, and it doesn't explain how there is no male on the CCTV of Amber with her friends.'

'So, he had to drug her here,' Samir pointed out, 'which means he would have had to have either been in here when she got home, or he met her along the way and was invited in, which again suggests that she knew him.'

Honor felt as though something was escaping them, some tiny piece of the puzzle. They would be questioning Amber's family and friends further, and would have to ensure that she was not seeing anybody or had any enemies who might wish her harm, but right now their quarry was a ghost, unseen and unheard.

Something the pathologist had told Honor popped back into her head.

'GHB takes time to have an effect,' she murmured. 'What if our guy spikes people's drinks in the pubs, then waits?'

Danny nodded slowly as he rolled the idea around in his head.

'Tough to do without being seen, but if he pulls it off, they start feeling rough after a while,' he said, 'decide to head home and *bam*, he grabs them.'

Honor visualised Amber making her way home through London, right past Bishopsgate, and on into Hackney. There were numerous narrow side streets there, routes she could have reasonably been abducted from without easily being detected.

'So why wait for her here?' Honor asked. 'What's the point in breaking in?'

Samir shook his head, unable to provide her with an answer.

Don't try to think like a sane person, Honor reminded herself. *Think like somebody driven by obsession.* She stepped back into the living room and looked around again. If their killer had indeed decided to wait for Amber here, then he too would have wanted to look around, even just to pass the time. *Yes, he is obsessed, so he would be obsessed with his victims. Being here would be exciting for him, an intrusion into Amber's personal space.* She let her eyes fall on the first thing that she saw in the room.

The mantelpiece on the left-hand wall, beneath the television, stood out. The row of framed photographs of Amber's family and friends, neatly arranged. She approached them and crouched down, observing not the images but the surface of the mantelpiece itself.

'Human nature,' she said as Danny joined her. 'These pictures have been moved recently. You can see the dust patterns where they were originally standing. The killer comes in here, waits, takes a look around to pass the time.'

'I'll let Forensics know,' came the reply. 'If this guy got in the least bit bored waiting, he might have moved other objects about, maybe left a print or a hair.'

The City of London Police Forensic Services Department had despatched a Scenes of Crime team to the site upon Honor's request, and within minutes they would begin to inspect every square inch of the property with a dazzling array of sensors and tools such as DNA17, fluorescent powder suspension, fingerprint detection tools and other in-house techniques that they used. Honor had requested their covert team to attend the scene, largely to minimise the public signature of the investigation.

'He'll have thought about that,' she said to Danny. 'Worn gloves, maybe even a hairnet. He's been too careful up to now.'

Honor pictured in her mind's eye Amber coming back here, perhaps under the influence of GHB already. She would have to unlock both the doors, get inside, lock them behind her and then make her way up the steep and narrow staircase. She might have been hazy, confused, lethargic, her consciousness wavering as she made it to the top of the stairs. She would have turned right, headed for the bedroom, slumped onto her bed, exhausted.

Honor moved to the bedroom door and imagined her abductor, waiting somewhere else, perhaps in the living room, watching in the darkness as Amber collapsed, before moving in and overpowering her. There would have been little struggle, perhaps none at all if Amber was already unconscious.

'You lay in wait for them, in the places they least expect,' she murmured to herself as she turned and looked at the rest of the apartment. 'They're home, they feel safe but they're weakened and confused: they're not prepared for you when you strike.'

Honor thought about that for a moment. The victim, utterly defenceless; the killer, utterly dominant over their prey, completely in control of the situation.

'Control freak,' she whispered, almost to herself as she wandered back into the living room, 'confidence issues, a history of violence perhaps.' She strolled to the windows of the apartment. 'Problems at home, parental abuse?'

Honor did not have a motive for the killings, yet, but she suspected that the desire to witness others endure their greatest fears as their own cause of death had its roots in the killer's past. Many who had suffered unthinkable abuse in their childhood sought their revenge by subjecting other, weaker victims to that same abuse. The cycle was never-ending, for it could never cure the sufferer of their nightmares or their pain, only bring those same afflictions to other, often entirely innocent victims, spreading the abuse like a cancer.

Honor realised that she was standing right about where Amber's abductor would have stood, had he wished to look down upon the approaches to the apartment, the window looking out over the waste ground to the south. From here, she could see the Shard behind tower blocks and other buildings amid Hackney's jumbled streets.

Danny's voice reached out from behind her.

'So, he gets her under control, but then he still has to get her out of here without being seen. How's he doing that?'

Honor said nothing, merely stared out of the window for a long time, wondering what he would have felt, standing here, waiting. Anticipation? Excitement? Fear? What if Amber came home with a male friend, someone who had noticed her excessive intoxication and offered her a lift home? He couldn't allow that, it would put him at risk, so he must have seen her leave the pub before committing to his plan. A vehicle then? Something on the CCTV might pick out if the pub was being watched, give them a clue, a lead that they could follow.

'Honor?'

'I don't know,' she replied to Danny. 'Something's missing here, he's either got help or he's got another route into and out of the square mile. We need to figure out how he's doing this, he had to get here somehow.'

She wanted to feel what he had felt, experience what he had, understand what was driving this killer to conduct his apparently motiveless campaign.

'Scene examiner's here,' Samir said from the stairwell. 'Send them up.'

She heard Samir call the forensics team into the building, but somehow, she knew that this man was not going to leave behind anything for them to find. Even if they located a hair, or skin, or some other genetic trace of him, she suspected that he had no criminal record, nothing against which they could match any evidence found at the scene. This man that they sought was of the most dangerous kind, unknown to police, with no trace of his crimes on the system, a lone wolf killer.

The scent drifted into the darkened realm of Jayden Nixx's consciousness, coming it seemed from far away on the fringes of the universe, a fetid odour that clung to the air like an infection. She coughed, shuddered, her world spinning crazily in an immense darkness as the foul stench coated the back of her throat.

She couldn't open her eyes, but she could hear a sloshing of water that echoed around her, bouncing back and forth. She realised that she could not move her limbs, everything numb and heavy. She swayed gently back and forth as she struggled to comprehend where she was and what was happening.

Slowly, with immense effort, she managed to open her eyes.

Black water shimmered below her as it sluiced past a pair of boots that forged their way along a narrow, brick tunnel. The pungent scent of raw sewage poisoned the air, and she hacked out a membrane-tearing cough as she tried not to throw up.

She realised that she was aloft, her body carried by a powerfully built man who bore her weight as though she were nothing more than a coat thrown over his shoulder. She could see his big, heavy boots crashing through a foul soup of human waste and churning water, the curved walls of the tunnel draped in sickening strings of biological debris. The rancid odours were like a living thing all around her, and she would have cried out in disgust were she able to command her body to move, but she could do nothing other than emit a feeble groan.

The man carrying her did not respond, but she felt him turn his head slightly, aware now that she was conscious. Jayden tried to lift her head, but it bore down with the weight of ages, forcing her to examine only the lower portions of the tunnel through which they moved. The walls were built from perfectly tiled patterns of carefully interwoven brickwork, and she dimly recalled the labyrinth of Victorian sewers that weaved beneath the city streets, hundreds of years old. The churning water sent a pulse of fear through her guts, especially *this* water, laced with a toxic microbial soup of faecal sludge.

The man trudged on, and as she struggled to make her limbs respond so memories fluttered through the field of her awareness as her senses began to reconnect themselves: she had been at the pub, and then she had felt ill, decided to leave, and then…

Jason.

She tried to speak his name, wondering whether he had in fact gone back on his word. He had been beside her when she had put her code in the security lock at the entrance to her apartment, so he could have seen the code and got inside the building, but then how had he got into her apartment so quickly? Only her friend Amanda had a spare key for emergencies. Jason had said they were going to call in on her, make sure she was okay, hadn't he?

'Jason?'

The name came out as a whisper, drowned out by the fetid water swirling below her. She could hear more of it crashing nearby, and she felt a wave of fear swell up inside of her as she realised where they were.

'Jason?'

This time, her voice was louder, and she sensed that the man had heard her because he hurried his pace through the water. She twitched her fingers, felt life coming back into her body as whatever drug had been put into her drink began to wear off. The nausea and the dizziness began to fade a little and she squirmed on the man's shoulder, trying to get off.

The man slowed, the sound of falling water louder now as he turned inside the tunnel and eased out into a chamber that was square rather than oval. She felt herself being hefted up, and then suddenly she was turned physically upright as though being held like a baby, two big hands beneath her armpits, and was pinned against a cold, damp wall, her feet still six inches above the water. More water spilled down the wall onto her hair and back, this time from above, and she twisted instinctively away from its icy touch as it trickled down her spine.

She tried to reach up for the man's face and claw at him, his features concealed beneath a hood, the only light a small clip-on torch that the man wore on his belt that reflected off the water in shimmering halos. The man turned his face away from her hands, then he dropped her down.

Jayden landed in six inches of foul water and she shrieked in horror, looked down to see her bare feet consumed by raw sewage sluicing through the chamber. One of her hands was gripped and wrenched upward, and before she could stop him, her wrist was clamped inside a tight metal manacle that was bolted into the old brick walls.

'No!'

Some of her strength returned and she swiped at his face with her free hand, her nails trying to claw his skin. The man batted her hand aside, grabbed it and pinned it against the wall as he pushed it toward another manacle. She screamed and twisted, her voice echoing like a banshee wail down the subterranean tunnels that branched off from the chamber

The man pinned her in place against the wall, looming over her, his strength far too great as he locked her wrist into place. His face was close to hers and on impulse Jayden lunged forward and sank her teeth into the skin of his jaw with primal savagery.

The man wrenched himself away from her bite as Jayden tasted metallic blood on her tongue. One big hand swiped sideways in the faint light and cracked across the side of her skull with enough force to snap her head sideways and crack her temple against the cold brickwork.

'Bitch.'

The word was hissed in the darkness, laden with rage. Jayden tried to spit at him, but he reached up and one giant hand smothered her lower face. He pushed her head back against the wall with a dull thud, stars whirling in front of her eyes as he reached into his pocket and grabbed a length of fabric that he then rammed into her mouth and tied around the back of her head.

Jayden's rage withered as he stood back and looked at her. In the faint reflected light of the torch, she saw the shape of his features, and with a startle she recognised him. Water trickled onto her head and she looked up to see a metal gantry nearby, beyond which was a vertical shaft with a manhole cover at the top. The light of the sky glowed faintly through small holes in the manhole's iron surface.

Jayden looked back at the man, and he slowly lifted off his hood. He spoke, his voice surprisingly soft for such a large man.

'Your time has come,' he said, his voice echoing in the abysmal darkness.

Jayden managed to keep her eyes on him, to show no emotion, but she was shaking now as the icy cold water cascaded down her back. The mess swirling around her feet made her guts clench as the man turned away from her. He waded through the water to the far side of the chamber, where Jayden could now see a series of thick cables running along the sewer walls and disappearing off down another tunnel.

'Optical fibres, telecommunications,' he said, his voice audible above the water crashing from a smaller sewer tunnel to her left and plunging into the chamber. 'Makes sense to route them through here, rather than dig new tunnels for them. They're going to come in handy.'

She watched with grim interest as the man produced a camera, and then he spliced into one of the cables and wired the camera into it. He taped the wires closed, and set the camera on a mount that was screwed into the nearby brickwork. Jayden knew without a doubt that this had all been prepared in advance, although she could not fathom why on earth somebody like this would go to such lengths to… *To what?* To kill her?

The man turned, and Jayden could see that the camera was now pointing at her, a little red light glowing in the darkness. The man pulled his hood up as he sloshed his way back to her side, smiling in the faint light.

'The weather's going to get worse today,' he said, and then his smile widened. 'Much, much worse. These tunnels can't handle the amount of water that's going to fall on the city, so you know what happens then?'

Jayden's guts turned to slime as tears sprang from the corners of her eyes and she began shaking her head. She knew what he meant, but it was all that she could do to beg for him not to leave her here. The man leaned closer.

'They flood,' he said. 'Right up to street level.'

Jayden began coughing on her gag, her heart hammering inside of her chest as the man went on, apparently oblivious to her mounting terror.

'The water management companies like it when the sewers flood,' he said. 'The force of the water cleans out the older sections of the sewers, kills all the rats. It provides a service. Normally, workers check the sewers routinely, but they won't for a while due to the rising water levels, the work is just too dangerous.'

He leaned against the wall and touched her cheek. Jayden jerked her head away from his gloved hand.

'You're going to be okay,' the man said. 'It's never as bad as you think it's going to be. Trust me, I've seen it all before; you're not the first, and you won't be the last. You'll soon be at peace.'

The man leaned in and gently kissed her on her cheek, and then he turned and strode away into the myriad, stinking tunnels of London's bowels. Jayden tried one last terrified shriek through her gag, but the nearby crashing water easily drowned her out. The last flickering light from the man's torch vanished into the darkness. She looked down at her feet, entombed in the fetid sludge, and noticed that the water had already risen an inch. She looked up, squinting into the water cascading down through the drain cover far above her, and she knew that the promised rainstorms hadn't even really got going yet. There was no escaping it - she knew that she was going to die here.

14

Honor walked into the Incident Room with Danny alongside her, in time to see DS Hansen put down the phone and offer her an uninterested glance. DI Katy Harper was at a desk near the front of the room.

'Anything?' Harper asked as soon as she spotted Honor.

'Nothing yet,' Honor replied. 'We think that he was there, but we're waiting for the examiner to process the scene. CCTV from the pub opposite the premises might help, but given the busts on St Magnus and Southwark, I doubt it.'

Harper sighed as she removed her spectacles.

'Mitchell should be back soon with the autopsy report on Amber Carson, not that it's going to tell us much that we don't already know. I'm hoping for a stray hair, DNA, anything that could give us a lead on the killer's identity. The media's going wild with this, they're going to want to hear everything from you as soon as you can.'

Honor sighed and rubbed her temples. 'I don't have a damned thing to offer them, boss, you know that. Unknown male, probably from the city, hunts victims based on their phobias. That's it. We tell them that, we're basically admitting we've got nothing.' 'Use your imagination,' Harper snapped, her voice quiet but taut with frustration. 'Baffle them with bullshit, just say enough to keep them off our backs. The briefing is scheduled for this afternoon.'

DI Harper turned and hurried away, leaving Honor standing in the IR wondering what the hell she was going to do next.

'Boss, you need to see this.'

Honor turned, hope blossoming in her heart as she hurried to Samir's desk and saw him staring pensively at his computer monitor.

'I think I've got something.'

Honor moved to stand behind him, and saw that he was watching footage from bars that had been frequented by both Sebastian Dukas and Amber Carson on the nights before their murders.

'I wondered if we might get lucky and pick up the same guy on both pub security cameras,' he said. 'I reckoned it was better to go back to the last moments that we know both victims were alive and see what shows up.'

Honor watched as Samir pointed to two camera feeds that were on his monitor: his left hand pointed to a figure in the bar in which Sebastian Dukas spent his last night, while his right pointed to a figure in the bar in which Amber Carson spent her last night.

Honor leaned closer. In both images, a man was standing beside the bar with a pint in his hand, surveying the pub. Frustratingly, he was positioned in such a way that he could not be easily identified, and the grainy nature of most security cameras meant that it was hard to distinguish his features, but there was no doubting that he was the same man: Honor could tell by both his physical size and also the way that his posture in both footage images was the same, and he seemed to be wearing the same kind of boots and hooded top.

'Both of these are from the nights of the two murders?' she asked him.

'Yep,' Samir agreed, clearly excited for sourcing a possible lead in the case at such an important time. 'This guy could be a regular who just haunts the same spot, but we have footage from outside too. Check this out.'

Samir selected another video feed, this one from a camera showing the *Crosse Keys* main entrance and exit. To Honor's delight, she realised that Samir must have been sitting on this for a while, gathering further evidence to support his assertion that the man in the footage was acting in ways that in a murder investigation would not be considered normal.

'In both pubs, and on both nights, he walks into the pub with his hood up,' Samir said, gesturing to the screens. 'It's been damp the last few nights, fair enough, but he always seems to manage to keep his face hidden from the cameras on the inside of the pubs too. Look here.'

Honor watched as Samir switched to interior footage of both pubs, running them alongside each other. The man walked into the bars, pulled his phone from his pocket and checked it while walking to the bar and ordering a drink. Then, the man moved to stand in a position where he could barely be seen by the cameras.

'Okay,' Honor said, thinking fast, 'but he's just going into a pub for a drink. It's not enough to put this guy's likeness out there to the public.'

'Not normally, no,' Samir agreed. 'But look how he checks his phone.'

Honor peered at the two reels of footage as Samir wound them back and replayed them. For a moment, she didn't notice it, but then suddenly it leaped out at her.

'He uses opposite hands,' she said.

'Yeah,' Samir nodded, 'he's always using whichever hand allows him to not reveal his face to security cameras inside the pubs, turning away from them.'

Honor stood upright and thought for a moment. The man in question must, by his actions, have known where the cameras in both pubs were to be able to conveniently position himself away from their direct line of sight on both occasions.

'Okay, he must have scoped the bars out prior to the nights of the killings,' she said. 'Can we get anything from the security footage in the days prior to the attacks?'

'I'm already on it,' Samir replied, 'but both bars don't open until around ten o'clock, and both only keep their camera footage for about a week before it's recorded over. It's gonna be a tight squeeze to get anything else on this guy before the press conference, and if he knows when they clear their footage, he could have scoped the bars out a month before these images were shot.'

'Do what you can,' Honor insisted, and then a thought hit her. 'How come we didn't see this guy before?'

'Because I was always watching the victim's movements before their deaths, not the rest of the crowds in the bar. We suspect that both victims had their drinks spiked in pubs before their deaths, right? So, whoever did it must have been close to them.'

Honor nodded, knowing well how victims of date-rape drug attacks often had their drinks spiked by deftly-handed rapists armed with tiny pills that could sink invisibly into bottles and glasses without being noticed. Then, all the rapist had to do was hang back and wait for their victim to gradually be overcome by the drugs, follow them, and pounce when their victim was unconscious.

'Watch the bar,' she said. 'See if we can catch this guy anywhere close to the victims when they're buying drinks, or when their friends are. If we can see anything happening, this could actually be our guy.'

'Will do,' Samir agreed.

Honor patted him on the shoulder. 'Good work, detective.'

Samir beamed as Honor hurried out of the IR and back to her own office, her mind now working overdrive as she thought about how to get the information into her briefing. This really could be somebody who was involved in the case, a first shadowy glimpse at their elusive killer. Or, as was so often the case, it could be coincidence, a random event, and they would be identifying, questioning and perhaps accusing an innocent victim.

Her desktop monitor pinged, and she saw that Samir had sent her copies of the images. She opened one immediately and zoomed in, squinting at the image in an attempt to figure out who the man was. His large build made him stand out a little against the crowd, something that he was obviously attempting to conceal, always positioning himself away from the action.

'Boss?'

Honor looked up to see Danny Green as he gently tapped on her open door and walked in. He had a few sheets of printed paper in his hand and tossed them onto her desk. Each was a statement from a high street bank, and each detailed monetary transactions going back three months for Wheeler Construction Company Limited, based in Southwark.

'Gary Wheeler?' Honor asked. 'Didn't he alibi out?'

'Sure, he did,' Danny replied. 'Fellow workers put him in a pub in the square mile the night of Sebastian Dukas's murder. Thing is, that doesn't rule him out as having committed the crime after leaving the pub, for which time we have no solid evidence of his story about going home being true.'

Honor leaned back in her seat as she cast her eye over the financial records. 'So, what's the story with his bank?'

'I got the Cyber Griffin section to do a run-through on Gary Wheeler's business and personal accounts, routine check to make sure there was nothing that we should be suspicious about. You can see by the figures that what his business turns over and what he makes each month on three personal accounts don't come close to adding up.'

Honor scanned the lines, and saw the discrepancies immediately: Wheeler's company was turning over a high-five figure-per-month income, with expenses taking

a large chunk out of that each month to leave around four thousand, but his personal income was swelling by up to six or seven thousand per month.

'Are these figures being reported to HMRC?'

'Nope,' Danny said, 'already checked. These accounts are tied to his name but are not on the list of his business assets, meaning he's not filing returns based on those incomes. There's no paperwork against them, nothing to say where the money's coming from.'

Honor scanned the pages one more time. 'It doesn't make him our killer.'

'No,' Danny agreed, 'but it means we'll have to check his routes home on CCTV to confirm he at least went home when he said he did. The problem we have is that we know our killer is moving without being seen, so even if he can prove he got home when he said he did, how do we know what he did next?'

Honor motioned for Danny to join her on her side of the desk as she turned her monitor around a little to face him.

'What do you make of this? Seen at the same bars the victims enjoyed their last night out, before they died.'

Danny leaned on the desk and peered at the images of the man standing at the bars that Samir had sent her. He said nothing for a few moments, then shrugged.

'Tough to call, but it's not impossible we're looking at Wheeler.'

'That's what I was thinking,' Honor said. 'We can't afford to waste any time. We need to bring him in, question him before the press conference, see if he's going to spill his guts.'

Danny nodded, reaching for his mobile phone.

'I can put uniforms on his construction sites and his home,' he said as he began to dial. 'We can get him in here and lean on him a bit, see what he says.'

'I'll tell the DI,' Honor said as she got out of her seat. 'Samir put me onto this footage, so he deserves the credit.'

'It's not solid yet,' Danny warned her as he waited for an answer on the line, the phone pressed to his ear. 'This could be a wild goose chase and our guy's still out there. You gonna tie this to what you said on the phone last night?'

Honor shrugged, unsure of herself, but these two latest revelations did provide some concrete foundations to the suspicion that Gary Wheeler might be their man, and it sure as hell gave her something to get her teeth into until something, *anything* better turned up. She could hear other detectives heading to the briefing room, and with a reluctant sigh she picked up her notes and read through them one last time before she walked out of her office and into the briefing room with Danny alongside her.

The DI and DCI were already there along with twenty or so detectives, all involved with their own cases. The fraud unit, normally front and centre in such meetings given the close proximity of the financial district, were now playing second fiddle to Honor's murder inquiry, which dominated the wipe board at the head of the room along with DCI Mitchell's imposing form.

'Good morning ladies and gents,' Mitchell said as the door to the room was closed behind the last officer to enter. 'Status briefing, no need to remind everybody that we have a press conference this afternoon regarding the Dukas and Carson murders. Honor, where are we?'

Honor took her breath, her own voice sounding loud in her own ears and yet painfully inadequate.

'We have two possible leads in the case,' she reported. 'The first is a member of the public seen in both bars that the victims frequented on the nights before they died, spotted by DC Samir Raaya. He's a well-built male who seems to try to avoid security cameras. It's not possible yet to determine age or identity, but we're looking into the possibility of tracing older CCTV footage – the guy must have first checked out both pubs in order to know where the cameras are.'

DI Harper nodded. 'You want to lead with that to the press?'

'It's worth us asking the public to help identify the man, to eliminate them from our enquiries. It's a tenuous lead, but if it plays out then we might be able to get this guy off the streets before he can strike again.'

'And the second lead?'

'Gary Wheeler, managing director of Wheeler Construction,' Honor replied. 'He's got a number of financial discrepancies that suggest he's running projects in the city that are probably for-cash jobs. If he lied about that, who knows what else he's hiding? It's also a tenuous lead, but Wheeler matches the height and build of the man seen in the pub CCTV footage prior to both murders.'

'You think Wheeler might be the perpetrator?'

'It's possible,' Honor nodded, 'we certainly can't rule him out, and although he alibied out of Sebastian Dukas's murder, we can't place him anywhere for certain after he left the pub he was in the night of the murder. Plus, his alibis are all from family or his fellow workers, any one of whom might have reasons to lie for his benefit. We're bringing him in for questioning to get to the bottom of it.'

DCI Mitchell nodded thoughtfully. 'What about the other CCTV sources like traffic cameras, or the river?'

Honor's skin flushed with heat a little as she replied.

'Nothing, boss,' she admitted. 'He must use some kind of local knowledge. Fraud have identified mobile phone signals connected with the Southwark homicide of Amber Carson as pinging somewhere between Spitalfields and Whitechapel, but beyond that we don't have more details other than what we can deduce from the killer's methods and suspected motivations.'

'Which are?'

Honor felt the other officers in the room all watching her now with deep interest, the blink moment upon her. She recalled Danny's warning. *Better to air it here, than get it wrong in front of a few million viewers on live television.*

'The murder of Sebastian Dukas occurred on August thirty-first, with Amber McVey's murder just afterwards, September first. Both victims were killed and displayed in a manner conducive with a killer who is seeking to make grand statements, showing a desire to be seen, to be noticed. Both murders occurred near the river, with Sebastian Dukas killed within a stone's throw of Whitechapel. Although I cannot offer anything of true substance to support my suspicion, I believe that in some way this killer is seeking to replicate, in a modern fashion, the fame and success of Jack the Ripper.'

The air in the room felt oppressive, unmoving. Honor stood motionless, staring at the DI as she stared back. Prickly heat tingled across the back of her neck and she felt her heart fluttering uneasily in her chest.

'You're giving the papers their headline before they've thought of it,' DCI Mitchell murmured with something that could either have been a smile or a grimace. 'You walk in there with that this afternoon and they'll be all over it by the following morning.'

'There's more to it than just the Ripper,' Honor said, eager to support her assertion. 'I've been researching phobias, and one in particular stands out: *Thanatophobia*, the fear of death, and of losing close friends to death. The killer's desire to see his victim's moment of death seems paramount in his work, we see that in his use of cameras to watch the victims' last moments. He's killing based on phobias, but many people with phobias also have a fascination with the *cause* of those fears. I think he's addicted, in the same way that some people became addicted to snuff videos a few years back, watching people die for real. That's got to have a cause, a trigger point somewhere in his life, something that drives him to pursue the same experience time and time again.'

More silence. Honor began to feel the room turning against her, even though not a single officer other than the DCI had said a word. It was too wild, too far out there and also too obvious a motive: any killer in the square mile could easily be said to be emulating the Ripper.

'Too neat and too *Hollywood*,' DS Hansen said. 'We need to keep anything about the Ripper out of this. Besides, there are too many theories now about how the Ripper didn't kill prostitutes, wasn't a surgeon and so on. Anybody basing their crimes on such myths is chasing rainbows.'

A murmur of agreement rippled through the gathering, Honor noting a few stifled chuckles. So much for the brainstorming.

'I agree, but we're going public anyway,' Honor pointed out. 'What better way to grab people's attention than an easy and memorable tag? They'll swallow it up, everybody will be talking about it, and our person of interest on the CCTV will be on every front page by dawn.'

DCI Mitchell nodded.

'And if they're innocent of any crime, they'll be holding a bloody press conference of their own when they sue us,' he replied. 'We can't walk on with that. We need something concrete or they'll tear us to shreds, and God forbid if this nutter comes up with another victim before then.'

'Yeah,' DS Hansen uttered, 'it's a nice idea but we can't afford to waste time chasing ghosts of the Ripper and miss something potentially useful. This killer's a narcissist, it's his own name that he wants to go down in history.'

Honor waited to see what the DI would decide to do with her revelation. She didn't have to wait for long.

'We stick with what we know, which doesn't sound like very much at the moment,' Harper said finally. 'Both families are on board with this, they want the killer found by any means possible, understandably. We'll brief the press and focus on the murders themselves, unless something better comes up before then. DS Hansen, what's the story with the Hollsworth fraud case?'

Hansen was about to reply, when the door opened and an officer poked her head through.

'DS McVey?' she asked, and spotted Honor. 'Gary Wheeler is downstairs in holding.'

Honor grabbed the information like an anchor back to safety and immediately turned to leave the room. As she made her way between the other detectives, she intercepted a few bemused glances. A whisper from Hansen drifted her way, chased by muffled sniggers.

'Don't forget your top hat and cape, McVey.'

Honor felt bile rise in her throat as she walked out of the room and into the corridor outside. She let out a breath that seemed to have been cooped up for hours, stale exhaust gusting into the cool corridor as she closed her eyes for a moment and sought a centre to herself.

'Are you okay, ma'am?'

A constable aged no more than twenty-five closed the door behind her, a look of concern on her face.

'Another day at the office,' Honor murmured in reply, her skin cooling as Danny Green and Samir Raaya joined her.

'That didn't quite go to plan,' Danny said.

'You know, I'm glad you're here,' she shot back. 'I'd be lost without you.'

'You know what I mean,' Danny replied as they walked. 'It's too much, even if you're right. Hansen and the others will latch on to it, say you're off your game.'

'They can say what they damned well like. Let's go see what Gary has to say for himself,' Honor snapped back, angry enough to take it out her partner.

Danny raised his hands in defeat but said nothing as they walked toward the custody suite.

15

Honor entered the interview room to find Gary Wheeler sitting with a cup of coffee on the opposite side of a plain Formica table. Danny accompanied her into the room, while Samir carried out further examination of the financial records with a member of the fraud unit in an adjoining room.

Wheeler looked perplexed but he raised his eyebrows in recognition of her and DC Green as they sat down. Honor noted that he was wearing a hooded top, just like the one worn by the person of interest in the pub CCTV footage.

'Good morning, Mr Wheeler,' Honor began, 'I appreciate you coming here at such short notice. I would like to remind you that you're not under caution, and that we're recording this interview. The time is, oh-eight-fifteen hours.'

'Why am I here?' Wheeler asked, genuinely confused.

'Got a busy day ahead?' Danny Green asked with a smile. 'Where are you working right now?'

A pair of quick questions that required no deception. *Watch the responses, the body language, gain an idea of what the suspect looks like when they're telling the truth.* Honor noted that Wheeler looked up to the left as he thought about his response.

'Up to my neck,' he said. 'Out near Hackney this morning, then down to Camberwell this afternoon.'

Wheeler was sitting straight, his gaze was clear, and he was cradling the coffee gently. He looked up to the left when thinking about the truth, which might mean he'd look up to the right when he was using his imagination, the hemispheres of the human brain affecting his body language in subtle ways that most folks didn't even know about.

'I see,' Danny replied, the smile gone now. 'Gary, we have some questions to ask you about your company's books.'

Wheeler eyebrows went up in surprise, as though they were about to run off of their own accord. Honor saw his shoulders rise and the coffee cup deformed a little in his hands as he squeezed it.

'The books?' he echoed. 'I thought that you wanted to know something about the church?'

'We check out everything in a murder inquiry,' Honor informed him, her anger at how the briefing had gone now fuelling a predatory instinct within her. She could hear it in her voice, cold and hard. 'There are some discrepancies in your income that we'd like to talk about.'

Gary Wheeler's eyes wobbled as though a seismic tremor had shuddered through them.

'Talk to us about how many people you employ on your sites,' Danny suggested as he gently laid down a file on the table between them, but did not open it, 'and about how many sites you're working, because what you're telling HMRC and what your bank statements are telling us don't add up.'

Wheeler, a big and rough-looking man, looked as though he was himself now staring death in the face. His pupils were dilated, his forehead suddenly glistening with a faint sheen of sweat. For a moment, Honor thought that Wheeler might buckle-up and fight back, but then he sagged.

'I've got a few off-the-books sites,' he said, his normally deep voice a whisper, 'I run them from time to time when things get tough, helps keep the money coming in.'

Honor leaned back in her seat, watching Wheeler for a moment before she spoke. 'How many, and where?'

Wheeler sighed, glanced up and to the left.

'Two in Hackney,' he said, 'another in Gainsford Street, south of the water.'

'Southwark?' Honor asked, and was rewarded with a nod. She exchanged a brief glance with Danny, the locations of both sites significant. 'And these sites, they're worked on by you, or by other people?'

'I'm the site foreman for all three,' Wheeler replied in a defeated tone. 'The workers are hired by me.'

'We're gonna need names,' Danny said, 'all of them.'

Honor was about to pull out a pen for Wheeler when she saw him wince.

'What?'

Wheeler rolled his big shoulders as he pulled his coffee closer, looking for all the world as though he wanted to dive into it and vanish from the room.

'I don't have any names.'

Honor stared at Wheeler for a long moment. 'You don't have any names? I thought your site foreman Cooper handled security and personnel?'

Wheeler shifted uncomfortably in his seat. 'He doesn't know anything about the other sites.'

'He doesn't know anything about them?' Danny echoed, his tone flat.

'I mean that the men were all hired for cash by me, no questions asked, I kept it to myself and…'

Danny shot up out of his chair as he slammed his hands on the table.

'This is a murder inquiry and you lied to us?!' he boomed as Honor got up and put a hand on his shoulder to restrain him. 'Didn't you hear about the victim in Southwark? Amber Carson was buried alive under two tons of fucking concrete and you're concealing information?'

'That's enough,' Honor said.

Danny fumed for a moment longer. In that moment it looked as though he could murder Wheeler with his bare hands. Wheeler cowered, said nothing, as whatever he saw in Danny's eyes quelled any resistance that he might have harboured.

'You lied to us,' Honor said to Wheeler as she and Danny sat back down. 'How many people have worked for you that you can't identify?'

Wheeler winced.

'Dozens,' he replied. 'We all do it! There isn't a contractor in the city that can complete without hiring cheap hands, the Polish and the Lithuanians, they're all over the place. My income dropped thirty per cent in three years, I had to do it to survive.'

Honor took a breath, closed her eyes for a moment as she tried to rise above

Wheeler's pleading tirade.

'You're telling me that there could have been dozens of people on your sites that we'll never be able to identify, people who could have accessed St Magnus Church and committed murder?'

Wheeler stared at her for a moment, and she could see that only now was he beginning to calculate the consequences of what he had done.

'Well, I, I hadn't thought of that, and it's not like they could just walk onto the site anyway and…'

'Obstruction of justice,' Danny snapped, staring at the desk as he counted off charges on the fingers of one hand, 'lying to a police officer in the course of their duty, fraud, health and safety, building regulations, insurance fraud…'

Wheeler's face began to collapse in on itself. Honor leaned forward, glaring at him.

'There are two dead people out there, one of whom was murdered on a construction site for which you're the foreman, another who died horribly yesterday on another construction site that one of your former employees might have been able to gain access to, and you've delayed our investigations for days. You know what "accessory after the fact" means, don't you, Gary?'

Wheeler's jaw dropped open and he stared back at her, wide-eyed. Before he could speak, Danny recited a legal line direct from memory.

'Whosoever shall aid, abet, counsel or procure the commission of any indictable offence, whether the same be an offence at common law or by virtue of any Act passed or to be passed, shall be liable to be tried, indicted and punished as a principal offender.'

Wheeler stared at them both, his mouth open but unable to speak, confusion writ large across his ruddy complexion as though he'd been slapped about the face.

'Complicity,' Honor enlightened him. 'Your actions after the fact have delayed an investigation that could otherwise have saved lives, meaning that you potentially caused the loss of a victim's life. It's called manslaughter.'

'But I haven't done anything!' Wheeler yelped.

Honor, still leaning forward on the table, fixed Gary Wheeler with her most dispassionate gaze.

'Your alibi was provided by work colleagues, who stated that they were with you the night of the murder of Sebastian Dukas until eleven at night, upon which time you went home. Sebastian Dukas died somewhere between eleven at night and six the following morning. In that time, we have no idea where you were.'

'I was at home,' Wheeler gaped, 'I went to bed and was up at seven in the morning.' 'So you say,' Danny uttered. 'Do you have any evidence to support that assertion?'

Wheeler performed a rapid mental calculation, then his expression changed and he leaned back and folded his arms. 'I can't disprove a negative.'

'Do I look like the kind of mug who's going to buy that?' Green snarled.

'You're looking at several charges, right up to manslaughter itself, if we find that your lies led to the death of Amber Carson!'

Danny yanked open the file between them and tore out a glossy, high-resolution photograph of Ambers' concrete-entombed corpse. He shoved it in front of Wheeler, who stared down at Amber's horrific death mask, one hand moving to cover his mouth as his defiance withered once more. Honor watched the big man carefully as Danny slid another image in front of him, this time the pair of shots of a tall, well-built man in the bars where Dukas and Carson had last been seen.

'Taken the night Dukas died, and the night Carson died,' she said as she pointed to the images. 'Tall guy, big build,' she observed, 'not unlike yourself. Same hooded top, too.'

Wheeler stared from one image to the other and then back to Amber's mutilated corpse, her mouth wide open and packed with dirty concrete, her eyes sunken black pits filled with soil, and then he suddenly jerked away from the table and jack-knifed as a thin stream of vomit splattered onto the floor between his boots. Wheeler coughed and began shaking as though he'd been plugged into the mains, his sobs filling the room.

'That's not me,' he gasped, unable to look or even point at the images of Amber. 'I don't care what you say, that's not me! I didn't kill anybody!'

Wheeler's voice trailed off into miserable, choking sobs. Honor had heard of people who could vomit at will, and she'd sat across the table from some of the best liars ever to walk the streets of London, but the chances of both skills manifesting themselves in the same person were slim, to say the least. Wheeler was sheened with sweat, his belly shuddering as he blurted another line.

'I want a solicitor! I want somebody here to help me! I'm not saying anything else.' Honor glanced at her watch: eight thirty-two.

'We'll terminate the interview for a few minutes, Mr Wheeler. When we return, we'll expect your full cooperation.'

Danny stood and stalked out of the room. Honor walked out behind him and closed the door.

'Bollocks,' Danny uttered. For a moment, Honor thought that he believed Wheeler to be deceiving them again, but then he shook his head and ran a hand through his thick hair. 'He's not our guy.'

'He's an Oscar candidate if he is,' she agreed. 'We could have dozens of suspects now, and we don't have names for any of them.' She put a hand to her head and then kicked the wall, just for the hell of it. 'Jesus Christ, we go from one unknown suspect to several dozen, we're going fucking backwards!'

Danny nodded but said nothing, staring at the floor, one hand resting on the pocket of his jacket where his cigarettes resided.

'I don't even know where to start. Visit Wheeler's off-the-books sites?'

'It'll be a start,' Honor agreed miserably as she considered how many alibis they were now going to have to confirm, and then only if they could track down every one of Wheeler's hired-hands. 'Many of them could be back in Poland, summer workers, travelling on EU open-borders, they could be anywhere. They're all going home anyway aren't they, fed up with the UK, Brexit, all that stuff?'

Danny shrugged, staring into the middle of nowhere as though inspiration was going to just leap up and slap him around the chops. *Shit.* This was more than a setback.

Wheeler's case was for another department entirely, something they could off-load onto the fraud unit or hand over to the MET, but there was no way they could pick out everything pertinent to their own case in short-order, and hand it to DI Harper in time for it to be fed to the dogs come the press-conference.

'We've got nothing,' Danny said finally. 'Just the guy in the CCTV, that's all. Wheeler is a bust unless he can come up with all the contacts he ever made on his other sites.'

In through the nose, out through the mouth. Honor closed her eyes for a moment and got a brief glimpse of a summer meadow, but it was overshadowed by dark clouds, rain falling like tears from a bruised sky. She snapped herself away from it, opened her eyes, reality for once better than the tainted solitude of her mind.

'Okay, get onto Wheeler, every bloody name he can recall. We confiscate his mobile phone, computers, everything, and get somebody onto collating contact details for every person he's spoken to in the last month. It's all we can do, maybe we'll get lucky.'

Danny straightened up. 'Will do. Er, could you send somebody down to clean up in there? I'll move him to another room.'

Honor nodded as she set off for her office, cursing Wheeler and his sodding hired hands. She stalked in and slammed the door shut behind her, walked to the window for no particular reason and stared through the glass at the busy streets bustling below. The roads were sheened with water that flowed along the gutters, turbulent clouds driving sheets of rain in swirling vortexes between the buildings. Cars were driving slowly with their headlights on, streetlights glowing in the gloom. It could have been mid-winter, not bloody September. So much water.

Like a terrifying premonition, she thought about the water, about the weather, about how everything the murderer seemed to have done was timed along with the rhythms of the city itself. *Water*. Somehow, she knew already that it was too late, that somebody else was suffering somewhere and nobody knew about it yet, nobody but her and the deranged lunatic Ripper-wannabe stalking the drenched city streets. *He wants the fame for himself, his own place in history. He wants noise, he wants attention, he wants people to know just how clever he has been. He's the opposite of you, Honor, the darker path taken. He doesn't want to hide away, he wants to be seen, to bask in the glory of his work and yet never be caught for it.*

The traffic rumbled past down below, and she heard the distant clatter of a drain cover as a stream of black cabs rattled over it. Hamlets Council had a lot to bloody answer for if they couldn't even fix a sodding drain cover that was…

Honor stared at the street below for a long moment, seeing nothing before her but the rain pouring down the window and images of Southwark Cathedral, the streets nearby, the apartment where Amber Carson had spent her last night before her death, and the manhole cover outside St Magnus church that tilted when she walked on it.

Honor whirled and yanked open her office door as she hit the corridor at a run and sprinted down to the Incident Room. She plunged in and shouted at the first person she saw.

'It's the fucking sewers!'

The DI, DCI Mitchell and the Borough Commander, Andy Leeson, all looked up from where they sat around a desk as though she were from another world. Several other detectives also stared at her in surprise. Honor reigned herself in and coughed.

'I mean, sirs, I think I know how the killer can move through the city without being spotted: he's using the sewers.'

Katy Harper and the two men stared back at her for a moment longer.

'I thought you were talking about the job,' DCI Mitchell finally replied, his beard twitching with amusement. 'Perhaps you should share your idea with the team?'

'Yes, boss, of course, I'll do that right away.'

Honor hurried to the board and wrote in big red letters the word SEWERS. The detectives in the room, one by one, finished their calls and turned to look at her.

'Okay, the one place we never thought to look for this guy was *down*,' she said. 'Beneath the city. What do we know about the city's sewers?'

Danny Green shrugged. 'Not much, beyond what I contribute to them every day.'

A few chuckles echoed around the room.

'We need to look into them,' Honor said.

'How deeply do you want us to delve?' Samir asked with a smirk.

'You think we can flush him out, boss?' Danny asked.

'I'll do the gags,' Honor shot back. 'Manhole covers are provided with rubber seals after major events in the city, visiting members of state and such like, so that we can tell whether they've been interfered with. We haven't received any reports of broken seals, so the suspect must know about them and either repair or replace them when he moves through the sewers. Contact Tower Hamlets, find out what we can about how far somebody could move through the sewer system. It's all really old, right, built by the Victorians?'

'Most of it, yeah,' Danny agreed. 'They fix up some areas from time to time.'

'Fine,' Honor said. 'We find out what we can, and then we get somebody to check it all out. It ties in with my suspicion that this guy is obsessed with the Ripper, he might want to spend a lot of his time in places that are old, from the same era. There aren't that many of them left, so it shouldn't take long.'

'Seriously?' Samir asked. 'You think that this guy likes to spend his nights in the sewers?'

'He might not like it,' Honor conceded, 'but it's the perfect way to move undetected.'

Danny Green reached for his phone.

'You can call Hamlets,' DCI Mitchell said to him, 'but they're not going to be able to help us much.'

'How come?'

'The weather,' Mitchell replied with a sweeping gesture of his arm to the office windows, where rain was spilling in torrents down the glass. 'The sewers will all be flooding and…'

There was a prolonged silence as they all looked at each other. 'Water,' Honor said. 'Hydrophobia.'

Before any of them could say anything further, a constable dashed into the Incident Room and searched with a frantic gaze for Honor.

'We've got another one!'

'What's happened?'

'Another video has been sent to a family in St Luke's, twenty minutes ago,' the constable informed her. 'Local station sent it direct to us, they already recognised what it was. Word's spreading fast.'

'Get it into the Incident Room, pronto!' DCI Mitchell's voice boomed. 'We all need to see this.'

'It's already here!' came a voice from a desk across the room.

Honor saw at once the television screen in the IR fill with the image of a young woman. Honor's heart felt as though it had stopped in her chest.

'Water,' she whispered to nobody in particular as detectives flooded into the room. The screen was filled with a woman's face and upper torso, her features twisted with horror and illuminated by a pale, red light that occasionally flashed in her retina as she fought her bonds. She was shackled to an old brick wall, her mouth gagged, and water was spilling down onto her from above. The camera revealed little else, and there was no sound.

'Who is she?' Honor asked.

'Jayden Nixx,' came the reply. 'Thirty-two, lives in Aldgate, single, that's all we know right now. The family are on their way.'

The borough commander glanced at Honor, his features a fusion of new respect and abstract disgust at what he was seeing on the screen.

'I'd like you to speak to them, Honor.'

Honor nodded, not even noticing the commander's conciliatory tone or his use of her given name rather than "detective". All she could see was Jayden Nixx thrashing against her bonds, and the ancient wall behind her.

'She's in the sewers,' Honor said, loud enough for everyone to hear. 'That's his next play, hydrophobia. He's going to drown her.'

Honor stared at the footage for a moment longer, then turned to DI Harper.

'Wheeler isn't our guy, we're pretty sure of that. I need somebody to lean on him and dig out everything we can about who's worked for him and when, any one of them could be our suspect.'

'I'm pulling MIT 1 off the Finley case for you,' DCI Mitchell replied, and rewarded her with a brief wink. 'We'll put them onto it.'

Honor felt something warm spill through her belly and she smiled broadly in return, an action that sent bolts of pain through her cheeks. She averted her gaze rapidly as hot flushes tingled up and down her throat, stunned at her own reaction. Christ, she felt like she was about to piss herself with excitement. A quick glance again at Jayden Nixx's ordeal killed off the primal joy in an instant, as did the voice of an IT technician working behind them.

'Guys, we've got a real problem here.' The detectives all turned to see the IT man look up. 'This footage, it wasn't sent to the family.'

'What?' DI Harper uttered. 'It was the family that called it in, wasn't it?'

'Yeah, but they weren't receiving it exclusively,' came the reply. 'That's what I'm trying to tell you: Honor was right, he's escalating. This isn't being sent just as an e- mail, it's live footage. It's all over the Internet, all over the bloody world.'

16

'It's *what?*'

DCI Mitchell's voice boomed like an artillery cannon as he whirled to the IT man.

'You Tube, viral sites, forums, it's all over the place!' the technician replied. 'Look for yourself, this is going to be global within the hour.'

Honor's heart sank as she realised that their suspect was still one step ahead of them and showing no sign of letting up. As she had predicted, he had escalated his crimes, and now he was seeking the public recognition for whatever damned crusade his twisted mind believed that he was embarking upon.

'Pull them down!' DI Harper snapped. 'Put Cyber Griffin onto this, get that stuff off the Internet.'

The IT guy shook his head.

'It's too late for that now,' he said. 'Even if we pulled down every site showing this footage in the next sixty seconds, which is impossible by the way, it wouldn't matter. People have seen it, they'll be sharing it, streaming it across the globe. Try to cover it up, and everybody is gonna ask; *what are you hiding from us?*'

Honor stepped forward as Harper fumed in silence.

'Contact all digital vendors of on-line streaming and point out to them that this is effectively a snuff video, someone's personal suffering being shared on the Internet without their permission and against their human rights. Have them pull as many live feeds as you can to at least damage the fallout.'

The IT guy picked up a phone as Honor turned to one of the Cyber Griffin digital fraud detectives.

'Get the BBC, Sky, everybody on the horn and tell them the same – we can't share this information and we shouldn't let this killer get his rocks off watching this girl die. We should also make every effort to trace the source IP address.'

'Will do, ma'am.'

Honor turned to Danny and Samir, not waiting for DI Harper or DCI Mitchell to give orders.

'He's escalating, just like we said he would, just like all serial killers do. This isn't about his fetishes or his obsessions anymore, he's jumped on the gravy train and he's enjoying himself. This is where he's most likely to start making mistakes, so we need to be ready to shut him down the moment something pops. Get onto the sewer angle and let's see if something there might help us identify him. Do they have cameras in sewers, or covering the entrances? Are there other cameras near to the crime scenes or the victim's homes that might have picked him up entering or exiting sewers? Find out what you can.'

Danny and Samir whirled to their desks as Honor turned to DI Harper.

'We need everything we can get onto this guy,' she said, and glanced at Jayden Nixx's desperate face. 'How long has she got, do you think?'

Harper shrugged.

'Hard to say, depends on how deep she is in the system. Hours, at most, given the heavy weather that's hitting the city and the entire South East. They've already raised the Thames barrier.'

The borough commander gestured to the television.

'She might not even be in the city,' he said. 'He could have taken her elsewhere to throw us off the case, ensure that she dies.'

Honor thought about that for a moment, still transfixed by Jayden's suffering. It was morbidly addictive viewing, and she understood now why he had created it, just as the Ripper's savage and bloody mutilation of his victims both appalled and enthralled Victorian London in the late 1880s.

'Shock and awe,' Honor said out loud as she thought about the way in which modern day events sought to gain media coverage, using ever-escalating sensationalism to capture an audience. 'He's playing to a crowd, just like the Ripper. He knows they'll be fascinated by it, knows that people won't be able to stop talking about it. But he also wants to be in the same places, recapture the same fascination. This is all about the old city for him: ancient churches and cathedrals, old sewers and streets. Jayden's somewhere in London, somewhere close by. He won't have left the city.'

'Are you sure?' Leeson asked. 'There's nothing in that footage to betray her location.'

'I can't be one hundred per cent sure, sir, no,' Honor admitted, 'but it doesn't fit his method so far. He could take her anywhere, but transporting her long distances increases risk for him, and I'm certain that he uses the sewers to move around. Given where she is now, it's more likely that she's somewhere within the square mile.' She shook her head as she watched Jayden's ordeal. Somehow it made it more personal, more terrifying than ever, watching somebody slowly die right before her.

'He's going to get his wish. His work is going to become famous now, whether we catch him or not,' Harper said.

'We'll catch him all right,' DCI Mitchell said as his voice rose to be directed at the entire room, 'and then we'll make the bastard famous for all the wrong reasons. Jayden Nixx has to be our priority for now, so I want every London Borough council informed of the incident, and every resource devoted to finding Jayden Nixx, is that clear?'

A chorus of "*yes boss*" shook the room. As if on cue, one by one, the telephones began to ring as the media picked up on the viral Internet feed and began calling frantically for more information.

DI Harper turned to Honor.

'I think that it's fair to say you've got the best handle on this case. What do you need?'

Honor thought for a moment, tried to get ahead of the situation escalating rapidly around her.

'I need a map of London's sewers,' she said. 'All of them.'

The *thrill* of it.

His nerves jangled, twitching to live currents pulsing through his synapses. His mind seethed with latent energy, primal drums beating ancient rhythms that echoed through darkened neural networks. Absolute power, absolutely unrestrained. He was committing the perfect crime; watching it live, yet far from the action. One of his legs bounced up and down on tiptoe, nervous energy spilling from him in mindless repetition.

He sat on his sofa and watched, wide-eyed, as Jayden Nixx shivered in the cold water that was plummeting down onto her head. Her long, black hair was curled into drenched locks that plastered her face, her arms outstretched either side of her, her cuffed wrists just out of shot of the camera.

The wall to which she was manacled was bare of any features – he couldn't afford council workers to be able to identify in which sewer conduit Jayden was imprisoned. That risked them finding her before she died. No, she was *somewhere* in the city's endless labyrinth of subterranean tunnels, and it would take a gargantuan effort to find her before they flooded.

He smiled, watching her without blinking, afraid to miss that crucial moment. Sure, he could rewind it if he missed it, but that just wasn't the same, was it? To be there, right there, and yet not need to be there at all, that was something that he owed to the immense power of the Internet, and now the rest of the world knew about it too. *The rest of the world.*

The knowledge that right now there were millions of people watching Jayden

Nixx's terminal moments sent a fresh wave of electrifying delight rippling through his nerve endings. *Millions.* Perhaps tens of millions. Hundreds of millions? The police, by now, would be once again caught up in the turmoil of the chase, once again out-foxed, out- witted and out-manoeuvred by a man they still could not identify. He glanced at a second television, this one tuned to a foreign television station's digital broadcast. It was beyond his hope that the BBC or any other official channel would display the footage that he had presented to the world, too afraid to risk the legal wrath of the politically correct. But other countries did not hold their reporting to the same standard, and even now he revelled in the thought of distant countries waking up to a sunrise and the terrible reports coming in from England, of the girl drowning in full view of the entire globe. It would be talked about for months, years, perhaps decades. This was not the kind of story that was forgotten the next day, like a conflict in some far-flung corner of the globe or a random stabbing on a derelict housing estate. No, this was something that would be in the public memory forever, a lasting, haunting memory that would stalk London's streets just as the Ripper had done.

He checked his watch: *two forty-eight pm*. He glanced to his right, out of the living room window, where a darkened sky shadowed the city. He stood up, willing to leave the television if only for a moment to check the weather, and was rewarded with a scene of apocalyptic rainfall, the roads awash, streetlights coming on as their sensors detected a lack of light and reacted to the supposed onset of evening.

The news stations had issued yellow alerts for heavy weather for the rest of the day and into the evening, with no let-up in the rainfall predicted until at least midnight. It wouldn't stop, and he knew that there was no chance that Jayden Nixx would be spared her fate. He glanced to his left, as though he could see through the rows of houses and beyond toward the Thames, where right now Jayden was incarcerated in her darkened subterranean prison and facing her death head-on.

'Soon, Jayden,' he smiled, shivering with anticipation. 'Not long now.'

The water was frigid, Jayden's feet aching with the cold as she strained against her bonds. Water splattered down onto her head from above, where it was running down the arched walls of the sewer and then falling away to land on her. She looked up, squinting into the falling water, and could see the shaft rising up and away from the chamber gantry, and right at the top, the manhole cover through which she could just about see the open sky through holes in the iron surface.

Water cascaded down through the drain cover, pouring in glistening sheets down the walls of the sewer and ironically keeping most of her clean despite the stinking mess flowing past her. She looked down, her entire body shaking as she watched the dark, microbe-infested water sluice by. It had risen above her ankles in the past hour and now it was rising faster by the minute. She felt objects in the water brush past her skin, chunks of unthinkable human waste coiling around her legs, the stench enough to make her gag.

She squinted up again toward the drain, wondering where she was and whether anybody would hear her if she were able to shout for help. The gag in her mouth was tightly wound fabric, and she had been working at it with her teeth in the hopes of slicing it away over time and freeing her lungs to scream. Her wrists were another matter – tightly fastened in place with what looked like Victorian-style manacles that might once have belonged on a slave ship or in a gaol.

Jayden turned her head to the camera attached to the far wall of the sewer, its tiny light casting a feeble glow into the chamber. She could not know whether he was watching, whether anybody was watching, but she had to assume that it was her only means of contacting the outside world. She would dearly have loved to have been able to communicate her location, like a *Hollywood* heroine who would somehow figure out a way to alert her friends to where she was, and escape alive to see her tormentor arrested and imprisoned for his crimes.

The water was rising. She looked down, her stomach in turmoil as she saw the foul soup churning around her calves; filthy wet-wipes, discarded food, thick drools of cooking fat and oils seething in a sea of bacterial waste as revolting in appearance as it was in smell. The stench permeated the air like a living thing, coating the back of her throat with slime as she fought against her bonds and tried to keep her breathing under control. She knew instinctively that to panic now would seal her fate, but her heart was slamming against her chest and her nerves were already shredded, jangling with shame and fear.

Water.

In her mind's eye Jayden saw herself as a little girl, playing near a stream with her friends. She saw herself trip in reeds near the bank, saw herself fall into the water. It had been the middle of summer, but the water had been icy cold as she'd plunged in. The shock of the cold water had caused her to suck in an involuntary breath, and with it, the water.

She had thrashed, coughed, gagged and choked beneath the surface, struggling for the last few seconds of her life but hopelessly tangled up in the thick reeds, the water that had looked so peaceful and inviting now cold, dark and dangerous. She had felt her consciousness slipping away, her limbs unable to move, and then, suddenly, a tremendous force had hauled her from her watery grave as a passer-by had rushed to her aid.

She had coughed up a thick mess of water soon after, never having actually fully lost consciousness. She had experienced every last moment of her near-drowning at the tender age of seven, and it had a lasting impact on her. She feared water with a passion. She could not travel on ferries or boats of any kind, and would avoid flying anywhere that required crossing large stretches of open water. She had only ever visited Europe, for it could be reached by crossing the English Channel in an airplane, and a former boyfriend had assured her that by the time an aircraft reached the middle of the Channel, they were high enough to carry on to dry land in either direction, even if an engine were lost. Were it not for that knowledge, she would never have travelled abroad at all. Jayden could not swim, and would only fill a bath with the bare minimum of water. She couldn't watch films or read books that had even the slightest hint of a drowning in them, and had huge admiration for anybody that could endure such an ordeal.

Now, she stared into the darkness as her mind began to unravel. She could almost feel the fragments of her sanity slipping away like a tree battered by ferocious storms, its leaves tumbling away into the maelstrom. She was going to drown here. Terror was building up inside of her in the same way that the water was rising in the chamber. She glanced down, almost afraid to look, and there in the weak light she saw the churning water rising toward her knees - black, dangerous and as cold as death itself.

Please, no. Not like this.

He was watching her, she was certain. Who the hell the insane man was, she didn't know, but she knew his face. She'd seen him before, in the pub, on the street, just here and there, somebody she recognised enough to say *hi*. A nice guy, a normal guy, who smiled at her when he said hello and never bothered her in the slightest. Now, in retrospect, she realised that he must have been following her, learning about her, knowing everything about her: where she lived, where she worked and with whom, her routines, her life, even her fears. What she didn't understand was, *why?* Who the hell was she to him? Why would he have gone to all of this bother to entrap her down here to die?

Jayden focused on his face in her mind, tried to ignore the sludge-laden water rising over her knees. There had to be a reason why she was targeted, something about her, perhaps in her past, that had provoked in him the need to kill her in this most cruel of ways? Had she rejected his advances? She didn't recall ever speaking to him at length, couldn't remember anybody who looked like him, and he'd seemed a fair bit older than her, maybe in his very early forties, so they couldn't have been at school or college together. Maybe university? But she'd studied in Bristol, a chance to escape the capital in which she'd been raised, to see another part of the country. He wouldn't have followed her all the way back here, would he?

The rush of the water was now becoming louder as smaller outflows began to join the deluge, blasting more water into the chamber. To her right, she could still see the exit pipe that she assumed must run down towards the Thames, the water flowing into it, but the level was quickly rising as the water simply couldn't flow out of the chamber as fast as it was pouring in from every other direction.

As the level rose, so the red light from the camera reflected on the surface a little more, and Jayden looked up to see various bits of debris hanging from subterranean power cables, loops and strings of material clogging London's bowels. She felt fresh terror surge through her as her worst fears were confirmed: the debris must have been caught there the last time the sewers had flooded, and that meant the water had in the past risen several feet above her head.

Jayden began to sob as fear closed its cold fingers around her, her tears adding to the deluge as she looked at the manacles pinning her in place and wondered if she could somehow pull them from the brick walls. Another thought crossed her mind: she could eat through her own arms and walk away.

Jesus, Jayden.

There was no way out. The rush of the water began to thunder through the chamber, and she realised that even if she could remove her gag, she would never be heard above the commotion. She looked up at the manhole cover, far above her, and saw that the sky had darkened.

The full force of the storm was now being unleashed on the city above. As she listened to the water thundering into the chamber, so she heard something else coming with it, a high-pitched whistling noise that seemed to emerge all around her at once. For a moment, she dared to hope that somebody, anybody, was coming to her rescue. But then she saw the lights.

Tiny, pin-prick lights, reflecting the light of the camera opposite. In the darkness, she saw shapes scuttling around the edges of the sewer, running along shelves in the brickwork and swimming through the foul mess swilling around her. Their eyes flicked this way and that, their noses sniffing the air as they tumbled into the chamber in their hundreds, trying to avoid the same terrible fate to which she was doomed.

A large rat swam toward her, its grey coat smeared with congealed waste, and Jayden shrieked through her gag as the animal's claws latched onto her nightclothes and it tried to scramble up her body and away from the rising water.

Honor McVey spread a large map onto a table in the Incident Room as every detective in the building gathered around her. Many of them were working other cases with other MIT units, but the extraordinary nature of Jayden Nixx's suffering had brought them across to the operation, and even some detectives whose shifts were about to end were there, Hansen among them.

'These are the sewers of London,' she said. 'It's our belief that the man responsible for the deaths of Sebastian Dukas and Amber McVey has been using them to traverse the square mile without being observed. The current ordeal of Jayden Nixx seems to confirm that.' She gestured to a man standing alongside her. 'This is Paul Sharp. He's worked for Hamlets Council for the past two decades and knows much of what's down there. Paul, tell us everything you know.'

Paul Sharp was a short, stocky man who looked both nervous to be in the company of so many law-enforcement officers, and excited to be involved in a major investigation. His grey, curly hair was receding and he wore square-rimmed spectacles as he glanced down at the map and cleared his throat.

'As I'm sure most of you know, the city's sewers were built between 1859 and 1865 to combat cholera epidemics, the result of raw sewage discharged into the Thames. There are six interceptor sewers with a combined length of around one hundred miles, many of which now channel what were once rivers that flowed through the city. Three of these sewers are north of the water, three to the south, and all use gravity to flow eastwards toward pumping stations. The one closest to the river, on the Embankment, is the lowest.'

'Can anybody gain access to them?' Danny asked.

'Sure,' Paul nodded, 'although why anybody would want to, I don't know. It's a rough place down there, dangerous for obvious reasons.'

'How far can somebody travel?' Samir asked.

'The sewers are vast and cover much of the city, over four hundred miles of them in total,' Paul replied, with apparent pride. 'But seeing as we're talking about the square mile, it's possible for a person to enter the sewers at Moorgate and come out on King William Street without ever being seen, although many of the drain lids are on the surface of busy streets, so they'd have to pick their moments.'

DI Harper spoke up, standing at one end of the table with her arms folded as she stared down at the map.

'Jayden Nixx is somewhere down there right now. Was there anything you could see in the video that might pin-point her location?'

Paul had been shown the live feed a few minutes before the briefing began, and had been suitably traumatised and appalled by what he had witnessed, but despite his great knowledge of the sewer system he shook his head slowly.

'Whoever put her down there was smart enough to place her somewhere such that it's impossible to identify from the footage you have of her. There's not enough of the surrounding area for us to tell. She could be literally anywhere, although I can narrow down the search for you.'

Paul leaned over the map and pointed to certain areas.

'She's fixed to a brickwork area, which rules out any sections of the sewers that have been reworked with modern concrete. That, and the fact that whoever put her there clearly wants to drown her, means that she is probably in one of the deeper sections, somewhere that will flood quickly and prevent you from reaching her. The deepest sections are those nearest the river, along Embankment.'

'Any idea on which side of the river?' DCI Harper asked.

'She's north of the water,' Honor said, speaking on impulse. She looked up to see Paul and DI Harper frowning at her. 'He's going to keep every killing that he can in the Whitechapel area, that's part of his design. Plus, I suspect he's enjoying this game of his and wants to see us scurrying about the city looking for her, while marvelling at his own creativity.' There was little reason to argue with her, but Honor gestured to the map. 'Still, we should obviously search both sides of the water, I'd just put an emphasis on anything to the north. Anything else, Paul?'

He sighed thoughtfully.

'She might be in what we call a *breather space,* the convergence of several interceptors into a chamber. The water falling on her head supports that – it's coming from something above her, possibly a manhole cover or roadside drain.'

'Rainwater?' Honor asked, and was rewarded with a nod. 'How can this guy have accessed the sewers so often without being detected?'

Paul answered with a grim smile.

'It's not exactly Piccadilly Circus down there. If you have somebody running about the sewers, they're not going to meet many other people, apart from the *drainers.*'

Honor frowned. 'Is that what the council workers call themselves?'

Paul shook his head.

'No, believe it or not, there are people who like getting into the sewers and taking a good look around.'

'You're shitting me,' Danny said, grinning as he nudged Samir.

'They're real,' Paul replied, apparently missing the pun. 'We catch them now and again exploring down there, mostly history buffs and such like. I can't imagine why they'd do it for free, it's bad enough when you're being paid. They even have forums to chat and share photographs of what they find down there.'

Honor turned to Samir.

'We can use that,' she said. 'Make a note to cross-reference the IP's of users of *Face Fear* and the drainer's forums. If we get a match, it could be our guy.'

The team stared at the map for a moment, at the vast extant of the sewers, and then DCI Mitchell looked up at the rain-soaked windows and the city beyond, sheets of rain falling in diaphanous veils from a heavily bruised sky.

'How long does she have?' he asked.

'A few hours at most,' Paul answered without hesitation. 'I can't tell how close the water is to covering her, so it's hard to be precise, but those sewers were designed for the London population of 1860, not today. Heavy rainfall over a short period of time can easily overwhelm the system, when the rainwater joins mixed sewers and backs up behind the treatment works or just overflows the sewers themselves. She won't make it much past last light, and there's no way Hamlets will send any of us down there with the flooding risk so high – one mistake and trust me, there's no way out.'

DCI Mitchell glanced at his watch, then turned to the team assembled before him. 'I want every MET patrol officer and vehicle informed and on the lookout for anything suspicious around drains and manhole covers in the city,' he said. 'Get in touch with the Marine Policing Unit and organise a dive team to be prepared to get in there if Jayden's location can be identified before last light. And get more people onto security cameras that cover areas where we have known access points to the sewers – maybe we can catch this guy in the act of putting Jayden down there and start back-tracking his position to where he lives in the city.'

The officers rapidly dispersed to their duties as Honor turned to stare at the footage of Jayden, still manacled to the walls of the sewer, her body drenched and shivering in the cold as water cascaded down upon her.

'Jesus,' DI Harper uttered. 'What the hell is this guy thinking?'

Watching Jayden's suffering was difficult in itself, here in a warm and safe place. It was human nature, to struggle to watch others in danger, suffering. To enjoy such a spectacle invoked natural thoughts of psychopathy, the actions of a sociopath devoid of such emotions as empathy and sympathy. And yet, this was something more. This was something that he enjoyed doing, an experience that he sought, that he *wanted*.

'The moment of death,' she murmured, more to herself than anybody else. 'He doesn't kill any of his victims quickly, he wants to allow himself time to get away and settle somewhere else to watch the victim's death play out.'

Harper raised an eyebrow. 'You think he's sitting somewhere with a beer and some popcorn, taking it this in?'

Honor couldn't be sure but she found herself nodding, as though her instincts were compelling her to obey.

'Something like that,' she said. 'This is the first time he's broadcast something, but it may not be the first time that he's watched somebody die like this.'

'The camera in the coffin,' Harper replied, then turned her head and called across to Danny Green. 'We get anywhere with the coffin camera?'

Danny shook his head, a phone to his ear as he covered the receiver with his free hand. 'Generic, along with the phone it was attached to. Can't be traced to a purchase order but I'm backtracking the serial number to try to link it to a supplier. The coffin's no use to us either as it was hand-made from rough timber, just thrown together.'

Harper shook her head. 'He's got to have left a trail somewhere, keep at him. What about Jayden's flat, her friends, the last people to see her alive?'

'Jason Sharp was interviewed and alibied out, says he left Jayden at the front of her apartment block and went home. Jayden's friends are on the record as having tried to visit her later that night, but she didn't answer her door. They thought she was asleep, and as Jason had said he got her home safely, they weren't too worried. We're getting CCTV coverage from the apartment block to review to confirm their story, but it checks out so far.'

Harper bit her lip. She was feeling the pressure, Honor could tell – it was like they were up against a ghost.

'Keep at him,' was all that she could say.

Honor nodded, and then something struck her about the victims. 'How old did you say Jayden was?'

'Thirty-two,' Samir replied to her.

Honor stared into space for a moment as her brain processed what she'd heard.

'Thirty-two,' she said. 'The victims are all thirty-two years old.'

17

The roar of the water drowned out Jayden's muffled screams as she watched countless rats swarming through the sewer, glistening eyes and thick, matted fur rushing past like a river of their own.

The interceptor pipe opposite was blasting jets of water into the chamber, a fine mist filling the air with a foul-smelling haze. The rainwater tumbling down onto her head was blissfully clean compared to the filthy deluge churning around her waist, a thick flotsam of scum clinging to her blouse as it slid past.

The rats scurried across narrow ledges around the circumference of the chamber, seeking any means of escape from the water. Jayden gyrated as they reached her, shaking them off until they were carried away by the flood. Her stomach twisted with anxiety as she saw them dragged below the surface of the foul mess into the exit sewer. She turned her eyes up to the faint patch of light she could see far above her, the slotted manhole-cover just visible. The sky was rapidly darkening, and she could see other, faint patterns of light drifting past. To her delight she realised that they were the glow from passing car headlights, life carrying on as normal just a few metres above her head.

Her feet slipped on the brickwork, the force of the flowing water now pulling sideways at her and causing her to lose her balance. She tried to keep her head up, pulling on her left arm to fight against the powerful flow of the fetid sludge now tugging her to the right, arms and wrists aching as she fought for grip on the slimy bricks.

The gag was still tight around her head, pulling her lips back in a fearful rictus as she chewed at the edges of it, trying to bite through the fabric. Her jaw ached but she could feel it starting to fray as she ground her teeth.

Rats tumbled from their precarious perches into the turbulent flow of effluent, and Jayden screamed through her gag as several swam through the muck and clambered onto her. Tiny claws dug through her blouse and into her skin as they scrambled up her chest and into her hair, tumbling off one after another as they lost purchase. She smelled their damp, rank fur, felt their claws tear at her skin like little razor blades as they swarmed onto her head, covering her face.

Jayden shook her head frantically, screaming, her heart shuddering in her chest as she fought the urge to vomit as human faeces and other grim debris was smeared from the rats onto her face and into her hair. The rats plummeted into the water again and were carried away, squealing until they were dragged under the surface, where bubbling mounds of foamy scum betrayed the mouth of the exit sewer.

Jayden was panicking now, frantic with terror as the water rose toward her and equally terrified rats closed in from all directions, seeking any means to escape the deluge. Another group scrambled up her chest and clambered up her bare arms, perching themselves on her wrists and hands as she shook and twisted, trying to dislodge the foul creatures from her body. Their claws dug in deeper as they swarmed across her, tumbling in a dirty little flood down her chest as they fought for the safest perch.

Several of the dreadful creatures leapt from her hands and onto the gantry nearby, scurrying away toward a ladder, which itself led up to the manhole. Through her misery Jayden looked again to the manhole, desperate for a means to escape her bonds and climb to safety.

More rats rushed toward her and she screamed as they swarmed onto her body. Jayden twisted away from them, and as she did so her feet slipped and dropped away beneath her. Jayden's heart skipped a beat as she was pulled sideways by the powerful current, and she barely had a chance to realise what had happened before she slid off the ledge and her head plunged into the foul water.

Time stopped in a moment of absolute disgust. Jayden's childhood terror in the river flashed before her eyes, and despite all that she had feared since she realised in that one terrible moment that it couldn't compare to what she was enduring now. The cold, dark, dangerous river of her nightmares seemed almost calm compared to this horrific sludge. It was all she could do to remember not to breathe and to clamp her mouth around the gag as she fought for her footing, only the manacles stopping her from being dragged to her death in the deeper sewers.

Jayden got one foot down and propelled herself up, her face breaking free of the water as she sucked in a deep breath of sickening, stale air with which to scream again. The rats had abandoned her the moment she'd slipped under the surface, and now Jayden shoved her head willingly under the cascade of rainwater pouring down from the manhole as she tried not to think about the billions of microbes now feasting on her skin. The gag was drenched, and nausea turned her stomach as she tasted the foul water soaking through into her mouth, lacing her tongue with effluent.

She pulled hard on her left arm to right herself, and as she did so her wrist slipped a little inside the manacles. Jayden's head whipped around and she stared for a moment at her arm, slick now with faeces and slime deposited by the rats in their headlong flight for safety. Jayden's heart soared and she pulled again on the manacle, felt her wrist slip a little more. A dull ache throbbed through her bones as they were compressed by the manacle, her skin rubbed raw, the constant damp threatening to tear the skin if she pulled too hard.

You can do it.

Jayden grit her teeth, and began to pull.

No.

He leaned forward on the sofa and stared at the screen, watching intently as Jayden's attention was diverted away from her suffering and onto something to her left. He saw there something that he hated, hated more than anything else in the world.

He saw hope.

'Don't you dare,' he growled, willing her to stay where she was.

It was only a matter of time, *so little time*. He could see the filth-laden water sloshing around her chest, a revolting slick of human effluent drifting across its surface. The rate at which it was rising was enough to convince him that Jayden's remaining lifetime could be measured in minutes. To see her freed from her bonds now would be the cruellest of blows, the very worst that could happen.

'It's your time,' he snarled.

Jayden struggled, twisting and turning and pulling on the manacles. As he watched, and saw the mess strewn across her skin, he realised what was happening – the filth was lubricating the manacles, and with such slender arms and wrists, it might just be enough for her to break free.

He sat perched on the edge of his sofa, thinking fast. He could go down to the manhole, maybe park his car right over it to ensure that she couldn't escape, but that would be too risky if the police figured out where she was. They by now would surely have contacted Hamlets Council, spoken to sewer workers who knew the area. But if he left now, he might miss the finale, the final moments of serenity that would herald the end of Jayden's life.

'She's ready,' he whispered.

No more fear.

An image of his mother popped unbidden into his mind. He sat for a moment, no longer focusing on the screen as he saw her there, finally at rest after so much suffering. At the time he had been unable to understand why, despite his overwhelming grief, he had also been relieved. He had been young, too young to understand what had happened, why it had happened. Confusion had reigned, and then fear, an overwhelming dread every time he awoke in the morning, every time he came home from school, every time he caught his father's eye.

He spat the image of his father's wrath from his mind, ejected it like the effluent flowing past Jayden Nixx. He no longer allowed those images into his mind, no longer wanted to see him as he once was; powerful, domineering. No. He preferred the current image of his father; lying there in the basement, as close to death as he would ever be yet without ever quite reaching it, enduring an eternal agony.

He smiled and allowed his mother's image back into his mind, untainted. They had survived together, her gentle touch and encouraging words his only ally in a world that didn't care. Now she was gone. The doctors had said that it was *inevitable* – he could remember the word, although at the time he had not understood it. Somehow, though, he had guessed by the tone of their voices that there was nothing that could be done. The next three months had gone by in a blur, and he had watched her wither away like a flower denied water, until her skin had hung from the rigging of her bones and her breathing had become so shallow, he could barely hear it. He had cried, every night, his father taking good care of his mother only now, when an inheritance was at stake.

She had finally passed in her sleep at the age of thirty-two, still young, still with so much to give. He had been aged nine, and with her had died any vestige of value for human life. In what universe could such a kind and gentle soul be snatched away by an illness so vile, yet a bully and drunkard spared? What justice was there in the favouring of an unpleasant man over a pleasant woman? What value was there to evolution, when the saviour died before the brute? The fact that she had gone to her grave bearing the wounds of many blows from his father's fists, always delivered where they would not be seen, had not lightened the burden that he had carried as a young man, and the years that had passed since had not quelled the growing furnace of hate seething within. He glanced at the door to the basement and allowed himself another brief, bitter smile. In all things, justice came with time. It might be slow, painfully so at times, but it came none the less. Karma. *What goes around, comes around.*

The last time his father had struck him had been when he was a sullen teenager, happier playing computer games in his room than being out with friends. His father had come back from the working man's club, drunk as usual, and as ever had found something that wasn't to his liking. The first blow had knocked him on his side against a wall, but his father's second blow had missed when he had ducked it and slammed his own fist deep into the old man's belly. Bloated with drink, the blow had winded his father, who had dropped to his knees, one hand on his flabby guts as with eyes wide he held up a placating hand. The same kind of hand that his mother had often held up, to no avail. And, so, the time for justice arrived. *What goes around...*

He could not remember how many times he had punched and kicked his father's body, driven by unnatural forces that had surged through him, fury fuelled by high-octane grief, demons freed from a lifetime of suffering. When he had finished, and looked down upon his father's unconscious and bloodied body, he had realised that he was alone in life, that there was nothing that really mattered, nothing that he cared about and nobody out there to care for him.

He had tied his father up, binding his ankles and wrists, then dragged the body into the basement, where he had then bound him to a single mattress. Then, when the time had come, he had force-fed him porridge laced with sedatives that had once belonged to his mother, used to fight the pain of the deadly tumours plaguing her every waking hour. He hadn't been sure of what he intended, but a day had become a week, a week a month, months to years, and his father had not moved from that single bed ever since. His muscles had wasted, his senses dulled by years of off-the-counter sedatives, his eyes sunken pits hollowed of life, suspended on the edge of the chasm of death for so long that he could not remember just how long his old man had lain there. But he wouldn't let him die, not until he had extracted every last breath from his body, every one of them spent incarcerated alone in the darkness, lost in a fog of purgatory.

He glanced back at the screen, saw Jayden still trying to free herself from her manacles as the water rose toward her chin.

'Not long now, Jayden,' he said. 'Not long.'

Honor McVey sat in the Incident Room in front of the feed of Jayden Nixx desperately trying to free herself from her bonds. Honor had barely been able to contain her disgust when she'd see the rats crawling all over Jayden, trying to escape the flooding sewer, but now there was a little lift in her heart as she saw that Jayden was fighting back, trying to free herself from her bonds. The Marine Policing Unit commander arrived in the Incident Room and DCI Mitchell moved to meet him.

'Anything?'

'Nothing,' the MPU commander replied. 'She could be anywhere, maybe even down in some long-forgotten shaft that we don't even know about.'

'There can't be that many places she can be hidden, surely?'

Honor listened to the MPU commander's reply and her heart sank again.

'A guy got lost in a London sewer a few years back after falling into a drain, and spent three days trying to find a way out. They reckon he walked five or six miles under there before he became overwhelmed with exhaustion and just started crying out for help. Luckily, people heard him through a manhole cover and the police pulled him out.' The commander gestured to the screen. 'That guy was only in a rainfall sewer, not one of the deep ones that your victim's trapped inside. Seriously, she could be anywhere in the city and even if we were looking for her without a deadline, it might take weeks.'

Honor stared at the screen for a moment.

'She's being filmed,' she observed. 'Are there power units down there, cables, something that somebody might splice a camera into?'

Paul Sharp, who was still hanging around in case he was needed for information, nodded.

'Cables run through most sewer conduits, mostly fibre, some power but nothing high-grade. It would take skill, but it's possible.'

'Could just be a mobile phone, like at Southwark,' DI Harper pointed out. 'The battery would last long enough to broadcast this.'

'But would it though?' Honor asked. 'Video runs batteries down real fast, and it's got to be wet down there. A phone wouldn't get a connection if it was that far below ground, but if a phone was wired into both…'

Paul's eyes lit up.

'The phone,' he said. 'We never get mobile signals below ground. If he's broadcasting this live, then he's got to be wired in, and that means she's opposite a fibre cable.'

'How much does that narrow down the possible locations?' DCI Mitchell asked. Paul turned to the sewer map.

'Enough to rule out the very lowest stretches, the cables are placed for reasonably easy access from roads,' he replied. 'That rules out some of the interceptors. If I were to put money into it, I'd say she's probably under a main road access platform.'

'How many?' Honor demanded.

'Dozens, but if you're thinking your killer wants to keep her inside the square mile, then we're looking at maybe thirty locations. Fenchurch, Monument, London Bridge and Bank all have major access features.'

DI Harper whirled to the MPU commander.

'Get on them,' she ordered. 'Start targeting any of the entrances in the square mile, especially Whitechapel.'

'Why Whitechapel?'

'Tell you later,' Harper replied.

Detectives hurried to start spreading the word as Harper paced silently up and down like a caged animal, glaring at the screen.

'Jesus, look at her, it's almost up to her chin. She's only got an hour at most.'

Danny Green watched the screen from his desk, his face stricken. Honor knew that he'd taken the death of Amber Carson pretty hard, and now he was being forced along with all of them to watch the whole thing again.

'We have to go public,' DCI Mitchell said.

'We can't give him what he wants,' Honor countered. 'There's something about this campaign that we're missing. All of the victims have been the same age. I think he's reliving something, over and over again, with each of his victims and he's desperate to share it, to share it with the world. We can't keep giving him what he wants, because it will just encourage him to continue. He's desperate for the attention.'

'And Jayden Nixx is desperate for her life.'

Honor tried to reply, but no words passed between her lips. She knew that there was no way they alone could locate Jayden in time to save her life, and a glance out of the Incident Room windows revealed a darkening sky and torrential rain pouring down on the city. She looked at her watch, conceding the inevitable. Her fears were as nothing compared to Jayden's ordeal. *Face them, as Jayden is facing hers.*

'Half-past five. Rush hour. If we go now, we can get the eyes of the entire city looking for her and the conference will hit screens in time for broadcast on the six o'clock news.'

Harper whirled away and called to one of the constables manning the phones in the Incident Room.

'Push it up,' she said. 'They'll be desperate to get in here anyway.' Harper turned to Honor. 'I need you in on that briefing.'

'I need to be here,' Honor replied. 'There could be something on that film that reveals where she is and…'

'There's nothing there,' Harper snapped. 'Briefing room, fifteen minutes. We need to face the music and get the public in on this before it's too late.'

DI Harper turned away from Honor before she could say anything more, and hurried out of the room to prepare for the press conference. They all knew that the major media outlets would send people at the drop of a hat, knowing already that there was a woman in jeopardy somewhere in the city and that the police were scrambling to find her.

Honor grabbed a remote and switched on another, smaller television, this one tuned to the BBC. Despite the random timing of her decision, she was met instantly with a report on the video now being viewed by millions around the world, and turned up the volume a little so that she could hear what the presenter was saying.

'… *there is no doubt that the video footage is being streamed live from somewhere in London, and that the individual concerned is a British citizen. Video analysis experts have confirmed the live nature of the feed, and inquiries have determined that at least one London family may have been questioned about the video. There are numerous questions being put to the City of London Police, all of which have so far gone unanswered, with officers saying that they cannot comment on an on-going investigation. Demands for a public hearing have so far also gone unanswered, but the question that everybody is asking right now, is whether the video of the trapped woman is linked to the series of bizarre murders that have been committed in the past few nights across the square mile…*'

Honor switched the television off and stared at the blank screen for a moment.

'Honor?'

She turned, to see Samir Raaya at the Incident Room door. 'Press are already here; DCI and borough are waiting for you.'

Jesus, she said fifteen minutes. 'They're here already?'

'They've been camped outside all afternoon,' Samir replied and shrugged. 'They've smelled blood.'

Honor felt her skin flush with colour as prickly heat irritated her neck. There was no use in putting it off any longer, she knew that she would have to face the cameras and the questions as the lead detective, and so with an expression of the damned on her face she grabbed her bag and walked on unwilling legs toward the door.

'You want me to go?' Danny asked as he stood up and blocked her path.

The temptation to say yes was almost overwhelming, but she glanced at the television screen and saw there Jayden, fighting to the last.

'No,' she sighed. 'I have to do this.'

'Give 'em hell,' Danny said and squeezed her shoulder before standing aside.

Honor didn't reply, her mind fixated on the glaring black eyes of cameras and probing questions, the demands that they would make of her, the accusations that she somehow already knew would fly.

She took the elevator down to the ground floor, her eyes closed on the way down as she built herself up to the dreaded moment. *Steel and ice.* She imagined an immoveable tower of solid metal and cold ice surrounding her, protecting her, a forcefield against the world outside. She imagined herself a foot taller than anybody else in the building, visualised herself walking with dignity and pride, finally free of all anxieties, always there with the right words, the right actions, the right solutions.

The elevator door opened and she walked along a corridor toward the conference room, feeling a good deal shorter than her imagination would allow her to believe. She could hear a bustle of conversation from within, could see journalists hurrying into the room, and when she walked in, she could see probably a hundred seats, all occupied but for a single empty seat on a raised dais, flanked by DI Harper, DCI Mitchell and the borough commander.

Her seat.

Heads turned as she strode into the room. She kept her head high and her pace firm even as her guts turned to slime within her. The room went out of focus a little and she feared a sudden attack of dizziness, which then provoked further paranoia that such an attack might be inevitable. She felt her balance waver as she walked between the rows of chairs, saw cameras turned to point at her, kept her focus on the wall behind the dais.

Cognitive Behavioural Therapy was of no bloody use to her now, as every sodding reporter in the room and by extension half of the damned country were watching her.

Behind the dais were images of Sebastian Dukas, Amber Carson, and Jayden Nixx. Honor noted that none of the gruesome video images of the victims had been used, and instead more casual images had been obtained from the families in order to portray the victims. Honor managed to walk up onto the dais without tripping or otherwise embarrassing herself, but her face ached, her teeth gritted in her jaw as she focused only on sitting down, arranging her bag and the microphone, and catching nobody's eye.

The assembled journalists settled down and Andy Leeson spoke into his microphone. 'Ladies and gentlemen, as you know there has been an on-going situation in the City of London which we have been working to resolve, and at this time we have decided that the time is right to enlist the public to assist us - in this case, to save a life. We are asking for help in determining the whereabouts of Jayden Nixx, who as I'm sure many of you are aware, was abducted from her home last night in the city and is currently being held, against her will, somewhere in the city's sewers.'

Although every single person in the room knew damned well that Jayden Nixx was being held in a sewer, obvious from the footage of her suffering, the mention of her name, a humanising of her condition and confirmation that it wasn't some kind of bizarre prank, drew a gust of shock from the journalists.

'Furthermore,' the commander went on, 'we believe that Jayden's case is not the first of its kind, and that her predicament may have also been faced in a similar way by two preceding victims.'

Another ripple from the audience, and not for the first time Honor sensed delight and anticipation, the whiff of a major story, the hunt for the truth unfolding. Honor found her towers of steel and ice harden as she determined that she would keep this briefing focused on the victims, not the spectacle.

'… you to the leading officer on this case, Detective Sergeant Honor McVey.'

The cameras switched their unblinking black gaze to Honor, other cameras flashing as they took still images, and for a brief moment she froze. *Everybody's watching you.* Honor hesitated, and then she thought of Jayden's terrible ordeal, and her own terror abated. *Get a grip, this is nothing compared to what that poor girl is going through right now.* The ice hardened, the towers steadied.

'Two days ago, we discovered the body of Sebastian Dukas hanged from scaffolding upon the spire of St Magnus the Martyr Church, near London Bridge. Initially thought to be a suicide, we now know that he was in fact murdered. A day later, Amber Carson was found buried alive in concrete outside Southwark Cathedral. The connection between the victims was that both suffered from extreme phobias: Sebastian Dukas was terrified of heights, and Amber Carson had a life-long fear of being buried alive.'

Gasps went up from the audience, followed by a barrage of questions. Honor sat in silence, not moving, not listening, waiting instead as the tsunami of noise broke against the unbending steel and ice. DCI Mitchell raised a hand as though he was parting waves, and the journalists fell obediently silent.

'We now also know,' Honor continued, 'that Jayden Nixx suffers from hydrophobia, a fear of water, as a result of a childhood accident. It is our belief that the individual behind these attacks is seeking victims based on their deepest phobias, and deliberately exposing them to those fears, with the express intent of watching them die.' Another rush of strained gasps as the journalists scribbled furiously and the cameras recorded every word that Honor said. For a brief moment, she thought of all the millions of people watching the broadcast, and wondered what they were thinking right now. Were they on the edge of their seat with anticipation? Behind it, in horror? She reminded herself to focus on the suffering of Jayden Nixx.

'Right now,' she said, loudly this time, and the journalists fell silent, 'a young woman's life is in direct danger and we don't know where she is. The storm passing over the country is flooding the sewers of London and she may only have an hour or so left before she is drowned. We have convened this conference with the express intent of asking the public for help in locating Jayden Nixx before she suffers the same horrific fate that befell Sebastian Dukas and Amber Carson. Furthermore, we are asking the public for assistance in identifying the man in this image.'

Beside her, a City constable held up a large printed board with an image of the man seen on CCTV in the pubs where Sebastian Dukas and Amber Carson had spent their last night alive.

'This man is a person of interest whom we would like to speak to, even if only to eliminate from our inquiries. He was caught on security cameras in the vicinity of two of the victims prior to their disappearance. If you know anything, if you've seen this man or anybody who has been seen entering or exiting the sewers of London via manholes or any other point of entry or exit, please call us on the phone number you can see on the front of this table.'

The journalists erupted into questions once again, prompting DCI Mitchell to once again silence them with a wave of his hand and select a single journalist from the crowd, an attractive woman with long dark hair who spoke as soon as the furore had died down. 'Are you telling us that this killer has been abducting people and taking them *below ground*, into the sewer network?'

'Yes,' Honor agreed, 'we think that he's been using an extensive knowledge of the sewer network to avoid detection by CCTV and security cameras.'

Another clamour, before a male journalist was singled out.

'The footage of Jayden Nixx is being viewed across the globe, and she may well die live on camera. How does this make you feel, as the lead investigator in the case?'

Honor stared at the man without expression.

'What I feel doesn't matter, it's what Jayden and her family feel that matters. Has anybody got a sensible question they can ask?'

'Detective?' another man asked. 'Were all of the murders filmed in this way? Why didn't we see footage of Amber Carson's murder?'

Honor sucked in a breath.

'It's my belief that these murders are not random, but a premeditated campaign designed to escalate knowledge of the killer's crimes. The murder of Amber Carson was filmed, but we were unable to release the footage publicly as that would have fed into the killer's plans.'

There was another rush of whispers and shocked stares.

'You knew that Amber Carson was dying and you were unable to save her?' asked another female journalist, from the back of the room.

'We were unable to locate her before she died,' Honor acknowledged.

'You *watched* her die?' asked another. 'Why didn't you go public with an attempt to find Amber?'

'Because Amber was buried alive,' Honor replied sharply, anticipating the question. 'There was nothing at all in the footage that could betray her location, whereas with Jayden Nixx there is at least a slim chance that she can be found before…'

'Amber's footage *was* broadcast though,' accused another, 'so there was a *chance* that she could have been located.'

'We were very close to saving her life,' Honor said, sticking to her guns. 'We were only moments too late, and yes, we were searching for the broadcast via Internet IP addresses. Sadly, we were unable to reach her in time.'

There was a moment of incredulous horror from the collective of journalists. 'You let her *die* rather than go public?'

Honor opened her mouth to reply, but it was DI Katy Harper who stepped in, her voice like a whiplash cracking the air over the heads of the journalists.

'Let's not forget who is the enemy here and who is trying to catch them. Apportioning blame for the loss of life in this case should be reserved for the killer, don't you think? Or are you suggesting that our detectives should be put on trial rather than the person committing the crimes?'

The journalist who had shouted the accusation blushed. Honor felt a warm pulse of gratitude toward the DI as the journalist visibly shrank into her seat, but another took her place in an instant.

'Sebastian Dukas died three days ago, and yet you don't have any suspects in this case?'

'We are pursuing several leads,' Honor replied, 'but as yet we do not have a named suspect. As I said, we believe this to have been a meticulously planned campaign, and right now all we're interested in is finding Jayden Nixx before it's too late.'

A moment later, a quiet female voice piped up from near the back of the room. 'Why do you think that they're killing their victims in this way?'

Honor saw the diminutive form of Priya Lakshmi, a freelancer, black hair and neat spectacles, a notepad in her hand. There was no accusation in her tone, no outrage, just inquiry and observation.

'We don't know for sure, yet,' Honor said, loathe to give the killer the fame they were so clearly seeking and yet knowing that she had to reveal some kind of insight for the journalists to run with. 'However, I suspect that the killer suffers from his own phobia, and that he's reflecting that fear onto his victims, deflecting it perhaps. The killer is almost certainly male, physically capable given the lengths he goes to keep his victims out of sight, and possibly suffers from something known as Thanatophobia, a deep-rooted fear of death.'

There was a genuinely interested silence as the journalists noted this new and unsuspected angle.

'So, he's playing out his own fears and watching the results,' Priya went on, 'a morbid fascination with his own phobia, and denial of his own mortality.' Honor was impressed, and encouraged.

'That would fit with our basic profile of the killer,' she agreed. 'There also appears to be a suspected obsession with Jack the Ripper. The killings are occurring at around the same time of year, and the killer appears to hunt in some of the older and more notorious areas of the city; Whitechapel,

Spitalfields, Cheapside and so on.'

'Where the Ripper killed,' Priya acknowledged. 'And the Ripper's victims were all innocent women, despite the misogyny of the original investigations, that much we're certain of. But this suspect is killing men as well as women, and he's doing it more quickly.'

'And without blood being spilled,' Honor agreed, warming to her own theme. 'The suspect may possibly be squeamish around blood, and certainly isn't up to being a slasher-killer in the Ripper's style. Only the first victim was murdered conventionally, via strangulation, and we think that only occurred because the victim recovered consciousness too soon, quite literally forcing the killer's hand. All of the victims were members of the same phobia forum, known as *Face Fear*, and all were drugged using GHB. We're encouraging users of the forum to take extra precautions: don't travel alone, especially at night, and don't think for a moment that you're safe inside your own home. We suspect that Amber Carson might have been abducted from within her own apartment, which was well secured, yet there is no evidence that she knew her abductor and killer.'

The journalists were writing furiously now, some holding hand-held recorders and hanging on Honor's every word. Things were going better than Honor could have hoped, and she was almost used to the cameras now. Another journalist raised a hand. 'Detective, I understand that you have only recently returned to work after six months off for a stress-related illness. Is it wise to have somebody suffering from such afflictions in charge of such a high-profile case?'

The air in the room vanished. Honor opened her mouth to reply but it seemed as though her lungs had been evacuated and now hung limp inside her chest. She gaped for a moment, a hundred pairs of eyes all staring at her in shock. Honor glanced to one side and saw DC Hansen standing with his arms folded, watching her intently. *Son of a bitch.*

'All detectives have to take time off for stress,' DCI Mitchell took to her defence. 'How many dead or mutilated bodies, murders, drug-overdoses and fatal automobile crashes do you think could you look at, before you realised that you needed time out?'

The journalist stood his ground.

'The question is a valid one,' he replied, 'and I'm not a detective.'

'I can tell,' Mitchell growled, and the borough commander stepped in.

'I think that what Detective Chief Inspector Mitchell is trying to say is that when a detective is assigned cases, they put their entire lives into them. Our detectives have been working through the night to solve this investigation, often sleeping on the office floor and not seeing their families for days. That's the side of policing that nobody sees. We're permanently under-staffed, yet forced to perform more work in less time than ever before. I think the question that you should be asking is; what kind of person does it take to perform this arduous work, *despite* the terrible stresses that they have suffered?'

Honor stared ahead over the heads of the journalists, unable to speak as tiny needles of pain lanced the corners of her eyes, her vision blurring. At once appalled and elated, ashamed and overjoyed, she didn't know where to go and neither did her emotions. The towers of ice melted, the steel fractured, and she felt her grief swell up inside of her.

'Terrible stresses?' a journalist echoed the borough commander's words. 'What kind of terrible stresses?'

Honor opened her mouth to reply, suddenly deciding to just hit them with the truth and have them cringe as she bared her soul, when a voice caught her attention.

'Detective McVey?' The voice came from the back of the room, and Honor looked up to see Danny Green beckoning her. 'We've got something.'

Honor stood up as though an electric current had been fired through her backside, grabbed her bag and hurried from the dais, aware of several cameras following her as DI Harper finished the briefing.

'Please broadcast this number as far and wide as you can, to help us locate Jayden Nixx before it's too late. Any piece of information could be of use, no matter how big or small and…'

Honor rushed from the room and straight past Danny, gasping for air as she walked as fast as her heels would carry her back to the sanctuary of the Incident Room.

'Are you okay?' Danny asked as he hurried to keep up.

'I'm fine,' Honor blurted without looking back. 'What's happened?'

'Nothing. I could see you were getting it in the face, so I thought I'd give you an out.'

Honor's grief teetered on the brink as tears spilled from the corners of her eyes, and suddenly she whirled and threw her arms around Danny's shoulders, buried her face in his chest and held onto him, her legs trembling beneath her.

She felt Danny tense up for a moment, and then his hands were on her back, gentle, nervous even. She stood for a moment, her breath coming in ragged gasps.

'Easy,' Danny said in a surprisingly soft voice. 'They ain't got nothing on you, okay?'

Honor sucked in a lungful of air and whirled away from him, before he could see her face and the tears staining it.

'Give me a minute,' she managed to utter, leaving him standing there in the corridor. Honor got to her office and slammed the door shut. Her chest heaved and her vision blurred as she staggered to her desk and slumped into her seat. One hand slipped of its own accord down to her belly, cradling it, and she shivered in the gloom. Her office light was off, and she heard rain splatter in ferocious waves against the window as the storm battered the city. She turned her head, too lethargic to get up and close the blinds, and saw veils of torrential rain tumbling from the darkened heavens. On the roads below, headlights slashed through rivers of rain, traffic lights blinking, their colours reflecting off the rain-soaked tarmac.

Jayden.

Honor drew in a ragged breath and with a monumental effort she switched on her computer and accessed the live footage of Jayden beneath the city's sewers, desperate for some last-ditch, last-minute way to identify her location before it was too late. She knew that she was just doing it to avoid confrontation, to avoid explanation, to avoid the whole fucking world, but she couldn't help herself.

The monitor lit up, the footage switched on, and Honor's morale sank even lower as she witnessed Jayden's terrible state.

18

Jayden wrenched her head back as the churning, black effluent bubbled and swirled around her throat, then pulled hard on her wrist despite the pain it caused her. Her hands were marginally wider than her wrists and the falling water from above was cleaning them of the filth that the rats had left behind, making it harder to pull them through the iron hoops.

She could do it. *I can do it. Don't give in!* The water was high enough now that it was pulling at her all the time, balanced on tiptoe on the slippery floor of the sewer to keep her head out of the water. She was jerking spasmodically with the cold, her uncoordinated movements threatening to dunk her once more into the foul mess.

The roar of the water was almost gone, the interceptor pipes completely submerged, but she could tell by the churning surface that they were still blasting more water into the chamber. She turned again, pulling at the manacle, gritted her teeth as she did so, and suddenly something gave not on her arm but in her mouth. The fabric of the gag wore through and suddenly, blissfully, it fell away from the sore corners of her mouth and she screeched in grim delight as it dropped into the water and slid away into the darkness.

'Help!'

Jayden screamed but her voice was hoarse, weary, and she was shocked to find out just how lethargic she was becoming. She had been down here for countless hours without food or water, not any that she could drink anyway, even the rainwater having first to run down the sewer's slimy walls.

'Help!'

Jayden tilted her head back and cried out, looked up at the distant manhole cover and wondered whether anybody could hear her above the wind, the rain and the thundering traffic.

'Help me! Can anybody hear me?!'

Her voice was amplified by the confines of the chamber. Jayden kept yelling, kept pulling on her restraints, her head turned upward to the dwindling light as the water bubbled and churned around her chin. Sobs of terror racked her body but she kept fighting, unwilling to let her last moments be those of defeat and despondency.

'Help! Somebody *help me!*'

Honor picked up the phone the moment she saw Jayden bite through her gag. 'She's calling for help!' Honor shouted down the phone to a constable in the Incident Room, as though she were living Jayden's final moments alongside her. 'Get people to open whatever manhole covers they can, anywhere!'

Honor slammed the phone down as she turned to her screen, willing Jayden with all her might to break free and find her way out of the sewers before it was too late. She tried not to think about the Marine Policing officer's story of the

London man who'd taken three days to find his way out of a sewer during dry conditions.

Black water roiled around Jayden's hair, which snaked on the surface around her, rainwater crashing down onto her head as she tilted her head back to try to stay above the surface. She had only minutes left. Honor leaned closer to the screen, and then it seemed as though time stopped around her, the rest of the world lost as she stared at the footage. Jayden was thrashing in the water, frantically trying to break free while screaming for her life, but in the deep darkness around her Honor noticed something: the light was changing.

She leaned closer. Jayden yanked her arms this way and that, the flotsam of sewage churning, rainwater cascading down upon her from above, but in the gloom Honor could see it. It was subtle, gentle, almost hypnotic, and for a moment she didn't realise it for what it was.

Red.

Amber.

Green.

Honor leaped out of her chair and ran for her office door. She plunged through it and ran into the Incident Room, yelling at the top of her lungs. 'She's near a set of traffic lights! Get the sequence and run it with traffic, find out where she is!'

Too late now.

He smiled, perched once more on the edge of the sofa, one hand caressing his crotch as he watched and waited. Jayden's thrashing began to abate as the water rose too high and she feared splashing raw sewage onto her face. She was screwing up her features in disgust and terror, eyes wide like saucers in the darkness.

He could see it now. That *face*. That *realisation*. The moment was upon her, the moment of no return, the moment of death. She would relax, resigned to her fate, unable to avoid it any longer. She had fought bravely - needlessly, but bravely none the less, and now she would be at peace.

'Well done, Jayden,' he murmured. 'Don't run from it any longer, it's all over.'

Jayden's wide eyes quivered as the water rose up beneath her nose, her body still now, shivering but motionless as she tilted her head back. Her hair floated in the sewage, her ears consumed until only her face remained, a pale pool of soft skin amid an ocean of filth. The rainwater splattered her face, keeping it clean until the last possible moment.

'Goodbye, Jayden,' he smiled.

The water rose up, and then suddenly Jayden yanked one arm with fearsome rage and her wrist shot through the manacle and broke free.

'No!'

Rage soared through him as he saw Jayden emit a grim howl of joy as she turned in the water, reached out for the other manacle, and pulled hard.

'No, stay where you are!'

Jayden's right hand shot out of the manacle and she instantly slipped off the ledge and plunged into the flow of the water, flailing wildly as she scrambled to stay afloat, her body entirely beneath the black water and only her arms visible as they thrashed for something to hold on to.

'Die! *Die now!*'

Fury rushed through his bones as he stood, watched as Jayden's hand caught on the very same manacles that had restrained her and she hauled herself out of the water, her face smeared with detritus, her hair matted and lank, her mouth open as she sucked in foul air and clung to the manacles that had almost killed her.

'No!'

He watched, mortified, as Jayden held her face to the clean water cascading down from above, ridding it of the filth, and then began pulling herself toward the gantry and out of shot. Directionless rage seethed like acid through his veins. He stormed up and down the living room, seeking a vent to his anger, and in a fit of fury he rushed down the stairs to the basement and lunged into the spare room.

The stench hit him first, that of faeces and decay, and he was brought up short. He turned on the light and looked down at his father's body where it lay on the thin, filth- ridden mattress. The face was at peace, devoid of suffering; mouth agape, rotting teeth bared between parched lips laced with sores, a purple tongue lolling down one cheek.

In his obsession with Jayden's suffering, he had left the old bastard alone for too long, long enough that he could die, and die without being watched. He cringed, folded over his own rage, screamed something unintelligible as he ran out of the room and grabbed a baseball bat that he kept in the basement. He rushed back into the foul- smelling room and swung it over his head. The bat smashed into his father's emaciated skull and the feeble bones split like eggshells. Black blood splattered the walls around him as he swung again and again, smashing the peace from that hated face, sweat beading on his forehead and his breath coming in ragged gasps.

The rage subsided and he hurled the bat aside, looked down upon the terrible damage that he had wrought. His father's skull was a tattered mass of dark blood and bone, one orbit shattered, the eyeball dangling from damp tendons. He looked at the remains for a moment longer, and then his stomach summersaulted inside of him and he turned away as he hacked up a thin stream of bile. He staggered out of the room, lost, unfocused, enraged and yet unable to vent that rage, even on his own hated father who was now forever beyond his reach.

He made his way back to the living room, looked at the television, and saw only water. The camera was now submerged, but the spot where Jayden Nixx had once been was empty. Whether she lived or died, he would no longer see it and had no control over it.

He fought the urge to thrust his fist into the screen, and instead turned to his notebook. He opened it, and managed at least a wan smile as he crossed Jayden's name off. She might yet die. *You can still do it.*

There were five canonical murders committed by Jack the Ripper, all prostitutes, most of the others being only loosely connected to the original slayings, and disputed by many researchers as being the work of copy-cat killers. No, the brutal killing of five innocent victims was all that he needed, like the worthless whores that Jack slashed into bloodied gore centuries before. Five slayings, each as gruesome as the other, brought to the attention of a global audience with their unique nature, their undeniable attraction. Sebastian Dukas; Amber Carson; Jayden Nixx, *if* she died; his own father. That was three, as his father didn't really count if he was being honest with himself.

He looked at the remaining names on the list. There were several, but he ignored them, including his father's, which had been at the very end of the list. His plans had to change now. There was no point in prolonging things, for the police would eventually identify him now that they had CCTV of him in the various pubs. He recalled the pretty girl behind the bar in the *Hoop and Grapes*, who would certainly recognise his face when the time came. The sewers were no longer a safe haven, so he would have to do things differently. He could kill the bar girl, but that might only draw closer attention to him. Jason, Jayden's friend, would also be able to identify him in a photo parade. His only chance now was to finish the game and vanish long before that happened.

His rage subsided into a cold, determined fury, and he added two fresh names to his list, focusing their images in his mind as a loose plan of action formed.

He would end this the way that the Ripper would have ended it, the way that it should end: with all those involved brought to peace, liberated from their suffering.

Jayden Nixx hauled herself up out of the foul water and onto a metal gantry that was slick with gloops of foul mess. She was shivering violently, and the water was now rising up onto the gantry, filling the oval chamber ever faster.

She staggered to the ladder, cold water cascading down onto her head, and managed to clamber up until she could reach the manhole cover. The sound of traffic thundering past on the road above was deafening, and although the water tumbling through the holes in its iron surface made it hard to see, she could make out the faintest hint of light off the clouds far above, flashes of light from headlamps, brake lights and what seemed to be traffic lights nearby. Weeping with joy, she reached up and pushed against the manhole cover.

The cover remained stubbornly shut. 'No,' she gasped. 'Help!'

She was exhausted, weeping, shaking and trying to control her trembling voice long enough to be heard.

'Help!'

Cars thundered by, and as she yelled so she felt something cold wash over her feet. Jayden looked down, and saw the filthy water rising rapidly up the ladder and into the shaft in which she was now trapped.

Weary beyond belief, she cried out for help again.

Honor stood in the Incident Room with Samir and Danny, anxiously clenching and unclenching her fists by her sides as she waited for a call from the traffic section. Every single set of lights inside the city of London was controlled by computer, and the sequence in which the lights controlled the flow of traffic was designed to alter depending on how much traffic there was and where it was heading. Sophisticated algorithms controlled that flow, and also provided a handy feedback loop that allowed technicians to monitor the light sequences of any junction in the entire city.

A phone rang, and DI Harper picked it up instantly.

'Fenchurch and Lime Street!' she snapped, and in an instant, officers were picking up their phones as Honor dashed for the door.

She hurtled down the stairwell outside with Danny and Samir close behind, and out of Bishopsgate station entrance, not even thinking about trying for a HAT car as she turned left and began running through the torrential rain pummelling the pavement around her. A forest of umbrellas parted like waves as commuters ducked out of her way, the wind buffeting her as she ran, ignoring the rain pouring in sheets around her.

Fenchurch Street was barely five hundred metres south of the station, and Honor knew the area like the back of her hand. Rush hour traffic would slow even a patrol car with its blues lit up. She ducked left into Bevis Marks, then right into St Mary Axe, full-tilt past the towering, glistening lights of the

Gherkin and Leadenhall, tore across Leadenhall Street and into Lime Street as she heard wailing police sirens soaring across the city like banshees, racing her to the scene.

The dizzying heights of the financial district's towers gave way to Fenchurch Street, the Shard's glittering heights on the far side of the Thames lost in the tumbling clouds. Honor burst out onto Fenchurch Street at the same moment as police cars converged on her position, their hazard lights flickering like exploding stars, the debris bouncing off glossy windows all around.

'Which one?' Honor screamed as she staggered, breathless, to a halt in the middle of the junction with Lime Street and Philpot Place, and looked at the road beneath her as the police cars screeched to a halt broadsides across the road, blocking all traffic from entering the area.

Officers swarmed in, and she felt her heart aching as she saw the drains and the manhole covers around her, water seeping from all of them to join the floods streaming along the gutters.

'Pick the biggest one!' Paul Sharp yelled as he got out of the HAT car and pointed to a triple set of covers right by a kerbside drain.

The cascade of rainwater on Jayden's head.

'Open them!' Honor yelled, her hair hanging limp and sodden from her head, her suit drenched, cold rain spilling down her face.

Police constables rushed to her side, and she was pushed clear as they forced metal hooks supplied by Paul Sharp into the holes in the manhole cover, where streams of water were pulsing like black blood onto the road, as though the city itself were bleeding.

As one, the officers hauled the manhole covers off and a great rush of water flooded out into the street. In the light of their torches, Honor saw Jayden Nixx's face rush up out of the water, her mouth agape, her eyes wide open, her limbs flailing. Officers grabbed her body, and for a moment Honor held her breath as Jayden was dragged onto her back in the road, flickering hazard lights illuminating her body as paramedics rushed in. Honor tried to get closer as fire engines and ambulances arrived, screeching upon the scene, and over the shoulder of a paramedic she glimpsed Jayden's eyes staring lifelessly up at the night sky.

'Clear!'

Jayden's body jerked as a defibrillator punched current into her wounded heart, again, and again and again. Honor stood immobile in the rain, watching as the paramedics shocked her repeatedly, and then, finally, they glanced up at her and shook their heads.

Honor stood in silence, staring down at Jayden's inert corpse, her mind numb, devoid of thought. She could not feel the cold or the rain, could see nothing but Jayden's death mask before her, twisted with the agony of her last breath, and something else, something even more horrible that wrenched Honor's heart from her chest and sent it screaming into a darkness she could no longer quell. *Dismay. Disappointment.*

They had failed Jayden. She had failed Jayden.

Honor turned away and started walking. She had nowhere to go, the rain pelting down on her head as though beating her into submission. She made ten paces until she reached an ambulance parked at an awkward angle near the traffic lights, turned and slumped against it as every last ounce of her soul drained out of her and poured away on the rivers of rain sailing away toward the Thames. Her forehead thumped against the metal side of the vehicle, slick with rain, her hair plastered against her forehead.

'Fuck's sake.'

She heard footsteps approaching, and sensed rather than saw Samir move alongside her.

'This isn't on you.'

His words were simple but honest. Still didn't mean fuck all though, not really, not when they were standing a few feet from Jayden Nixx's corpse. A daughter, a sister, a mother, an aunt, a friend, a *person*, all ripped from life for nothing more than a murderer's deranged passions. Honor didn't say anything in reply, couldn't bring herself to speak, to think, to do anything.

'It isn't on you,' Samir repeated.

Honor put one hand over her face and willed him to just piss off and leave her alone.

'Tell me that you understand, it's not on you.'

'It's not on me,' she replied through her hand. 'I know it's not on me, Samir.' Cold fury ripped through her from out of nowhere. She whirled to face him and stabbed one finger into his chest. 'When you've faced a few dozen more of these, when you've got children of your own and when you've done more than follow me about like a lost puppy, you'll understand that "it isn't on you" means *fuck all*.'

Honor barged past Samir and stormed away, shoved her hands in her pockets and ducked her head down against the miserable rain plummeting down all around them. Other detectives were on the scene now, Danny Green standing among them with his hands hanging loose by his sides, the rain glistening on his skin, his thick brown hair as wet as hers. Honor felt immediately compelled to tell him that this wasn't on him, and her rage instantly broke up into shame and dismay. *Christ.*

She turned back to the ambulance, but Samir was already gone. She stood for a moment, staring at where he had been. *It's not on him, either.* Everything was collapsing around her, like some awful nightmare breaking through into reality and shattering what little life she had left.

'He likes you.'

She turned. Danny wasn't looking at her, instead watching as Jayden Nixx's body was rushed into an ambulance. Although dead-at-the-scene, they would still try to revive her again at the hospital, hopeful that the cold water might have slowed her organs down enough to prevent brain damage.

'What?'

Danny pulled out a cigarette, struggled against the rain to light it as he spoke. 'Samir. He likes you.'

Honor didn't really know what the hell Danny's point was, and wondered fearfully if this was just one too many for him and he'd lost himself. Like she was losing herself.

'Samir's fine,' she uttered.

'You know what I mean,' Danny replied, the cigarette stubbornly refusing to catch. 'You just won't let yourself see it. He's right, it's not on you, or him, or me or anybody else but the arsehole who put Jayden down there.'

Danny got a light going and sucked in a huge lungful of smoke before letting it bleed from his nostrils in lethargic blue coils.

'You're in danger of losing your shit, Honor,' he said finally, his eyes almost black in the night. 'You're pushing people away, one by one, because you think you're alone. Trouble is, alone is precisely what you'll end up.'

Honor hastily erected what was left of her defences. The last stand.

'You can play doctor another time,' she snapped. 'I want CCTV from this spot, and any other entrance to this sewer, from the past forty-eight hours. This guy had to get in and out of here and I want to see him do it.'

Danny didn't move. He simply watched her as he drew on his cigarette again, the tip glowing red, provocative, accusing.

'We're chasing our tails,' he replied. 'We need to get ahead of him.' 'How about an idea, genius?'

Danny's gaze narrowed but he said nothing for a moment as he drew again on the cigarette. He let out the smoke with a sigh, as though weary of trying to breathe.

'We can't put specialist search teams down there until the flooding subsides, and that's not going to happen tonight. I'll handle the scene here, and update CRIS. Go home, now. Get some rest,' he said, and turned away from her.

19

The city lights flickered like glittering stars arrayed across a bleak and uncaring universe. The rain was still pouring down, the higher buildings' lights glowing in misty halos to illuminate the tumbling clouds.

Honor stared out across the city from her apartment, seeing everything, seeing nothing. The wineglass in her hand was half empty, forgotten as she sat in comatose silence, thinking about everything, thinking about nothing. The room around her flickered like the city lights as the television silently played the BBC News channel, and endless cycle of reports from the incident in Fenchurch Street that was already global knowledge, and alongside it the press conference in which she had taken part.

Honor had lost count of how many times her name had been mentioned, broadcast to a nation reeling in horror at the way in which the City of London Police had handled what had become one of the most sensational criminal cases in British history. A frenzy of headlines was being spewed across news networks, heightening the public's awareness of the case as the media gorged on the carcass of Honor's failure.

The Ripper Returns.

Shadowy killer once again stalks Whitechapel. Your worst fear is this killer's greatest strength.

City of London Detectives under fire for their handling of greatest criminal pursuit since the hunt for Jack the Ripper.

She could see her own face on the screen out of the corner of her eye, the same piece of footage replaying over and over again. The media outlets had not focused on her appeal for assistance, nor her analysis of the criminal behind the killings. All that they were showing, repeatedly, was the same journalist's question and her own faltering response.

'Detective, I understand that you have only recently returned to work after six months off for a stress-related illness. Is it wise to have somebody suffering from such afflictions in charge of such a high-profile case?'

Honor hadn't known how to react. She couldn't have known how to react, as it would never have crossed her mind in a million years that headline-hungry reporters would sink to such a low, just to generate public outrage at the force's supposed failure to do the "right thing". Of course, the broadcasts failed to show DCI Mitchell's timely intervention, and the journalist's resulting shame. They focused only on the attack, never on the defence.

Don't take this on if you're going to dry up like that in front of a few million viewers. She had relived that briefing a hundred times, delivering withering put-downs, witty ripostes, leaping out of her chair in righteous outrage to slam the journalist for his callous line of questioning. *Who do you think should be in this chair, the killer himself? How dare you call into question our efforts to try to catch this maniac? Who do you think you are? There are detectives here working eighteen-hour days trying to put a stop to this man!* But none of it helped at all, for none of it had ever happened but within the tortured crucible of her own mind.

You failed her.

She should have fought back. She should have stood her ground. She should have done *something*. And yet she had sat there, unable to speak, unable to shoulder the burden of her own guilt, her own grief, her own utter contempt for herself and her life. The journalist was right. Hansen was right. Danny was right. She shouldn't be handling this case. She wasn't up to it anymore. The truth was hard to bear but she had to face it. She was broken, so much so that she barely felt the tear trickling down her cheek, her misery so commonplace that it felt like a companion, someone to hold on to.

She made a resolution for the following morning. She would walk hand-in-hand with her misery into Bishopsgate, and tender her resignation to DCI Mitchell. A brief image of DS Hansen's delighted sneer as she turned tail and ran from her career sparked a faint flicker of defiance, but the image of Jayden Nixx's tortured face snuffed out what resistance she had left with a cold gust of self-loathing.

It's over. Stop fighting. You're not coming back, not ever.

Honor took a sip of her wine and instantly felt a little better. With the decision made, she felt unexpectedly relieved. She could get into this, just hide behind a bottle a day and watch the world go by. Take some job where she could work from home and never have to face the world outside. Hell, the Internet made anything possible, right? She'd never have to walk out of that bloody door, nor ever let anybody through it again.

On cue, the door buzzer rang.

Honor sighed, dazed by the universe's bleak sense of humour, too weary to even be angry any more, but she didn't move. Whoever it was, they weren't bloody well coming in.

'Honor,' came a soft voice. 'It's Danny.'

Balls. Honor sat for a long moment, staring at the blackened city outside, and then she found herself standing up and walking to the door, as though she were not in control of her own body. She unlatched and unlocked the door, opened it. A shaft of warm light beamed into the darkened apartment, Danny standing there with a bottle of wine and what smelled like a Chinese takeaway. Honor belatedly realised that she hadn't eaten for more than twelve hours. Samir was standing next to him, hands in his pockets and a pensive expression on his face.

'Sorry,' Danny said as he glanced at the darkened apartment, 'were you sleeping?'

'No,' Honor blurted, her mind addled by the wine and an empty stomach. 'I was just thinking, forgot to turn the lights on.'

Danny nodded, watching her. 'Thought as much. Brought you dinner. I reckoned you wouldn't want to go out and that you'd forget to eat again, so I brought the rest of the world to you instead – China in one hand, Italy's finest in the other.'

Honor stared at the wine and the food and instinct once again took control.

She ushered them both into the apartment and shut the door, popped the latch on before she switched on some lights, embarrassed by her own sloth.

'Nice place.'

It was said in such a way that she could have harboured a corpse on the sofa and Danny would have said the same thing. She saw his gaze linger briefly on the image of the ultrasound on one wall, and then he set the takeaway down on the coffee table as she fetched some cutlery, plates and extra glasses.

'Got it a year ago,' she replied as she handed them knives, forks and plates.

Danny sat down on an armchair and Samir onto a bean bag as she re-took her place on the sofa and poured them some of the wine they'd brought. Chilled Prosecco. Standard, safe, bloody nice with Chinese. She handed it over, feeling as though she were going through a transient out-of-body experience. A moment ago, she had been dwelling on a life lost, chiefly hers, and now she was eating Chinese and trying to be merry. Everything was out of place, as though she were watching a dream play out before her, no scene connecting with another.

'Tough day,' Danny said as he tucked into a prawn cracker and gestured to the television.

Honor grabbed the remote and shut the bloody thing off.

'I don't want to talk about it,' she said, stuffing down a spring roll and avoiding eye contact.

Danny shrugged. 'You should talk about it,' he said. 'That's what's wrong.'

Honor felt anger rise up within her, quick, easy, but when she looked at him to retort she saw the pensive look on his face and remembered how she'd spoken to Samir beside the ambulance on Fenchurch Street. The rage subsided into shame once more, as though she didn't suffer enough already.

'Look, I – I'm sorry for what I said earlier,' she said to Samir. 'I didn't mean any of it.'

'I know,' Samir replied. 'It's okay, I get it. I mean, I don't get it, but I know it's not you.'

Honor wasn't sure what to say. *He likes you.* She hid behind another spring roll and tried to change the subject.

'Anything to report from the Incident Room?'

Danny shook his head, stuffing a spring roll into his gob as he replied. 'They're on the hunt, Harper just doesn't sleep. I'm going to head back in once I've had some kip, give them a hand. We're certain that we're gonna get good images of this guy entering the sewers at some point.'

Honor nodded, realising that she had been sitting here moping about when there was still work that badly needed to be done. The publicity would probably get them more hands in the investigation, but that wouldn't help much if somebody wasn't at the helm.

'What are you going to do?' Danny asked her. 'What am I going to do about what?'

'You know what I mean.'

Honor chewed her food as an excuse not to answer straight away. *I'm going to quit. I'm going to sit here and spend the rest of my life drinking myself into a bloody stupor. How about you?*

'I'm working on it.'

'You're thinking about quitting.'

Honor shot him a sharp look, stunned that he could see through her so easily, or perhaps admiring that he'd throw a wild-card and hit the target.

'What makes you think that?'

'You're struggling,' Danny said. 'It's getting in the way of what you're doing, getting in the way of your work, and we all know it.'

Honor glanced at Samir, wondering why he was here and not Danny alone, then wondering why that was an issue for her. Samir shrugged and nodded.

'Looks that way.'

'Says the walk-in detective?'

Honor had meant the comment to carry some jest, but she saw no humour on Samir's expression.

'Doesn't take a detective to see that.'

Honor tried to focus on eating, but she felt suddenly vulnerable in her own home. She shouldn't have let them in, she realised. She wasn't ready for this shit, wasn't really ready for anything. Who the hell were they to come in here and start telling her what was wrong? Samir had only been on the job for a year, was probably stacking fucking shelves or something before that, and…

'What happened to the baby?' Danny asked.

Honor's train of thought slammed to a halt. *Jesus Christ.* The flames within gusted into life and flared dangerously. That Danny would ask her something so personal in front of another officer she'd known for just three days shoved a flaming stick up her arse that sparked an inferno in her belly.

'You really want to know, Danny?' she snapped. 'I was three months gone with my first child when I found out that my husband was having an affair, okay? My whole life fell apart, I got diagnosed with acute stress, and for some reason the change in hormones triggered a natural termination. I miscarried, lost the baby, lost my husband and lost my whole fucking life!'

Honor tossed her fork onto her plate, her appetite withered amid churning adrenaline, grinding regret and loathing for herself, for her past, for now, for everything. Danny sat in silence for a moment, then nodded.

'I see.'

Honor stared at him. 'You *see*?'

Samir was watching her as though he was circling a wounded predator, the nervous suitor in the Black Widow's web. Danny, on the other hand, merely nodded as though they were discussing the price of bloody apples.

'I see what's eating at you, and it makes sense,' he replied. 'Hiding all this stuff away, hiding yourself away, it's not fixing anything, it's not making you feel any better, right?'

Right. Fuck off, Danny. You're right, but I can't let you see that. I can't let anybody see that. Why the hell *can't* I let anybody see that? Honor tucked her legs beneath her. 'I don't think that anything is going to just *fix* things, funnily enough. Losing a child kind of does that to people, but you wouldn't know.'

Danny continued to eat, not letting her anger get to him. Jesus, why was he putting her through a bloody interrogation after the day that she'd had? The lighting in the apartment was low enough that shadows abounded around them like slumbering demons.

'I lost my mother when I was young,' Samir said softly, 'so I do know something of what you're feeling, actually.'

There was a quiet dignity about Samir's reply that furthered her shame. She sighed, the boil of her indignation lanced once more.

'I'm sorry to hear that.'

Danny mopped up after his meal and tossed the napkin onto his plate.

'And I lost my wife to the job. You're sorry for a lot of things, just like all of us. This isn't your first rodeo, you don't need to hear this crap, but I'm done with you sitting there hating yourself. There's no reason to beat yourself up over what happened. You didn't fail Jayden. I didn't fail Jayden. The department didn't fail Jayden. Nobody did. That man out there, this is all part of what he wants, just like you said. Notoriety. Discord. Conflict. The media feed on it like bugs on a corpse, they love it, and so does the public, although they won't admit it to themselves, but there's a reason headlines sell. There's only one person to blame for everything going on here: what's important is that the person to blame isn't you.'

Honor sat for a moment in silence. She looked down at her food, and reluctantly picked up her fork and started playing with it, unable to think of anything to say, like an admonished child who didn't quite understand what they'd done wrong.

'You're the person who's meant to fix it all,' Danny added. Honor blurted a bitter little laugh. 'I can't fix any of it.'

'You can,' Danny insisted. 'That's what you won't let yourself see. You think that you're less than you are.'

'Since when the hell are you a psychologist?' she asked, but this time managed a smile, even though it felt as though she was trying to bend an iron bar with her lips.

'Armchair shrink,' he smiled back, 'pub philosopher and full-time know-it-all. I don't know what I'm talking about, not really, but it's instinct – I can see what you're going through because I'm outside of it, not consumed by it. I can see the answers, what I would do if I were you, but they're no good to you because you need to solve this your own way, the way that works for you. I suppose that's what I'm trying to say – do this all for *you*, nobody else. Stop surviving and start fighting.'

Honor leaned back and took a sip of her wine. 'Sounds easy if you say it quickly enough, right?'

Danny nodded, gulped down a mouthful of wine, then pointed at her over the rim of his glass.

'My dad used to tell me that the best way to handle stressful situations was to treat them like a dog would: if you can't eat it or hump it, just piss on it and walk away.'

Honor sprayed a fine mist of wine into the air. Endorphins flushed her system with a warm embrace and she realised it was the first time she'd laughed in as long as she could remember. Samir noticed it too, grinned quietly.

'You light up when you laugh.'

He likes you. Honor stifled the giggles, stared at her plate. Samir wasn't somebody she was interested in, not in that way. She instead found herself looking at Danny, scruffy-haired, cocky, a born scrapper and yet more insightful of the human mind than she'd have given him credit for. The light in the apartment seemed warmer, the demons banished into dark recesses, afraid of the light.

'I can't go back,' she said to him. 'The press crucified me in that conference and it's all over the bloody planet.'

'Yep, you're famous for screwing up on one of London's biggest investigations.' 'That wasn't the supportive appraisal I was hoping for.'

'I know,' Danny replied, 'so what *are* you looking for?'

Honor didn't know. She really didn't bloody know. She shrugged.

'That's what I thought,' Danny said, as though reading her mind. 'You've got to change the way you look at things. You think that you can't go back to work, that you're a laughingstock?'

Again, she shrugged.

'It's bullshit,' Danny snapped. 'You've convinced yourself that you're worthless. Everybody in that office knows that you've conquered every unknown since you started work on the case. You were the one who first deduced that Sebastian Dukas was murdered. You were the one who first suggested that the killings were an attempt to emulate Jack the Ripper. You were the one who figured out he was using the sewers to travel across the city unobserved, and you were the one who narrowed down where Jayden Nixx was. Every detective in the department knows all of that, and right now every one of them thinks that you got a bad deal in that conference. They're disgusted at the way you were treated, and so am I.'

Honor now felt ashamed at herself for sinking so low, for not being able to separate herself from her anxieties.

'I didn't know,' she said, unable to think of anything else worthwhile to share.

'That's right, because you were sitting on your arse feeling sorry for yourself. You need to stand up. You need to fix this. You're not a pariah at work, you're held in high esteem.'

'The rest of the world sees me as a failure,' Honor protested. 'The department will have to fire me due to the public pressure. I can't fix that.'

Danny watched her for a moment.

'Can't you?' he asked, and then leaned forwards. 'Catch him. Find this bastard and bring him to justice. Prove them all wrong. Prove *yourself* wrong. That's how you fix this – by doing nothing more than your job.'

Danny picked up his glass and drained his wine, then he got to his feet.

'I need to get back,' he said. 'Grab a shower and some kip before I head back into work. Do me a favour - get some sleep, get over this and get back into the office as soon as you can, okay? I don't think we're going to catch this guy any quicker if you're not alongside us.'

Honor stood up, surprised that Danny was leaving so soon, and then instantly wondering why she felt that way.

'I will do,' she promised, surprised all over again that her voice sounded calmer in her own ears. Danny had an unexpected way with words that seemed to have quelled the black chasm inside her into an ocean of gentle swells. Or maybe it was the bloody wine, she couldn't really tell.

Danny shot Samir a glance, and Samir belatedly stood up and joined Danny as he headed for the front door, opened it, and stepped outside.

'We'll see you in a while. Did I forget to mention that we got CCTV of a tall man in a hooded top entering Jayden Nixx's apartment block before she returned home?'

'Jesus, Danny! Yes, you bloody forgot!'

'Jason is also on the footage, as well as Jayden's friends, but they are all seen leaving again,' Samir added. 'The unidentified male in the hoodie enters the building, but isn't seen to leave.'

Honor's mind raced.

'He found another way out,' she said, 'one not covered by the security cameras.'

'They have them covering the entrances,' Danny confirmed, 'not so much the exits. He's our guy, and we already checked Wheeler out – it's definitely not him, he was with his solicitor at the time. The apartment is covered by a camera and a security pad, with a four-digit keycode pass.'

'He knew the code?'

'We're checking up on it,' Samir said. 'First thought was that it might be Jenson Cooper, Wheeler's manager, as he has skills in that area. But he didn't fit the security system and he has an alibi; he's on camera headed home about the same time that the abduction took place. Again, same goes for his contractors, O'Rourke and the others clearly seen heading home after work. Somebody, somewhere, knew that code and could access the building ahead of Jayden.'

'We searched Jayden's apartment, but nothing was found,' Danny added. 'Forensics are there too. The apartment manager said that although they change the door codes once a month, it would be easy for someone to note the code by watching others enter the building ahead of them. We're checking to see if this guy shows up on previous footage, but it's gonna take a while. So,' Danny said with a grin, 'you need to come back in the morning, right, or this arsehole might yet slip away again, and we don't want that, do we?'

Honor managed a smile. Danny turned and walked with Samir away from her through the door to the stairwell, leaving her with a simple choice: fight or flight?

There wasn't much time.

He moved with quiet efficiency, his hood up against the rain still pelting the city streets. His route carried him through Whitechapel, always hugging the backstreets, moving from shadow to shadow like the dangerous thoughts flitting through the vaults of his mind.

This was how the Ripper had moved, unafraid, unchallenged. The alleys were no longer as narrow and dangerous as they had once been, apartment blocks in place of warrens of cut-throughs and alleys that had been the Ripper's lair, but nonetheless the rain kept people inside, and moisture in the air cast the light from streetlamps into diaphanous orbs. Although much of the old city had been demolished and new buildings erected after the Second World War, he knew the locations of all the 18th century buildings that remained.

But now he ignored them, for the time of worshipping the past was coming to an end. Now, the time to honour was his own. Would, someday, citizens walk these streets and think of the great killing campaign conducted by a mysterious figure in the early 21st century? He liked to think that such a thing might happen, hundreds of years from now. His legacy was becoming legend, and he walked with urgency but also in high spirits again, for he was close to his goal. Jayden Nixx had died, and his next victim was close at hand.

Emily Wilson, aged thirty-two, an office assistant who worked up near Hoxton. A fanatical tennis fan and skilled player in her own right; married, no children, lived in a rented apartment in Whitechapel, right on his doorstep. The target was perfect, and although his plans for her had been set for a few weeks' time, the recent discoveries by Detective Sergeant Honor McVey and her team meant that he needed to revise his timeline.

McVey was something of a mystery. The woman intrigued him intensely, and he'd watched her recent press conference with great interest. The media had torn into her, as expected given what was happening in the city, but she had shown great dignity despite the unwarranted attacks. McVey represented the greatest threat to his plans, to his grand design, and so he had taken the time to investigate her. It had not taken long. London detectives found themselves in the papers and on the news more often than people would at first think, and he had soon been able to track her down via former school friends, associates, colleagues and other people who either knew her, had known her, or were connected to her in some way in the digital age. Within an hour he had figured out where she lived, some of her routines, her likes and dislikes, the times she travelled to and from work, and some of her history. And there, he had been delighted to discover, was the source of his greatest interest: Zach Arnold, a thirty-four-year-old computer graphics artist, and his new fiancé, Natalie Delray, thirty-six. What interested him was the fact that Facebook photos on friends' profiles featuring both Zach and Honor showed them clearly as a couple perhaps just a year previously, and yet now Zach was engaged to another woman.

He smiled. Something there was afoot, and he knew that he would need to research a little further. He had listened to her assessment of him as a killer and had enjoyed it, duly impressed at her insight: her only mistake was in assuming that he was somehow deranged, a man suffering from mental health issues. In truth, he had never felt more of purpose and conviction than now, his nerves jangling to primitive chords as he hurried along, revelling in the darkness and shadows and rain spilling from black skies.

Emily would be home soon, and he didn't want to miss her. He hefted the rucksack he wore into a more comfortable position as he walked, but that was easier said than done, as the contents writhed and tumbled within, caressing his back as he strode through the deserted back alleys. Detective McVey had noticed that he avoided the sight of blood. That didn't mean his victims should. If they wanted blood, he would give them blood.

Emily Wilson staggered out of *Legends* nightclub and sucked in a deep lungful of air, stunned at how drunk she felt. A group of her friends spilled from the club in a colourful little flood onto the glistening pavements, the rain falling more lightly now, which was just as well as they struggled with umbrellas and coats. The whisper of the rain competed with a dull thudding bass coming from within the club as they said their goodbyes, huddled together beneath a canopy of umbrellas before turning their separate ways and heading home.

Emily was not used to staying out this late, nor drinking as much as she had done. However, Lucy's birthday did come but once a year, as she had told her friends repeatedly as they downed tequila shots and danced the night away. The club had been busy, filled with students who looked considerably bloody younger than Emily, another sign that her clubbing days were long behind her. So, it would seem, were her drinking days as she swayed unsteadily, her heels clicking on the wet pavement. She hadn't had *that* many, had she?

Emily breathed deeply on the cool air, keeping her mind focused as she walked along the main road. *Stay close to the traffic*, her husband Alex had advised her – *never cut through back alleys, or across the common*. Despite her weariness she obeyed, avoiding the darker recesses as she made her way into Whitechapel. It wasn't a long walk, but the rain and her increasing fatigue made it more laborious than usual, and she was glad when she finally reached her front door, one in a row of small townhouses. Emily had been lucky – her late father had bought several homes in London, back in the 1960s when property had been cheaper, and four years previously she had inherited one of them in his will.

With some struggle Emily managed to unlock her front door, feeling as though she was sixteen again and suffering the after-effects of too much sangria, as she staggered inside and then locked the door behind her. With a sigh of relief, she slipped out of her coat and shoes and dumped them on the floor, too tired to bother putting them away. The house was dark, unsurprising given it was almost half past one in the morning – Alex would be long asleep.

She made her way up the stairs, swaying dangerously and leaning on the bannister for support. Jesus, this was really out of hand – Lucy had a lot to answer for. She made it to the top of the stairs, feeling as though every breath was becoming harder to make, but she was beside her bedroom now and she could see Alex asleep beneath the covers. Emily crept into the room, not wanting to wake him, then slid out of her dress and underwear in the darkness, one arm against the wall for support. She had never wanted to sleep so much in her life, and with a grateful sigh she slipped under the covers alongside Alex, felt the warmth of his naked body as she snuggled up against him and heard him shuffle about.

'Sorry, I didn't mean to wake you,' she murmured softly.

Beside her, Alex turned over, and in the dim light Emily saw the face of a complete stranger smiling back at her. She opened her mouth to scream but one large hand clamped over her jaw and she felt the man's large, naked body press against hers with immoveable force. Pinned beneath the sheets, her consciousness beginning to waver, she felt a rough hand slide up and down her naked body, caressing her gently as her world faded into blackness.

20

Honor walked into Bishopsgate at six-thirty in the morning, enshrouded within a suffocating bubble of anxiety. She had no idea how the team would look at her, whether they would mock her, ignore her or just not notice her at all. Danny had told her without any shadow of a doubt that they were all on her side, but her stomach was tumbling as she rode the elevator up to the second floor and walked into the Incident Room fourteen heart beats later.

Detectives were already hard at work behind their desks, and a few said "good morning" to her as she passed. Despite the horrible mauling she had endured at the hands of the press, there seemed little further reaction from them. She had been forced to watch the morning news before leaving, as much to update herself on the situation as anything else and, as expected, she was still the face of the investigation.

Slightly buoyed, she made her way to her desk.

'Got something here, boss.'

Danny was at his desk, hands burrowing into a pile of papers while he watched CCTV feeds on his monitor, clearly seeking evidence of their quarry's movements around the times of the killings. He looked like he'd been there since the early hours, his sleeves rolled up and his tie loosened, wearing the same shirt he'd had on the night before.

'Tell me it's good news,' Honor said.

Danny looked at her, saw the determination in her expression, and grinned. 'It's good news.'

Honor felt her heart lift a little more as she joined him at his desk and surveyed the paperwork he was amassing.

'Okay, this is what we've managed to pull on Gary Wheeler's extracurricular business enterprises,' he announced. 'There's nothing on paper, *per se*, because the labourers were all hired for cash and the contracts were under the carpet.'

'Cheap labour,' Honor agreed, knowing how many people liked to employ immigrants, legal or illegal, for rock-bottom wages and no-questions-asked. 'Most folks are happy to employ cash workers on their sites, keeps the paperwork down. Any links with our guy's movements?'

'No, nothing,' Danny said, 'but I've been able to make calls to the same numbers that Gary used, and those individuals were able to put faces to names on pretty much everybody that worked for Gary in the last couple of months on a cash-in-hand basis.'

'That's amazing,' Honor said, genuinely impressed. 'Anybody stand out?'

'They're surprisingly clean, only a couple of minor arrests between 'em. Looks like most are just labourers working the city. A few are contractors, moonlighting here and there for the extra cash, weekend work mostly. But that's not what I wanted to show you.'

Danny turned his screen to face her, and there she saw four images, each frozen still, all taken at night on grainy CCTV cameras, and all showing the same figure emerging from manhole covers in side streets. Large build, hooded top.

'The same guy from the pubs,' she said, no doubt in her mind. 'Is it the same guy seen entering Jayden Nixx's apartment?'

'Looks that way. He's even got the same hooded top on from one of the pub shots that Samir found,' Danny grinned in delighted reply, his eyes sparkling. 'Ain't no doubt about it - this is the bastard we've been looking for.'

Honor dragged a chair alongside Danny and sat down, peered at the image. He was a big guy, that much was obvious, and although the resolution was not sufficient to identify him, there was no doubt that he was Caucasian, at least six feet tall, maybe fourteen or fifteen stone. Age was impossible to tell, but there was no denying it – either he was about to become the unluckiest *"drainer"* of all time, or he was a serial killer with a penchant for phobia victims.

'Everywhere,' Honor said. 'The media, on posters, everywhere. I want to take this to the last pub he was seen in and question the bar staff. If we can get a decent description and a photofit, we could identify him by dinner time.'

'I'm on it.'

Honor looked up across the Incident Room. 'Where's Samir? I thought he was coming back in with you last night?'

'He didn't show. He's been working long hours on this one, probably got his head down for a bit.'

Honor nodded vacantly. Samir didn't seem the type to change his plans at the last moment without telling somebody. She pulled her mobile phone from her bag and rang Samir's number. The phone rang for a few moments, and then went straight to answerphone. She left a message and then shut the phone off. Danny was watching her with interest.

'No sign?' he asked.

'He's not answering. Any more gems to share with me, Sherlock?'

'I'm putting together his movements,' he replied. 'If I'm really lucky, this guy will walk home after one of the killings and I'll be able to track him all the way to his door. We know it's in Whitechapel or the surrounding areas, he's only got so many routes he can take.'

'I'll ask DI Harper to put more bodies on this,' Honor promised. 'And tell Samir to start on it too, as soon as he shows up.'

Honor made her way out of the Incident Room and down the corridor to the DI's office. Harper was at her desk as always, trays filled with forms and other paperwork as she looked up. There was an odd expression on her face, a mixture of both delight at seeing Honor and something that she couldn't place, the scars of a war going on behind the façade.

'Come in,' she said, waving Honor forward. 'Tell me you've made an arrest and he's confessed to everything on live television.'

Honor smiled. 'I wish. We have him on film using the sewers. It's not enough for a positive ID but Danny and the team are tracking him. It's only a matter of time.'

Harper nodded as she sat down opposite. Katy looked tired, which was a shock to Honor, as Harper seemed to have the energy of ten robust women. She realised that she had never once seen Katy falter since she'd joined the force, all those years before.

'How are you holding up after those bastards mauled you all night on TV?'

Katy was concerned for Honor, yet Honor could see that there was something she too was covering for. She wondered why she had never seen it before, why she had never noticed?

'I'm okay,' Honor replied, feeling oddly buoyant. 'You?' Harper stared at her, as though caught out. She blinked.

'All good. We need that footage out to the media right away. People can't climb in and out of a sewer without being noticed, somebody would have seen something.'

'He carries a fluorescent jacket about with him, and some tools,' Honor informed him. 'Most people probably barely notice what he's up to, but we'll have the networks informed within the hour. I want this arsehole in custody by tonight, or at least to know who the hell he is.'

'I'll inform the borough commander,' Harper said. 'I have a meeting at seven this morning, but I'm back by eight-thirty and can get a progress meeting organised for next steps. You think you can ID the suspect by then?'

'You give me enough people I can,' Honor replied. 'I'll head to one of the bars he was in, start trying for a photofit – that should speed things up a little.'

'Good.'

Harper sat for a moment in catatonic silence, staring not at her but past her as though she were momentarily no longer in the room. Honor hesitated. Sometimes it was better to walk away, to not provoke someone into sharing their feelings, but at other times that was just an excuse to not get involved.

'Are you okay?'

Harper blinked again, stared at her for a long moment. She opened her mouth as though to say something, but then swallowed it back.

'Rough night,' she said finally.

Her shoulders were sagging slightly, head bowed, as though the ramrod-straight back had suddenly withered and folded under the weight of some unseen burden.

'If you want to talk…,' Honor offered.

Harper hesitated. She could see there were a million words fighting for space, yearning to escape, but somehow unable to. Harper forged a glimmer of humour back onto her face. She looked as though she was chewing a wasp.

'I appreciate that, but you're the one who's just returned from leave due to stress, and now you have the press on your back.'

'I've been there,' Honor agreed. 'I know how it feels.'

Harper sat for a moment, catatonic, and suddenly her robust nature seemed fragile, the upstanding, stoic resilience a veneer for something else, a shield that she hid behind, as Honor did her columns of steel and ice. On impulse, Honor stood, realising that to confront Harper like this was making her feel uncomfortable, just as she had felt uncomfortable when Danny had so brazenly challenged her to look at herself.

'Just ask,' Honor said. 'Don't fight on alone, it's not necessary and it just makes things worse.'

Honor turned and headed for the door, thoughts immediately filling her mind of the killer she had to catch, *would* catch, and of her determination to never quit until she succeeded.

'My husband left me.'

The words reached her as though from far away, drifting on the wind. Honor stopped at the door, stared at it for a moment in the hopes that inspiration would strike her with perfect words. When nothing happened, she turned. DCI Harper was staring at her desk, her hands flat on the surface. Honor said nothing, waited for more.

'Just couldn't take any more,' she said. 'The long hours, the crimes, the misery of it all. Walked out two weeks ago. He said he felt as though he'd raised our family alone.'

Harper's voice cracked, raw with a volatile fusion of rage warring with grief, confusion clashing with frustration. She looked at Honor, devoid of understanding, pleading for enlightenment.

'It's me that has to suffer all the long hours, all the misery,' she said. 'Why am I to blame for it?'

Honor felt her own heart fracture within her as she saw this towering personality, a rock, the most stable person she had ever encountered, begin to crumble like ice calving from the face of a giant glacier. She held onto the door handle as though it would anchor her to reality.

'He doesn't understand,' Honor replied. 'You have to help him to see what it is that you do, what we all do. If he knew, if he could see it, he'd never leave you.'

Harper stared at her, as though she had not heard a word, frozen in time. Then she turned away, voice cracking with restraint.

'Report back when you have something concrete on our suspect.'

There was something in her tone that told Honor to get out of the office, to leave her be for a while. Honor, a master of wanting to be alone, recognised the condition when she saw it. She opened the office door, but then with unthinking reflex she looked over her shoulder at Harper.

'I've looked up to you ever since I became a detective,' she said. 'You're not alone, ever.'

Harper did not respond, sitting in absolute silence. Honor pulled the door shut, wondering briefly whether the pragmatically minded DI would put her affairs in order before opening her office window and hurling herself out of it. That thought then provoked another, about whether she should report the DI's mental health to the Health and Safety officer, before Katy did something she shouldn't. Already, Honor's OCD was running away with itself. Danny's calm advice drifted into her thoughts, and she swatted the paranoia aside.

Give it an hour, see what happens.

Honor felt pressure mounting on her shoulders again, the blissful light-footed arrival at work already a distant memory as she headed back to the Incident Room and began thinking about updating the CRIS database. She was halfway there when she heard the cry go out, and dread blackened her heart once more.

'We've got another one!'

Emily felt the cold first.

Slowly she felt herself coming awake, her senses reconnecting themselves in the darkness. Her skin was cold, goose bumps rippling on her arms, and she instinctively tried to pull them in to her body to warm up, but she could not move them.

With a force of will she opened her eyes and stared up at her bedroom ceiling. For a few moments, confusion reigned, her brain unable or unwilling to engage itself with her surroundings. She was at once both safe at home and yet aware of danger lingering on the fringes of her awareness. She felt cold again, and tried once more to pull her arms in.

They would not move.

Wearily, she turned her head to look at her right wrist, and saw that it was hand-cuffed to the bedpost above her head. She wondered whether Alex was teasing her with some kind of bizarre sex game or…

Alex. He had been here last night, but now he was nowhere to be seen, and there was a pungent scent on the air, as though somebody was cooking a fry-up from stale ingredients.

'Alex?'

Her voice was meek in her own ears, muffled. She wanted a drink of water but there was none by her bedside, which was odd because she always fetched a glass before bed and…

She had been drunk, exhausted, and she'd climbed into bed alongside…

Emily yelped in fear as she recalled the stranger waiting in her bed, the horror as he had smothered her. Adrenaline surged through her system and she tugged all of her limbs in an instinct to escape the room, but all were cuffed to the corners of the bed, the metal scraping painfully at her wrists and ankles. Emily sucked in huge breaths of air, past the gag that she realised was tied tightly around her head.

'Alex?!'

There was no response to her muffled cry, and as she pulled her head off the pillows to look at her body, so she smelled a strong odour of cooking oil. She coughed, staring at her skin and saw that it was plastered with a slick film of food waste. Emily's stomach turned over, not at the smell but in horror, for she could not understand what was happening and the confusion was as terrifying as anything that she had ever witnessed in her entire life.

Emily looked down the length of the bed to the bedroom door, to call again for her husband, and it was then that she saw it.

Her body was naked and smothered with thick layers of biological waste, as though somebody had basted her with the contents of their food recycling bin. An odour of decay filled the room and the cold touch of the food on her skin chilled her, but that was not what focused her attention. Between her legs was a canvass sack, and the sack was writhing as something alive moved within.

Emily's heart began to thump in her chest, her senses zipping back to her as fear clenched her heart in a cold grip and began to squeeze. Somehow, she already knew what was inside that sack, and the creeping horror that enveloped her was like something alive. Her breath began to whistle inside her throat as her oesophagus contracted, her eyes wide with terror as she stared at the writhing sack and heard multiple enraged squeals coming from within it. The bag was touching the soft skin on the inside of her thighs, pulsing with life entrapped within.

'Oh God, please, no.'

The bulging mass of life writhed, creatures fighting with each other, fighting to escape, and as Emily watched so she saw sections of the canvass sack begin to fray as tiny teeth and claws fought tore at it, driven by the scent of food.

'Alex!'

'Oh, for fuck's sake.'

Honor saw the monitor in the IR streaming live footage of a bedroom, a naked woman shackled to a bed, her body smeared with a slick of grimy food and oils. The camera was set up in such a way that the victim's head was out of shot. Between her legs was a writhing bag of who-the-hell-knew-what, obviously fighting to get out.

'Is this live?' Danny asked.

'Same as before,' came the reply from an IT tech' behind them. 'It's bouncing around servers; we're trying to track it down but it's all over YouTube and the Internet. We'll get it taken down as soon as we can.'

Honor stared in disbelief as she took in the scene. A modern bedroom, double bed, digital clock in one corner of the room, big window out of shot to one side where light was coming in, but the camera wasn't pointed at it to avoid revealing the location.

The location.

'Don't take the feed down.'

Honor said it without thinking, instinctively knowing that something was up, that something had changed.

'What? We can't leave it up there, the IPCC will have our heads!' Hansen snapped. 'This woman's naked and live all over the Internet!'

'She's going to be dead all over the Internet if we don't find out where she is,' Honor fired back, 'and the only people who might know are those who have seen that bedroom before. We need the public's support on this one, and I'm pretty damned sure that whoever that poor woman is, she'd agree with us. Wouldn't you?'

There was no argument from Hansen as Honor turned again to look at the footage. There was nothing much to reveal where the woman was, the camera mounted on the ceiling over the end of the bed and pointing down at it. A little of the carpet was visible, a little of the walls, and half of a bed-side cabinet to the victim's right-hand side, whereupon sat the digital clock. The time on it was just visible as being eight-fourteen in the morning, and a quick glance at her watch convinced Honor that this was both live and probably coming from the city.

'How long do you think she's got?' Honor asked. 'And what the hell is in that bag?' 'I'm guessing rats,' Danny replied.

Honor shook her head, appalled beyond words. There was every chance that the rats in the bag were starving, hence the food waste strewn all over the victim's body. The poor woman was going to be eaten alive, and Honor had no trouble in figuring out what her phobia was.

'Get on the *Face Fear* forum,' she ordered Danny. 'Contact everybody who has ever been on them who suffered from musophobia, and have them call us. Cross reference them with anybody who lives in Whitechapel, or the square mile.'

Danny hurried to his desk and picked up a phone with one hand while hen-pecking his keyboard with the other. Honor moved closer to the monitor, stunned at the creative malice of their suspect. This was something a step beyond even the other murders, the live-streaming of a woman being eaten alive. The killer was escalating, just as all serial killers did, but this guy was in a league of his own.

'The media's on to it,' came a call from across the office. 'The news stations are picking it up!'

'Make sure they blur out everything they damned well should!' Honor yelled back. 'But let them run with it. Somebody might recognise something.'

Honor turned and saw DI Harper enter the room, her back straight again and her eyes casting like a hawk's over a field, seeking prey. Honor she was struck again by how Harper's coping mechanism was much the same as her own, that even a woman like her was as vulnerable to anxiety as she was. Honor's grief and her suffering were not unique, were not something to be endured alone, for it seemed that everybody was suffering in their own way.

'Why has he changed his method and gone live straight away? There's been no call in.'

DCI Mitchell was staring at the screen now, watching the feed and the writhing bag lodged between the woman's legs.

Honor moved to stand alongside him. 'I hadn't thought of that. There's been no word from the woman's family, so they're not receiving this personally first.'

'That's what bothers me,' Mitchell said. 'He keeps changing his MO. I think you're wrong, Honor. I agree that this is a calculated campaign, but he's starting to reveal himself for what he really is. He's a coward, a man who likes nothing more than to revel in the suffering of others weaker than he is. He's getting off on this, and watching us squirm as we try to find these victims before they die.'

Honor nodded, staring at the screen as she thought for a moment.

'This isn't an elaborate set-up, and it's live, so he must know that we'll identify the woman and the location before long.'

'What makes you think that?' DI Harper asked. 'We can only see the bed; her face is covered.'

'Somebody must know her and recognise the bed, the sheets, perhaps even her body. He's risking too much, making it too easy for us. It's a distraction,' Honor said, letting the hunter's instinct run free within her. 'He's up to something else, and this is to keep us occupied while he goes about it.'

Now the rest of the MIT team were listening in, Danny included.

'We can't split resources, he knows that, so maybe he's playing on it,' he suggested, 'keeping us running and chasing our tails while he sets up something new, something bigger.'

Honor knew that they had to get ahead of this guy for once and for all, and DI Harper was clearly thinking the same thing.

'Bring MIT 3 off the Ismael Sheridan case and into the Incident Room, and call the MET and SO15, let them know we've got another one,' she ordered. 'We need bodies on the street and more hands to take calls. How long before this is on the main networks?'

'Minutes,' Danny replied. 'They'll be running the footage by ten o-clock.'

'Keep cross-referencing members of the *Face Fear* forum with females who have a fear of rats,' Honor said, and then added; 'And focus on addresses with east-facing bedrooms, the sun's coming through the window to her right, you can see the light moving.'

DCI Mitchell's eyes widened as he shot her a sideways glance. 'You keep surprising me like that, as much as you like.'

Honor felt her stomach plunge into a warm pool of bliss and somehow managed to smile and turn away from him before the colour rose in her cheeks and she flushed a vibrant shade of red. Danny didn't miss either the exchange or the high colour on her cheeks, but he said nothing as he averted his gaze back to his computer.

'Samir,' she said, suddenly remembering. 'Has he still not come in?'

21

Emily lay on her bed and pulled at the cuffs binding her to the bedposts, while trying to ignore the writhing sack of creatures propped between her legs. Whoever had put her there had been careful to make sure that the cuffs on her wrists were attached to a point where they could not simply be pulled over the top of the posts, a horizontal cross-member preventing them from moving. Her ankles, however, were restricted only by how far her legs were stretched, and they were stretched just about as far as they could be, with little room for manoeuvre.

Think! What would Alex do?

Alex. My God, where the hell *is* he? Did something happen to him? Why was he not here when she got home? Random thoughts fluttered through her mind, fears that he had run away with another woman, sent a man to kill her to take the inheritance he would get from their home. But they had been happy, hadn't they? They had only recently enjoyed a week in the Mediterranean, sangria and sun and sex and dozing on the beach. Everything had been fine.

The sack between her legs brushed against her inner thigh and she smelled the putrid odour of rotting food once more, was reminded that everything certainly wasn't bloody fine now. She could hear them, inside the bag, screeching, breathing, predatory bodies fighting to get out, to get to her. She felt herself shaking as the canvass sack surged toward her, as the animals within fought to reach the food just beyond their grasp. The sack touched her genitals as she felt tiny claws poking through the canvass.

'Shit, get off!'

Her voice was muffled behind the gag as she tried to pull herself further up the bed, but her legs were taut and there was no way she would be able to escape the horrible creatures within when they swarmed over her body, a gigantic feast upon which they would gorge themselves. An image flashed through her mind of police officers rushing into the room to find her deceased body, her skin long gone, rats burrowing into her corpse as they gorged on…

Emily stomped the image out of her mind as she tried to focus on how she could escape. Her heart was battering at the walls of her chest and her breath was coming in short gasps, sweat beading on her skin despite the cool room. She was going to die here, unless she managed to do something about it.

Fight back. That's what Alex would have done. What was it he always said? *I wasn't put on this earth to take shit from anyone.* The only way out of this was to face her fear, to conquer it. She had to push down the bed, to give her legs enough room to try to hook the ankle cuffs off the bedposts.

Emily took a few deep breaths, tried to control her panic as she prepared herself. Then, with every ounce of her will, she began extending her arms, pushing herself down the bed, shuffling along and pressing her most sensitive organ right up against the swarming bag of rats.

She cried out in horror, flinched away as the creatures within the bag went haywire, scrambling this way and that. Tiny claws gouged at her groin and thighs, lances of pain as the animals scratched her soft skin. Emily, her breath clawing at her throat, pushed again and shuffled down the bed. The sack was now pressed hard against her, and she was sure the animals within could smell her body, her skin, her organs, so close to them now. Their tiny claws scrambled in a frenzy but the canvas sack held as Emily pushed herself down the bed until her arms were now outstretched as far as they could go.

Emily immediately pulled back a little, getting herself clear of the sack and denying the animals within their chance to taste her. Her skin pulsed with little pinpricks of pain as she fought to control her breathing. Her heart actually ached within her, felt as though it was going to burst as she looked down. The sack was still between her thighs, but her legs were now bent a little at the knee.

With some effort, her limbs trembling, fear running like acid through her veins, Emily picked up her right leg and began trying to hook the other end of the cuff over the top of the bedpost.

'She's trying to get free.'

Danny spotted it first, saw what the woman was trying to do. Honor turned from her computer screen, where footage of their suspect was being fed to her as MIT detectives back-traced the man's movements from the *Hoop and Grapes* pub, trying to identify from where he had travelled.

Honor stood as she saw the trapped woman try to pull the ankle cuffs off the bedposts, and wondered how the poor girl must be feeling. Honor could see at once that freeing her legs wasn't going to save her, but it might give her enough movement to fight against the rats if they broke free.

The phones were ringing off the hook, calls from concerned citizens who had seen the footage and were sure that they knew who was strapped to the bed. The trouble was that the calls were coming in from all over the country, nobody having of course any idea *where* in the country the woman was being held.

'Anything solid yet on the calls?' she asked.

'We've got officers from multiple forces chasing their tails following up on them,' DCI Mitchell said from one of the desks, where he had commandeered a telephone and was helping out. 'It'll take days for them all to be checked out, and we know that Whitechapel is the only area of real interest – nothing so far from there.'

Other detectives and constables were also manning the phones, the public now their only real chance of getting to the mystery woman before she was eaten alive on television. Honor glanced across at Danny, who was holding a phone to one ear and using a mouse with the other. He caught the glance and shook his head, placing one hand over the receiver.

'Nothing on *Face Fear* yet, but we can't access all of the profiles, some people are better at hiding their data than others.'

Honor knew that they wouldn't have time to get a court injunction to allow access to user's private data, even in a life-and-death case such as this one, and there was nothing else that they could do but keep looking for the killer they sought and hope that somebody, somewhere, would see the footage and call in.

Honor glanced at the screen, and spotted something. 'She's got an ankle tattoo, right leg, outside!'

Her voice carried across the Incident Room as every detective looked up and saw what looked like an esoteric, flowery mural winding its way from the woman's ankle up to the lower calf. The angle of the camera on her body had denied them that knowledge until she had started trying to free her leg.

DCI Mitchell shut off his current conversation on the phone and immediately began dialling news networks to inform them of the new information. Honor got out of her seat and began pacing back and forth, primal fight-or-flight energy firing through her synapses. This was the worst part - the anticipation, the chase, the desire to locate and free the victim. It consumed a detective's being, the rest of the world blurring into the distance like a hunter seeking its prey.

Honor realised in that moment that this was precisely how their killer felt, but for the entirely opposite reason: *anticipating* the kill, the pain, the bloodshed. Yet, this was the opposite of the path that his previous abductions had taken – there had been no blood, no gore. Honor was struck by a realisation so terrible that she could barely bring herself to confront it.

'He's reacting to what I said.'

A few heads looked up at her, Danny Green's one of them. 'What?'

Honor swallowed, her throat thick with loathing. 'I said that he wasn't a slasher- killer like the Ripper, that he didn't do blood.'

Danny glanced at the screen, got it immediately. 'It's not on you. He's working with phobias, that hasn't changed. He had this one planned long before we showed up.'

Honor shook her head slowly.

'That's not what I mean. I know it's not on me, but he's changed his plans because of what I said, I'm sure of it.'

Danny opened his mouth to answer, but a female constable's trembling voice broke in before he could say anything.

'Oh Jesus, the bag's opening.'

Emily turned her ankle this way and that as she tried to unhook the cuff from the bedpost. She'd managed to shuffle it to the top, but it was catching there and she couldn't quite free it. Her thigh ached with the effort of keeping her leg in the air, her vision starring as a volatile toxic of fear, nausea and adrenaline surged through her body. The canvas sack tumbled and shifted just inches from her, and she sensed a new and terrible odour coming from within.

Blood.

The animals were fighting, tearing at each other's bodies as they tried to escape. The knowledge that these animals were cannibalising each other sent a fresh wave of loathsome terror through her and she fought again to release the handcuff from the bedpost. The light coming through the bedroom window was brighter now, and she could hear cars driving past on the road outside. She tried to scream through the gag, but her voice was muffled sufficiently that nobody would be able to hear her, even though the bedroom window was open.

Emily let her leg rest for a moment, her ankle hanging painfully as she caught her breath for another try.

And then the sack ripped a little. A twitching nose and sharp little white teeth poked through, tiny claws ripping and tearing in a frenzy at the opening.

Panic pulsed like lightning through Emily's spine and she frantically lifted her leg again and began unhooking the cuff. She had no idea what she was going to do with her legs when the sack finally tore open, but she was sure as fucking hell she'd be better off with them freed. *Kick the sack off the bed.* Deny the little bastards their breakfast and put one in the eye of the sadistic bastard who had put her here.

Emily shoved herself as far down the bed as was humanly possible, her groin bumping against the writhing sack to a squealing crescendo from the contents, and she ignored the pain of their claws as she unhooked her right leg and the metal cuff slipped over the bedpost and her leg broke free.

Emily screamed around her gag as the canvas sack began to split and tear. Raw terror poisoned her veins as she saw dozens of rats swarming within, their fur dirty, smeared with something that smelled like sewage, their bodies emaciated, blood streaming from open wounds and staining white teeth.

The opening widened and one of the creatures poked its head out, black eyes staring at her as it fought to escape from the ragged hole. Three more tried to scramble free at the same time, blocking each other's progress.

Emily screamed, swung her right foot down and shoved it under the roiling sack. With a heave of effort, she pushed the sack over her left leg and then kicked hard. The glistening black bodies of the first rats poked out of the sack and then the whole thing slid off the side of the bed and thumped to the floor.

Emily pushed herself down the bed and lifted her left leg, was able to unhook the other cuff as she heard rats scurrying *en masse* from the sack, swarming across the room. The sheets were on the bedroom floor, bundled out of sight of the camera, so the rats could not climb up them to reach the bed, but she felt certain that if she didn't somehow free herself, it would be but moments before they found a way to her.

A noise to her right caught her attention and she turned in time to see a rat the size of a small cat as it scrambled up the curtains nearby and onto the windowsill. Her heart rattled dangerously as she saw the creature turn, sniffing the air, and then it pivoted around, its tail stiff to balance itself as it turned to look straight at her.

Another joined it, and then they were climbing the bedside table on the other side of the bed, scrambling up the front of it, their claws using the gaps between draws to haul themselves up with hellish speed.

Emily squirmed against her handcuffs, fighting in the hopes that she could slip her slim wrists through them before the rats made it to the bed, but the cuffs were tight and there was no time to break free.

The rat on the windowsill coiled itself and then leaped into the air to land with a thump on the bed beside Emily. Emily screamed and rolled over to crush the rat beneath her weight before it could bite into her. Another jumped and landed this time on her belly, razor sharp claws plunging into her flesh with pangs of fearsome white pain. Emily screamed and rolled away in time to pin two more rats beneath her back as others flooded onto the bed and then they overwhelmed her, a dirty black flood of fur and claws pouring across her body.

Emily screamed at the top of her lungs through her gag as she writhed and fought for her life, teeth and claws tearing into the food on her body and with it, her flesh and blood.

Honor stared, stricken with horror, at the screen as she saw at least twenty large rats swarm onto the woman's bed and begin devouring her. The phones were ringing all around in the Incident Room but it was as though she could not hear them, her entire being focused on the poor woman now suffering such a hellish demise and…

'We've got her!' Katy Harper shouted. 'Newark Street, Whitechapel! The mother's called it in! Her name's Emily!'

'Despatch all available units!' DCI Mitchell yelled as he grabbed his jacket. 'McVey, with me! Green, you too! Where the bloody hell is Raaya?'

Honor grabbed her bag as the three of them rushed from the Incident Room and ran down the stairwells to the street outside. This time there would be no sprint to Whitechapel, as a CID car was waiting for them outside the station for just this purpose. Mitchell got into the driver's seat, Honor beside him and Green in the back as Mitchell started the engine, switched on the "blues" and promptly hit the accelerator.

The CID car lurched out into the street, traffic parting before them as Mitchell slammed the car through the gears and thundered south toward the water. Within two minutes they were east-bound on Aldgate and into Whitechapel, joined by a screaming procession of ambulances and patrol cars all converging on Newark Street.

'We've got the number,' Honor said as she consulted the car's internal computer screen. 'Paramedics are on their way, uniforms are already breaking in, it's an upstairs flat.'

Mitchell did not respond, his eyes fixed on the road as they pulled hard right into Newark Street. Narrow, rows of old Victorian three-stories, built from the same bricks the Ripper would have seen as he stalked their confines. Two ambulances blocked the street along with three patrol cars as Mitchell screeched to a halt and the three of them tumbled out and ran to the front door, where four uniformed constables were waiting.

'Is she alive?'

Honor's voice was twisted up, high-pitched, filled with far more passion than she would have thought possible, as though she herself were strapped to the bed.

'I don't know,' came the officer's reply, 'the paramedics are up there and…'

Honor barged past him and tore into the flats, rushed up the stairs with DCI Mitchell and Danny right behind her. She turned onto the third-floor landing to see one of the apartment doors busted open, a "big red key" leaning against the wall outside, the police officer's affectionate name for a heavy, hand-held battering ram. Honor hurried to the doorway and immediately saw a rat looking up at her, its nose twitching and its black eyes sparkling. Though she knew the animal was blameless, she drove her heel down onto its neck and heard its spine snap like a dry twig as she stormed into the bedroom and saw the room littered with rat corpses, officers stamping on them as two paramedics fought to save Emily's life.

'Clear!'

Honor heard a familiar whine as a defibrillator wound up, and to her horror she saw Emily laying on her back, naked, her body smothered in red claw marks, bites and streams of dark blood that ran like tiger stripes down her flanks. Her eyes were open, one looking up at the ceiling, the other staring sideways, her tongue hanging limp from her mouth.

The charge hit her body and Emily surged, arms still cuffed to the bedposts. The paramedics plunged back to her body.

'Nothing,' one of them said.

'Hit her again!' Honor snapped.

It wasn't her place to tell them what to do, and the dirty look she got from the paramedics told her so. The defibrillator charged again, Honor watching and willing and hoping and trying not to let the black chasm of defeat swell up again within her.

'Clear!'

The charge hit Emily's bloodied corpse and she jerked again, but this time she suddenly sucked in a surge of air that whistled through her throat as her eyes flew wide and regained ocular unity.

'Christ,' Honor uttered in relief, one hand slapping against the wall for support. Danny gripped her shoulder with one hand for a moment.

'Now we've got you, you bastard,' he uttered as he watched Emily recover consciousness.

Emily's gasps for breath were replaced with a terrific shriek of terror and pain that rose up like a demon screaming to escape the room. The paramedics swarmed over her as she began to thrash, tearing at the handcuffs still holding her in place as blood began to stream from the countless, deep wounds torn into her body.

'You're okay, it's over, you're safe.'

The paramedics held her down while Honor watched, until one of them could get a needle into her. A uniformed officer produced a key to unlock the cuffs, and moments later the paramedics gently lifted Emily's writhing form onto a gurney.

'When can we talk to her?' Honor asked. 'She may know who did this.'

'When we say so,' the paramedic snapped. 'She's suffered a cardiac arrest from what just happened to her, so she's gonna need some time, don't you think?'

Honor watched them carry Emily from the room, their boots crunching down on the bodies of rats that had been stomped left, right and centre, their corpses littering a carpet stained with their blood. Honor followed them out of the room and through the hall and was about to head for the stairwell when she noticed that the kitchen door was closed. She exchanged a glance with Danny, who walked across and shoved it open.

The room was a galley kitchen, long and narrow, with a small radiator at the far end beneath a window. Handcuffed and bound to it was an unconscious man, perhaps thirty years old, blood from a headwound caking his face, his eyes swollen and bruised.

'We've got another one in here!'

22

Bleach. Disinfectant. Cleaning fluids.

Honor had always hated the scent of hospitals, and the Royal London Hospital in Whitechapel was no different. Ironically, the odour of such cleanliness reminded her of nothing but sickness, the domain of the terminally ill.

She sat with Danny in a waiting room, where they had spent the past two hours waiting for the chance to speak with Emily and Alex Wilson. With them was a digital composite artist with a laptop computer, the hope being that they would be able to construct a definitive likeness of the man responsible for the attempted murder of Emily. All three of them were munching down sandwiches bought from a deli around the corner, likewise all three of them using their mobile phones to stay in contact with the Incident Room.

Under police instructions, Emily and Alex were being held in private wards with no members of the press allowed: the last thing that Honor wanted now was information reaching their suspect that might give him the chance to escape before he could be apprehended. Honor was certain that he intended to disappear when this was all over, that he wanted to spend the rest of his life basking in the infamy and mystery that would surround his gruesome crimes for decades to come.

'They're ready.'

Danny, Honor and the artist stood up as a nurse beckoned them to follow her into a private ward. The private wards each had a single bed, but one of them had been refitted to contain two, Alex and his wife being treated together by two nurses. One of them, a stocky woman with a stern expression and keen eyes, saw Honor and Danny arrive and hurried to the door.

'They're both out of intensive care but they've endured a terrible ordeal, especially the wife,' she reported in a soft voice, low enough that the patients behind her could not hear. 'Emily suffered a cardiac arrest as a result of what she went through, and she was lucky the paramedics were able to revive her before she suffered permanent brain damage. Her husband, Alex, is suffering from severe concussion after a blow to the head which almost fractured his skull. They would appreciate *gentle* questioning.'

Both Honor and Danny nodded as the nurse stood back and allowed them into the room.

Emily and Alex were on saline drips, Emily wearing an oxygen mask, her eyes sunk into deep, bruised pits. Honor glanced at the countless injuries she had suffered and had to force herself to breathe normally. The rats had taken chunks out of thirty per cent of her body before City Police had crashed through her door, and now she was covered in a patchwork of medical dressings. The nurse was treating a particularly deep and nasty wound where it looked as though a rat, or rats, had actually started burrowing into her body as they ate.

'Hi Emily,' Honor said, forcing a gentle smile onto her lips that made her jaw ache. 'How are you holding up?'

Emily looked at her with eyes flat and dark, as though the life was still sucked from them, a reluctantly beating heart trapped within an unwilling body.

'I'm alive,' was all that she gasped.

'I'm Detective Sergeant Honor McVey, this is Detective Constable Danny Green,' Honor said as she showed Emily her warrant card. 'We're detectives with the City of London police. Can we ask you a few questions?'

Emily nodded. Beside her, Alex nodded also, the movement clearly causing him great discomfort.

'Did either of you see your attacker?' Honor asked.

For a moment neither of the Wilsons moved, but then both nodded and a surge of hope lifted Honor's heart.

'Did you recognise him?'

Alex nodded slowly, his eyes closed, presumably due to sensitivity to the light, and then Emily also nodded.

'Where from?' Danny Green asked. 'Do you know his name?' Emily spoke softly, her voice feeble.

'No, he's in the pub sometimes. He used to look at me a bit, I thought that he fancied me or something, but he was never any bother.'

'Would you recognise him if we were to build a photo-fit of him?' Honor asked, and was rewarded with a nod from Emily.

'I'd fucking recognise him,' Alex uttered, squeezing his eyes shut as he did so. His voice was tight with pain but also anger. 'He came to the door, asked if we'd lost a ginger cat he'd found outside the apartments. I said no, we don't own a cat, but then he jumped forward, got his foot behind my ankle and pushed me over. I fell onto my back, and as I came up, he whacked me with something and that was it, game over.' Alex opened his eyes, squinting. 'But his hood came off, I saw him clear as day.'

Honor felt excitement rising within her.

'We have a computer with a database of faces that we can use to build a likeness of your attacker,' she said. 'We believe that this man is the same individual responsible for a string of murders over the past few days. Can you help us to identify him, and bring this all to an end?'

There was no hesitation – both Alex and Emily nodded, a tiny spark of light flickering angrily back into life in Emily's eyes. Danny turned and waved their fellow officer through, who came to sit between the two patients with his laptop. As he prepared to start, Emily pulled out a couple of images of the man in the pubs that they had captured on CCTV, along with more of him emerging from manholes near the crime scenes.

'Could you both take a look at these and see if anything looks familiar?' she asked. Emily and Alex both looked at the images, and Alex nodded first.

'Oh yeah,' he snarled, 'that's him, that's the guy. The build, the hoody, everything fits.'

Emily frowned uncertainly. 'I don't know, I only really remember his face, but it does look a bit like him. He always had a hoodie on when I saw him in our local pub.'

Honor took back the images.

'We'll be in touch with both of you, and I'm sorry that we couldn't get to you sooner. We did our best.'

Emily looked up at her.

'This isn't on you,' she croaked. 'Please just find that bastard, so I can spend the rest of my life watching him rot in prison.'

Honor turned with Danny and walked out of the private room. As they set off down the corridor outside there was an urgent spring in her step.

'This is it,' she said. 'If we're lucky, he won't have time to pull off another attack.' Danny nodded, but was more cautious.

'He'll be pissed if you're right about him,' he warned. 'That's another failure, one that will end with him being identified. He's going to want to flee, to hide.'

Honor didn't give a damn where he ran to.

'It doesn't matter, once we know who he is, he could go and live on the other side of the world and we'd find him eventually. This is where it ends, Danny. He's running out of time.'

There was nothing that he could say.

He sat in front of the television, watching as the news channels reported on the last-second City Police rescue of Emily Wilson from her home on Newark Street, Whitechapel. News crews were all over the property, held at bay by police cordons as forensics teams swarmed the home, seeking evidence with which to track him down.

They had contaminated the moment. He had seen her die, seen her gasp her last as rats swarmed over and into her defenceless body. She had writhed in agony as the famished rats began to devour her, and then she had gone into a rictus of a kind he had never seen before; eyes wide, mouth agape, features twisted with a new, fascinating kind of pain, just before the light in her eyes had dwindled out like a dying star. The moment had been beautiful, precious, but it had been stained with the sudden appearance of the police and the paramedics, who had rushed in and revived Emily less than a minute later, as he had lain, sated and sweating, on his bed.

And there was the blood. He could not get the blood out of his head. The rats' feeding frenzy had been shockingly gory and the moment had been contaminated by it, spoilt, ruined. *It just wasn't the same.* His hand had been forced and now his campaign was being derailed, his grand design mutated by the police, by Detective Sergeant Honor bloody McVey.

Now, he sat naked and watched the news for a moment longer. He had killed the live feed the moment the police had appeared on the footage of Emily's room, denying them the chance to identify his location, but that was not what he now feared the most. *Emily Wilson was alive.* He had seen her, and she had seen him. She could describe him, perhaps even identify him. It wasn't impossible. The police would put together an identikit or whatever they were called these days, and that would jog the memories of bar staff and other people who would have seen him moving around the city. The husband had also seen him when his hood had slipped free. He had hit him hard with the bat, thought that he would be dead, but he too had somehow survived.

His image would be on every television channel within hours, which left him with very little time to complete his task. Five canonical victims: Sebastian Dukas, Amber Carson and Jayden Nixx were all deceased by his hand. That still left two more to go, with both Emily Wilson and her husband now recovering from their wounds. There would have been five by now, if they'd had the decency to just die and be done with it. He could have stopped, could have finished, could have melted away into history and revelled in the legend that he had created. Now, he was facing exposure and perhaps, though he could not bear to contemplate it, arrest. The only saving-grace was that the use of Emily Wilson's ordeal had given him the distraction he needed to move freely through the city: the police were undermanned, overworked and their resources always stretched to breaking point. All he had needed was to dangle the right kind of carrot in front of them, and then make his move.

He looked at the news feeds replaying the recent footage of the rescue, watched Detective Sergeant Honor McVey arrive at the crime scene in dramatic style, an un- marked police vehicle screeching to a halt and detectives tumbling out. He had heard their sirens from his own living room, and had briefly rejoiced in the knowledge that they were surely too late.

He sat in catatonic silence for a few moments more, contemplating his next move. He had made plans, of course, quite extensive plans both to cover his escape and to obscure his guilt of any crime. But now he still had two more kills to make.

He stood, cleaned himself up and dressed, then walked downstairs and opened the basement door. A waft of putrefaction from his father's rotting remains stained the air. He made his way down the steps and looked at the bed, whereupon lay his next victims, bound and naked next to each other, terror in their eyes. For them, the best would be saved to last. These two *had* to count, for if everything worked out as he had planned, he would vanish into obscurity and nobody would ever know quite how he had done it.

'Your time has come,' he said to them with a smile.

*

'Are you sure about this?'

DI Harper sat behind her desk and watched DS Colin Hansen closely.

'I don't like it, and I didn't want to bring it up, but it seems obvious. The suspect could have been right under our noses the entire time.' Hansen sighed theatrically. 'Samir Raaya has not been seen for over twelve hours. He's been privy to every inch of the investigation. He's not answering his mobile phone and he's not answering his front door.'

'You've been there?' Harper asked.

'I'm beginning to fear for his safety,' Hansen replied. 'The guy isn't showing up and he hasn't called in, and Honor's so busy chasing the suspect that I fear she's lost touch with the obvious – Samir Raaya is perfectly placed to *be* that suspect.'

DI Harper sat for a moment longer, thinking about it. Samir Raaya was one of the new direct-entrant detectives, part of an initiative to bring new bodies onto the job. The entire MET and City Police forces had suffered terrible manpower attrition due to politicians more concerned with money than public safety. As far as she could recall, Samir had been an electrician before that, marking him out as somebody with the potential skills to have orchestrated the campaign – the CRIS database was littered with evidence of technical skills possessed by whoever was behind the murders.

'He's also perfectly placed to become a victim,' Harper countered. 'His face has been all over the news the past couple of days.'

'Most of the victims have been female.'

'Most, not all. If the killer wanted to get at Honor, it would be the perfect way to do it, abduct a colleague.'

Hansen surprised her, thinking about that deeply for a moment.

'Leverage,' he suggested, 'it could be enough to force Honor into doing something rash. She's not been herself, not since she was off sick with stress. This case is getting to her, you and I can both see that. The longer this drags on, she's going to become more of a liability than an asset, and we both saw how things went down at the press briefing. She folded right there and then. If Samir's become a victim, or a suspect…'

Harper didn't let Hansen ride high for long. 'She's the best detective we have.'

Hansen's skin coloured slightly, but he kept his cool. 'All the better to look after her, right?'

Harper contemplated her options, but now that Hansen's suspicions had been raised, she could hardly ignore them. If the remote possibility came to be that Samir Raaya, a City detective, was in fact behind the killings, and she had failed to act on the suspicions of another of her detectives…

'Okay, we raid on the pretence of officer safety, not that he's a suspect.'

'Understood,' Hansen replied, getting up out of the seat and hurrying for the office door.

'Hansen,' Harper said as he reached the door, 'this works both ways. If Samir is in fact a victim, and we lose valuable time chasing our tails here…'

Hansen hesitated for a moment.

'If he's a victim, he's going to want us out there looking for him. I know I would.'

'This is bullshit.'

Honor could not conceal her contempt as she fumed alongside Danny. The call had come in a moment ago, directing them to Samir Raaya's home.

'It is what it is,' Green said. 'Hansen's made his play. We'll follow the forced entry team and see what there is to find.'

Danny drove as they headed to Meath Road in Ilford, where Samir owned a one-bedroom flat on a street of terraced houses, most of which had long ago been converted. The forced-entry team were already waiting for them in an adjoining street when they arrived, keeping out of sight of the apartment before the strike.

Honor got out of the car in time to see DC Hansen directing the forced-entry team assembled on the pavement.

'The owner of the apartment could be the suspect or they could themselves be a victim, we just don't know yet. The suspect, whoever they are, is cunning and may have anticipated this move, so be on your toes. We don't know what we'll find when we go in there, so be prepared for anything, and that includes booby traps or weapons.'

Hansen turned as she approached, and raised a placatory hand.

'I know what you're thinking, but Samir's absence is out of character and highly suspicious.'

Honor fumed, her fists clenched by her side, Green standing alongside her as though poised to stop her from swinging for Hansen.

'This playing of games has to stop,' she uttered. 'We don't have time for it.'

'It's called police work,' Hansen snapped. 'DI Harper signed off on it, and we've got uniforms backing us up. Do you want to waste any more time or shall we get on with it?'

The entry team, fully kitted with helmets, defensive pads, body-armour and face shields, set off down the street at a jog and reached Samir's apartment within thirty seconds. Honor followed behind, desperate to intervene if Samir was found at home and for some reason had simply not been able to make it into work. She tried not to think about the worst possible scenario, one in which the killer had decided to extinguish Samir's life in revenge for his own murders being derailed by either his victims' struggles for life or, now, the police intervening at the last moment.

The police team rushed up the side alley of a small two-storey, and with several swings of the "big red key" and the sound of shattering PVC and glass, the door was smashed in and the team piled into Samir's apartment. Honor and Danny held back outside as the officers stormed through the apartment to repeated calls of *"Clear"*. A moment later, one of them poked his head out of the shattered door and waved them inside. The entire operation had taken less than thirty seconds.

Honor stepped through the debris of the shattered door and saw Samir's apartment, a simple affair, cheap sofas in a living room that looked through a bay window over parking spaces. A flat-screen television dominated the room, a couple of pictures of Samir's sister and family at a wedding, a newspaper left on the coffee table in the centre of the room alongside a games console.

'He's not here,' DC Hansen said. 'We're checking the communal garden, but we found this on the door mat.'

The officer held up two unopened letters. Honor took them from him. One was just a junk flier for a local tandoori restaurant, but the other was a utility bill.

'He's not been here for a while,' she said to Danny.

'He might have anticipated *us* being here,' Hansen countered.

There was nothing that she could say in reply. Moments later, they were called into the bedroom. Hansen walked in first, with Honor and Green behind him, and they all stopped as they saw a large wipe-board on the wall in front of a narrow desk. On the board, which was one laid out in a similar style to the one back at the Incident Room, were the names of some of the victims, plus further names that they had not encountered before, and several trinkets that Honor carefully approached. On the desk were a number of watches, rings and other belongings.

'What's the betting these belonged to the victims?' Hansen beamed, folding his arms across his chest.

'Wow,' Danny uttered. 'You got there fast, genius.'

'Yeah,' Honor replied. 'Very neat, don't you think? *Too* neat.'

'Done in a hurry,' Danny agreed. 'Most of that writing up there is fresh, but the dates look as though they're designed to make us think it's the result of months of work.'

'Oh, come on,' Hansen uttered. 'How close to the bottom of the barrel do you two want to get before you'll admit that there's something going on here?'

'It's called police work,' Honor replied with a smile that conveyed no warmth.

Honor tried to think as the entry team clattered their way out of the building. Samir's apartment was filled with evidence of him being the person they sought, and yet it was just as clear that he wasn't the culprit. Or was it?

'He could have arranged it this way on purpose, knowing it would make us think that he's a victim,' she said, hating her own words. 'Hansen could be right. It could be Samir, and he's playing us.'

Danny nodded, deep in thought as he stared at the board before them. 'There are a lot of names there we've never heard of.'

'I know,' Honor replied as she looked around, careful not to touch anything. She noted that the bed was perfectly made, untouched. 'If this is the work of our guy, whoever he is, he could have been at this for years.'

'Until he decided to escalate and go public,' Danny agreed, his hands in his pockets as he surveyed the room. He leaned down and looked along the length of the desk. 'Very fine layer of dust, undisturbed. Nobody's been here for a day or so.'

'And Samir vanished right after the Jayden Nixx drowning,' Hansen pointed out. 'Who was the last person to see him?'

Honor swallowed thickly. 'We were. He came with Danny to my apartment; we had a takeaway. Rough day and all that. He left about eleven, said he was going to get his head down then head back into the office.'

'Where he never showed,' Danny said. 'Last I saw of him was walking away from Honor's apartment toward Waterloo.'

'Samir's been missing over twenty-four hours,' Honor agreed. 'Either he's our guy and he's running, or he's been abducted himself. His face was on the news, same as mine.'

Danny looked at her, and although she knew what was coming, she didn't like it one bit.

'You're off this one, Honor, DI Harper won't let you run the case now that Samir might be involved,' he said. 'There's every chance that he'll come for you next, whoever's behind all this. Do we know if Samir has any phobias?'

Honor shook her head. 'He never mentioned any, but the campaign has changed. The killer can't use the sewers again, everybody knows that's been his MO until now. He's on the run or otherwise deceiving us, misdirecting us. If I leave the case now, he'll know about it, it's the last thing we should do.'

'DCI won't see it that way,' Hansen said. 'Mitchell won't want you in harm's way until this case is in the bag.'

'That'll take the heat off,' Honor argued. 'It'll take somebody else time to get up to speed on this guy. Trust me, the suspect is planning his escape – he wants to vanish into history, just like the Ripper. When we get that photofit, everything's gonna change.'

Danny was about to reply when Honor's phone rang and she answered it, seeing DI Harper's name on the screen as she switched it to conference.

'Honor McVey, Detective Sergeant, Danny and Colin are here.' 'You'd better get back here,' Harper said, her voice sombre. 'What's happened?'

'Can't talk about it on the phone, Honor,' Katy said, her tone setting Honor's neurons racing with anticipation and dread. 'There's been another abduction, but you're going to have to come back to the station to hear about it. Bring Hansen and Green with you, this one's urgent.'

23

Honor felt a growing sense of dread burgeoning within her as she joined Danny and Colin and headed back to Danny's car. They were back at Bishopsgate within thirty minutes, Danny and Hansen alongside her as they headed up to the IR. DCI Mitchell had obviously been informed of their arrival, because he came out of his office and blocked their way.

'I'm afraid that you can't go in the IR, Honor,' he said.

'I know what you're thinking,' Honor replied, 'that Samir Raaya is a colleague and that I can't be on the same case if he's under investigation. It won't affect my job, boss, I…'

'It's not about Samir.'

Honor's oratory came up short and she stared at the DCI for a long beat. There was genuine concern on his features, and a terrible fear rushed like poison through Honor's veins.

'My parents?'

'They're okay,' Mitchell replied. 'There's been another abduction, and the family are asking for you directly to talk to them about it. They're in the custody suite.'

'They're asking for me?' Honor repeated, dread coiling like a venomous snake in her belly. 'Why? Who's been abducted?'

DCI Mitchell pulled her to one side in the corridor and spoke quietly.

'A woman named Natalie Delray, fiancé to a Zach Arnold. I'm told that you know him.'

Honor's heart seemed to stop beating in her chest, and every last girder and glacier of steel and ice within her collapsed into a smouldering heap in the darkness that swelled in her chest. Those names. *Them.* Delray, and Arnold. People she hated with a passion that was difficult to describe, let alone control.

'Delray,' she managed to utter. '*She's* the next victim?'

'We think so,' Mitchell said. 'Whatever the suspect is up to, whoever they are, this just got personal, Honor. The family wants to talk to you, I accept that, but Detective Constable Hanson will run the case from here, with Danny in support. I don't want you on this for obvious reasons, okay?'

Honor nodded without even thinking about it. Jesus. Delray.

'They're in suite four,' Mitchell added. 'Danny, go with her, if you will?' 'I'll be fine,' Honor said, too quickly. She sucked in a ragged breath.

'Go with her,' Mitchell repeated to Danny. 'Hansen, the IR, get up to speed and be ready for a briefing in thirty minutes.'

'Yes, boss.'

Hansen turned for the IR without a word and left them in the corridor. Before she could change her mind, Honor walked down to the custody suite, her mind numb, her legs seemingly carrying her of their own accord as she and Danny were met by a FLO and escorted to the suite.

'You sure about this?' Danny asked as they walked. 'I can interview the family.'

'No,' Honor replied, unsure of why she couldn't just let Danny go in there. 'I can deal with this.'

The door to the suite was open, and despite her not wanting to turn into the room, like a nightmare that refused to stop unravelling she followed the FLO inside and was greeted with the first sight of her ex-husband in almost twelve months.

Zach Arnold sat on a chair alongside his mother, an elderly but formidable woman by the name of Rosemary. Zach looked pensive, stubble on his jaw, black hair in disarray, eyes clouded behind thin spectacles. Rosemary looked concerned but in control, holding her son's hand. On Zach's other side were the parents of Natalie Delray, Stephen and Alison, whom she had never met. To see them here, like this, was so utterly bizarre that Honor stood in catatonic silence as the FLO introduced her.

'This is Detective Sergeant Honor McVey, she's in charge of the investigation.' Normally, this would be where Honor would try to be warm and greet the bereaved, the suffering, the lost or the confused, try to get to the bottom of whatever horrendous crime they had endured, but now she simply stood and stared. Her colour flushed up and she missed a breath, tried to get some sense of control back in her mind. *Get your focus on solving the problem. Don't distract yourself, distraction doesn't bloody work. Confront the issue.*

Honor turned and sat down on the nearest available chair, more for something else to do other than stand staring at them. Rosemary Arnold sensed Honor's discomfort and reached out, one hand touching her forearm.

'We're so sorry, for all that's happened.'

She meant it. Rosemary's eyes were filled with the same discomfort that swam deeply in Honor's. She wanted to accept the apology –what had happened was hardly Rosemary's fault, but Honor sank back into her seat a little and managed a fleeting smile as she introduced Danny Green.

'Can you tell me what happened in the hours leading up to Natalie's disappearance?'

Honor kept her voice even and her expression neutral, not looking at her ex-husband. *Don't give the cheating bastard the satisfaction of seeing you squirm.* Her frayed nerves hardened and she began to feel more in control as she surveyed the family. Zach was now sitting with his hands folded between his knees, moving them constantly. A silver band adorned his ring finger, different to the ring he'd worn when he was engaged to Honor. He seemed unable to meet her gaze as he spoke, looked as uncomfortable as she was.

'She disappeared this morning, somewhere between work and home. She always calls when she gets into work. When she didn't, I called her mobile but she'd switched it off. I called the office, but she never showed up.'

She'd switched it off. How would he know? Could he have done something, or did he know nothing and simply assume that she was the one who'd turned the phone off? Could go either way, but despite being a duplicitous bastard, she'd never have pegged Zach for a killer - he just wasn't the type.

'Do you know where she was last seen?'

Zach shrugged. 'By me, I suppose, before she left home this morning.'

Honor made some notes as she asked him what route Natalie took, on what transport, rough ideas of times. It wouldn't be hard for MIT to track down her movements and identify where she had been abducted, but whether they would be able to tie in their suspect to the attack and whether he would be identified by then were unknowns. The fact that Samir was now on the suspect list made her shiver inwardly – he knew about what had happened to Honor the previous year, about the affair, about how her husband had ended up sleeping with Natalie for God-knows-how-long before he'd been caught out, before he had lost her their…

Honor briefly closed her eyes and tried to keep her thoughts on track.

'You called the Major Incident Team at this office with the news of the abduction,' she said. 'Why?'

Zach spoke, his voice soft, meek even.

'We got an e-mail,' he said, and handed her a piece of paper which had clearly been printed from a computer.

Honor took the paper, careful to ensure her hand did not come into contact with Zach's as she looked down at it. The page was a standard Internet page, a private e-mail account belonging to Zach, and in the centre was a message from an e-mail address that belonged to Natalie;

You've seen the killings in Whitechapel. Natalie is next.

Honor stared at the message for a moment longer than was necessary, partially to conceal her own emotions, and partially because she was surprised. This was another break from method for their suspect, another pivot. This was possibly a copy-cat attack, unrelated to the string of murders they were investigating, although the choice of target was of course far too great a coincidence. Samir knew about the cognitive behavioural therapy, about the OCD, about the affair and the loss of her child, about pretty much everything. He also knew how much she valued her privacy, how much effort she made to keep her home life separate from her work life – that would all be shattered by the "public's right to know". Everything about her life would be processed and splashed across every news outlet and television station in the country, exposing her to the worst possible kind of public scrutiny.

'You cruel bloody bastard,' she uttered.

It came out louder than she had intended. The family members stared with shocked expressions as she looked up from the page.

'Excuse me for a moment,' she said, then stood up and hurried from the room.

Danny Green followed her outside and closed the door, an urgent look on his face. 'You think this is our guy, or a mimic?'

Honor shrugged.

'He's targeting people close to me,' she replied. 'He knows about them, knows about how they're connected to me.'

'Samir knew that information too.'

'He knew enough to know who to go after,' she said, but then frowned. 'What I don't understand is why anybody would target Natalie Delray. I can't stand her. It's not like they'd expect me to be moving heaven and earth to find her.'

Danny frowned but said nothing as they turned away from the suite.

'You need to stay clear. I'm going to ask the MET to put a car on your house in case this freak, whoever they are, makes a play for you directly. There's nothing more you can do, and with a photofit in play it's only a matter of time before we identify the suspect. Go home, get some rest, you've done enough already.'

Honor sighed. 'I want regular updates, okay? I don't want to be left in the dark.'

'I'll keep you posted, promise,' Danny said. 'Hansen's a jerk, but he'll get the job done.'

Honor fetched her bag as Danny headed back to the IR, and within minutes she was standing outside the station, her umbrella up against a fine drizzle falling from a laden sky. She'd used the custody entrance, down an alley alongside the station, and now she used it to conceal herself from the paparazzi gathered in front of Bishopsgate, hurrying away from them before they spotted her. She walked a single block, then fished out her mobile phone as it buzzed in her pocket.

'Honor McVey, Detective Sergeant?'

'Detective, it's Paul Sharp. The flood waters in the sewers have subsided enough that your team can get into the crime scene. Do you want me to call the Incident Room and let them know that…'

'No,' Honor cut Paul off on impulse.

She desperately wanted Danny alongside her, but she knew that she couldn't contact him unless she had something concrete to offer. It was starting to get dark, and she knew how hard-pressed the IR team would be. They would appreciate the help.

Bullshit, Honor, you're lying to yourself. If there was something in the sewers that might lead to an arrest, she wanted to see it for herself.

'I'll be there in twenty minutes. I'll pass on what I learn to the IR from there.'

24

'You're not going to like this.'

Honor stood in Fenchurch Street next to Paul Sharp within a small Hamlets Council cordon arranged in the middle of the busy high street. Cars splashed cautiously around the cordon, passers-by watching them from beneath umbrellas up against the rain.

Paul gestured to the open manholes in the road.

'That said, they got flushed pretty good so most of the really bad stuff was swept away. It's not as terrible down there as you're probably thinking.'

Honor winced at his choice of words as she glanced sideways at him. 'Never going to be good though, is it?'

Honor donned a set of thick overalls, boots, gloves and a hard hat provided by Paul, before she gingerly followed him down into the sewer on a ladder that was slick with slime. The sounds of the city faded away above her, and air that she might have once considered polluted was replaced by a pungent odour that made her cough.

'You'll get used to it,' Paul said cheerily from somewhere below as he stepped off the ladder onto a metal gantry. 'Your brain will shut it out soon enough.'

The stench was thick, coating the back of her throat with something slimy that made her want to wretch. As she stepped down onto the gantry, her gloved hand brushed against debris that hung from the rungs in thick grey gloops.

'Jesus,' she uttered, recoiling away from the mess. Jayden had spent her last hours alive in this hellish dungeon, surrounded by the detritus of mankind.

'Wet wipes,' Paul informed her. 'We tell people not to flush them, but they never listen.'

Honor tried not to think about what the grey, stringy wipes might have been used for as she watched Paul climb down off the gantry onto another small ladder and step into ankle-deep water that was flowing through the sewer chamber. Despite the repulsive stench and the questionable flotsam on the surface, Honor dredged up sufficient fortitude to climb down the second ladder and step into the water alongside him.

'This is an original Victorian section of the sewer,' he informed her as though revealing the treasured secrets of the universe. 'It's over a hundred and fifty years old. Those pipes coming from upstream are interceptors, that take most of the waste water to be processed, while this chamber marks the point where drain water overflow is guided down to the Thames and is discharged into…'

'Where was Jayden trapped?' Honor asked, managing to open her mouth to speak for the first time despite the fear of ingesting a festival of airborne bacteria.

Paul gestured to a spot right behind her.

'There, against that wall. She would have been standing on that little ledge.'

In the gloom, Honor could see two manacles hammered into the brickwork, the ones that Jayden had managed to escape from before her appalling death only minutes later. She waded through the mess flowing past her boots, stared up at the spot where Jayden had fought so bravely. Thoughts of all that had been taken from Jayden's life rushed through Honor's mind: Jayden had been a sister, a daughter and an aunt to her sister's little son. She had been a normal, decent, hard-working woman trying to make her way in the world, only to have this done to her, all to quench the lust for suffering that was her quarry's hallmark.

Honor turned, and looked at the far wall of the sewer. There, she could see where a set of cables had been spliced together.

'Is that where the camera was?' she asked Paul.

'Yes. The camera was sent straight to Bishopsgate so that they could try to trace where it was purchased.'

Honor nodded, knowing that her MIT would be running barcodes and components through relevant databases in an attempt to locate where the camera was bought. It was likely though that the camera was bought for cash as a private sale, keeping the new owner's identity under wraps for as long as possible.

Honor waded her way across to the far wall. 'Who owns these cables?'

Paul shrugged. 'British Telecom, I suppose, it's not part of anything we deal with. They're fibre-optic, I think.'

Honor reached the wall and looked up at the cables. The various types were bundled together in brightly coloured groups, all heading off through the sewers in various directions. In front of her, just above head height, one of the cables had been severed and then re-joined. The splice had been where the camera would have been mounted on the wall of the sewer, and she could see four small screw holes in the brickwork where the killer would have had to drill for the camera mount.

There, running through the splice, she saw a manufacturer's name.

Nexus Cables Ltd.

Honor stared at the cables for a moment as her mind flashed back to a site three days ago, the church at St Magnus the Martyr. Tall, well-built male, responsible for the site CCTV security. *It's all state of the art, but they're not active yet.* Honor whirled and splashed her way across the sewer as she launched herself at the ladder.

'It's not *that* bad down here,' Paul protested as he began to follow her up.

Honor clambered up the ladders and burst out onto the surface, the sky dark now and gusts of fine drizzle swirling down through a halo of streetlights.

'Bored of the stench already?' Paul asked with jovial curiosity as he followed her up onto the street. 'I thought you'd be down here for…'

'It's O'Rourke,' Honor said as she tore off her hard hat and began scrambling to haul off her overalls and boots. 'Kieran O'Rourke, the contractor who works for Gary Wheeler.'

'He alibied out, didn't he?'

'He was seen heading home before the abductions took place,' she replied. 'Doesn't mean he couldn't have sneaked out again, especially if there is a concealed sewer entrance anywhere near where he lives.'

Paul watched her kick off her boots, which were smeared with unthinkable mess. 'DI Harper was concerned that your friend Samir's the culprit, you said they're still running with that.'

'It's piss-weak,' Honor snapped back. 'Samir doesn't fit the bill physically, and if he's been abducted by O'Rourke then there's every chance Samir's in as much danger as every other victim.'

'Wow,' Paul said, interested. 'How do you know, by the way?'

'The cables in the sewer were spliced with the same make of cable that O'Rourke was fitting to the security set-up at St Magnus. Same size, colour, everything. He fits the bill, and we haven't seen him for days.'

Honor sucked in a breath of clean, fresh air as she tried to ignore the stench that seemed to have clung to her hair and clothes. If O'Rourke was their man, he would by now have Samir held against his will somewhere, possibly as insurance against his own arrest. The fact that she could not help in the case to apprehend him provoked a spasm of frustration that threatened to send her over the edge into self-destructive rage.

She dug into her pocket for her mobile phone, felt it vibrating, heard it ringing as she stepped off the road and onto the pavement. In the darkness, the screen glowed with Samir Raaya's name. Honor pressed the answer button and held the phone to her ear.

'Samir?'

The voice that answered her was not Samir's, but a soft London accent that she recognised all too easily.

'Samir is indisposed, Honor, and if you attempt to locate him, I can assure you that he will not survive the night.'

Honor stood on the pavement, frozen as though in time. The rain fell on her but she didn't notice it streaming down her face as she stared into the darkness.

'I know who you are,' she replied. 'It's over, Kieran.'

There was a soft chuckle on the other end of the line.

'No, Detective,' he replied, *'it's only just beginning. Your story starts here. If you call anybody, try to warn anyone, Samir will meet a terribly unfortunate demise. Do you understand what I'm saying to you?'*

Honor remained catatonic in the rain, the phone sheltered by her hair as it plastered the back of her hand.

'Yes,' she said finally. 'You have Natalie, don't you?'

'St George in the East, ten minutes. If you try anything, Honor, anything at all, you'll only have memories of Samir to keep you company. I'm watching.'

The line cut off. Honor stood in the rain, pedestrians passing her by, the streets laden with queuing cars, their bodywork slick and shiny in the wet. She lowered the phone from her hand, still staring into the middle distance as she tried to figure out how the hell O'Rourke could be watching her right now. Her first thought was that he was bluffing, but the adept way in which he'd avoided

CCTV and security cameras during his killing spree left her in no doubt that he was capable of watching her for at least a part of her journey.

'Anything else you need, detective?' Paul asked as he closed the nearby manhole covers with a metallic thud.

Honor shook her head and walked off with her hands shoved into her jacket pockets, her head down as she thought hard. She barely heard Paul's disgusted retort of *"bloody charming"* as she abandoned him.

The city seemed to close in around her as she walked, dodging pedestrians by unthinking reflex. St George in the East was just off East Smithfield, Whitechapel, an 18th Century Anglican church, classic architecture. She could make it there in maybe ten minutes if she walked, but she wanted to make it harder for O'Rourke to track her. If she went for the DLR at Tower Gateway, she could get off at Shadwell and reach the scene a few minutes quicker than he might be expecting. It wasn't much, but anything she could do to buy herself a little time to think or survey the scene would be worth it. Honor hurried to Gateway and up the steps to the overhead line, her mind filled with desperate thoughts. She could call somebody at Bishopsgate, get Danny and the team to meet her at the church. What the hell would O'Rourke do anyway? Samir didn't have any apparent phobias that she knew about. Was this O'Rourke's end game? Was this how he intended to finish things, leaving Samir in the frame for the murders?

The train whined into the station, blissfully only half-full, as most commuters were heading out of Canary Wharf toward west London at this time of night.

Honor sat down, her phone in her hand in case O'Rourke called again. He'd used Samir's phone. Any investigation would see only the phone records, which would further support the notion that Samir was behind the murders. DS Hansen would use that to further his own cause, pushing MIT 2 out onto the margins as an unreliable, tarnished team led by an unpredictable and unstable DS. DI Harper would see through it, of course, but she would have a hard time defending Honor against such a breach of the force's security, a crippling blow to public confidence in the City of London Police. Harper would have to be seen to make amends, and that might mean publicly shifting Honor to another MIT team or perhaps out of the force all together.

She saw the signs for Shadwell appear far too quickly, and briefly toyed with the idea of riding past them to Limehouse and coming at the church from the east to fool O'Rourke, but then rejected the idea. There was little to gain. She stepped off the train at Shadwell, and walked down through the station onto Cable Street.

The church was located about two hundred metres to her right, off Canon Street Road. She walked swiftly through the rain sweeping in diaphanous veils from blackened skies, gusting on the squalls battering the trees and sending vortexes of dying leaves spiralling to the streets below. Rows of three-storey Victorian houses lined the street to her left, modern high-rise flats to her right, all concealed behind rows of trees that swayed and rustled in the wind. Most of the entire block of houses had stood here since the time of the Ripper, the area one of the most dangerous in the city at the time. Honor felt herself drawn into O'Rourke's mind, the one that occupied some distant, murky Victorian London that now, at night and in the rain, seemed closer than ever before.

Canon Street was quiet, the church still completely concealed from view behind the rows of Victorian houses, but when she finally reached the entrance, she saw the towering spire before her, flood-lit in all its Hawksmoor glory. It soared two-hundred feet into the night sky, three-hundred-year-old stone reaching for the turbulent heavens. Honor slowed, dwarfed by its immense architecture, the trees lining the approach trembling as wind-driven rain swept across the grounds. She could see that there were

lights on inside the church, the promise of warmth within, and yet she also knew that O'Rourke was almost certainly in there, awaiting her.

Her phone shrilled loudly in her pocket and she jumped out of her skin. Honor answered, her heart thumping against the walls of her chest.

'Good, Honor,' O'Rourke intoned. *'You're almost there.'*

Almost *there*. O'Rourke wasn't here, then, he was somewhere else, watching somehow.

'What do you want from me?'

'Go into the church, Honor.'

'I'm not doing anything without proof of life.'

There was a moment's pause, and then she heard a new voice. 'Honor!' Samir yelled. 'Don't do anything he says or…'

A twisted, hellish scream of pain soared down the line, then O'Rourke's voice once more.

'Your choice, Honor. If you want to see him live, do as I say. Go into the church.'

Honor began walking, slowly, toward the big church doors. 'Then what?' O'Rourke's reply was laced with malice.

'Climb the spire, Honor. Right to the top.'

Danny Green walked into the Borough Commander's meeting and immediately intercepted a half-dozen suspicious glances as the door was closed behind him. DI Harper, DCI Mitchell and Borough Commander Andy Leeson were all present, about a dozen constables and most of the MIT teams there too, as well as the Detective Chief Inspector of their borough, DCI Graham Holloway. DS Hansen had broken off his briefing as Green entered the room, and now he offered Green a shit-eating grin.

'Thank you so much for joining us.'

Green, his hands in his pockets, said nothing.

'I was just updating the team on the raid on Samir Raaya's apartment,' Hansen continued. 'We found numerous items inside the apartment that belonged to victims Amber Carson and Jayden Nixx. Items included clothing and jewellery, all of which are now being forensically examined for evidence that might lead us to their killer.'

Green said nothing, waiting for Hansen to continue.

'The media are broadcasting images of the suspect captured on CCTV and we're taking calls all the time, so hopefully we will soon have a confirmed identity for this bizarre and cruel murderer, a fair bit quicker this time around.'

Green again said nothing. The fact that MIT 2 had done all the investigative work in order to allow Hansen to pick up the glory didn't bother him at all, for he'd seen it many times in his career. All that mattered to him was identifying the suspect and apprehending them as soon as possible - he didn't care who took the credit.

'We're convinced that Samir Raaya has used his position here at City of London Police to execute one of the most audacious and terrifying campaigns of murder that the city of London has seen, and it's my opinion that he is attempting to emulate the work of Jack the Ripper, to become a modern-day version of the legend.'

Green managed to keep his mouth shut, but even he was barely able to conceal his contempt for Hansen's determination to reap everything that Honor had sowed, to claim her insight and work as his own. He could see DI Harper watching with an equally stony expression, but she was also staying quiet.

Green's mobile phone buzzed in his pocket and he fished it out to see an incoming file sent from the digital artist they had left at the hospital to speak with Emily and Alex Wilson. The file download icon turned slowly on the screen, and then the image flashed into view and Green's heart almost leaped into his mouth as he recognised the face in the digital photofit that he had been sent.

'Shit, it's O'Rourke!'

His outburst silenced DS Hansen mid-stride as Danny rushed over to DI Harper and DCI Mitchell, shoved the phone at them.

'Positive identification of the attacker of Emily Wilson,' he snapped. 'This is Kieran O'Rourke, an employee of Gary Wheeler, the building contractor who worked the site at St Magnus the Martyr church, the location of the first murder. Emily's photo-fit is perfect, and we haven't seen him since.'

'Didn't he alibi out?' DI Harper asked.

'Yes, he did, and there was nothing on the security cameras at the church,' Green replied. 'But he was the one who installed the damned things. He could have shut them off. We knew that was possible, but everything else checked out just fine and he was compliant and even helpful. His alibi must have been falsified. Honor was right, Samir Raaya can't have been responsible for the killings.'

DS Hansen's voice cut across Danny's.

'We found the victim's clothes in Raaya's apartment! How much more evidence do you need to stop this fantasy?'

Green spoke not to Hansen but to Mitchell and Harper.

'O'Rourke could easily have placed those items in Samir's apartment, and if what Honor feared was true comes to light, Samir's in as much danger now as any of the previous victims. He's one of our own. We need to move on this, right now!'

DI Harper didn't wait for the Borough Commander's approval.

'Get everything we have onto him,' she snapped. 'I want his address searched right now, apprehend him on sight.'

As officers rushed to organise the search, Danny turned to DCI Mitchell. 'Did you put a constable on Honor's home?'

'Yes,' Mitchell replied. 'She hasn't shown up there, last time I checked.'

The meeting broke up as dozens of officers and detectives burst from the conference room and dashed for phones or the stairwell to the car park. Danny didn't even look back as he rushed out to the Incident Room while fumbling to dial Honor's mobile phone.

Honor walked inside the immense interior of the church, saw the knave soaring up into a large oval ceiling, rows of pews amid softly glowing lights that gave the church a serene presence that belied the sinister nature of her visit.

'Keep walking, Honor,' O'Rourke said down the line. *'The stairwell to the belfry is on the opposite side of the nave.'*

Honor obeyed, guessed that O'Rourke could see her on some of the church's security systems. He would have known how to hack them, how to access everything, the man capable of entering any security system that he had devised. That was the problem with any security system – it was only ever as secure as integrity of the person who had installed it.

A set of steps climbed up from the nave toward the belfry, doubling back on themselves repeatedly as she climbed, the phone still held to her ear.

'You're wasting time, O'Rourke,' she said. 'You failed with Emily Wilson and she's able to identify you. It's only a matter of time before you're in custody.'

'Time you don't have,' came the calm reply. *'By the time they work out who I am, this will all be over and I will be gone. It's your time now, Honor, you're almost at the top.'*

Honor reached a platform in the belfry, and immediately detected the scent of rain and cold air. A tension formed in her gut, twisting it with latent fear as she stepped out onto the belfry platform. The baffles were closed on all sides but one, where they had been removed entirely, and she realised that the floodlighting on that side of the church had also been switched off. To her horror, she could see three scaffolding planks lashed one on top of the other, stretching out into the absolute darkness outside, slick with rain. Honor froze where she was.

'Don't stop, Honor,' O'Rourke murmured slowly, accusingly. *'Your destination is at the end of the plank.'*

Honor's guts turned to slime within her as she stared at the stone arch and the wet plank vanishing into the night.

'What the hell are you playing at?' she demanded.

The response that came down the line was not O'Rourke's voice, but Samir's, and it was a hellish scream of unimaginable agony that screeched into her ear and echoed around the belfry like panicked bats seeking to escape. The horrific scream faded away, and O'Rourke's voice reached her again.

'I won't tell you again, Honor. If you want Samir to live, walk the plank.'

Honor crept toward the open archway, the stone aperture about as tall as she was and maybe eighteen inches wide. The planks were lashed firmly in place, and she could see that something was lashed to the other end, and that there was also a small bag on the end of the planks. The wind gusted, driving rain across her field of view, and then she saw the body dangling beneath the end of the plank.

Natalie Delray was hanging by her wrists a couple of feet below the end of the planks, her hair tangled and roiling like snakes in the wind, her mouth gagged as she swung back and forth. Her eyes were wide with terror, her face stained with tears, and her limp body told Honor that she was under the influence of GHB, unable to move.

Honor felt her phone vibrate in her hand and looked at the screen. A message had appeared there, a call waiting from Danny Green. Honor's thumb hovered over the answer button, desperate for his presence and assistance, but knowing that if she answered the call, O'Rourke would know about it and Samir would…

'Now, Honor!'

O'Rourke screamed the command into Honor's ear and she took her thumb off the screen as she stepped forward onto the plank, ducked her head slightly to fit through the archway. She couldn't help the whimper of terror that escaped from her lips as she saw the sheer two-hundred-foot drop to the ground open out below her, and her knees buckled as the strength was robbed from them.

Honor crouched down onto her knees, gripped the plank with both hands as she slid her mobile phone into her pocket, careful to leave it on speaker. There was still the hope that the police would think to track its location and find her, although she felt pretty sure that they would have no reason to do so unless Emily Wilson came through and identified O'Rourke.

Her arms felt feeble, her guts churning as she crept out onto the planks, just like the ones they had found at St Magnus the Martyr church. She guessed that the three were strong enough to bear her weight and that of Natalie dangling from the other end, but her fear overcame her and she froze, her feet still inside the archway.

An agonised scream of misery emanated from her pocket as whatever hell O'Rourke was putting Samir through continued. Honor felt tears spring to her eyes as she began shuffling along the planks, one agonising inch at a time, the wind buffeting her and the rain pelting her skin and making the surface of the planks ever more slippery. The church car park was two hundred feet below, parked cars like little toys, the tops of the trees swaying in the wind. Vertigo turned Honor's senses on their head, her legs pulsing with terror, as though every puff of wind threatened to hurl her into the abyss. Samir's tortured scream faded away as Honor inched her way forward. Her knees were tucked in and touching each other, her elbows dragging on the surface of the plank, her knuckles white as she prayed that the wind would not be strong enough to blow her off. She kept her head down, her nose almost touching the plank, desperate not to see the horrendous drop below.

'Almost there, Honor,' O'Rourke intoned, *'just a little further.'*

Honor crept another few inches, the bag almost within her reach, but her heart was fluttering dangerously in her chest and her limbs seemed unwilling to respond to her brain's commands. The planks began to bow as she moved further out, moving up and down in the wind and she screeched in terror, froze where she was. O'Rourke's voice reached her from her jacket pocket.

'Good, Honor, very good. Now, check the bag. In there, you will find a knife.'

Honor's fingers crept along the surface of the plank, and she pulled the bag toward her with one finger, terrified that any further motion would send her plunging to her doom. It was small, just a leather satchel, and despite her shivering she managed to open it by pulling it onto its side and reaching inside, moving nothing but her fingers. Her hand touched something hard and sharp, the blade. She eased it out.

'Good, that's the knife.'

How the hell can he see me? Honor looked down, her guts convulsing as she saw the vertiginous drop yawning below, but then she saw Natalie's terrified face looking back up at her. Around Natalie's forehead was strapped a band to which was attached a small camera, which stared back at her from Natalie's forehead like a third, cruel black eye.

O'Rourke's voice reached her once again.

'Cut her bonds, Honor,' he said slowly, relishing every word. *'Send her to her death and gain your revenge, or Samir's life will end.'*

PHOBIA   Dean Crawford

25

'We've got another one!'

Danny shut off his phone as a uniformed officer rushed into the Incident Room and picked up the remote to the wall-mounted television, switching it to BBC News in time to catch a fresh report coming in. The screen filled with a spinning, gyrating view of a plunging two-hundred-foot drop to a darkened car park, the sound of a woman crying, rain spilling from the night sky.

'… the latest shocking footage being broadcast across the Internet of a woman dangling from great height somewhere above London, which may possibly be connected to recent broadcasts of victims being trapped in situations that reflect their greatest phobias…'

Danny stared in disbelief at the footage, which was hard to follow as it seemed that the person involved was actually wearing the camera. The point of view swung this way and that, a blur of imagery, the lens flecked with spots of rain water.

'We need to know where they are,' DCI Mitchell boomed, one arm pointing like a shotgun at the screen.

'She won't stay still,' DS Hansen complained, squinting as he tried to pick out details of the surrounding area.

Danny took a pace forward, thinking fast. 'Rewind it, and start playing it forward at one-quarter speed.'

The officer complied instantly, snapping the footage back by ten seconds and then advancing it slowly forwards. The footage was still blurred, but now they could see the car park more clearly, trees, some kind of grounds, streetlights on nearby roads with rows of houses.

'Could be anywhere,' DI Harper said as she examined the footage. 'Got to be something like a church spire, like the one at St Magnus, or maybe Southwark cathedral, we know he's used them before.'

Danny nodded in agreement and glanced at his computer monitor, which was feeding him footage from the body cam of a City Police team rushing into Whitechapel. 'Forced entry team is almost at O'Rourke's, they'll be inside within moments, but he's not going to be there.'

The BBC News footage swung around, the image blurring as whoever was wearing the camera pivoted about and looked up into the night sky. They were treated to a shot of the victim's wrists, lashed to the end of three scaffolding planks placed on top of one another, and on the end of the planks a face, hair matted with rain, features twisted with a volatile mixture of grief and determination, a large knife in one hand.

The officer with the remote froze the image on instinct.

Danny stared wide-eyed at the face, captured in one terrible moment of time on live television for the entire world to see.

'Honor.'

'Cut her loose, Honor.'

O'Rourke's disembodied voice spoke to Honor from her mobile phone, willing her on. Honor crouched on the end of the wavering planks, the wind and rain lashing at her, threatening to hurl her to her death far below. Natalie Delray's bleating face stared back up at her from the end of the rope, as able to hear O'Rourke as Honor was. *'She ruined your life, Honor,'* O'Rourke intoned, *'she's brought you nothing but pain and misery. She took everything from you, your life and your husband.'*

Honor held the knife in her right hand, the blade just inches from the rope now separating Natalie Delray from certain death.

'She took your baby from you, Honor.'

Honor felt her heart fracture as she saw in her mind's eye the ultrasound image of the child that had once grown within her; a tiny, innocent life, untarnished by the callous hand of fate until the moment when Honor had realised that her entire life was a lie, that the one person most devoted to protecting her and supporting her had been deceiving her for months, perhaps for their entire relationship.

'She took your baby from you, Honor.'

O'Rourke's voice was soft, soothing. Honor could barely feel the wind and the rain as she crouched on her knees and elbows, stared down into Natalie Delray's eyes. This woman had taken her life apart, shattered her every dream, killed her first child, this woman who now dangled by a thread, her entire future in Honor's hands. In O'Rourke's hands. Honor should have phoned Danny, she should have called somebody, done something, but she hadn't, and now she was stuck here and facing an impossible choice. It was on her. This was all on her.

'She's not worth the gift of life, Honor, not like Samir here. Save him, take her life and free him. Nobody would blame you, it's an impossible decision, you're under duress. Cut down one bad person to save one good person, Honor, you know that there's no other way.'

Honor stared down at Natalie for a moment longer, and then she heard the sirens screaming across the city, carried by the gusting winds. From one corner of her eye she detected flickering blues racing through the streets, rushing to her aid, to end all of this. O'Rourke's voice drifted through her consciousness like a cruel phantom taunting her from the edge of death itself.

'Time's almost up, Honor. Who's it going to be? Whose life do you wish to spare? Your colleague, Samir? Or the life of the woman who ruined your life?'

Another horrific shriek of agony from Samir soared from the mobile phone. Honor gritted her teeth.

'You took everything from me!'

Her cry emerged from somewhere deep within, raw and wild, and went howling into the savage night. Natalie shook her head, tears mixing with rainwater on her face, blood smeared on her wrists from the grinding, rough rope.

'You killed my baby!'

Honor could no longer really see properly, the rain blurring her vision, her crippling fear momentarily tamed by rage. Natalie again shook her head with shuddering, uncoordinated jerks, the GHB in her system wearing off slowly. Honor heard her begging through her gag for surcease, pleading for some chance to explain.

'The police are almost there, Honor,' O'Rourke murmured. *'Do it, now, or Samir will be lost forever.'*

Honor gripped the knife tighter in her hand, pressed the blade against the rope, and suddenly she knew that she had no choice. There was nothing that she could do, no other way out of this, and Samir did not deserve to die. *Samir does not deserve to die.* Her baby had not deserved to die. Somebody has to pay. *There has to be justice.*

Honor pressed the knife against the rope and with a shriek of helplessness she hacked the blade back and forth.

O'Rourke stood in front of a small laptop in an abandoned warehouse in Spitalfields and watched, enraptured, as Honor hacked at the rope. Excitement pulsed through his loins as he glanced at Samir's mobile phone beside the laptop. Then he looked to his right, where he held a knife that was thrust through the bridge of Samir's foot. The police detective's naked body was sheened in sweat despite the cold, bound by ankles and wrists, lying on the damp floor of the warehouse and writhing in pain.

O'Rourke watched the rope fray as Honor hacked it apart, heard Natalie's muted cries of terror. Natalie looked down to the car park two hundred feet below her, screaming and crying in desperation.

Then the rope parted as Natalie screamed and she tumbled into freefall.

O'Rourke gasped as he saw the ground rush up, the footage blurring left and right as Natalie plunged to her death in a frenzy of streetlights, rain and wind. The unforgiving tarmac of the car park flashed toward her at terrific speed and then there was a deep thud and a sickening crunch. The footage snapped to a motionless, side-on view of the car park, specks of rain falling silently onto the lens.

O'Rourke stared at the screen in mortified delight as a maniacal chuckle blurted from his lips.

'She did it,' he said as he turned to Samir. 'She actually did that for you.'

For a brief moment O'Rourke saw an unbidden image of his mother in his mind's eye, her tenderness, her kindness despite all that she had endured, and for the first time he felt a moment of shame for what he had put Honor McVey through. He turned to where Samir writhed still, and then he grabbed the detective's foot and yanked the blade from it.

Samir cried out as blood spilled from the wound.

'You're a lucky man, detective,' O'Rourke murmured. 'I know what it means to have somebody who cares for you, as Honor cares for you.'

Samir gritted his teeth against the pain, but said nothing. O'Rourke looked down at his victim.

'A shame, then, that it's all for nothing. You're number five, Samir.'

O'Rourke switched off the laptop computer, then took the mobile phone and switched it off too. He pulled out the SIM card, then dropped the phone onto the concrete at his feet and drove one heavy boot repeatedly down upon it, shattering the phone. He then picked up the mangled remains and tucked them into his pocket.

The he turned and looked down at Samir.

Danny stared in utter astonishment as Natalie Delray plunged two-hundred-feet and smashed into the ground. A rush of whispers and gasps of horror fluttered like phantoms around the Incident Room, the woman's death broadcast to countless millions of people.

'Jesus,' DS Hansen uttered, 'she just committed murder in front of the whole world. I *knew* she wasn't up to the job!'

DCI Mitchell called across the room to Danny. 'They've entered O'Rourke's property, one dead body confirmed at the premises but it's not Samir. They're searching now, but O'Rourke's not there either.'

Danny tried to assimilate what he was hearing, but none of it matched up. Honor had said that O'Rourke was changing his MO, keeping them on their toes, distracting them to avoid capture. He was so deep in thought that he barely noticed his mobile phone buzzing in his pocket. He reached down, lifted it to his ear and answered without taking his eyes off the television screen.

'Green, detective constable.'

'We just had a tip-off, O'Rourke was seen entering a disused building, Princelet Street, Spitalfields.'

Green shouted the information, the phone still against his ear. 'Princelet Street, Spitalfields, O'Rourke's in a disused building!'

DI Harper and DCI Mitchell were in motion in an instant, calling in units to hit both ends of the street and cut off any escape for O'Rourke as Green spoke into the phone.

'Do we know who the tip-off came from?'

'That's the thing, it came from Detective Sergeant Honor McVey. How would she know where O'Rourke was?'

Danny thought for a moment, then he shut the line off.

'I'm heading down there. I think I might know where O'Rourke will go.'

DI Harper didn't reply, she simply waved her hand vigorously in the direction of the door. Danny dashed out of the IR and ran down the corridor outside, betting the farm that he could get one step ahead of O'Rourke before he could vanish into history.

The police sirens screeched into Whitechapel, their blues flashing as multiple vehicles pulled into the car park of St George's in the East church. Honor could see them from where she crouched on the end of the plank, numbed by the cold wind and rain, frozen with terror. The dark abyss beneath her was real and tangible, but the darkness within had vanished. Her rage, the terrible, corrosive anger, had withered and fled into the wild night, leaving her only with her crippling fear of heights and a voice that spoke softly to her.

'You can do this, Honor. Just ease backward, one shuffle at a time. The plank's not going anywhere, you are. Just keep backing up, nice and slow.'

Honor's limbs wouldn't respond, shivering uncontrollably, fear writhing through her body like something alive.

'One inch at a time, Honor. You'll be safely back inside within a minute. You can do this.'

Honor managed to get one leg to respond and shuffled backwards along the plank, staring down at the woodgrain beneath her to avoid having to look anywhere else. Paranoia suggested she might not back up in a straight line and plunge off the side, and she froze again.

'You're doing great, keep going. You've got this.'

Honor shuffled again, moving backwards one tiny movement at a time, and slowly she edged back inside the archway and into the interior of the belfry, her fingers aching as she clutched the boards. The rain stopped falling on her as she crept back into the darkness, could hear drops of water dripping and echoing around the belfry, could smell the cool stone and old timbers, and then she staggered off the planks and collapsed onto her knees, her entire body shaking like a leaf as she heard police storming up the steps toward her.

The tears came then, a tsunami of regret, hate, fear and a dozen other emotions she didn't even fully recognise. She threw her hands to her face as the knife clattered to the stone floor, crouched over her grief as she heard someone climb off the plank beside her and throw arms around her shoulders, wrapping her up.

Honor felt herself slipping away into a swirling maelstrom of repressed emotions. Police boots thundered into the belfry and then came to an abrupt halt as they saw the two figures clutching each other, sobbing in the darkness. The officers' jaws dropped as one.

'How in the name of arse…?'

Natalie Delray's hair was as heavy and soaked as Honor's, her limbs trembling with cold and an infusion of adrenaline. She kept her grip on Honor and kept talking. 'It's okay, Honor, we're going to be okay. I didn't know about any of what you said, Zach never said a word. What baby?'

Kieran O'Rourke hurried out onto Princelet Street and made his way down the street outside. The rain was falling, the skies dark, the streets deserted, and he smiled. *Your time has come.*

He made his way down to the famous Brick Lane, then turned north. His destination was Dray Walk, a tiny side alley off Brick Lane and one of the oldest locations in the city. Now home to hip shops and boutiques, at this time of night it was deserted. The Brick Lane entrance was blocked by shutters after the close of business, but he knew that he could gain entry via Hanbury Street. There, near Quaker Street, conveniently placed out of sight, was a manhole cover used by Thames Water to maintain a watch on the Whitechapel sewers. From there, he could traverse Monument and travel north all the way up to Bank, where he had parked a Fiat that he'd bought for cash a month earlier.

O'Rourke hurried through the narrow confines of Dray Walk until he saw Quaker Street ahead, and the two large manhole covers he needed to access. He would need to be quick, but he was conditioned to this now and had already checked to make sure that he could lift and access the sewer inspection sites easily.

He would make for Scotland first, and from there he could find passage into Europe and start afresh, somewhere new, somewhere different, where he could live in peace and watch the furore that would erupt as the police strived and failed to bring him to justice, his name passing into legend.

O'Rourke reached Quaker Street, looked left and right and found it empty, devoid of vehicles or pedestrians. Quickly, he slid the rucksack he carried from his shoulder and pulled out a metal hook designed specifically for the task of lifting the manhole cover. He hooked them into place and heaved on the cover.

Two police cars surged into Quaker Street from opposite ends, their lights blazing, tires squealing as they converged upon his position.

'No!'

O'Rourke whirled to flee back down Dray Walk, in time to see a detective rush into view.

'Game's up, O'Rourke.'

O'Rourke recognised him, Daniel Green, a detective constable, one of McVey's people. O'Rourke reached for a knife in his jacket, and his hand began to quiver. He couldn't run, couldn't escape. The police vehicles screeched to a halt and officers flooded out. He could hear them yelling, warning him that they were armed with Tasers, ordering him to show them his hands.

He pulled the knife out, and Danny Green slowed, raised a placating hand.

'Easy,' Danny murmured. 'Ain't no sense in taking yourself down or anybody else, Kieran. Take it easy and put the blade down.'

O'Rourke put the blade to his own throat, the metal cold to the touch, callous, uncaring, savagely sharp. His arm began to shudder uncontrollably. No way out. He had to die. *Put the blade through.*

An image of the blood spilling, hot and thick, down his throat turned his guts upside down and a bolt of nausea lodged in his throat. *Cut, now!* His arm shuddered as he tried to dredge up the will to face death, gritted his teeth, groaned with fury. An image of Emily Wilson's blood spilling from her body as she was consumed by rats stayed his hand, but the police were almost upon him now. There was no longer any time. He should go as the Ripper would have chosen to go, swift but violent, a glorious escape from an impossible situation. He needed to die a man's death. *End it, now!*

'Armed officers, TASER equipped! Put the knife down, now!'

The blade sliced into his flesh and unbearable white pain seared his skin, hot blood spilling down his throat, and he yanked the blade away.

Danny Green lunged forward and grabbed O'Rourke's wrist, twisted it upward and sideways. Pain ripped through O'Rourke's shoulder as the blade clattered to the ground and he was forced to his knees. Within seconds, a constable was binding his wrists in metal handcuffs as Danny Green's voice echoed up and down the narrow London street. 'Kieran O'Rourke, you're being arrested under the suspicion of murder. You do not have to say anything, but anything that you do say…'

Revelation and realisation reached into the depths of his mind, too late, as they so often were. *In all things, justice came with time. It might be slow, painfully so at times, but it came none the less. Karma. What goes around, comes around.*

'Thanatophobia,' Danny Green said as he hauled Kieran to his feet. 'Honor was right, you didn't have the spine to take your own life. Move!'

O'Rourke said nothing, utterly compliant as he was forcibly cajoled toward a waiting patrol car, the rain falling silently all around him on one of Spitalfield's oldest streets, every building standing at the time the Ripper had stalked London.

Coffee, even from a Styrofoam cup, had never tasted so good.

Honor sat on the back step of an ambulance, a blanket around her shoulders, the coffee clasped in her hands. Her legs were still shaking, her guts churning from a radical injection of adrenaline, but she was alive. *Alive.*

'Christ, there you are.'

Danny Green ran toward her, concern writ large on his features as he rushed to her side. He reached her, crouched down and wrapped her up in an embrace.

'I'm okay, more or less,' she said, her voice feeble. 'Shit, Danny, I need a cigarette.' Danny released her, pulled out a cigarette. He lit it for her, and one for himself, and she dragged down a lungful of nicotine that nearly sent her flat on her back. She blew out a billowing cloud of smoke and instantly felt mildly nauseous.

'You've earned that one,' Danny said, surprised but understanding.

'Samir?' she asked.

'On his way to hospital with head injuries,' Green replied. 'O'Rourke stomped him out but didn't finish the job. I don't know his condition yet. Officers got to him based on your tip off, just after you'd killed…'

Danny cut himself off, his features tortured, torn between relief and regret for what she had done.

'Natalie is fine,' Honor said.

Danny stared at her for a moment, not getting it. Honor tilted her head toward another ambulance. Danny glanced across at it and almost choked on his cigarette as he saw Natalie Delray sitting on the back step. Danny looked back at Honor, who reached behind her and produced an evidence bag containing the camera that had been strapped to Natalie's head. The strap had been hacked in two.

'Told you the fucker would make a mistake eventually,' she uttered with a grim smile. 'If he'd suspended Natalie by her ankles, it'd be me in custody right now.'

Danny Green shook his head in wonder, ran a hand down his face as though to wipe it free of weariness and pain.

'You cut the camera, not the rope,' he said. 'How the hell did they ever put DS Hansen in your place?'

Honor shrugged but said nothing. She took another drag on the cigarette, but as her jangling nerves continued to calm, she realised that she wasn't really enjoying it at all. She tossed it and crushed it under her heel, blew the smoke out along with what felt like a lifetime of pain and watched it coil away into the damp, miserable night.

'She helped me,' Honor said. 'Natalie helped me back inside the church.'

Danny looked up at the planks, two hundred feet above them. 'Bloody least she could do. But if you cut the camera strap, you'd have had to hang off the edge of the planks to reach her, right?'

Honor nodded, said nothing.

'Christ,' Danny uttered. 'That's some brass balls, right there.'

'She didn't know, about the baby I lost, none of it. It was all kept from her. She said Zach told her he left me because the work made me too cold, unemotional. He couldn't understand me anymore.'

Danny watched her for a moment, chose his words carefully.

'Things in our heads often look different to the way they're seen by others.

How did you know where O'Rourke was?'

'I didn't,' she replied. 'I cut Natalie's gag right after the camera, and she told me where O'Rourke had taken her, along with an Asian guy she'd seen, which must have been Samir. I called it in right away, then I just froze up. The GHB in her system was wearing off, so Natalie guided me to help free her hands, and got us off the planks and into the belfry. Turns out she's got a hell of a spine and isn't afraid of heights. Where's O'Rourke now?'

'In custody,' Green replied. 'I got lucky, and caught him trying to use the sewer entrance off Brick Lane; seemed like his only way out of Whitechapel once we were on to him. He tried to cut his own throat, but lost his nerve.'

Honor thought for a moment, and then smiled. 'Thanatophobia,' she said. 'He couldn't go through with it, right?'

Danny nodded, puffed happily on his cigarette and blew the smoke away from her. 'Meek as a lamb once I took the knife from him. And guess what – he had a bite mark on the left side of his jaw, and the pathologist said that at autopsy she discovered that Jayden Nixx had skin caught in her teeth. What's the chances of that skin matching Kieran O'Rourke's do you think?'

Honor closed her eyes and leaned back against the step of the ambulance, suddenly weary beyond belief. 'We've got him.'

'Yeah, which means you're on leave until further notice,' Danny said.

'I want O'Rourke in that interview room, first thing in the morning.'

'Mitchell wants you to rest for a day or two, until this all dies down. So does Harper. The close nature of the case might mess up anything we put in front of

CPS, if they conclude you were compromised or under stress during interview. We can't risk blowing the prosecution on this one.'

'Bollocks. I want O'Rourke,' she growled.

'Don't shoot the messenger,' Danny said, hands in the air. 'You're alive. How about small mercies?'

Alive. Honor realised that she'd never felt *more* alive than now, sitting here, shivering and exhausted after days in the presence of death and misery. The similarity with what she suspected O'Rourke experienced during his campaign wasn't lost on her, and it made her shudder. Yet the delight and the relief that she now felt was not caused by death, provoked by suffering; rather, the catalyst was the end of the trauma. O'Rourke was in custody, and no more innocent lives would fall victim to his insane campaign.

Honor stood up, face to face with Danny.

'I want to see him, just once, behind bars where he belongs. Can we at least do that?'

26

Bishopsgate custody suite was strangely devoid of suspects as Honor walked back into the station and was buzzed through. The fifteen cells were often packed with a volatile collection of drunks, drug-abusers and other ne'er-do-wells swept up off the streets every day and night by city officers. Although she couldn't be sure, she suspected that the ongoing campaign of murders had attracted the attention of more than just the general public, criminals themselves equally fascinated by the investigation.

Honor walked past a series of lockers behind the custody bridge, atop which was a jaunty pile of constables' helmets, their red and white check-flash and gold badges vivid against black.

'He's in five,' the custody sergeant said to her, gestured to one of the cells.

Honor stared at the door. 'What do we know about him?'

Danny spoke softly.

'You were on the money. O'Rourke's mother died aged thirty-two, cancer, left him alone and in the care of a father with a history of alcoholism and domestic abuse. Father drops off the radar when O'Rourke turns eighteen, maybe nineteen. Turns out he was still alive, but strapped to a bed in O'Rourke's basement. He's been there for over twenty years.'

'Alive?' Honor asked, horrified.

'Forced entry team found him dead, smashed up with a baseball bat,' Danny replied. 'Murder was recent but the body was emaciated. They said it was like looking at archaeological remains. The autopsy will tell us more, but they're thinking he was barely alive throughout that time, kept ticking over by his son.'

The obsession, with the moment of death, Honor thought, played out in reverse upon an abusive father. O'Rourke had kept him barely alive for two decades, hovering on the verge of his own terminal demise, tortured for every single second of his existence at the hands of a psychotic son with nothing left to live for. The fact that O'Rourke had lost his mother at a young age, leaving him to face his father's wrath, had probably been the trigger point – either that or O'Rourke coming of age and turning the tables. O'Rourke was no psychopath, merely a twisted, sickened man constantly seeking to avenge the loss of a mother, a grievance he'd never been able to get over.

'You sure you want to do this?' Danny asked as he followed her in.

Protocol demanded that another officer accompany her, to prevent any legal defence from claiming that she had interfered with the suspect. A personal connection to the victims could be used as reason for the Crown Prosecution Service to reject or alter the case against O'Rourke.

'Yes,' Honor replied. 'Has legal counsel been assigned yet?'

'He hasn't even been interviewed yet, just processed,' the sergeant replied. 'They're going to start work on him in the morning, although we've got him under suicide watch just in case.'

Honor smiled softly. 'I wouldn't worry too much about that.'

'I do,' Danny said. 'I don't want him suddenly growing a spine and taking his own life. I want him behind bars for the rest of his life.'

Something about the way Danny said that gave Honor an idea. 'Put me in cuffs.'

The sergeant raised an eyebrow. 'Say what?'

'Do it,' she said, 'and lead me to the cell.'

The sergeant glanced at Danny, who nodded. Reluctantly, the sergeant cuffed her, and then she walked to cell five, approached the door slowly. There was an open observation window in the door at head height, a female officer sitting on a chair beside the door. Although Honor knew who was sitting within the cell, it was as though she didn't want to approach, as though somehow there was something waiting for her that was far more terrifying than just a man within.

Danny hung back as Honor walked to the window, took a breath, and looked inside. Like all cells, the interior was spartan and well lit. A single, slab-like bed protruded from the back wall, and a sink adorned the wall to her right. There, on the bed, was a man laying with his back to her, his arms folded around himself. Big shoulders, a tall man, yet strangely seeming smaller in real life than she had come to imagine.

'Kieran.'

She said his name softly, almost as though it fell from her lips of its own accord. Slowly, the man rolled over and she saw the recognition in his eyes, the flare of surprise and then a deep veil of shame, the pall of the defeated. For a moment she thought that he would roll over again and turn his back to her, but curiosity got the better of him and he turned to sit on the edge of the bed, keeping his distance from the door.

'I wondered when we would meet.'

His voice sounded utterly unthreatening. Honor realised that there was no way on earth that she or anybody else, upon encountering this man on the street, would have had any idea of what he was capable of.

'You kind of made our meeting inevitable.'

Keiran glanced briefly past her, saw the duty sergeant behind her, the awkward set of her shoulders, and she saw him realise that she was in cuffs.

'You were very brave,' he said. 'It was a shame that your colleague had to die, but five victims were what I needed, and I got them. You were all too late.'

A smile. A pyrrhic victory for a narcissist. Honor kept her features composed.

'None of it was worth it, Kieran. You think you're the next Ripper, but you failed, in everything.'

She saw a flame of defiance spark back into life as O'Rourke stood and paced toward the window. Now, she could see his formidable size, but again, somehow, she was no longer intimidated. She knew this man's character, that of a coward, a man who had been unable to face up to the same fears that he had so cruelly inflicted upon others.

'Five victims,' he repeated, 'all killed in spectacular ways, with you, the last victim, to suffer your crime for the rest of your life. You shouldn't have gone up against me, Honor, you weren't up to it.'

The smile, again. O'Rourke was stooping slightly to see her through the window.

Honor raised her chin.

'You got what you wanted,' she replied. 'Why did you do it? Why kill like that, innocent people? What was the point?'

'The point?' Kieran echoed, as though surprised that she did not yet understand. 'Why would there be a point? There's no point to anything, Honor. We live only once, and then we're all gone. Nothing matters, nobody matters. We're all just dust and ashes once we're gone, right? Why not leave a mark to be remembered by?'

Honor felt cold. There was nothing in O'Rourke's eyes, blank discs shining with fanatical delight that was as empty as it was frightening, a soul without empathy, but not one that had been born empty of love or hope. This was a man shaped by his life, by the cruel hand of fate, unable to deal with the blows it had dealt him.

'If that were true, then you'd feel no grief at the loss of your mother.'

Kieran's smile slipped, cold hatred flaring in his gaze like a blade catching the light. 'You know nothing about my life or...'

'You took your grief out on others, because you couldn't get over the loss of your mother.'

Kieran said nothing, grinding his teeth in his jaw but unable to break his gaze. 'Kept your father in agony for decades,' Honor went on. 'Funny, Kieran, how you put so many people through such horrific torture, and yet when it came to your turn to face your fears, you failed miserably.'

Kieran's eye twitched as Honor edged closer to the window, their faces only inches apart, and spoke softly.

'Every single one of your victims overcame their fears and fought for their lives, but you, you just folded and ran away like the coward that you are.'

'You know *nothing*! You're just like all the rest!' 'I am,' Honor replied. 'I owe you one, Kieran.' O'Rourke's rage subsided into confusion.

'I haven't got over the loss of my baby,' she said, so softly that she could barely hear herself. 'That was a life taken from me, but it was nobody's fault. It just happened. I need to talk about it, so I will, so I don't end up like you.'

Kieran's outrage tried to reassert itself, but she could tell that his twisted mind couldn't find a way to turn her brutal honesty into a victory that would soothe his tortured ego.

'You'll never get your baby back,' he hissed, lips twisted into a grimacing grin.

'I know,' Honor replied. 'Just as you'll never get your life back. But me, I'll walk away from this.'

'You'll suffer in a cell just like me,' O'Rourke snapped, 'for the rest of your life.'

Honor stepped back one pace from the door and looked over her shoulder. 'You can remove the cuffs, now, Sergeant.'

Honor looked back at Kieran, and saw the confusion on his features as he watched the cuffs being removed.

'Five canonical victims,' Honor said as the sergeant took the cuffs off her wrists. 'So you believe, but of course that's not how it played out at all. Sebastian Dukas died at your hands, because you screwed up his dose of GHB. Amber Carson died a horrific death, but Jayden Nixx escaped. Both the Wilsons survived their ordeals and have identified you as their attacker.'

Kieran's features began to collapse. 'You killed Natalie Delray, and your detective lays dead on the floor where I left him.'

Honor said nothing but she smiled now, a long, slow smile that she could see further infuriated Kieran with every second that she kept it on her face.

'You're going to spend the rest of your life in prison for murder!' Kieran shrieked at her, spittle flecking the glass.

Honor shook her head, and with one hand held up the evidence bag with the camera and its severed strap. Kieran's eyes locked onto it, and in an instant, she saw a devastation crush his warped dreams as she spoke softly.

'Natalie Delray is alive and well, and Samir Raaya is recovering in hospital,' she replied. 'So, in fact, you only really killed two people, as I'm guessing your father doesn't count to you. Still, the campaign itself will ensure that you'll spend the rest of your life behind bars, unable to bring your own suffering to an end.'

Honor lowered the bag back out of sight, turned on her heel, and walked away from the door.

'You won't forget about this!' O'Rourke yelled after her. 'The world won't forget about this!'

Honor paused, looked over her shoulder, then walked back to the window.

'I certainly hope so,' she replied quietly. 'Your greatest legacy might well become as an example of how we catch the next serial killer, because unlike the Ripper, you screwed up just about everything.'

Honor reached up and slammed the window shutter closed before she turned again and walked back to the custody bridge. Her heart was battering the walls of her chest but she felt suddenly buoyed by the confrontation. She turned and walked away from the cell, heard O'Rourke screaming something unintelligible from within, but she knew now that she would never see him again.

'Turning the screws,' Danny smiled as he walked with her. 'You've got a hard edge that I really quite like.'

Honor shook her head. Like the victim who beats a bully, she found that there was little surcease in victory when so many had lost so much. Sure, she'd got O'Rourke, but the pain that had driven him was no different from the pain that swilled deep within her, one that she knew she must confront and move past, in as much as any person could.

'I just wanted to pull his chain a bit,' she replied as they walked back through the custody suite. 'I'll never come face to face with him again, never give him the chance to argue his case. That'll hurt a narcissist like him more than anything else, hopefully.'

Danny checked his watch. 'I'm going to head home, see my girls before bed.'

Honor turned to him. For a moment she didn't know what she wanted to say, only that she knew she had to say something. She tried, but nothing came out. Danny leaned on the wall at his side, his hands in his pockets, saw her try to speak and somehow come up short. One side of his mouth curled up in a little smile.

Sometimes, every now and again, Honor realised that you didn't have to say something, you already just knew. Danny watched her for a moment longer, and then he pushed off the wall.

'I've got your back,' he said simply.

As they were buzzed out of the custody bridge, she noticed a lot of activity outside the station, flashing cameras, commingled voices. Above the noise, DCI Mitchell's voice rumbled as he addressed the media.

'I'm gonna head out the side entrance,' she said to Danny, keen to avoid the chaos on the street outside B-Gate.

As she turned, she saw a wall-mounted television showing the BBC News channel, with her face upon it. For a moment her shoulders sank as she realised that they were still tearing her apart, even after all that she had done.

'Jesus, I just can't get away from this shit.'

'It's great, isn't it?' Danny said as he saw her face on the television.

'You're kidding, right? The national character assassination? It's not my finest hour, Danny, thanks for reminding me.'

Danny looked at her, confused, and then he got it.

'You haven't seen the news since you caught O'Rourke,' he pointed out. 'Everything's changed. Millions of people are talking about what you did.'

'That's kind of what I didn't want.'

'They're talking about you bringing O'Rourke in,' Danny added. 'How you fooled O'Rourke, saved a life and captured the perpetrator. It's all they're talking about, on the news, everywhere. Some are even saying you engineered the whole pursuit, put yourself in harm's way just to bring him to justice.'

Honor wasn't sure what to make of that. 'It's BS,' she replied. 'I almost got killed.'

'Kind of the point,' Danny acknowledged. 'They know what you went through and it was all on film, right there, live on television. There's not a news network in the world that isn't showing it, so now they're looking at you for all the right reasons. You did this.' He stepped closer to her, and gently poked her in the shoulder. '*You* did this.'

'You gonna head out that door and face the media, or keep hiding in the shadows?' Danny asked her.

Honor glanced again at the station doors, her stomach turning over upon itself at the thought of facing the media once again. Truth was, the attention was the last thing that she wanted, victor or no. So what did she want? For a moment, as always, she couldn't tell. Then, she turned to Danny.

'Come with me?'

Danny nodded, grinned, and gestured the way to the doors with a grand sweep of his arm.

'After you, boss.'

Honor took a breath, steeled herself, and walked toward the station doors. Danny opened them, and she saw DCI Mitchell turn to face her, ranks of reporters and cameras and flashing lights, the dark night sky, the traffic thundering past on wet roads, the scent and the presence of London filling her universe.

And then the applause from the deep ranks of reporters, cheers, the broad grin on DCI Mitchell's face as he stood back to let her come forward from the doors, the gentle, friendly nudge from Danny's elbow to get her moving. Honor couldn't manage to crack a smile, but she found herself walking down the steps, no longer as afraid as she used to be.

It's on you. It's all on you. Everybody is watching you. Everybody is interested in you. Everybody cares.

***

ABOUT THE AUTHOR

Dean Crawford is the author of over thirty novels, including the internationally published series of thrillers featuring *Ethan Warner*, a former United States Marine now employed by a government agency tasked with investigating unusual scientific phenomena. The novels have been *Sunday Times* paperback best-sellers and have gained the interest of major Hollywood production studios. He is also the enthusiastic author of many independently published novels.

Printed in Great Britain
by Amazon